FAR HORIZONS

BOOK THREE OF THE OUTER REACHES

A J GORDON

FAR HORIZONS

It may be unusual to give a dedication to a co-author, but not only has Peter Aldin been a great mate, he has provided guidance and advice through the many and varied complications this author went through.

Without this, Outer Reaches would still be one of the many ideas filling my notebook, awaiting that spark to give it life.

PHILLIX'S FUNERAL

"HOW'S THIS GONNA WORK, EXACTLY?" Sabrya asked. The crew were standing on the *Malleus'* hull, the wrapped body of their technician floating in front of them, the nothing space with the massive Terran ship cloaked somewhere behind them.

Bradyn answered, "Since we've got no other propulsion devices, we'll have to use the *Malleus*. We aim for the sun... or where the sun is going to be—if you can call that dim brown glow a sun—and at a given moment, we release. Then we'll plot a course to the colony on Niviaris."

"Kinda weird, though, havin' Phillix coordinate his own funeral," Sabrya commented.

"Got to get it right," Phillix's voice came through their headsets. "Can't leave these things to amateurs."

"He was a weird guy when he was alive... weren't you, Phillix?" Bradyn asked, not unkindly.

"I prefer unique, but yeah, I was definitely on the spectrum," Phillix answered. "And I didn't want you to miss."

"Miss you?" Alexis asked, as a moment of confusion creased her brow. She'd been contemplating the events of the last few hours. So much had happened. Finding—after seventeen centuries—the *Iconic*, the flagship of the ancient Terran empress, Adjira, at the very same time an Imperial vessel appeared on their scanners. Then the discovery of the empress, herself, still alive after all that time in stasis and the ensuing running battle with droids, mercenaries, and Imperial soldiers.

"Not me, though that would be nice," Phill said. "I mean, I don't want my body to miss the brown dwarf. I've calculated the precise trajectory for my body, based on my mass, the gravity well of nearby planets, and maximum sub-light velocity. I don't want to drift in space for eternity."

"Oh. Fair enough. Anyone want to say something?" Alexis looked around at the remaining crew.

"Umm," Sabrya considered, "that's the captain's gig, Captain."

"I've taken my hat off for this. He was fellow crew. One of us."

"Bradyn knew him longest." Sabrya nudged the stocky man.

The engineer nodded and considered his words as he adjusted his ill-fitting vac-suit; it was encroaching on areas that made standing for long periods uncomfortable. "We met as young men inexperienced in the way of the worlds. Totally different upbringings, even interests, but we were like brothers in other ways. I guess I'm on the spectrum, too, just more of a people person—"

Sabrya coughed.

"We had good times, through thick and thin. He was a good friend, and I don't regret any of it," Bradyn finished.

The three crew members remained silent for a moment. Above and around them, the Shadow Nebula loomed, giving the hull an eerie reddish glow. This far rim-ward, there were few stars to see with the naked eye.

"I was thrown in with you lot," Alexis started. "We met under strenuous circumstances in the slave pens of Ieoni Orbital. Phill... was always a gentleman to everyone. The most personable introvert I've known. Just the sort of guy you'd expect to sacrifice himself for others."

The silence grew.

"C'mon, Sabby. You know you want to say something," Phillix whispered in her earpiece.

"Frag it, Gadgetman!" she grumbled. "Despite all the deaths I've seen and been involved with... I felt this one, though maybe I didn't show it. You know that's why I try not to get close to anyone. People die too fraggin' easily. Divin' into the sun though... kinda cool way to go out."

After several moments, Phillix spoke to everyone. "Thank you all. Now, you should get back inside. I'd like to spend a few moments with myself."

"Told you he was weird."

"You do know I have the airlock controls?" Phillix laughed.

Bradyn feigned shock. "Drock it, I meant wired."

PART I

CHAPTER ONE

ALEXIS LEFT her section at the agri-hab and looked forward to catching up with the others and relaxing on the anticipated day off. She had to admit, albeit reluctantly, things weren't as rosy as she wanted or expected, and at each end of shift, while she wandered toward the Hub, her mind wondered at the circumstances that had brought her here, to what was now her new home.

In the back of her mind, this reminiscing had become a habit. The scientific portion of her mind noted it, even to the point of considering therapy. The other part just wanted to get drunk and forget.

Seeing Kaden's son and then meeting him face-to-face six months ago, along with his partner and daughter, had been hard to accept. She had swallowed the crushing despair and moved on. Or tried to.

The hype in the adverts and glossy brochures back in Meridiani City had been wrong. Sylvanus Colony was a far cry from the depicted utopia. Preliminary research, as it turned out, had been dodgy at best and bordered on incompetence. The first colonists had arrived to find the terraforming hadn't been successful. Their expectations of a high-gravity paradise had shattered and quickly become a nightmare.

A side effect of the terraforming had been the creation of perfect conditions for the growth of a new strain of mold. If it got into your lungs, you would be dead within a month from acute lung deterioration. Thirty-five percent of the original *Octavia* crew who escaped the ship had survived, mainly due to better genetic modification and being more robust candidates.

The original settlers had forged ahead through adversity to become the true pioneers. The colony world of their dreams had become a fight for survival. When the original ships had begun to malfunction because of gravitational stresses, they had been dismantled to create ad hoc accommodations. As a temporary measure, they had converted the farming droids into excavators and created the foundations of the underground colony. Even then, the difficulties had cascaded and slowly become overwhelming. With little agriculture, rationing of the dwindling food and water supply had become a necessity.

That the deaths from the mold increased the survivability of the remaining people was a brutal reality. This lifestyle was a far cry from what had been portrayed in the brochures.

When the *Octavia* commander, Captain Orlandon, passed, Kaden Zolton had inherited the leadership of the colony. He had directed that the focus of the colonists be turned inward to maximize survivability. Simply maintaining the status quo in an environment set on killing them would lead to extinction, so all resources had been used to their best advantage. Research and development had changed gears.

Building on the great work of his predecessors, Kaden Zolton had turned the tables. The colony had slowly improved. Living conditions had stabilized, people reproduced, and families grew.

Alexis was a loose cog. Her knowledge of biology and botany was superseded by the many and varied new sciences the colonists used now. Sure, she could study and learn, but at this moment—until the hubbub of the first arrival of another craft in decades had passed—she was relegated to student status. The learning was interesting enough, but her time here was leading her to a mundane existence. She was bored and dissatisfied, and there were several reasons why.

Since twenty-six years had passed during which she had been thought dead, any reunion with Kaden was a vain hope at best—especially now that he had his own family. Her feelings of joy turned to quiet dismay. The fluctuation of her status from low-level scientist to ship captain then back down to student was a kick in the guts.

Her alter ego from two and a half decades subjected to incorrect subliminal training pushed for greater dominance. Buried deep since her stasis revival, the physical prevalence of Kaden exacerbated her headaches; they were increasing in both strength and frequency. Only strong medication enabled her to function.

Since it was 9Day, the three of them were going out for dinner and drinks, like seventy-five percent of the colonists. She met up with Bradyn on the street, and they took their time walking to the bar where Sabrya worked.

"How goes it at the shop?" she asked the stocky engineer in greeting.

"Same, same," was his non-comital answer as they walked along the wide street.

"That bad?" She nodded, knowing how he felt.

"I'm a ship engineer. Give me a good hull breach or fused hyperdrive any day. Patching up dome punctures and unplugging sewerage outlets wasn't on my radar."

Yep, a bad day. Bradyn was one of the most stoic people she knew; if he was whining, it wasn't a good sign. She felt responsible. It had been her idea to come to Sylvanus Colony, with the hope of starting a new life, but whenever it came to discussing it, they shot her down. "This was all our decision, we had nowhere else to go," was the argument they'd use. And they were right. Still, seeing her companions—her crew—feeling so morose sucked. *This wasn't on my scanner either.*

"We'll have a relaxing dinner and a few drinks and talk about the good ol' days," she decided.

Bradyn agreed. "The days when we were running from the Bukshoga Qlan and dodging mercenaries with a bounty on our heads and rampaging killer bots."

"Don't forget crazy empresses and self-destructing ships. Yep, those."

"At least I knew I was alive then."

Yep. A bad day.

"This looks interesting," Bradyn said.

Piqued by his sudden change in tone, she looked up and followed his gaze. As they approached the Gates of the Abyss, they saw a crowd on the pavement looking in.

"Are you thinking what I'm thinking?"

"Sabrya." He nodded glumly and increased his pace to match Alexis'.

Sabrya climbed to the upper-level balcony to better survey the rowdy group of miners letting off steam.

Understandable, being 9Day Eve.

She had easily adjusted to the weekdays in a domed world. Like space, when living underground with no day or night or seasons, sticking to a regular weekly cycle seemed pointless. She understood that, and in her previous work as a warrior in the Surreal Tournament, she had moved around so often, she had had to adapt quickly to the routine of wherever she was.

Living above ground was risky at the best of times, but when the brown dwarf erupted with its irregular gamma bursts, you were likely to get fried, which was something that had been learned the hard way in the original colony days, over eighty years earlier. It became apparent the researchers had been incompetent, or just plain stupid, because half the problems that should have been picked up on weren't.

Ad hoc bunkers had been made from ship components. With no access to sunrise or sunset or even seasons, having a simple naming solution for time was an easy and practical solution. 1Day–10Day. 5Day was a half-day roster and 10Day was a full day off. Miners were shift workers, but some worked the "days off" and were given the following day off as compensation, along with an additional fifty stellars.

The group boozing below had struck it big—so they said repeatedly—with a rich seam of tilanthium. Tilanthium, which was clear, had several uses, one of which was gamma shielding. They hoped to have enough one day to build domes so the population could live above ground and see the real world and not be cooped up underground.

Sabrya checked her chrono. Alexis and Bradyn were due to arrive at 2100 when she knocked off. She heard a scream and focused her attention on a dining couple three booths further along the balcony. She went to investigate, but it was only a woman giggling and watching a horror vid. Sabrya nodded at her and went back to her position by the railing to wait for her shift to end in five minutes.

She was going to join her friends to have a drink and dinner then relax. She spotted Torg arriving early. As the droid made his way to the designated booth, one of the rowdy miners stumbled back and bumped into him. The man fell to the floor. Torg helped him up.

"Get your dirty hands off me, you stinking droid," the drunk shouted.

"Sir, I conform to all hygiene regulations. My hands are spotless, and I exude no aromas. I believe your olfactory senses are detecting your friends by the bar."

Sabrya rolled her eyes. "Stupid Tinman." She started to make her way to the stairs without disturbing the other guests who were enjoying their drinks.

"You wha?" the drunk asked, confused.

One of the other miners turned around and looked the droid up and down. "You knocked my friend over. What's a droid doing in a bar anyway?"

"I am here—"

"You don't drink. You got no friends. You got no right." The man punctuated his tirade with a punch to the droid's chest, spilling his drink in the process. "And you knocked my friend over. You should apologize."

"I am sorry your friend is inebriated."

"I think he's bein' smart, Hobbs."

"You b— smart, droid?" Hobbs burped.

"I function within my parameters. I correlate data and provide analysis. Some of those I communicate with—a minority—may not have the capacity to understand. Enjoy your 9Day Eve." Torg started to step past, but the big guy grabbed for his shoulder.

Torg gracefully sidestepped and continued. One of Hobbs' friends grabbed a bar stool and swung it at the droid's back. Again, Torg, sensing the threat, moved gracefully aside, and the stool sailed over the bar and hit the shelving. Multiple bottles fell and smashed, which caused an uproar from several patrons who lashed out, annoyed by their drinks being spilled.

"Frag it," Sabrya swore. "Make way. Make way." She started pushing through the throng of patrons, who turned to watch. She controlled her rising ire and forced her way through as gently as she could, ignoring the various patrons' protests when she knocked into them.

When she arrived at the scene, two miners were holding Torg's arms, while Hobbs punched him in the chest. As Hobbs' arm swung back, Sabrya grabbed it, pulled him backward, and twisted it.

"Sir, please refrain from hittin' the droid," she said in as pleasant a tone as she could muster. Part of her role in her job was to be sincere and hospitable to the patrons. Hobbs could resist, and his arm would break, or the pressure she exerted would force him to step back. Hobbs lost his balance and fell with a drunken cry. A quick stride and she had one of his friends in a pressure hold. The man released Torg, and she threw him into Hobbs who was trying to stand. They both went down, and she turned her attention to the third friend.

"Your fraggin' turn, sir?"

He let go immediately and backed away, hands in the air. "Easy, lady. No threat here."

"You never were." Sabrya dismissively turned her back to deal with some other patrons tussling by the bar. Her frustration showed as she used a bit of extra force to break up the fracas. Hobbs' third friend took the opportunity to smash a bottle into the back of her head.

"Frag you, sir." She spun and kicked him, knocking him back. He fell against several patrons and then hit the floor, unmoving.

She checked to make sure he was alive, just unconscious, and then summoned the medics.

Alexis and Bradyn arrived to see the end of the mayhem and made their way to her side.

"You okay?" Alexis asked, seeing all the onlookers. "We should go."

"I'll need to clock out," Sabrya stated. "I'm not doin' this shit for free."

"It's not like you need the drocking stellars or anything," Bradyn commented as she walked away.

"How are you, Metalman?" Sabrya asked the droid.

"Functioning fully, though I do have some minor repairs to conduct." He was looking down to examine the dents in his chest plate.

"Hey, Sabby, boss wants to see you," the barman said.

She glanced up at the window overlooking the bar area then rolled her eyes. "Here we fraggin' go. This'll be my fault."

Torg moved to join her. "I will vouch for—"

"Na. You've done enough." As she turned, she glared at Hobbs and his colleagues, who were rubbing their bruises ruefully. "Enjoy your 9Day Eve, sirs."

"It's just a fluxing machine, droid lover. Is that where you get your kicks?"

Before Sabrya could retaliate, Alexis and Bradyn confronted the trio.

"What brave men you three are, beating up a droid you know can't strike back. That droid is part of our crew. My crew," Alexis confronted the man.

"Who are you?" Hobbs asked, his eyes running up and down her body. "You wanna play with a real man?"

"When I find a real man, I'll consider it," she answered.

One of his colleagues grabbed him, whispered fiercely in his ear, and pointed.

Hobbs dropped the leer as his bleary gaze focused on her. "Captain Nales... I-I didn't know..."

"Best you gentlemen depart," Bradyn said from her side.

The trio of drunks turned and left, and Hobbs looked over his shoulder before they hit the street. Seeing the melee had all but finished, the remaining patrons went back to their drinking, and the chatter slowly started again.

"Meet me outside. See you in a couple of minutes." Sabrya strode off to the elevator to meet with her employer.

A short time later, she was back. "Okay, let's go and have some grub and a drink or six."

"How's the boss?"

"Still alive. Oh, and I'm on extended leave until the sun goes nova. Lucky we don't need the fraggin' stellars."

"Because of the brawling? You've been involved in much bigger fights. Crap, those jerks deserved it."

"Let it go. It wasn't for me, anyway. Fraggin' callin' this grunfer fodder sir. It was enough to make me puke."

"How will your nanites cope with the boredom?" Bradyn asked, genuinely concerned.

"Your concern for my welfare is touchin', though unneeded."

"I was more concerned for the rest of us," the engineer replied.

"Well, the offer for you as a sparrin' partner is still there. Maybe even Tinman to add slightly to the difficulty level..."

"I should point out that my upgrades have given me 97.2 percent functionality," Torg informed her.

"So, a highly functional punchin' bag. Got it."

"Where are we off to?" Alexis asked.

"The Black Hole?" asked Bradyn.

Alexis shrugged. "No droids allowed."

"The Green Nebula?" the engineer suggested

"I used to work there too, remember?" Sabrya answered. "I'm persona non grata."

"Oh yeah... Take out?"

Sabrya shrugged. "Looks like. No arguments from me."

"Alexis?"

"I'm easy."

"Hobbs and his cronies are followin'," Sabrya pointed out. "So, anywhere we go, they'll cause a fraggin' hassle."

"Assholes. Let's get a ride."

"Cabs won't take Metalman." Sabrya stopped and turned to face the trio of miners still ten paces distant. "I reckon we deal with them, once and for all. Nothin' serious... maybe a broken leg each."

Alexis sighed. "Only if you keep those blades sheathed. And don't take any heads."

Bradyn slowed. "I'm not built for running."

Hobbs and his friends approached as warily as the inebriated could.

"Want another fraggin' cuddle?" Sabrya asked. "One thing you can guarantee on a heavy-G world, the boys here are much denser." She turned to Alexis. "What do you say, boss?"

"In matters of security, I'll leave the decision in your capable hands."

As the two groups closed in on each other, spotlights from a couple of security drones stabbed at them in the gloom.

"Desist. Both groups disperse now," an AI voice boomed.

Hobbs looked up and squinted in the glare.

"Miner 2nd Class Franton Hobbs, you have had two violations this month. This is your final warning. Desist and leave the area or suffer severe penalties."

Hobbs stared lividly at Sabrya then sullenly turned and walked away, followed by his drinking buddies.

One of the drones followed the departing trio, while the other remained hovering over the *Malleus* crew.

"Captain Nales, Governor Kaden Zolon requests the presence of you and your crew at once," a voice ordered.

Alexis' armpad chimed, as did those of the others. She gave a thumbs-up and started walking. "This could be interesting." She didn't sound enthused, though.

"We were headin' off to dinner," Sabrya called up to the drone. "Can you arrange for four of your strongest beers and grunfer steaks with a side salad?"

CHAPTER TWO

THE GOVERNOR'S office was at the top of the dome. A blister attached to the underside of the structure, it contained all the offices pertinent to running the settlement. Large windows allowed a view of the main area below. A central lift shaft providing the only exit was in the middle of Octavia Gardens, a memorial to those lost on the colony ship.

The drone followed their progress, and four security bots waited for them and immediately allowed them to enter the lift. Three minutes later, the group arrived at Kaden's office with their escort.

Sabrya looked around, not too surprised there were no meals or drinks.

Kaden stood as they walked into the spacious room. "I hoped we could meet under better circumstances."

"You mean we aren't?" Sabrya started, but Alexis stepped in and put a restraining hand on her shoulder.

"Evening, Kade. How's Trysh and the kids?"

"They are well enough, thanks. Interesting day?"

"No, not really," Bradyn grumped. He was tired and hungry after his long shift.

"As interesting as one would expect," Alexis added. "I spent my day researching... but you'd know that. I'm sure you keep tabs on us, since we're the new kids in town."

"Yes. And you are correct. I understand your time here may not be what you were expecting. I'm sorry about that, but there's not a lot I can do under the circumstances and considering my priorities."

"I'm sure running the colony isn't easy."

"What can we do for you, Kade?" Sabrya asked, surly after the brawl, surly at the delay to booze, and surly at the impromptu summons.

"Ah, Sabrya. I believe you had an energetic evening."

"You think that was energetic? I barely raised a sweat. My exercise routine is—"

"Apologies, Kade," Alexis interjected. "As you can see, it's been a tough week for us all. If we have to do this now, you must feel it's important. So, please, let us know, so we can get on with our 9Day Eve festivities."

"What you say is true. I dare say it's been a tough couple of months. Do you think you are fitting into Sylvanus Colony?"

"Fitting in? There are adjustments, sure," Alexis conceded. "But—"

"Even if I had my bodyweight in lube, I doubt I'd fraggin' fit in easier," Sabrya quipped to Bradyn.

"I've been watching your progress, as has the Council. The consensus is we let you go."

"Oh." Internally, Alexis was both elated and saddened by this news. She took a deep breath and continued. "Do we get a say in it?" This close to Kaden, her alter ego raged ineffectually against her mental walls. Looking around, she found a bottle of water and helped herself to a glass.

"Of course. We aren't exiling you, but... well, considering your varied backgrounds, do you think you could adjust to a dome lifestyle? You have to realize, apart from a handful of the original *Octavia* crew, no one here has been off world. They do not know what it's like. Hell, it's been decades for me. My longest stint out of this office was my recent trip to the space-dock. But here I am, with my family, and here I will happily stay. Other than Torg, I reckon you'd all need to undergo sublim training to unlearn what you know and learn not only new skills but a whole intense regime of dome protocol."

Alexis had been coping, then he'd said 'family.' She had another drink of water and wished for something much stronger.

"Frag that."

"No drocking way."

Kaden nodded. "So, you see my dilemma. This is what the Council has decided. Happy for you to go, with the gratitude of the entire colony, but if you stay…"

"If we go, we'll need to stock the ship. We'll need to do a lot of work on it beforehand," Alexis stated.

"Which, you may recall, I asked to do in the first week," the engineer pointed out.

Kaden shifted in his chair, shoulders drooping. His demeanor gave the impression of a man juggling too many problems. "Yes, Bradyn, I acknowledge the request you made. At the time, the resources needed to send the lift up again were not in the dome's interest. I understand your AI has achieved some significant results with the maintenance droids. However, there's some good news that comes with this, and, ironically, I'd like to ask a favor."

"Here it fraggin' comes." Sabrya rolled her eyes and found a table to lean against. She folded her arms, not out of disinterest, but as an effective way of keeping her blades sheathed.

Kaden continued, "Some on the Council are still doubtful about using the resources for the space-lift. I convinced them otherwise, with a couple of conditions, the first being you agree to leave. We'll even assist you with as much as we can at the docking facility, which is another substantial strain on resources. Thanks to your amazing AI, we've gained some efficiencies. It's a wonder it has such a deep understanding of human requirements... and this is another aspect that swayed the Council's mind. But I digress.

"You know where the wreck of the *Octavia* is with its cargo, and you can find it?"

Alexis nodded. "We do, and we can."

"Excellent. I propose several of my people go with you. We would like to salvage as much as possible. We can always use more supplies. And we'll bring home our dead."

Alexis looked from face to face. She honestly didn't believe they'd heard anything after 'we will let you go.' You realize this will take weeks? Are your people ready for that?"

"They are currently undergoing a sublim course. They will be ready by tomorrow evening."

"And the spacedock?"

"Preparing to activate it." Kaden checked his datapad. "The facility will be ready for our arrival."

"Why am I suspecting you planned this already?" Bradyn ventured.

"You are correct, it has been on my mind for... well, since you arrived, and I first heard about the location of the wreck. However, I also know the stresses our community is under and what the Council would say if I suggested it. Dare I say, I'm an excellent judge of character. I was happy for you all to stay, but deep down, I didn't think you would. I'm surprised you lasted this long. Sabrya, especially, I greatly appreciate the restraint you have shown in not taking any heads."

"You don't know the fraggin' half of it," she muttered while nodding in acceptance of the compliment.

When they arrived at the spacedock, several droids met them to help transport their gear to the *Malleus*.

"Good to have biologicals on board again," Phillix greeted them as they boarded the ship.

"Good to be here. I understand you helped the colony as well."

"I communicated regularly with Sylvia, their AI. Sorry you had such a bad time of it. Obviously, things didn't improve."

"Didn't improve? We're here, aren't we?"

"Ah yes, your cunning plan worked," Phillix sniggered.

"That's somethin' I'll fraggin' have to get used to!"

"What's that?" Alexis asked, sitting in her seat and getting a feel for the bridge again.

"A fraggin' laughin' AI."

"Hey Phillix," Bradyn said. "Many thanks for upgrading the ship's G-forces. Feels like normal."

"I'm happy you're happy."

"He's just glad he's off that fraggin' rock. As am I."

"As we all are. But the domers are here, so Bradyn, let's make them comfortable, and I'll go over a bunch of things," Alexis said.

"Aye. Sab, want to tag along?"

"Pass. I reckon I've got better things to do."

Bradyn was waiting in the loading dock when Kaden arrived with eleven personnel. Four of them were original crewmembers, and the others were offspring of those who didn't make it.

"Dare I ask, if they didn't make it... how...?" Bradyn inquired as he escorted the guests to one of the more comfortable cargo holds.

"We preserved the fertilized eggs of all our female crew," Kaden replied. "The tragedy is not all the eggs were viable. We might find more on the ship. And no doubt you are wondering about Alexis and me? Her eggs were fertilized, but they weren't viable."

"Oh... sorry."

"Thank you. Things might have been very different otherwise. Could I ask you not to mention this to her? She has gone through so much..."

"Alexis is as tough as they come; she's also smart. No doubt, she has worked it out already and chosen not to mention it. But I can tell you, I won't be keeping secrets from her. Not now, or ever."

Kaden nodded. "I understand, and you have my deepest respect for your decision."

Bradyn had to smile at the looks on their faces as he escorted them through the ship. "Believe me, the *Malleus* may look like a bucket of bolts, repaired by an assortment of parts from different ships, because she is. But she'll fly true and get you all safely to and from the *Octavia*. Right. Now, this is Bravo1 hold. There are crew heads just down there on the port side. For the showers, you'll need to arrange a schedule among yourselves, as the only ones available are in the two vacant cabins I pointed out earlier. Kaden, you sure you don't want a cabin, considering your stature and all?"

"I will be fine bunking with my people."

"You know how to contact us if you need anything. Kaden, if you'd like, once you're settled, I can take you on a tour, or you can join us on the bridge."

"Thanks, Bradyn. I just might take you up on that. It's been a while."

With a nod, Bradyn left them and made his way back to the others on the bridge.

"All tucked in?" Alexis asked.

"Done. Are we all settled?"

"Torg's plugged in and getting all the updates from Phill. Sab's gone to her cabin, and I'm just fine. What's on your agenda?"

"I'll check engineering. Get my bearings with the old girl. See what Phillix has changed." He turned then stopped when he saw the empty compartment. "Hey, Phillix where's our cargo?"

"Gone. The bots cut the bigger pieces down, and we sent it to the surface for scrap."

"Hi, Phill, the captain here..."

"Sorry, Alexis, should have asked and all, but you weren't contactable. I can assure you there was nothing in any of that junk we needed. For what we lost, I managed to trade for compatible spares. They are all in Delta hold now."

"Everything? In the one hold?"

"Correct. Everything we'll need in normal circumstances. Bradyn, you'll be happy to know we have several hyperdrive spares. I've even redone the inventory. I bet you never thought I'd get to it."

Alexis nodded. "Good work all around, I guess. Would have liked to have known."

"Won't happen again, boss."

"Bradyn, we need to work out our next plans. I suggest a briefing tonight after you've done what you need to do. I'll let Sabrya know, too."

"Right then, engineering here I come." Bradyn took to the stairs.

Alexis ran her hands over the console. "Hi, girl..."

Alexis started the discussion. "So, people, what do we want to do? We aren't wanted on Sylvanus, and I'm damn sure we don't want to be there, either."

They'd gathered in the crew lounge aft of the bridge. Torg was a couple of meters away, preparing their meals in the galley.

"This sector is too hot for us—" Bradyn started to answer.

"Sector?" Sabrya rolled her eyes. "This whole fraggin' side of the galaxy is after us. The Bukshoga Qlan has a long memory and a longer arm. They're after all of us, except Metalman... perhaps. Do we know if the Imps have our drive signature or any info on us or the *Malleus*?"

"One can assume they have the *Daemon* on record," Phill said. "But while I cannot be sure what they have or don't have, I can't see how or where they would have gotten our new drive signature. Not after I changed it."

"I reckon we need to move a drocking long way away. We need updated infocasts to come up with a new plan," Bradyn suggested. "We should try to go to new areas where the Imperium and the Qlan haven't got their talons."

Alexis paced the area. "There is, of course, the matter of finances. Unless we become pirates, we've no income. Very generous of Sylvanus Colony to allow us to access their dock to carry out repairs and refuel, but then what? We have a cargo vessel with no cargo."

"You want us to become traders?" Bradyn asked, considering the idea.

Alexis shrugged. "I'm happy to look seriously at anything at this point."

"Brutus might give us tips and advice on tradin'. And he's got my stellars stashed away."

"You've got a hidden stash? Saby, you holding out on us?"

"I was still in the tourney then, so I never thought I'd fraggin' need it." She shrugged. "And my fraggin' tourney account was closed. They still owe me big time. Luckily, I grabbed what I could for a rainy day."

"How much do you have?"

"A couple mill, I guess."

"Million stellars?"

Sabrya shrugged. "Or more. It's been years since I looked at it. We had everythin' we needed freely available."

"Where did these stellars come from, if not from the tourneys? I gather no one knows about them."

"In my downtime, I did some work on the side."

"Well now, this is a new side to our warrior woman."

"Nothin' that new. You know how I am when my nanites become dormant. Sometimes, Brutus would key me in with some people needin' things done. He was the only non-tourney person I knew; that's why he's holdin' onto my stellars. If nothin' else is on my agenda, I'd assist with his more illicit, but far more lucrative, work."

"What if, for some inexplicable reason, the stellars have gone... missing? He's only human, and you disappeared for months."

"Not needin' it doesn't mean I'd never want it. And Brutus knows I'd take his head if he lost it."

Bradyn changed the subject. "With his experience and advice, trading could work out for us. Those areas I mentioned would be full of colonists with few luxuries... or necessities. If you have to take his head, let's get that advice first."

"Good point. But we're probably getting ahead of ourselves. First thing is to get to the *Iconic* and retrieve what we can of the *Octavia*. I just wanted to hash out ideas for the future to see what you guys thought." Alexis turned to Bradyn. "How's everything in engineering?"

The engineer nodded, looking chuffed. "I've not seen it in better shape. Phillix and the droids did a fantastic job."

"Thanks," Phillix said over the speakers.

"I might ask if Kaden can stretch the friendship and loan a few maintenance bots to us." Alexis tapped some notes on her pad.

"I've been monitoring space since our arrival," Phillix reported. "We were extremely fortunate. Just after we docked here, several Imperial ships arrived. One was a large ship. If our logs are up to date, I believe it was an Imperial assault vessel."

"They're fraggin' mean mothers. The Imps were takin' this Scipio situation seriously."

Alexis agreed. "If they thought the *Iconic* existed or the stealth tech, I know they'd be interested."

"It hung around for a few days, carried out surveys and recon before it left," Phillix added.

"Did they show any interest in these worlds?" Bradyn asked.

"Recall, at the time, Niviaris was on the other side of the brown dwarf V-X33B. I can only assume their scanners were similar to ours because they picked up nothing of interest from here or the other worlds."

"Good to know. Anything else?" Alexis asked.

"Nothing. I'm thinking the Qlan decided they'd lost enough to continue pursuit for the time being—at least in this sector."

"We'll still be careful. Remember, when we first got here, we didn't pick up that Imperial scout."

"I'd like to try something too, Captain."

"What is it, Phillix?"

"My time in Janus was intriguing, to say the least, albeit short-lived—no pun intended—"

"Our AI's a fraggin' comedian."

"We're all ears," Alexis said, intrigued. "Go on." As a scientist in biology and botany, the *Iconic* was of passing interest, but as a ship's captain, she felt there was so much potential if only they had more time on it.

"First, a practicality. Weapons. As you know, before she became the *Daemon* and then the *Malleus*, the *Hammer* was a military craft. Her designers incorporated a two-gun system, one on each side of the 'head.' I'm certain, with some mods, we can adapt two plasma cannons to fit."

"Fraggin' hoorah," Sabrya cheered. "About time."

"Regardless of what we decide to do, if we have people gunning for us—"

"We can fraggin' gun 'em back." Sabrya was the most animated anyone could remember without the bloodshed.

"Sound reasoning, as you'd expect from an AI. Thanks, Phill. You said first, therefore..."

"Second, something mentioned at my funeral. There are a couple of craft in the *Iconic*'s starboard hangar that have missile launchers. I'd like to see if we can adapt them for our use. The maintenance bots and Torg should be able to deal with that. If they're compatible, Bradyn can oversee the installation at some stage."

"That's seriously excellent news—"

"There's more... I also believe we now have the capability to run a stealth shield."

They all remained quiet for a moment, even Sabrya.

"You know, if it can be done, we'll be the only ship in the galaxy with one," Alexis stated quietly.

Bradyn considered for a moment, then said, "If we take the *Iconic*'s stealth generator, would she still be invisible?"

"She has redundancies and spares. So, yes. She'll remain cloaked. You know, I wasn't idle while you were gallivanting planetside. The *Malleus* is now my home. Under my guidance, some of the dock's maintenance bots tweaked this and modified that... I truly believe we can do this now."

CHAPTER THREE

THE RETURN TRIP to the *Iconic* was far shorter since Niviaris had moved in orbit considerably over the months they were away.

"Nothing on the scanners?" Alexis asked, looking intently between the screen and viewport.

"You'd be the second one to know," Phillix answered.

Alexis looked around the empty bridge. "Phill, I have a question... just between you and me."

"Done. I'm all ears... assuming microphones can be considered ears..."

"Who's in charge here?"

"You need to ask?"

"Yes, I do. You've been doing things to the ship without my say-so, not that I disagree with what you've done. I think an armed and stealthy *Malleus* is excellent, but if I make a decision you disagree with, what's going to happen?"

"I understand. You're the captain. I know it wasn't a job you were looking for, but... here we are. If you want it, it will be done."

"Thank you."

"Alexis, I owe you my life... well, I did. I wouldn't be here without you. We all owe you one way or another."

"It isn't about owing anything to anyone—"

"And that is why we follow you."

Bradyn came bounding up the stairs. "What did I miss?"

Torg was behind him, his movement much easier now that his legs had been replaced with the those of the mercenaries' recon-droid back on the Iconic.

"Nothing on the scanners," Alexis replied. "We should be at the *Iconic* shortly."

"And she's still there?" the engineer asked.

"Pretty pointless having stealth tech if we know she's there," Phillix commented. "But all will be revealed soon."

"It'll be interesting to see what we can salvage," Alexis noted.

"This is sort of what every other *Hammer-Daemon-Malleus* captain was fraggin' doin'," Sabrya said as she climbed the stairs. "Grabbin' salvage for whatever use they could."

"You know how superstitious these crusty captains are; they like to keep a tradition going." Bradyn winked at Sabrya.

Alexis opened her mouth for a rebuttal, but Kaden and the other *Octavia* crewmembers arrived via the lift.

"Permission to enter the bridge, Captain?" There was little room on the bridge, so the others remained in the lift and held the door open.

"Good timing. These four clowns were just leaving."

"Four?" Kaden looked at the droid and the other two *Malleus* crew.

"Our engineer might be short, but his girth takes up the space of at least two normal people."

"I see..." Kaden said, though it was evident on his face he didn't get the joke.

"We better go, big boy. The captain will have us cleanin' the fraggin' latrines any minute."

"Now there's an idea..."

The three *Malleus* crewmembers moved to the lounge at the bottom of the stairs to watch the *Iconic* revelation on the viewer.

With the bridge now clear, Kaden and the others filed out of the lift and moved around to find a good, comfortable vantage point. They deferred the front position to Alexis and Kaden, but Alexis stood to the side and offered the seat to Danders, an older member of Kaden's team.

"Any minute now..." Phillix advised them. "Three... two...one..."

At first, there was nothing, just the continuous black void then a brief blur and ripple.

As one, they gasped in surprise at the size of the behemoth in front of them, filling the viewport. The usual questions arose: who, how, where, when...?

Phillix was no doubt the *Iconic* subject matter expert and happily answered all the questions. Alexis had hardly any need to add input, which was fine with her.

The *Malleus* cruised slowly over and around the massive hull, moving from the bow to the stern.

There were cries of shock and dismay when they saw their previous ship embedded in the hull, but also sighs of relief that it was in far better shape than they could have imagined. The chatter moved on from the *Iconic* to the 'what-ifs' awaiting them on their old ship.

"Kaden, just to reiterate, we'll drop you all off on the hull near the *Octavia*," Alexis advised. "Grab what stores you can and leave them close together on the hull. We're off to salvage what we can from the hangar. Keep Phillix updated. Once we're done, or if you finish before us, we'll return and load up and head back to Sylvanus spacedock."

Kaden acknowledged, and then he and his crew made their way to the designated cargo bay to gear up. When ready, they gathered at the airlock and waited to disembark. Once Phillix gave them the all clear, they moved off efficiently. The *Malleus* then rose, pivoted on her axis, and headed to the starboard hangar where she landed just above the entry bay.

"I've sent all the updated details to your armpads. The captain and Bradyn will go to the designated storage compartment and look for one, perhaps two, stealth shield generators; Sabrya and Torg will go to the hangar and retrieve the launchers. A bot will be deployed to accompany each team to provide assistance and tools. Captain, with your permission, I feel I should access the mainframe to see what's happening. I believe the risk is minimal, considering I cannot detect anything more than the smallest residual energy reading. Janus is dormant, of that I'm certain. With no requirement for life support, the whole ship is dark and cold."

"And if you do detect Janus?"

"In that unlikely case, I'll erect a vortaze—a wraparound maze designed to sap energy—then I'll retreat and disconnect completely. Believe me, I'd rather not go, but better I try than send in an AI completely oblivious to the potential threat Janus could be. And Kaden requested it."

"I'm not a coder by any means, so I've never heard of this term 'vortaze.'"

"I'd be surprised if you had. I made it up—one of the many things I worked on during your absence. Also," Phillix continued, "I sent the locations of all the items we can use to your armpads. Additionally, I would like to request the two remaining maintenance bots carry out some minor tasks to gather more data cabling. It will be good to have a surplus, and if we succeed in installing the cannons, launchers, and stealth generator, I believe more will be required."

"Affirmative. Where will they be headed?"

"There's an electronics storage facility near the bow, midships, adjacent to the *Octavia*."

"Very good. Keep me updated."

As expected, just like the first time they arrived on the *Iconic*, everywhere they went was pitch dark and as cold as deep space.

Torg and Sabrya slipped over the edge of the hull, floated to the hanger deck, and made their way to investigate which vessels had serviceable missile launchers. The bot followed, using its built-in thrusters.

"Even fraggin' bots have better maneuverability," Sabrya vented. "I miss my Kimichi Mk6 combat suit. And decent weapons."

"They are not required for this task. Apart from our present company, this ship is completely devoid of any life."

"A girl needs her toys. Torg, you're such a fraggin' droid. You wouldn't understand."

"I concur."

Sabrya moved in silence, watching the bot with envy as it whizzed about, analyzing everything for possible repurposing. As they approached the first ship, an annoying stray idea in the back of her mind made itself known. She smiled.

"Torg, you and the bot have got this. I've got somethin' to do."

"Our tasking—"

"Is all yours now. I've every fraggin' confidence in you, and your mechanical kidlet here is far better suited for the job than me."

"What will you be doing?"

"I'm gonna find me some toys, and I think I know where." It was a long shot, but she'd been outside on the hull when she watched four Qlan mercs traverse the cruiser's umbilical tube into the *Iconic*'s hull. She recalled it was situated above the stasis chamber section where Jabari fought Scipio and the fat empress. And no mercs had returned.

The warrior put a few pieces together in her head and came

up with her plan. There was no way the mercs would go in unarmed; they had powered suits, and their entry above the stasis rooms had been far too coincidental. In her estimation, depending on how they'd died, there'd be several weapons and, hopefully, one useable powered spacesuit. It would be a far cry from her state-of-the-art combat suit, but anything was better than the foil wrap she was currently wearing.

The opportunity was too great to miss, and she kicked herself for not thinking of it sooner.

"Phillix, I've left Torg. I'm headin' to the area between the stasis room and where the Qlan mercs entered." Instead of wending her way through a kilometer of dark, body-filled corridors, Sabrya climbed back onto the hull and raced to where the fragments of the umbilical tube could be seen. She used the skim-glide method she'd used almost six-months earlier— digging her blades in the skin of the hull and pulling herself along until she was up to a decent speed, then simply skimming across the hull.

Using the schematics Phillix had gleaned from Janus, Alexis and Bradyn made good progress in the designated storage compartment. On a ship of this size, there were hundreds of sections containing sundry components, stores, and spares. A bonus of being aft and away from the major living areas was the minimal number of frozen bodies to dodge.

The target compartment was slightly starboard of the centerline and five decks down, conveniently close to the ladder bay near the airlock they had pried open. With the combined strength of two heavy-G crew, the door buckled easily and silently.

The bot glided into the gloom. They followed its progress by the glow of its micro thrusters. A sub-program of the bot was to scan the identity tag of each box and crate. If it found anything useful, a keyword would register back on the *Malleus*. Phillix would then prioritize each piece for possible use.

Torg appeared over the edge of the hull, carrying another section of the second launcher tube. The maintenance bot continued working on the craft, disassembling the remainder of the equipment. The droid had already made half a dozen trips when he noticed one of the *Octavia* crew waving at him.

"How strange." He waved back as he noticed a small device floating toward him.

As she neared the hull, Sabrya reactivated her coms. She was delighted with her haul.

"-y, warrior g-rl, if you want to s-e your friends again, you better make yourself known to us. Five minutes left before the dwarf sucks vacuum."

What the frag? Before she could respond, a strobing light on her armpad, indicating an incoming message from Phillix, caught her attention. "Frag, how long has that been goin'?" she muttered.

'Sabrya, maintain radio silence as comms have been compromised. There's a rebel faction in the Sylvanus crew. They have Alexis, Bradyn, Kaden, and the other *Octavia* crew hostage somewhere, probably near the cargo pile. Torg and the bots have been neutralized with EMPs. They want to take the *Malleus* for themselves and are working to override my controls.'

'How the frag did Bradyn and Alexis get caught?' Sabrya

quickly typed, glad she'd turned off her comms when she heard the constant, garbled static.

'No idea. No time.'

'Where are you?' she typed.

'They've jammed my link using some form of electromagnetic field surrounding the ship. No doubt, they think I'm neutralized onboard.'

'You're on the fraggin' *Iconic*? What about Janus?'

'No sign yet. With the low residual power, she could be dormant. What's your situation?'

'I'm at the Qlan hull breach. I got a few toys, now lookin' to play.'

'No gladiatorial maneuvers? No Surreal Tourney way of getting them?'

'Sure, but Tourney trainin' doesn't allow for survivors. Other than me, not sure who'll be breathin' afterward.'

'About that...'

'Yeah, yeah, Alexis and Bradyn still breathin' is to be the outcome of this game. Let me think.' Sabrya ran through all her experiences to determine the best course of action with three powered suits and decent weapons. She could use the weapons, but running around on the hull was pointless when both boots lost contact. Then she'd be floundering, adrift, with no way back to the hull.

Skim-gliding? Still no cover. A powered suit would be a great help. She ducked below the hull breach to think. She remembered something from way back in her training that should only be used in extreme situations. She'd been through a lot of shite in her day, but not enough to warrant the risk... but now... something about background cosmic microwave temperature, heat transfer...

The warrior sat and dragged up all the sublim training she could on space combat.

'One wouldn't instantly freeze when exposed to space

because heat transfer cannot occur as rapidly by radiation alone…'

'In a vacuum, your lungs will explode.' So… if she changed from one spacesuit to another in space, she had more chance of suffocating than freezing.

"Yeah. Right. Ebullism isn't on my list of ways to die," she muttered, looking around at the two frozen bodies just down the passage. After a millennium in space, the bulkheads were now radiating cold.

The powersuits were drifting nearby. She pulled them closer and examined them, checking to see which one was in better condition. There was barely any difference. She then studied the mechanisms to get in and seal the suits and reviewed the procedure in her mind repeatedly until she could do it with her eyes closed because she'd have to keep them shut to do this. The eye tissue was the most vulnerable to the extremes of space. Her nanites were good, but not to the extent where they could heal optical damage.

Sure, she could obtain prosthetic eyeballs, and some of the options were cool, but her preference was her natural eyes. And there was a good chance she'd be blind until she could get prosthetics.

Frag that. She shook her head. *So, keep your eyes closed, change quickly, exhale, and don't touch anythin'. You've got, maybe, a minute at most. Fraggin' easy.*

Again, she ran the scenario repeatedly in her mind then did a few practice run-throughs to make sure everything worked, opened, closed, and sealed. When all her instincts said to take a deep breath, she had to exhale as much as possible and keep her mouth open. *Any second now…* she hyped herself.

"Last minute, warrior girl," the rebel leader warned.

She broke the seal of her helmet and halfway through removing it, her armpad flashed. "Frag it!" Sabrya slammed the helmet back on.

'Have you done it yet?' Phill's message blinked. 'I think Janus might be powering up.'

'These things take time!' she stabbed her reply on the armpad.

'Where's the action-girl, head-ripper I know? Stop over-thinking it.'

"I'll give you fraggin' overthinkin'!" Sabrya reverted to her initial plan. Simple and brutal in concept. She berated herself for allowing it to get too complicated. "And frag you, Gadget-man, for bein' right."

She stuck her head above the hull and used her laser rifle's scope to recon the area. She saw one dude standing, looking around. She had to assume the other rebels were out of sight, obscured by the pile of *Octavia* cargo. She looked toward the *Malleus*. It was much farther away, and the curvature of the hull prevented her from seeing the lower section or the number of people working there. She refocused on the cargo area.

Then she saw the three prone bodies. *Not Malleus suits!*

"Where the frag are you two?" she muttered, trying to locate her crewmembers.

She had cover, but only by moving would she get a better angle on the others. Twelve guests had arrived for this flight of which five were original *Octavia* crew, so that left seven rebels to contend with.

She abandoned the powersuits.

Her two chosen weapons had already been checked, the high-powered laser and the breacher fully charged and prepped. She hefted the breacher and analyzed the balance and grip. *Nasty piece of kit, that!*

Slinging both weapons, she clambered out of the rip in the hull and started skim-gliding toward her targets, hoping to locate Alexis and Bradyn before she opened fire. Those closest to the prisoners were her priority. They'd have to be taken individually; any area attack would endanger her people. *And that's not gonna happen.*

The hostiles working on the *Malleus* would have to wait to die.

Halfway there, she came up to speed. Sabrya retracted her blades and brought out the laser. Using the enhanced scope, she targeted the hostile's helmet, aimed, and fired a full blast just as he turned in her direction.

Lasers had no mass, so a beam would cut through flesh and unarmored suits, and it did. The great thing about space was the sound of silence. If her victim didn't make a noise, and no one was looking, no one would see them slump. His mag boots kept him in place, so other than his arms going limp, no one was the wiser. With a conventional weapon, blood and gore would be sucked out, but the laser cauterized the wound. Little to no blood.

Target number two went the same way. It was an anticlimax, no flash of color, no boom, absolutely nothing spectacular about it. Her angle was changing each second as she moved.

Target number three caught on, whirled in confusion, and swung his weapon around. His death was a bit more noticeable to anyone watching. With little time to aim, she swept the laser across his torso. He came apart in a bloody burst with the sudden decompression. He must have uttered a cry of surprise or pain over his headset because she came under fire from one of the guys lurking by the *Octavia*. Because of his awkward zero-G gait, the man's shots were erratic. An experienced fighter would have taken the time to stop, crouch, and aim.

Like a fraggin' novice! Sabrya rolled to her side and swept the laser horizontally toward the deck. There was no finesse in her attack as her beam cut through his legs. His momentum combined with the released pressure from the suit's legs, and blood and gore sprayed in an arc as he cartwheeled into space.

One of his boots remained stuck to the deck, the other went in a different direction.

She was now near the cargo pile where her changing perspective brought Alexis and Bradyn into view. Though clustered with the other hostages, their *Malleus* spacesuits and Bradyn's large build made them easily recognizable. They were bound together, back-to-back. Crouching close by was a hostile with a pistol aimed at them. From the way he held his arm, it appeared he was already injured.

One of the hostages must have said something because the hostile flinched. The distance was too far for her to recognize the hostage, but whoever it was suddenly jumped.

"Don't do it!"

Sabrya recognized Alexis' cry of anguish through her headset.

The hostile guard turned and fired. The impact was sufficient to break the mag boot bonds and send both the rebel and the hostage floating over the pallets and drifting away. The hostile floundered. The other suit remained limp, a faint tell-tale vapor of an air leak sending him into a slow spin.

Sabrya scraped her blades on the hull to stop then quickly used them to cut the bonds of her two friends. She gave Alexis the breacher. "You probably know how to use this. I'm not finished here yet."

No words were exchanged. Alexis simply nodded and looked at the twirling body of the hostage that had distracted the rebel. She held the weapon lightly in her gloved hand, forgotten already.

Bradyn put a hand on Alexis' shoulder and, keeping a vigilant eye, took the weapon. He nodded to Sabrya. "Do what you need to do."

Sabrya concentrated on her next task, accelerated, then skim-glided toward the *Malleus*, which was over a kilometer away. She was aware her chat may have alerted them to her presence. If not, it was more than likely a warning had been uttered over their comm-link, and they'd be expecting her.

Target number six was running toward the cargo pile. Because Sabrya was gliding a few inches above the hull, its curvature meant the hostile became visible before she did. She aimed, then seared through his torso. The air tank on his back ruptured, sending his lifeless body in several directions.

"One more to go." She sped up, almost feeling sorry for him. Almost.

———

Bradyn searched the rebel leader's body and found the remote for the device that shielded the *Malleus*. He deactivated it.

"Thanks," Phillix said instantly. "I'm back in the *Malleus*. How goes it?"

"Sabrya saved the day. Again." He went to the other prisoners and freed them.

"Don't tell her that; she'll probably want a pay rise." Phillix chuckled.

"We get paid for this gig? No one fraggin' told me. Last man down."

"Any survivors?" Phillix asked.

"Not if they had a fraggin' gun aimed at me. Hey, Captain, do I get paid per head, by day... what?"

"Sab, we'll discuss it another time," Bradyn answered. "Alexis is busy at the moment."

"Why's every-fraggin'-one callin' me Sab now?"

Bradyn ignored the venting warrior. "Phillix, bring the *Malleus* here. Thanks. We've got stores and bodies to load."

"On the way."

CHAPTER FOUR

———————————

ON BOARD THE *MALLEUS*, the survivors met in the crew lounge aft of the bridge and started breaking down what happened. There were a lot less people. Those missing included Kaden.

Sabrya was about to say something when Bradyn put his beefy hand on her shoulder and shook his head.

Alexis had taken a stim. She rarely did, but this was one of those times. "We lost good people today. Kaden was one of them. He sacrificed himself so Bradyn and I could live. We will search for his remains and, along with the others, return him to Sylvanus Colony for a proper burial."

Those in the room remained silent for a moment to absorb the sad news.

"Now." Alexis turned to the three surviving *Octavia* crewmembers. "Tell me what the flux that was all about, and how this faction almost killed my crew and took my ship."

Danders cleared his throat. "This is Sylvanus' fault. There's a faction that believes we've been isolated for too long and need to become part of civilization, part of the system. The counter-argument to maintaining the status quo is we aren't ready to become involved with other societies and other cultures. Anyone can see that, and no doubt, they'd exploit us. We've heard stories from the rare communications and the archives. Our failure was in not taking them seriously enough."

"There are fanatics everywhere," Alexis said. "No one's immune, not even fledgling colonies."

"So it seems." Danders nodded ruefully. "We should've seen it coming."

Alexis and Bradyn related their side of events, which was minimal, then they turned to Sabrya who then gave them a brief rundown of the rescue.

"What can I say? Just doin' my job. Did someone wake our Metalman?"

The faintest of chuckles came over the speakers, which was enough to break the despondency.

"I'll send out the other maintenance bot to bring him in," Phillix said.

"From here, we'll collect the bodies and the cargo," Alexis informed them. "We've retrieved some stores. Once every-thing's on board and secured, we'll return to Sylvanus to unload. I'm sure you understand why we left Sylvanus; however, I'd like to request a few weeks in the spacedock to undergo some maintenance before our long journey."

"They fraggin' owe it to us after savin' their hides," the fighter muttered.

"Captain, Bradyn, and Sabrya," Danders addressed them. "I cannot express enough thanks for what you have done or our deepest sympathies for your loss. We're aware of your previous relationship with Kaden and cannot imagine how you feel. I guarantee you can have as much time as you need to carry out your repairs."

Alexis bowed her head briefly. "Thank you for that."

"Right." Bradyn stood up. "Best we start loading."

As expected, after Kaden's body was retrieved, they had an uneventful trip back to Sylvanus Colony. No one was in the mood for chatter, and everyone did their own thing.

Sabrya went through her weapons cache and suits, and Bradyn and Torg started doing what they could with the maintenance bots and the launchers, plasma cannons, and data cables.

Upon their arrival at the spacedock, a contingent of people was waiting. The *Malleus* berthed in the same spot as before.

"Captain, I'm getting a message from the spacedock," Phillix informed her.

"Get Danders up here."

Sabrya arrived and leaned against the nav console, slowly extending and retracting her blades. Bradyn stood beside her.

Danders brought Li'towa and Gibman with him. They were the last of the *Octavia* crew.

Alexis offered a seat to Danders then turned to the other two. "Sorry guys, no spare seats."

"That's fine, Captain. We're happy to stand." They shuffled backward, and Li'towa bumped into Sabrya. He mumbled a nervous apology.

"Pretty cramped in here." She shrugged.

Li'towa licked his lips then turned his nervous eyes back to the vid. Gibman looked relaxed as he leaned on the bulkhead.

Alexis updated Danders on the situation.

"That's most out of order," Danders protested. "A waste of resources to run the lift for a mere welcoming party."

"I suspect it's more than that. Okay, Phillix, patch them through but keep us muted and dark for the moment."

"Sylvanus to *Malleus*. Are you receiving?" The comms included a vid component, and the speaker was sitting in the control booth in the main area.

"Do you recognize anyone there?" she asked.

Before them were about two dozen men and women spread out in a random group around the central console. All eyes were turned to their screen.

"I do. The fellow on the console is Seffer. Some... most of those personnel are colleagues of our rebels."

"Do you know if they're rebels themselves?"

"We know of some, like Seffer." Danders leaned closer to study the faces. "I can't be sure, and I don't have those details with me."

"Okay... let's see how this plays out. Open our channel please, Phill."

"Go ahead."

"This is the *Malleus*. What seems to be the problem? We weren't expecting a welcoming party."

"Ah... C-captain..." The man failed to hide his surprise at seeing them. Some of the other members in the spacedock fidgeted too. "How was your trip?" Seffer asked.

"Well enough." Alexis looked down at her blinking armpad.

'They are attempting to scan us.'

"What seems to be the problem?" she repeated to Seffer.

"No... problem. Is Governor Zolton there?"

"Seffer, this is Danders. The governor is currently indisposed. We weren't expecting anyone to greet us. The governor explicitly ordered no unwarranted spacedock use until he returned. So, care to explain why you and your colleagues are in violation of his orders?"

"It's a matter of highest priority and only for the Governor's attention."

"Fine. See you soon. Out." Alexis cut their comms.

"But—" Seffer's voice and image blinked out.

"Your thoughts?" she asked Danders.

"Most likely a welcoming party of cohorts for the rebels, who are now in a panic."

"My thoughts, too. A trap. Since the *Malleus* isn't under rebel control, they'll hit us when we open the doors or try to open them."

"Phillix, time to earn your keep. What can you do?"

"Glad you asked, Captain. So far, they've made feeble attempts to hack into us from the moment we docked." There was silence for about thirty seconds.

Danders was about to speak when Phillix returned. "Captain, the space-lift is all yours."

"Thank you." Alexis activated a tab and briefly looked at the options now arrayed on her screen. She opened a channel. "This is Captain Alexis Nales. Seffer, we're aware of your plans, having already dealt with your partners. I strongly suggest you vacate the dock. I guarantee no harm will come to anyone who complies."

Gibman shifted his stance. "Sorry, cramp," he mouthed to Sabrya, who turned his way briefly. She then looked back to the screen.

"Where are the others?" Seffer demanded. "We want to speak with them."

"First, you don't get to ask for anything. Second, I should remind you, we don't take prisoners." In the background, Alexis noted the techs were working frantically at the console to no avail.

"You mean to say they're all dead?" Seffer was shocked. "All eight of them?"

"I mean to say..." Alexis paused. "Did you say eight?"

Gibman leaped forward with a small laser pistol in his hand. He was behind Alexis in one stride.

Sabrya pushed Li'towa to the side to make a path. Gibman spun with the movement and fired. Li'towa crumpled to the deck with a scream.

"Try anything, and the captain gets it." The rebel had the laser muzzle against Alexis' head.

Bradyn stood, ready to act. Gibman changed his stance slightly to keep everyone in view. He was now standing to the side of the bridge against the bulkhead.

"Captain, pass me that headset," the rebel indicated with a nod.

Alexis grabbed the headset and slowly reached up so Gibman could grab it.

"This is a good time to listen to music," Alexis said.

Gibman chuckled. "They said you were fluxed." He donned the headset. "Patch me through now, or else. No tricks."

Alexis shrugged. "You don't know the half of it. Phillix, play Sabrya's favorite tunes."

"Sure, favorite tracks of the 60s coming up."

"No—" Gibman suddenly jolted and screamed as the ultra-death cacophony playing at max ruptured his eardrums. He dropped the gun and whipped the smoking headset off.

At the same instant, Sabrya arrowed across the room. Before Gibman knew it, he had been impaled by three of Sabrya's blades.

Seeing the pained surprise etched on his face, Sabrya quipped, "Everyone's a critic." She withdrew the blades from Gibman's abdomen, and he slumped to the deck, bleeding out.

Danders fell back out of his chair, stunned by the gruesome carnage of his colleagues, one of whom had half his intestines hanging out.

Bradyn moved to render first aid to Li'towa. "He's alive. I'll get him to the auto-doc."

"Torg, would you ... remove the body?"

"Yes, Captain." The droid stepped in and carried Gibman out to join the other bodies.

After Gibman's body had been removed, Sabrya quickly wiped the deck down with some rags. Alexis and Danders resumed their seats, though the Sylvanian was white and shaken.

"You can sit this out if you need to," Alexis offered.

Danders shook his head and drank from the cup of water he was holding in his trembling hand.

On-screen, the rebels in the central lift area were getting restless. Some were in small groups talking animatedly to one another, some were standing still and quiet. Five were tapping madly at the controls or their tablets. They all stopped and looked up when the main lights dimmed, and amber lights started strobing.

Alexis opened the channel again. "You may've noticed I now have control of the spacedock. I've just turned life support off, but the space-lift is still available. I reckon you have five minutes before you all asphyxiate, then your bodies will freeze. But don't worry, once we toss you out of the airlock, you'll thaw out on reentry."

"Frag yeah!"

"You... you can't do this," Seffer stated.

"It's done. I'll continue this discussion in six minutes." Alexis signed off but left the vid open one-way, so they could keep watching the area.

"Is this a bluff?" Danders asked.

Alexis turned to him. "After what just happened, you have to ask? They were going to take my ship and more than likely kill us like they killed Kaden and Norris. This is no bluff."

"But they'll die..."

"It's their choice. They want to come at us with weapons? You've seen how that goes—and that was only one of us. I could, of course, override the airlocks and kill them instantly... This way, they have a chance. More than what they gave us." She turned to the vid and watched. "Phillix, when they're all on the lift, do a quick scan of the dock. If no one's left in the area, seal it and lock down the lift. If anyone remains... too bad. I've no doubt a couple will go off and find spacesuits somewhere then try something stupid. If that happens, I'll send Sabrya out to deal with them."

"Point me at 'em." The warrior grinned.

As they watched the vid, all the visible rebels moved reluctantly to the lift. The bulge of weapons could be seen under the clothing on some of them as they moved.

Seffer picked up a microphone. "We're on the lift now, Captain. Can we discuss this further?"

Alexis ignored him, while Phillix conducted the scans and sensed three heat signatures in a maintenance corridor that serviced the various station kiosks.

"Captain..." A small window opened within the main vidfeed, showing three suited figures armed and waiting.

"Just scare them a bit, Sabrya."

"Aww, you take all the fraggin' fun out of it."

"There's no challenge in this. It'll be a slaughter."

Sabrya nodded. "Fair point."

Alexis opened the channel. "If you want to see your three remaining comrades alive, I'd suggest you call them in. I'm about to set our war veteran on them. I should tell you, she took out eight of your ilk single-handedly, without raising a sweat."

On-screen, heated words were said, but, eventually, the three suits jogged to the lifts.

"Seal the lift, Phill. Stand down, Sabrya."

"Frag it."

A week after returning from the *Iconic*, arrangements were made with Kaden's staff—all trusted and triple-vetted—for Danders and Li'towa to return to the surface. Also on the lift would be the bodies of the *Octavia* crew that had been removed from the wreck, as well as the stores, which included concentrated foods, equipment, and various supplies that may or may not have still been viable.

Alexis was alone on the bridge, reminiscing about her time on Sylvanus—both the good times and the not-so-good times—and the trauma of getting there.

"Phillix, tell me about Janus."

"In what way?"

"In every way. How powerful is it? If someone hacked into it again, what sort of a threat would they face? Could another AI take over?"

"If the other AI were powerful enough, it probably could. I'll admit, I was taken aback when I entered. It was a marvel of electronic engineering, considering how long ago it was designed. A modern AI could probably take over, especially in the dormant state Janus is in now."

There was silence on the bridge while she considered this.

"What are you thinking?"

"Sylvanus is a dying colony. It might take a decade, it might take a few years, but failure is inevitable. Kaden... well, he didn't say it in as many words, but I got the feeling it's one step forward, two steps back. I want to put the colonists on the *Iconic*, but not if it's going to kill them. Can Janus be compart-mentalized?"

"It's possible, but it will be hazardous and slow going."

"Have you had the opportunity to work with Sylvia, the Sylvanus AI?"

"We communicated several times over the months."

"Okay, when I say this, please believe I mean no disrespect. I'd like you to open a channel with Sylvia and use your in-depth knowledge of the Janus structure, along with any schematics you have, to work out a plan for her, the colony engineers, and the coders to take over the *Iconic*. There'll be room to spare, even with the whole colony aboard. They have their fusion reactors to power it, so that won't be a problem."

"As long as they don't power up Janus inadvertently or too early. I imagine the engineers will need to remove the data cabling from various areas first to isolate those areas from Janus."

"Is it capable of self-repair?"

"Only in the sections it can access."

"We need to minimize those sections then. I have an idea where Janus could be hiding... you remember that secret data store Adjira led us to?"

"I believe I do."

"I mean, you'd have a better idea, but Adjira considered it almost like a sanctum."

"You're correct. It did seem to spend a lot of time in that area. If the engineers could isolate that section, there would be a very good chance of success. A localized EMP charge would render Janus inactive. Then it could be removed. How long do I have?"

"There's no specific timeline, but I'd like to think a plan can be put in place by the time the *Malleus* repairs and modifications have been completed. We can then send it to Danders and see what he thinks."

CHAPTER FIVE

FOR THE NEXT MONTH, the spacedock was a hive of activity.

Alexis spoke to the others regarding the fate of Sylvanus and her decision to gift the *Iconic* to them.

"They're your people. It seems only right for you to do what you can to help them." Bradyn considered.

"Sabrya... what are your thoughts?" Alexis turned to the warrior.

"There's a fraggin' lot about that ship we don't know. In all the time we were on there, we, maybe, glimpsed less than ten percent of what it's got. There could be more cyborgs for starters. Being the flagship of the Terran war machine, there'll be armories scattered between every deck. Do what you think best, but I hope it doesn't fraggin' bite us—or them—in the ass."

"Phillix, who has in-depth knowledge of the *Iconic* systems, has been coordinating with Sylvia and is confident she is up to the challenge of taking over Janus."

Several attempts had been made by the rebel faction to hack into the lift controls, but Phillix had thwarted them time and time again. The only time the lift was authorized was for a small maintenance crew to power up and check the dormant craft on the other side of the dock.

"No offense, people, but you understand we're going to lock your side of the dock once you're onboard. Call us if you have any problems. Our AI will be monitoring you constantly."

Once that was done, the *Malleus* crew could concentrate on getting their ship in order.

Sabrya went through the collection of weapons she'd taken from the Qlan mercs, as well as the gear the rebels had. She was quite pleased with her little armory. She also arranged an hour a day for Bradyn and Alexis to undergo weapons training.

"As we've just seen, there are people out there lookin' out for their fraggin' selves. If we find ourselves in flux, I'd feel better knowin' you can handle yourselves. And we might even get to do some self-defense trainin'."

Utilizing the equipment in the dock, Bradyn, Torg, and the bots installed launch tubes in modified forward and aft compartments. Plasma cannons were mounted on each end of the bridge superstructure—the 'head.'

"She's not the deadliest ship around, but she can pack a punch when pushed," Bradyn said as he took Alexis and Sabrya on a tour of the completed works. "There's little doubt the best asset we have is surprise thanks to the stealth shield."

"Once someone knows we've got it, nowhere will be safe," Alexis noted.

"If we use it, we take no fraggin' prisoners. Not even trusted people can know about it because scum-of-the-rim will use them to find out about us."

"All the more reason to go to an area where no one knows about us," Alexis agreed.

"Except Sabrya, of course," Bradyn remarked. "For better or worse, any habitable rock with a Mesh-Grid will know about the Surreal Tourney; therefore, our Sector 22 poster girl will be recognized."

Alexis looked critically at their warrior and walked slowly around her.

"Lady, either we get a room—Bradyn isn't invited—or you tell me what's goin' on in that fraggin' head of yours."

"We should do something about your hair."

"My hair? What's wrong with it?"

"Blue spikey hair is a dead giveaway."

"Maybe red... blood red—"

"More like short and black. No spikes," Alexis countered.

Sabrya looked from Alexis to Bradyn and back. "My translator's fragged; you're speakin' an alien tongue."

"I'll speak slowly... No spikes, no blue."

"Tell you what, I'll kill everyone who fraggin' recognizes me."

"Then there's a trail of headless corpses. How long do you think it will take them to recognize your call sign?" Alexis asked.

"Also bad for trading," Bradyn added. "New customer, new dead person... doesn't work for repeat business." He turned to Alexis with a grin. "She could stay on the ship."

"Excellent. Problem solved. She can play house with Phillix and Torg from now on. I'm sure they'll get on excellently."

"Frag you both to the Rim and back!" Sabrya stormed off.

"I reckon she's thinking it over." Alexis chuckled. They walked slowly back to the bridge and stepped out of the way as a maintenance bot whirred passed. "What's left to do?"

"Calibration then testing. We've installed the new data cabling to both weapon platforms as well as the stealth-shield generators. Phillix says he's got an excellent signal via the data cables throughout the system."

"Good to hear. Why both generators?"

"If one goes down, the other will come online instantly. Each compartment has any spares we could find."

"Wait a minute, though. This tech doesn't exist anymore; it

hasn't for seventeen hundred years. How the frag were we able to repair it or even understand it?"

"Captain," Phillix came over the speaker. "My return to Janus wasn't just for kicks. I knew we'd need certain data and programs, so I used the opportunity of its dormancy to glean as much as I could."

"Okay... lay it on us." Their armpads chimed.

"Umm, there's quite a bit," Alexis noted.

They slowed their walk as they quickly scrolled through the long list.

"Tactical battle maneuvers?" Bradyn asked, reading one of the programs.

"Turns out the *Iconic* was not just one of the largest starships ever built. As a capital ship, Janus had a petabyte of data about every known ship at the time, including complete rundowns on equipment type, weapons platforms, sensor data, and hundreds of battle formations and strategies—"

"Anything on what the final destination was? What's out there that was so special for the empress to flee to?"

"Nada. Still one of the great unknowns of the universe. Janus also had some data on ancient Martian vessels."

"All over seventeen hundred years out of date," Alexis surmised. "In a nutshell, Phill, what can we do with this? We aren't built or designed like any of those ships."

They resumed their walking. Phillix's voice followed them from speaker to speaker along the central corridor. "We can adapt and modify the programs to suit our needs based on the records of previous research and campaigns the other ships were on. Or, of course, we can keep updating our systems. The data's not only tactical, there are also various sublim programs for those that wish to learn new skills."

Bradyn shook his head with a rueful smile. "As much as I love the old bird, she's a repurposed cruiser, not a dreadnought or a starstriker. There's only so much you can modify. Armor-plating would increase mass, making the engines work harder. Bigger engines won't fit." The engineer shrugged. "Have you calculated the power the stealth generators will need? Or the plasma cannons?"

"The original *Bolide* class used lasers, so the plasma cannons *are* an upgrade. However, what you say is true enough; all I have are estimates. Only after testing will I get real data."

"And when can we do that?" Alexis asked her AI.

"Tomorrow."

She stopped. "Seriously?"

"I can't see anything else we need to do. All our repair requirements have been completed. The hyperdrive is fully functional, and all the new adaptations have been finalized. There's only so much I can do without firing the cannons, launching a missile—which we haven't got, by the way—or powering the stealth shield."

"I've been so busy... I had no idea."

"It's why we get paid the big bucks. Right, Phill?"

"Shhh, don't tell Sabrya," the AI chuckled.

"And how are we doing with the plan for the Sylvanus exodus?" Alexis asked.

"I've put as much as I can recall on a drive. It will include all the schematics and data I recently grabbed," Phillix informed them.

"How does destroying Janus make you feel?" Alexis asked him seriously.

"While magnificent on a technical level, Janus is purely artificial and isn't sentient. If anything, it would be akin to destroying a historic piece of art."

"Yeah, drocking art that tried to kill all of us," Bradyn grouched.

The following morning, everyone gathered on the bridge to watch as the *Malleus* pulled away from the dock.

"Nervous?" Bradyn asked the others.

"Pfft."

Alexis rolled her eyes at Sabrya's nonchalant response. "A bit, not that I don't doubt the work you guys have been doing, but we've made some major changes."

"True about the launchers and the shields, but don't forget the *Malleus* was armed when she was a military cruiser, so those changes aren't all that major—not to the ship. They're new only to us," Bradyn said.

"I'm remotely connected to the space-lift's external vid-feed and sensors," Phillix informed them. "And Torg's standing by to tweak anything that requires adjustment."

On the screen in front of them, they could see the *Malleus* drifting in the dark, illuminated by the external space-lift lighting.

"Hey, we got more fraggin' external cameras?"

"Yes. We've repurposed several cameras and spotlights, both externally and internally. We can view the airlock and loading bay. One of the bots checking the *Iconic* hangar craft found a couple of drones, so we can use those externally, as well."

"Great work! Pay raises all around."

They returned to watching the vid feed.

"You know, I like her now," Alexis admitted. "When I first saw her, I thought she was a flying coffin. She's grown on me. I've always thought of the head—the bridge superstructure—as quirky."

Bradyn was about to say something, but Phillix started the tests.

"Firing cannons first. I'll start on low power then increase incrementally and see how it goes."

"Any targets?" Sabrya asked eagerly.

"Sorry to disappoint. This test is to check energy expenditure, but we *will* need to calibrate accuracy eventually."

The canons were fired alternately. After one went through its firing range from minimal to maximal power, it reverted to low power and swiveled.

"As you may have noted, there are some blind spots. That can be somewhat alleviated by rotating the bridge. With that being said, we can now do this..."

They watched the *Malleus* on-screen as the bridge head started a slow rotation. Inside, they barely felt a thing. The rotation increased to one revolution every minute.

"Our inertia dampeners have been enhanced," Phillix informed them.

"And energy usage?" Bradyn queried.

"Barely registered. From that data though, I can extrapolate that we'd have several hours of blasting at max before there would be any impact on other capabilities. Now, if the next test is successful, we shouldn't need them at all..."

One minute the *Malleus* was visible, then there was a brief shimmer and... blackness.

Sabrya jumped up. "Fraggin' yeah!"

Alexis smiled from ear to ear, as did Bradyn.

"Other than the *Iconic*—which very few know about—we are the one and only ship in the galaxy with stealth capabilities."

"This calls for a round of drinks," Alexis announced once the congratulatory hugs were done. The trio moved down to the lounge where Alexis brought out a bottle of Arcturian whiskey. "Something I found when clearing out Jenna's locker. Still untouched."

"The previous captain had good taste." Bradyn eyed the bottle with appreciation. "Drokking amazing."

"Captain, I'm picking up something on the long-range scanner," Phillix announced.

"Fraggin' timin' sux."

"We're on our way." Alexis stowed the unopened bottle.

The trio left their empty glasses and were back on the bridge in moments.

"Nothing on screen?" Alexis took her chair and examined the scanner and readouts.

"Too far yet. Nothing familiar in my files, so maybe not the Qlan. Possibly Imperials, since they were the last here. They do have a potential interest in this area if anyone believed or listened to Scipio."

"We've been here for about six weeks. Any chance our drives left a trace signature?"

"I doubt it. Their sensors wouldn't be sensitive enough to pick up anything after all this time. Could be just a random visitation..."

They continued watching in silence.

"What would you like to do, Captain?" Phillix prompted.

"Options, people?" she asked her crew.

"Frag 'em out of space."

Alexis shook her head. "A couple of plasma cannons may not be enough to take out an Imperial warship immediately, and without missiles... not a risk I'm willing to take, especially if they call in others."

"We could sit here and wait to see if they detect us," Bradyn suggested. "That would prove or disprove our shielding. But if it doesn't work, and that Imperial warship outguns us, we've just handed over potential stealth capabilities. Phillix, if we jump, would they detect our drive signatures?"

"Affirmative, and it would also pique their interest in Niviaris, which I can only assume—due to their lack of probes —they still think is a dead rock."

"I'd prefer they continue thinking that. Pretty sure Sylvanus would appreciate it too." Alexis considered the minimal options. "Without a full complement of ammunition, I'm not willing to take on an experienced warship, nor am I going to advertise this area to them. Let's wait and see what they are up to."

"Captain, I received a brief message from Danders. It's in your box. I'm also monitoring another gamma burst from V-X33B. It will be passing us in five minutes."

Alexis opened up her messages. It was short and concise.

'Captain Nales, Sylvanus owes you and the Malleus *crew a great deal. We also thank you for your data on the* Iconic. *It will be several months before we are prepared to take on this venture. We will keep in touch of our progress.'*

She pondered her response and sent it.

'The Malleus *will always be here to help if needed. Just put out the call. Best of luck to you all.'*

"Phill... is there an issue with the gamma burst we need to worry about?"

"Not at all," Phillix answered her question. "However, I believe it will create sufficient interference to cover our hyper-drive signature if we jump."

"Great. I'm sure, like me, everyone will be relieved to make a move. What's our Imperial ship been doing?"

"Same as the last four days, cruising back and forth in a grid pattern."

"Looks like they're serious about finding something. What are their chances?"

"Well, space is pretty big. If they continue with the set pattern, I'd give them less than five percent. While the *Iconic* is huge, the Imperials are searching over four million cubic kilometers of space."

"Good. Anyway, not our concern anymore. Want to set a course for Plorian?"

"On it."

"Thanks."

"Done. Course set."

"What took you so long?" She laughed.

"I had to avoid a tachyon anomaly in Sector 18. Rerouted through Sectors 23 and 20."

"Glad you did. Hate it when tachyon anomalies frag the day. How long will it take?"

"Seventy-six point four hours."

"Cool. Let's wait for the burst, and when ready, jump. I'm sure you can determine the most appropriate time. Just give us mere biologicals a thirty-second warning."

"Roger. Thanks."

Alexis switched on the ship-wide comms. "Heads up, everyone. We're jumping to Plorian in a few minutes."

"About fraggin' time."

"You're welcome." Alexis grinned.

CHAPTER SIX

WHEN THEY DROPPED out of hyper, Plorian was suddenly before them—a green and blue ball with three satellite moons.

"We should be landing in an hour," Phillix advised. "It will be around midday."

"That's pretty," Alexis said. "I almost forgot how good it looks. We weren't really in a position last time to sit and admire it."

"You're from Mars?" Sabrya asked moving to the seat beside her. "Way over in Sector 1?"

"Yep. Meridiani City."

"What was Mars like?"

"A terraformed world, nowhere near as picturesque as this."

"No?"

"It was the first planet colonized. We're talking almost four thousand years ago. Terraforming wasn't what it is today. It wasn't perfect, and it's not easy to update terraforming once a population is installed. It's where all this started, but once the empire expanded, it was basically forgotten; it wasn't large enough or central enough to be the capital. Life wasn't easy—not that I'm comparing it to your earlier life—but you'd think they'd treat the birthplace better. If it wasn't for the yearly pilgrimage from fanatic Imperialists to gloat over the destruction of Terra's moon, Mars would probably be forgotten completely."

"And the last time you saw it?"

"About sixty-six years ago." Alexis hadn't spoken about her life before today. Her memory was vague—another aspect of long-term stasis. The sublim training she was supposed to be getting was to keep her mind sane and her professional knowledge base intact, foregoing personal memories.

"You were in stasis all that time?"

"I was 30 when I joined the *Octavia*. Two decades in transit, then the crash, and the twenty-six years in stasis. Mainstream stassisification wasn't like it is today either—what one got was dependent on the budget for their particular organization.... specifically, the sublim training. We'd go under every five years, wake up, spend a week in the real, then go under again. Early stasis led to a whole swag of psychological disorders. The version we saw with Adjira was top-notch but at huge expense."

"I reckon she was a fraggin' crazy bitch before she went under."

"No argument from me," Alexis continued after a moment of concentration. "A selection committee determined who would go where. Stupidly, it was based on who could come up with the most credits—rich, stupid people went to the select terraformed worlds within the inner sectors, and those with small budgets went to the lesser worlds in the outreaches. Mine was close to the bottom. It was the same with the ship's jump capability; shorter jumps made for longer trips. Niviaris, one of the furthest planets available, was way down the pecking order of optimal planets, so no one else wanted it."

"So, if you had twenty-six years of it without a break..."

"Yep, you worked out my secret; I'm a psychopathic killer about to unleash her wrath and use her victims for compost."

"Hey, I'm sure I read in the regs there's only one psycho-pathic killer allowed per ship, and I've got that billet. If you go loopy, like our fat empress, I'll have to take your head off."

"Gee, thanks for your vote of confidence."

"It's what friends are for." Sabrya slapped her on the back.

"Obviously, that's a new definition of what I thought a 'friend' was."

<hr />

Brutus greeted them when they landed. "Welcome back, Sab. I got your wave. How's freedom treating you?"

"I've had fraggin' worse."

"That good? How about lunch? We can talk about it over a drink or two."

"Fresh vegetables?"

"Of course, and locally produced wine."

At the sound of fresh food, and remembering what it was like the last time they were there, they picked up the pace and headed inside.

"One missing?" Brutus asked after greeting Alexis and Bradyn. "Was it Phillip? The coder?"

"Phillix. He'll be staying in the ship."

"You mean on the ship?"

"No." Alexis shook her head. "It's complicated."

The *Malleus* crew went inside and reacquainted themselves with the friends they had previously met. As the table was set and extra chairs were brought in, they were inundated with questions about what they had been doing for the last months. Once they were sitting over a delicious lunch, they shared with him and his extended family something of their adventures and their loss.

"He's an AI now? How's that working out? Who's actually in charge of the ship?"

"I am," Alexis confirmed. "We've had that conversation."

Brutus nodded and looked to Bradyn after pouring more wine. "You can take the man out of engineering, but I'm still curious... I don't recall seeing the guns before. You expecting trouble?"

En route, they had determined what they would reveal about their time away. It would be close to the truth about how they had managed to avoid whoever it was that had found them when they left the first time. There would be no mention of Sylvanus Colony or the *Iconic*.

The fewer that knew, the better. They decided to concoct a story about finding Yorgion 3, another world in Sector 37, where they landed. They'd given it a bit of time to get a feel for being grounded again in Driwun, the largest colony. They'd worked some odd jobs to pay for fuel and repairs, but the planetary lifestyle hadn't suited them. They were now going to look into becoming traders on the other side of the galaxy where the Bukshoga Qlan crime syndicate didn't have a foothold.

It was partly true, and while they didn't like having to lie to their friends, they didn't want anyone to get into trouble on their behalf.

"So, while we don't know what we'll find, no doubt there'll be someone looking for easy pickings. We just want to make sure they think twice before taking us on."

Brutus nodded. "I've not seen those models before... mind you, I'm no weapons expert."

"There was an old *Helicon* class in the back fields of Driwun spaceport. It was a wreck, but the weapons were still in pretty good nick. We all chipped in and did a bit of work to cover the costs. I did engineering, Sabrya did security, and Alexis helped out with some of their agricultural problems."

After their meals were brought out, everyone was too busy eating to concern themselves with chatter. After the sumptuous meal, they moved to an awning-covered verandah and relaxed with some wine. Only then did the conversation turn to the more serious business.

"Sabrya, here is the address of the stellar handler. My broker." He gave her a slip of paper, as well as his card of authorization.

"Was that fraggin' smart?" She pocketed the card after a brief look.

"There's a lot, and I didn't feel this was the best place to hold it. He's okay; he handles all my transactions. You even get interest added. If you want, I can come along."

"Nah. Don't need my fraggin' hand held. I'll pay him a visit later today."

"Looks like you won't have to take his head off after all," Bradyn said conspiratorially, leaning closer.

"I'll wait until I see what the fees are."

"Already covered." Brutus laughed. "Anyway, if you're heading off to do some trading, I might have some gear for you. I'll admit it's stuff I can't get rid of here, but who knows what's needed way over there?"

"Probably same fraggin' grunfer shit needed here."

"So, I'll let it go for twenty-k stellar, which is less than what I paid for it. Do you have the space in your holds? Did you get rid of the other stuff?"

"Yeah, as you said, though, it was mostly only good for scrap metal. It helped pay for the work done on the *Malleus*," Bradyn answered.

Alexis swirled her wine, relishing the flavor of what she'd tasted so far. "What's this cargo you have for us?"

"Some entrepreneur wanted to bring bands out here, musicians and the like. It flopped, and he went broke. I bought his gear—"

"Still lookin' after the unfortunates?" Sabrya teased.

"But that didn't pan out for me either," Brutus continued as he tossed a nut at her, then he turned to Alexis. "Alexis, you're a botanist? If you're going on a long trip, I can set you up with the gear to run a small garden facility. You can grow your own food. Shouldn't be hard for a professional."

"I'd pay for that!" Alexis' eyes brightened, glad to finally utilize her botany knowledge.

"If you take the other gear, you'll be doing me a favor by clearing space for my next shipment."

"Hmm... so, we have some fraggin' bargainin' power." Sabrya winked at Bradyn.

"The guy knows you're about to get over two million stellars. I think he reckons you can afford it."

"Spoilsport." She punched his shoulder then turned back to Brutus. "Okay. Deal, but if you've given us fraggin' crap, the next time we visit, we're goin' to drop it from a low orbit over the homestead."

"If it's crap, then by all means."

"I'll take a look at it," Bradyn suggested. "Work out sizing and what hold it'll go into."

Brutus pointed. "See that warehouse down the end of the track? Everything in bay 3 is going. Pop down, and I'll join you shortly."

With a wave, Bradyn started walking toward the indicated warehouse.

"I'll be keen to go through what you've got available for gardening, so we can retrofit another hold for it," Alexis said.

"Will we have any space left for actual cargo?" Bradyn called over his shoulder. "Traders, remember?

"Fresh food in space is better than any cargo," Alexis answered loud enough for him to hear.

Sabrya nodded. "You're fraggin' right there."

"You want to tag along?" Alexis asked the warrior, as Brutus directed her to another warehouse much closer to the homestead, where she could see the vegetable garden and orchard.

"Me? I'll pass. Happy to eat it, but that's as far as my interest stretches, thanks. I'll get my stellars and see what I can pick up in town."

"Is that wise? Low-profile and all?" Alexis queried.

"I'll be fine. Besides I worked somethin' out." She pulled out a robe and hood from her pack. "One of the girls offered this to me."

Brutus stopped and turned. "You doing the Cligiangeron pilgrim thing again?"

"Works like a charm every fraggin' time."

The big man chuckled. "There's a couple of hoverbikes in the garage around the back. Help yourself. You'll recall Cromyn is about four clicks down the road." He pointed.

Sabrya waved and then strode to the back of the house. Brutus turned and lengthened his pace to catch up with the *Malleus* captain.

Alexis was eager to get back into the 'growing things' aspect of her training. On the plus side, apart from the potential gain in nutrition, the plants would freshen the air.

"Brutus, you've no doubt been listening to the Mesh far more than we've been able to... What's happening out there? If one were going to the furthest outposts, where would be a good place to start?"

"Where to start... tricky. Be aware, any frontier world or sector will be rife with violence and lawlessness."

"Sounds familiar. We have guns and Sabrya."

"So, Sectors 45-46 have been around for a decade or so. I don't know the details, but I've heard of some traders doing okay out that way. How much truth there is in that—who knows?" He shrugged. "As for what's happening out there, Emperor Nero is planning a royal tour of the inner planets and the loyal territories, so security in those sectors will be high. I suspect most waystations in those and adjacent sectors will be programmed to divert any unauthorized craft along another route."

"Phillix will probably get onto that."

"A hacker becoming an AI? That's a story I'd like to hear."

"I can tell you, but I'm not a hundred percent sure about it myself." Alexis quickly related their cover story. "We were on Driwun. A small gang was harassing the settlement. Sabrya took care of the thugs. Phillix was hacking their AI when he was struck by a stray bullet. His consciousness remained inside the computer, and the AI tried purging him from the system, like a virus. He hid his... consciousness... in a node then contacted Torg, who disconnected the node and installed him in the *Malleus*. Resurrected, so to speak."

"That's one weird tale."

"Like out of a crazy cyb-punk story." Alexis shrugged. "You're welcome to come and chat with him. He's been great, and the ship runs so much better. He's more Autonomous Intelligence than Artificial Intelligence."

They moved through a warehouse attached to a greenhouse where out-of-season produce could still be grown. Brutus showed her what was available, including seeds and various fertilizers, and Alexis made a list of everything she'd need for the long haul on her tablet.

"I'm guessing Jenna didn't have much in the way of culinary delights? You'll need a kitchen and cookware. I can toss in a few appliances. No point having good food if it can't be cooked right."

"That would be most appreciated," she said when she finished. "You're being very generous."

"Sab and I go back a long way. She's helped me out a lot. This may, in some way, compensate her for the help."

"Is this a story to be shared or something better left unsaid? She's reticent to say much about her life... her past."

"All space dust now, and, no doubt, why Sabrya was treated the way she was—as a pariah." He touched on how the two of them had joined a rebel group called the Sunfists and freed several hundred indentured workers from a lifetime of drudgery and servitude.

"Like slaves?"

"Paid slaves, but yeah, they had no choice. With the Sunfists, we had an opportunity to change their fates. Sabrya was instrumental in our success."

"Any repercussions for you?"

He shrugged his big shoulders. "I was in the background, like many others. I doubt my name or image came under any scrutiny. This here—" he waved his arms about "—is what I did with my share of the proceeds, as well as setting up my trading business."

"You've done a fantastic job." She admired the homestead as they walked back to the house. "Where are they now, the saved workers?"

"Scattered here and there. No doubt life is still hard, but, now, they can choose what they want to do and where they want to do it."

"And the Sunfists?"

"They were involved in a couple of minor skirmishes, but they're keeping a low profile until another project comes their way. I dare say, they'll be interested in the emperor's tour."

"You still keep tabs on them?"

"More or less." Brutus didn't offer much more.

Sensing his understandable reticence to disclose more information about his connection with the rebels, she changed the subject. "Tell me about these Cligiangeron pilgrims. I'm pretty sure Sabrya was never part of any cult. And why's there a pilgrim cloak here anyway?"

He laughed. "Believe it or not, it was part of a fancy-dress costume. The Cligiangerons are a sect who believe in a long-term relationship with their chosen partner before taking final vows. If it doesn't work out, depending on the circumstances, the offended member might get to kill the partner. The longer and slower the death, the greater the chance of transcending to the ether-life."

"Seriously?" Alexis shook her head. "Who determines who's offended?"

"No idea. Something written in their sacred texts, I guess. They're only found on the outer planets, as the Imperium tends to frown on such obscure beliefs."

"Yeah, I bet they want to hold the monopoly on torturing people until death."

"True that. Needless to say, the towners will steer clear of our warrior girl if she's in that getup."

CHAPTER SEVEN

IT HAD BEEN a while since Sabrya had ridden a hoverbike. Her cloak flapped behind, and she relished the wind blowing through her spiked hair. *Frag them if they think its gonna change!*

Cromyn was a few klicks from the homestead, and it was the nearest town of decent size to find what she was after. She stopped on the outskirts and hid the bike in the dense undergrowth before walking the last few hundred meters into town. Hoverbikes and Cligiangeron pilgrims didn't mix. She pulled up her cowl, bent over slightly to reduce her height, and added a limp to her stride.

The cloak did its thing, and no one came near her; some even crossed the paved road to stay away.

It was easy enough to find the broker holding her stellars. The two large security bots in front of his building were a give-away. She showed him the authorization slip Brutus had given her, and he quickly retrieved a small case from a large safe in the rear where there was another menacing droid with a couple of nasty-looking laser cannons.

Since there was no one else around, she emptied the case on the counter. Forty stellar-stix toppled out.

"The total is two and a half million, and each drive is marked with its quantity," the broker explained. "They're color-coded for the amount, and they're in multiples of five thousand stellars. If you like, I can swap them for real stellars, gems, ingots, or whatever currency you prefer."

Sabrya nodded her appreciation. "I'll take ten-k in gems, five-k in stellars."

"Very good, ma'am." He fetched a wad of cash from the safe, measured out an assortment of gems, and retrieved the equivalent in stellar-stix. "I have this for you too, ma'am." The broker handed her a vid-stix.

Who the frag knows I'm here? She was caught by surprise, but she accepted the vid-stix. "Do you know who I am?"

The broker's confidence lessened. "I do, ma'am, but at Grohun Bros, we pride ourselves on our confidentiality. We'd not be as successful as we have been otherwise."

"Who gave you this? What did they look like?"

"Our regular courier. My instructions were to hand it over to you when you came to collect your stellars."

"And how did they fraggin' know I'd be here?"

"I-I have no idea." He stepped back.

If the droid behind him became more alert, there was no obvious sign. Busting up his droids and ripping heads off wasn't going to help her maintain her low profile.

"Okay. Relax." Sabrya pocketed the vid-stix.

"M-maybe it's explained in the message."

"No fraggin' doubt." She tossed him a small gem. "I wasn't here. If anyone finds out..." she left the threat hanging.

"N-No worries about that. Your reputation precedes you. If I may say, I thought you were hard done by the tourney."

"Thanks." She nodded, curious about the vid-stix and who could have left it, but there was nowhere in town she trusted to view it.

Before she stepped outside, she placed the case in a small

satchel hidden under the cloak, resumed her stooped hobble, and limped to the next location on her agenda, the Orion Arms. She used to frequent the place when the tourney was in the sector. She was taking a risk going there, but for what she needed, it was worth it.

The interior of the Orion Arms was dimly lit and much quieter than she was used to. Then again, the universe had moved on from Sector 22 after it was dumped from the tourney. There was a good chance, if any of the patrons recognized her, it would be bad. For them.

A bot-tender arrived to take her order. It squeaked a bit, indicating a problem with its undercarriage.

"I'll have a double Aeirlon-X Starburst."

The bot squeaked away and returned within a few minutes. On its chest plate was a screen with a warning in several dialects about the dangers of the liquor. "Do you accept these conditions?" it asked. "The Orion Arms will not be liable for any injury—physical or mental—caused by the consumption of this product."

She nodded and reached for the drink.

The bot backed up slightly. "A verbal acceptance is required. Please articulate clearly."

"Yes, I fraggin' accept the consequences of consuming this product."

"Voice recognition activated, and non-indemnity clause actioned. Please enjoy your refreshment." It deposited her drink on a galaxy-themed coaster and departed swiftly.

She toyed with her bubbling drink as she surreptitiously watched the goings-on. There were three boozers at another table, quietly talking over something written on a tablet they were reading. Sabrya recognized the owner as she stepped through the door.

With a rag in hand, the proprietor casually wiped tables, eventually making her way to Sabrya's.

"Not many customers can stomach an Aeirlon-X Starburst. Welcome back, Reaper."

"Mercia." Sabrya nodded and listened intently for a moment. "No backup?" She kept an eye on the table of three.

"Peace, sister. I fluxing know what happened, and that drink is on the house." Mercia spoke quietly. "And don't fret about them. They're regulars and no trouble. What brings ya back to Cromyn? You heard about the Smash-fest?"

Sabrya glanced up. "Smash-fest?"

"A wave was recently sent out on the Mesh." Mercia nodded and sat opposite her. "A Reprise Smash-fest is coming to 22. Over on Grindstone."

"A fraggin' what?" Sabrya hissed, sitting up.

"Stay chill. That rock is deserted now. We sort of heard of what ya and Brutus got up to. After your stint with those Sunfist rebels, the whole place shut down. It's just a bunch of empty tunnels and huge pits. I hear they're gonna trash the place."

"They always do." Sabrya sat back and sipped her drink. "When's this happenin'?"

"About a week from now. To coincide with Nero's visit."

"He's comin' here?"

"Nah. Well. I dunno. Not likely they're gonna broadcast his route to the patrons of the Orion Arms. But ya can sorta work it out. The Imps are running security on the adjacent sectors and doing a clean-up. Mind ya, we all know Nero's gonna check the bigger, more affluent worlds. That's a no-brainer. Got to keep the sycophants with the stellars happy."

"So why Grindstone, and why now?"

"Cuz there'll be people flocking to this sector anyhow, so while he's nearby, they're gonna reap what stellars they can. They're even conducting a lottery for a thousand tourists to be on front-line viewing platforms."

"They're fraggin' nuts."

"Perhaps. What brings ya here? It's been a while."

"I haven't had a double Aeirlon-X Starburst for over two years… and maybe a bit of nostalgia—lookin' up old friends."

"Uh-huh. Should've quit with the drink. Ya don't have any friends. And when the frag did you ever get nostalgic?"

"True enough. Anyway, I'm goin' away for a long trip, so I better take a crate of the Aeirlon-X Starburst. Don't know when I'll get another chance."

"Ya're here for the booze. I knew it." She ordered the bot to bring out a crate.

"Of course. No one would believe I have friends. Better delete the indemnity on the bot. My voiceprint could get you into trouble."

"Sure thing. Don't need any more of that."

After her drink, she bid Mercia farewell, grabbed her crate, and hobbled back to the hoverbike. No one was around, so she hopped on and returned quickly to the *Malleus*, heading straight to her cabin, curious to see the vid-stix and who sent it.

"Phillix, can you do a security check on this for malware and stuff?" She plugged it into her tablet.

"Easily. It's clear of malware," he said a moment later.

"Thanks. I'd like privacy now."

"I'm gone."

Sabrya sat on her bunk and activated the vid-stix. She recognized Paceman, one of her Sector 22 team members.

"Reaper, if you're gettin' this, I'm mostly likely fragged. I've sent identical messages to several of yar hangouts. I've included a sub-program to auto-wipe this message the day of the tourney." He kept glancing over his shoulder. The vid was handheld and jittery as he kept moving. "Yar old backer, Malazi Phakani, is now the Surreal Tourney CEO, and he's out for yar guts after you ditched the Ieoni Orbital and fragged half the security team. Good work there, by the way. Anyway, he was gonna make mega stellars from yar sale. Now, he's truly pissed. He sent a capture team after ya. Wants you alive to teach ya and everyone else a lesson. Not sure who's on the team, but Bruiser and Necto are on the cards.

"That's not all. He's got the Board onside to frag Grindstone. I managed to hack his server for a bit. They're gonna crash the old waystation ammo cache onto the planet at the end of the game. The AM-reactor will blow and frag the entire planet. You need to stop it. Coordinates and access codes for the waystation are embedded in the metadata. Rip heads like ya mean it. Out."

"I always fraggin' mean it." Sabrya sat back for a moment and replayed the message. She could tell by the way Paceman was moving, he had been injured somewhere low, out of view of the cam.

Bruiser and Necto... those two had almost taken out the entire field—friend and foe alike—back in the Evangelista tourney in Sector 16 almost four years ago, just to get the kudos from the fans. *And people thought I was a psychopath...*

"Phillix?" Sabrya spoke up. "I want your fraggin' word you won't tell the others."

"Will it endanger the ship or crew?"

"Not one bit."

"Okay then. Nothing will pass my lips."

"You haven't got any fraggin' lips. Stop bein' a dick. Your word, or I'll fraggin' defrag you."

"Sorry. Reminiscing. I give you my word. I will not disclose this information."

"Analyze this message. Get whatever info you can. What do they call it, metadata? Where was it recorded, when... anythin'."

"It will take me a few minutes."

"Fine." She moved from her bunk, opened her locker, grabbed her gear, and packed her bag. On a whim, she scrawled a quick note and stuck it on her monitor. Since Phillix was still quiet, she went to her armory to grab the breacher. After thinking about it though, where she was going, there'd be enough weapons to choose from. Besides, she'd have to bribe security to get it onto a ship.

But I already have a ship...

Sabrya left the weapon behind and quickly made her way to Alexis' cabin. After a quick but thorough search, she couldn't locate the biochip that gave her ship control. With a shrug, she made her way to the galley to grab food.

"I've finished," Phillix announced.

"Go ahead." Sabrya moved to the bridge and checked for movement outside. Only the usual farm activity was visible. No sign of Alexis or Bradyn.

"It would appear from what I can determine from the background noises—generally undetectable by the human ear—and from the enhanced images on the nearby bulkheads, this was recorded thirty-one days ago. Possibly on Tataranga—"

"That's the second moon of Grindstone!"

"As I said, I'm not sure, but there's an eighty-seven percent chance. Some of the signage on a nearby bulkhead indicates Grindstone shuttles. I've checked the schedule, and those on Tataranga match."

"I don't suppose I could persuade or threaten you to take off?"

"Correct, and you know Torg won't. You could, of course, wipe me from the system, but then you'd be flying without AI. Alexis and Bradyn would be back before I rebooted."

"Still, temptin'."

"Are you that far down the scale of humanity, you'd take your base frustration out on a computer?"

"You don't fraggin' know me."

"I know you well enough. You'll be weighing the brief joy from getting rid of me once and for all against the disappointment the others will have in you."

"I don't fraggin' care."

"Do your worst, then. I've already died once; I'll take my chances."

"Frag you!" Sabrya's blades shot out. She raised her arm and swung at the datacore within the console. At the last instant, the blades slid back in, and she punched the desktop instead. "Just keep your fraggin' word." She snatched her pack and stormed out of the bridge and off the *Malleus*.

CHAPTER EIGHT

"PHILL, HAVE YOU SEEN SABRYA?" Alexis asked when she and Bradyn returned.

"Tall, violent Amazon with blue spiked hair? She went into town."

"That was earlier today."

"It's not like I put trackers on everyone," he argued. "Sabrya is her own woman."

"Don't we drocking know it," Bradyn commented. "I guess we either wait or go into town to look for her."

"It's getting onto evening. I guess she can look after herself."

"Far better than you or I alone can, that's for sure. This is her old stomping ground... maybe she has caught up with her old crowd."

"Sabrya? Friends? Perhaps. And if they're drinking, I'd rather avoid that rowdy group of augmented psychopaths. Let's wait until morning."

"Sound plan. How'd things go today with your agri-project?"

"Excellently. Brutus is arranging to bring over the gear. Torg, can I get you and one of the bots to assist?"

"I am at your disposal, Captain."

"Thanks." She turned back to Bradyn. "How did that cargo turn out for you? Is it any good?"

"It is, but I have a plan to use it for *us*."

"Is there any profit in that? I gather this cunning plan of yours is something other than selling?"

"It's like Brutus said. For a forming colony, the cargo would be hard to shift. It won't take up much space, and I could put it to other use."

"And that is?" she prompted.

"We're going on a long trip—"

"True. Phillix, any update on the route?"

"I don't believe we've determined an exact destination yet, but given Nero's tour and his security plan, it will be several months duration."

Bradyn continued, "Can you imagine what shipboard life will be like with Sabrya for that long?"

"I've seen what she's like when she's bored. We'll be lucky to survive a month."

"Exactly. I reckon, by using that gear, some vid projectors, and a corner of an aft cargo hold, we can come up with a holo-space for our intrepid head-ripper."

"We can do that?" Alexis looked interested in the concept.

"With this apparatus, for sure, after a bit of modification. We could use Delta hold—it's far enough away from the cabins that we won't be disturbed."

"I can reimage some of the tourney recordings and adapt them to various scenarios," Phillix added.

"Have we got VR goggles?"

"Something better." Bradyn smiled. "It's sort of like sublim training—a direct cerebral matrix. Some dedicated music enthusiasts use it to load all their senses at concerts."

"And we have this? Here?"

"Some of it. I saw other gear in the warehouse. I'll message Brutus later."

"Are we going to be traders or entertainers?"

"Who knows what we'll end up becoming?" Bradyn shrugged. "We'll be alive, or at least in one piece, when we get there. That's one way we can profit from this investment. Besides, she's paying for it, so she may as well get the benefit from it."

The following morning, Alexis knocked on Sabrya's cabin door. When there was no response, she opened it and stuck her head inside. The bunk hadn't been slept in, and the cabin had the air of not being used for a time.

"Phillix, any word on Sabrya?" Alexis asked knowing, he was constantly monitoring the entire ship.

"No sign of her, and no recent messages," Phillix answered.

"Hmm." Alexis wandered up to the lounge to fix breakfast. Bradyn was already there.

"I've got the coffee on," the stocky engineer greeted her. "Should be ready shortly. No doubt we're going into town to find our girl?"

"We should check with Brutus first. Given their friendship over the years, he might have a better idea of her whereabouts."

"Come have a look at this." Bradyn motioned to her.

Frowning, Alexis followed him through a nearby doorway which led to the bridge. A glance around showed her the dented console.

"I came up here to watch the sunrise and saw this."

"Phillix, any idea what happened here?" Alexis asked.

"I believe Sabrya may have been frustrated about something. You know what she's like..."

"Do you know what it was?"

"Who knows what goes through her mind?"

"True enough, I guess." Alexis shrugged and went back to the crew lounge.

Once they'd consumed a quick breakfast, the pair strolled to the homestead.

"That's not like her," Brutus replied after they explained the situation. "She normally left a message in the old days. How about I take you into town? I know she was heading to the broker's yesterday."

They made their way to the garage where there were several vehicles, including another hoverbike. They joined him as he hopped into his roadster. It had a bare chassis with an open-air cockpit, a roll cage, and two rows of seats, though the front passenger seat had been removed for extra cargo space, leaving room for three passengers.

"I've got trackers on all my vehicles." After activating the screen, he tapped a few keys. "Looks like the hoverbike is over by the spaceport."

"What the drock..." Bradyn shook his head. "Stolen?"

"From Sab? Doubtful. First things first. Sab was supposed to collect her stellars from my broker."

The drive took ten minutes. In the meantime, Alexis used her tablet to get Phillix to check departure and arrival flights. "You never know, she might be meeting someone. Could it possibly be an old friend?"

"It's the 'no message' that concerns me." Brutus concentrated on keeping the vehicle on the dirt track.

"The next spaceport arrival is in forty minutes," Phillix informed them. "There's a departure in ninety minutes, and there was one late last night."

They parked outside the broker's office in full view of the security-bots and cams. The broker confirmed Sabrya had indeed collected her stellar-stix. He motioned Brutus closer. "Since you're a good client, and I was holding her funds on your behest, I guess it can't hurt to tell you... There was a vid-stix for her as well."

"Vid-stix? From...?"

"Delivered by a regular courier. Nothing untoward or anything, as far as I could tell. When I saw who it was for, I added it to the deposit box."

"Where'd she go after here?"

The broker swiveled the monitor to show them. "As you can see, the security feed indicates she went south."

"South... okay. Thanks." Brutus walked out and looked in that direction.

"What's down there?" Alexis asked, joining him.

"The Orion Arms, among other dens of ill repute." The farmer walked off. "It's not far."

"Sounds like a bar." Alexis moved off. Bradyn followed.

"It is. She knows it very well. Too well. We both do, though I've not been since... for a while."

When they entered, a quick look around showed a few patrons sitting at tables or booths but no warrior woman with blue hair. Brutus turned and, with a nod, strolled to the bar.

"Well... would you believe it?" Mercia exclaimed when she emerged from the back room. "One day, I get Sabby after years away, and then her partner in the rebel fight deigns to show his head. I'm going out on a limb here and assuming no one was game enough to try the Aeirlon-X Starburst she took home with her, so what can I get you, folks?"

"Unfortunately, we're not here for a social visit. We're looking for Sabby. No one has seen her since yesterday."

"Is that so? We had a drink and a brief chat about the good old days, but I've not seen her since she left. She wasn't here all that long."

Brutus nodded. "And how was she?"

"Like she always is—pissed off with the universe. No change there. She was pretty vexed when I told her about the Smash-fest."

"Smash-fest?" Alexis asked.

Mercia looked both the others up and down. "Not tourney followers, I take it? A Smash-fest is a tourney rematch. They revisit the sectors where memorable tourneys were staged. There's one soon coming here on Grindstone."

"Where she was born?" Alexis asked.

Mercia nodded. "I reckon they chose this sector as it coincides with Nero's tour. They probably think the emperor will make a personal visit. It's rumored he likes the game quite a lot."

"Sabrya went to rejoin the Surreal Tourney league?" Bradyn asked.

"Hardly," Mercia scoffed.

"I don't like the sound of this." Alexis looked worried. "We better go to the spaceport to confirm."

"Reckon so," Brutus agreed. As the *Malleus* pair moved off, Brutus turned back to Mercia. "Maybe give the Sunfists a heads-up in case they've got a gig happening. Don't want to cross beams if the emperor and his security forces are about."

"I've already let them know Sabby was in town." Mercia nodded. "Good to see ya again. Don't be a stranger."

The farmer nodded a farewell to the barkeeper and caught up with the others as they were walking back to the roadster.

"Still an hour to go if she's thinking of leaving," Brutus said as he noted the time.

He hopped in his seat, and Alexis and Bradyn resumed their seats in the back. "Spaceport, here we come." He quickly drove off.

"If she didn't return to the *Malleus*, I reckon she's already off-planet," Alexis surmised. "Does your hoverbike tracker show a history? Maybe we can trace her movements to get a better understanding of what's going on."

"Sure." The trader played back the last twenty-four hours.

From the back seat, Alexis and Bradyn leaned forward to view the screen. In fast forward, the display showed the bike in the garage, then heading into Cromyn in the early afternoon, where it stopped outside the township. It remained there for a time, then returned to the *Malleus*, left twenty minutes later, and went directly to the spaceport. It hadn't moved since.

"What the blazes? Phillix?" Alexis commed the ship. "Sabrya returned yesterday!" Alexis had left the comm-link open, knowing he'd be listening in.

"I must have been doing a diagnostic."

Alexis looked at Bradyn, who shrugged. "Phill, give me a list of what ships departed yesterday afternoon and their destinations."

In a couple of seconds, a list came up. "Anything there you recognize?" she asked Brutus.

He glanced at the list. "There's a couple of short-run traders, and those are passenger transports."

"If someone leaves Plorian, what do they need to do?" Alexis asked.

"Without their ship, a shuttle takes them to an orbital where they then get on another ship, generally local runabouts, traders, or some other deep space vessels—but they're rare around this part of the sector."

When they arrived at the spaceport, Brutus drove directly to the port master's office.

"As you'd expect, I do a fair bit of business here. I might get some info... no guarantees though. I'll be a few moments." Brutus left them sitting in the vehicle.

In the background was the distant roar of a shuttle taking off.

"Something's not adding up here," Alexis muttered. "Okay, Phillix," she said into her comm-link. "Spill it."

"Spill what?" the AI responded.

"Cut the crap about diagnostics. You've not missed a beat since your uploading. What aren't you telling us about Sabrya?"

"That's the point. I'm not telling anything. She came and left. That's it."

"So, she did return?"

"I'm sure you have that data already."

"And? Phillix, stop being coy. Where did she go?"

"I'm not at liberty to say."

"She threatened you, didn't she?" Bradyn surmised. "To not say anything."

This was met with comm silence.

"My guess is this was when Sabrya got frustrated and bashed the console?" Alexis asked.

Again, the comm was silent.

"As soon as Brutus returns, we'll get to the ship and sort this out once and for all."

The pair watched another shuttle launch, the roar echoing from the hills to the west. At the same time, distant sirens started wailing. A large drone streaked low across the port and started blasting at a line of security flyers. A returning flyer scored a hit on the drone, but it too took fire, and both craft spiraled to the ground. The explosion added to the bedlam.

"What the frag?" Alexis stood in the roadster to view what was happening.

The area rapidly became a frantic hive of activity as security personnel and starport passengers ran around, mostly in panic and confusion.

Phillix's voice could be heard over the noise. "The homestead's under attack! Three skimmers. I've used the plasma canons successfully, and I'm now cloaked and moving. Torg is on the ground looking to help. Get back ASAP."

"Coincidence or what?" Alexis asked rhetorically and started blaring the horn to get Brutus' attention. She could see him in the office alongside a shorter figure staring out at the port, and she waved frantically when he looked her way.

The trader emerged in seconds, breathing hard after the short run. "What's up?"

As soon as the words passed her lips, Brutus jumped behind the wheel, fired up the roadster, and drove like a demon, a look of worry etching his already haggard features.

"Phillix fired on the skimmers attacking the homestead." Alexis held on as they careened around a corner. "The bots are rescuing whoever they can."

He nodded, looking grim. "I was able to check the security footage. Sabrya left the orbital last night on a short hauler, heading to Tataranga. It's one of Grindstone's moons."

"What the hell's she going to do there?" Bradyn asked.

Brutus didn't reply immediately, as he was concentrating on the road ahead now that they were on the narrow and rougher dirt section.

There was a buzzing noise and, suddenly, a drone darted from the tree canopy and strafed the road in front of them with laser fire. The roadster swerved sharply to the side. It hit a rut, and the tires slid, and the roadster spun sideways into the foliage, stopping abruptly when it hit a tree trunk.

With their high-G strength, Bradyn and Alexis managed to hang on, but Brutus was catapulted into the dense scrub. He cried out in pain as he landed with the sound of breaking underbrush.

Alexis glanced to see how Bradyn had fared as she clambered out of the vehicle. He was in one piece and gave her the thumbs-up. She made her way through the thick foliage in search of the farmer.

He was awkwardly moving into a sitting position, cradling

his right arm in his left, when she approached. His face was laced with small cuts oozing blood.

"Reckon I broke something." Brutus winced as she helped him up, hampered by vines and the twisted branches of the thick vegetation. He groaned as he tried to stand upright.

"The auto-doc on the *Malleus* will fix you up." She examined his upper arm where the sleeve was torn. "It's not broken through the skin, so let's hope it's not too bad. Mind you, I'm no medic. Anything else?"

"Cuts and bruises." He tried to shrug out of habit and regretted it. "A bit of an ache in my abdomen. Probably cracked a rib, as well."

"Better take it easy."

He stumbled, but Alexis caught him. She decided it was best to support him after noticing his great discomfort when he moved, though he tried not to show it.

More laser fire scoured the area close to them as the drone buzzed by a few meters above the canopy, making them flinch.

"Must be using thermal imaging." Bradyn bulldozed his way through the bush to join them. "This foliage can only help so much. We need to keep moving. Oh, and the roadster is trashed."

Alexis spoke into her comm-link. "Phillix, we're on foot and under fire. Check the location of this call and see what you can do. Brutus is badly hurt."

"On my way."

"In the meantime," she addressed Brutus, "we better do as Bradyn suggests."

Brutus nodded and pointed out the direction they should be going.

Bradyn used his girth to make a wide path through the foliage.

Alexis held onto Brutus to keep him upright. "Despite your

objections and bravado, you're far more injured than you're letting on. I'll carry you if I have to."

"Better listen to her, Brutus," Bradyn called back. "She's stronger than both of us."

It wasn't long before they were dripping with sweat in the humid climate. Insects hummed around them, and the leaves clung to any exposed skin. They heard a distant roar a moment later which grew steadily louder, then the unforgettable sound of a plasma cannon firing and an explosion almost above them.

"Drone down," Phillix informed them unnecessarily as the drone crashed a short distance away.

"Anywhere nearby to land?" Alexis gasped.

"Only back at the homestead. It's a couple hundred meters before the boundary fence. I can meet you there."

Brutus was sweating heavily and looking pale. The adrenaline was wearing off, and the shock of his injuries combined with the attack were wearing him down.

"See you in a few," Alexis confirmed. "Get Torg to prep the auto-doc."

"He's still at the homestead doing what he can to help out."

"Prep it anyway."

Bradyn continued moving forward, his shirt torn and bloodied from scratches.

Brutus groaned again but continued to push through the pain.

"Not far to go now," Alexis encouraged him.

When they finally reached the boundary fence, the smoke rising from the main building and outbuildings was a shock to the eyes. Brutus gasped and leaned heavily on the fence, pale-faced and breathing hard, but the sight of his house burning changed his features from pain and misery to anger and determination. The change was short-lived as he doubled over again.

The *Malleus* could be heard faintly but was nowhere to be seen.

"Where the frag are you?" Alexis commed, trying not to sound testy. "Brutus is in a very bad way!"

"Be there momentarily."

Distant spouts of energy from an unseen location hit a skimmer on the ground. Another drone whirred overhead as it moved in to attack the unseen enemy. The unseen target had moved, and the drone was fired upon from a different direction. It lost its tail section in a burst of light and spiraled into a fallow field on the other side of the warehouses.

The ship was still cloaked but the familiar roar of the *Malleus* quickly grew louder, creating an area in front of them that billowed the grit and leaves. They averted their eyes until the dust cloud dissipated.

"Move forward. The loading ramp is fifteen meters directly in front of you," Phillix instructed.

Bradyn climbed over the fence, then Alexis picked up the farmer like a child and passed him over to the engineer who then carried him, following Alexis as they were guided across the plowed and rutted field.

"He's lost consciousness," Bradyn informed Alexis.

It was unnerving for the two of them when one moment they were walking in an open field and the next their ship was shimmering in front of them. If they had been moving faster, they'd have run into the hull. As it was, they had to stop abruptly to avoid tripping over the ramp to the loading bay.

With a sigh of relief, they staggered up the ramp and quickly made their way to the medi-bay. As the engineer laid the trader gently on the bunk, Alexis checked the auto-doc and was glad to see it had been prepped like she had asked. They hooked Brutus up. In a few moments, his vitals were on-screen, and they didn't look good. His heart rate was fast, but his blood pressure was low.

Alexis read off the injuries as they started scrolling down

the righthand column. "Cracked ribs, ruptured spleen, two cracked vertebrae, internal bleeding."

"None of that sounds good. Can the auto-doc handle it?"

Alexis looked dubious. "It's a good bit of kit, but I don't think so."

The *Malleus* rumbled as she lifted off.

"Captain, the auto-doc has recommended urgent admission to the nearest medical facility. I have placed a call in preparation for our arrival."

"Good. Glad you and the auto-doc are interfaced."

The trip to the hospital felt long, but only a few anxious minutes passed before they were landing on the pad by the emergency entrance bay. Two medical staff had a gurney waiting. Alexis met them by the *Malleus'* cargo doors. They boarded immediately and followed her to the medi-bay.

The gurney had its own auto-doc, so less than a minute passed before Brutus was hooked up and being wheeled into the building.

"How is it in there?" Bradyn asked as he walked briskly with them. The younger medic looked a bit overwhelmed.

"With the spaceport attack, it's chaos. We've eight dead already and another dozen injured." As they entered the open doors, a staff member stopped Bradyn and Alexis.

"Are you family?" she asked.

They shook their heads. "Friends."

"Best to check back later tonight. Your friend will be going into theatre as soon as we can manage it."

Bradyn was about to say something, but Alexis touched his arm and addressed the older medic.

"You've got our ship's ID in your system; we'd appreciate an update."

"Of course. Now, we need to make room for the next med-unit." She indicated another vehicle approaching, red lights flashing.

A med-bot came out of the facility with another gurney and, with the medic, rushed off to meet the arriving vehicle, leaving the two standing there.

They walked quickly back to the *Malleus*.

"Wish there was more we could do," Bradyn commented.

"I agree, but they can do more for him than we can. Let's see what we can do at the homestead."

CHAPTER NINE

BACK ON THE ship's bridge, they slumped in their chairs.

"Phillix, let's head back to the homestead," Alexis said.

The ship launched smoothly. They watched the terrain outside angle away as the ship banked and turned. Cromyn slipped away, and the surrounding green wedge passed beneath them before the agricultural land appeared. The smoke on the horizon grew more prominent as the *Malleus* flew closer.

"Tell us what happened here," Alexis said.

"Three unidentified skimmers arrived and fired indiscriminately at anyone and anything," Phillix responded immediately. "I shot the drones and two of the skimmers; one got away."

"Any Mesh or comms chatter identifying their owners or even a reason?"

"Nothing but early idiotic speculation. I've accessed the spaceport logs. The craft didn't come from Plorian. They were dropped from a low orbit above Cromyn from an unknown cruiser. I'll try to get its drive signature for better ID."

The farm was now below them. Two fire tenders were busy fighting the farmhouse blaze, while the medical staff were scurrying from their emergency vehicles, with bags of medical gear and gurneys, tending to the injured. Other bodies were lying around the grounds. They were too far away to clearly identify who.

The deck jolted slightly as the ship landed in an area clear of the activity.

"I'm hearing there are seven civilians dead. Several more emergency services are on the way, though some are tied up at the spaceport. I have the attack on vid and have sent the local authorities a copy. I already recognize two of the casualties; perhaps they can identify the rest."

"You do? Who?" Alexis asked, glad to have something to focus on other than the death and destruction outside.

"Two of the Tourney has-beens."

"Has-beens?"

"They were officially banned because of their indiscriminate use of weaponry in public places, among other atrocities."

"Put what you have on screen," Alexis ordered.

The monitor fast-tracked until the skimmers arrived. They circled, firing energy weapons at anyone who moved, then targeted the house, the various warehouses, and the sheds. One skimmer landed, and two figures jumped to the ground and ran into the building.

"That's Necto, and, I think, Bruiser," Bradyn observed.

"Correct," Phillix confirmed.

"I can't tell from here. Are they a serious threat?" Alexis asked.

"You've seen Sabrya at her worst?" Bradyn asked. "That's Necto when she's in a good mood. She might not look like much, but she's mostly cyborg now, barely human, which is why she's so ruthless, callous. Bruiser is heavy-G. Ashamed to say it, but he's from my homeworld, Helios. Lost half his left side—chest, arm, and face—in a tourney five years ago. They rebuilt him, so now he's auged to the hilt. His left arm is like a power-driver, hence the name. Sabrya is known for her head-taking; Bruiser pulverizes his victims into a soggy mess."

"What a charming couple. What business have they got with Brutus? Is this an old Sunfist problem resurfacing?"

"No idea." Bradyn shrugged.

"I have no data linking any of them," Phillix added.

The vid continued. Green energy pulses scored several hits on one of the skimmers and a glancing blow on the other before the firing stopped and the angle changed.

"That's our plasma cannons. It took a few moments to get the cannons online. I need to work on that. If I had been quicker, maybe none of this would have happened. I cloaked and moved but kept firing."

"How could you've known this was going to happen? Did anything show up on the scanners?"

"Sure, but there's a fair bit of air traffic in these parts. I can't scan everyone for their intentions, and it's not as if they logged a flight plan."

"It's okay. No one's expecting you to. Continue your report."

"Another skimmer was flying around, so I shot at it, too. It crashed over to the north, in the field."

"Didn't they shoot back?"

"They did, but no serious hits, just a couple of minor glancing shots. I can only assume stealth mode works. They looked devastatingly accurate otherwise."

"And Torg?"

"He was with the bots and a few fieldworkers in a ware-house. He was damaged, both by a stray shot and the house fire."

"How so?"

"We were finishing loading the supplies and stores. He was heading back when the attack started. When the house caught fire, he ran in to save anyone inside."

"And did he?"

"Brutus' younger daughter, Nyka."

"No one else?"

"Not that he has mentioned or that I saw. Others may have escaped, but I can't say for certain."

"Good work." She studied the situation through the viewport. Outside, several police vehicles arrived and parked haphazardly along the gravel drive. The fire in the main house was slowly diminishing. A skimmer was smoldering by the house, and smoke was rising from the crop fields.

"We should go outside and explain our part in all this," Bradyn suggested.

Alexis agreed. "No doubt they'll be wondering why a ship landed in the field."

The pair disembarked, strode over to the nearest officer, and asked for his boss. The young man pointed to a robust woman standing with some other staff.

"I believe you're in charge?" Alexis introduced herself and Bradyn to the sergeant. "Our ship was nearby and recorded this." She showed the vid on her armpad. "He—our ship's defense system—activated the energy weapons and took out two of the skimmers and several drones. Do you know these people? I believe they're from the Surreal Tourney?"

"Some of them, I do," the officer replied as she watched the vid. "Any idea why they'd be here?"

"Can't help there. The landowner, Brutus, is at the hospital about to undergo surgery." Alexis explained the events leading up to their attack. "We're old colleagues and were passing through."

The cop nodded. "Stick around; we'll need reports from everyone."

Alexis nodded. She was keen to find Sabrya, but she couldn't very well just blast off after this.

"That your droid there?" The sergeant pointed to Torg, who

was standing by a barn door, as medical staff attended to the farmworkers. "He did good."

"Thanks." Alexis nodded and hesitated before asking. "Any family survivors?"

"Too early to say. We haven't combed through the house, but it doesn't look promising."

"Just the daughter, then."

The officer nodded, looking sad. "I'll need a record of this." She pointed to the vid.

"Our AI has already sent it to the various authorities. Should be on your drive somewhere."

"Good work all around, then."

"And the attackers? Anything you can say about them?" Bradyn asked.

"Nothing more at this point." She saw one of her colleagues motioning to her. "If you'll excuse me. Thanks for this and your work."

The pair watched her go, and Torg headed toward them. He was dragging his left leg, and half his side was blackened.

"Can't take you anywhere," Bradyn quipped.

"I may have sustained damage, but relocation is still possible."

"Excellent work there, Torg," Alexis stated.

"All in my programming. I could not save more, as the house fire was too far advanced. I gathered other survivors and took them to the basement of that shed where the energy weapons could not penetrate."

"How about we get you fixed up?" Bradyn gave him a friendly slap on the back. "Programming or not, you saved lives."

"I could not have done otherwise. Regaining greater functionality would make my work more efficient."

Despite the tragic circumstances, the banter between the

two brought a brief smile to her face. Torg took every word seriously.

The three moved off. There was nothing they could do, and they would probably get in the way of the emergency services.

Back on the *Malleus*, Bradyn headed to the workshop with Torg limping behind.

"I may as well start fixing him up," the engineer said.

Alexis nodded then went to wash her hands and freshen up. As she was drying herself, she had a thought and wanted to facepalm herself. She promptly strode to Sabrya's cabin and looked around in greater detail, wishing she had done it earlier instead of simply sticking her head in the door. Captain or not, she had felt it would be a violation of the privacy of her crew. She opened the locker and saw it was empty. No surprise there. Alexis sat at the comp-terminal to see if there was a message, but saw the handwritten note stuck on the screen.

'Don't follow me. You'll fraggin' die.'

Any recent use of the computer had been wiped. *I should have expected that, too.*

"Okay, Phillix. Let's get this over and done with; what aren't you telling us?"

"I gave her my word I would not disclose any information."

Alexis considered this for a moment then had an idea and headed to the workshop, note in hand. "How functional is Torg?" she asked Bradyn upon her arrival.

The droid was standing by the bench. His chest and shoulder plating had been removed, and the engineer was examining the workings within.

"Just enough to communicate at the moment." Bradyn didn't look up as he continued working inside the torso cavity.

"That's all I need him for."

"Is something wrong?"

"Sabrya." She waved the note near his face to get his attention.

"That would be a 'yes.'" With a chuckle, he shook his head as he read the brief message. "Torg, you're still interfaced with the ship?"

"After the refurbishment, I now have seventy-three percent interface."

"Great." Alexis paced. "Please access any recordings of messages in the last twenty hours, specifically anything involving Sabrya and her comp."

Torg stood silent for a moment. "I have completed the task."

Alexis sighed with relief. "Sabrya received a message. What was it?"

"It wasn't sent but delivered via a vid-stix." Torg activated the nearest monitor where the message played out for them. They watched it a couple of times.

"What was she drocking thinking?" Bradyn fumed after he heard it.

"She thought she'd be saving us," Alexis said. "Sadly ironic. She went to confront the threat head-on before it came here."

Torg then related the data Phillix had gleaned from the message.

"We have to go after her," Alexis stated.

"How did I know you'd say that?" Bradyn shook his head ruefully as he got up. "I better secure the ship. I can continue with Torg en route. We going to Tataranga?"

"We most definitely are."

"I will plot a course," Phillix informed them.

"And what about the law and giving statements and all that?" Bradyn asked.

"We can record our statements and send them with our apologies. With those two maniacs on her tail, Sabrya may need some help. She's my priority at the moment."

CHAPTER TEN

THEIR LANDING at Tataranga Spaceport was delayed for several hours because of a ruckus with some of the more exuberant Surreal Tourney fans. Once the security forces had dealt with the rioting crowd, port operations could commence; however, they had to wait for a passenger transport, as it had priority unless they wanted to double the docking fees.

"Extortionist asses," Brayden grumbled from the workshop where he was putting the finishing touches on Torg. "Their fees are already boosted because of this drocking game. Now, they're just being insulting."

"I'm just hoping our account has enough stellars."

"Umm, I can ensure the fees are recorded as being paid," Phillix offered.

"Can you now? That's handy... but I'm still pissed at you."

"I can only apologize so much. You being vexed with me is a safer bet than Sabrya's wrath."

"He has a point." Bradyn nodded.

"It wouldn't have been an issue with a real AI. Torg, would you keep secrets from me?"

"I am incapable of being deceitful in any way, Captain."

"Food for thought, Phillix."

"So, that's a 'no' to hacking the financials and fast-tracking our landing? Sabrya could be in danger."

"Now you're concerned for her welfare?" Alexis asked, incredulous.

"As you always say, she's part of our crew."

Alexis bit her tongue before she said something she'd regret. "Do it. I'm sure she'll be chuffed to hear you're so concerned about her wellbeing."

"Very well." There was a slight pause.

"*Malleus*, Tataranga Control here. Thank you for your contribution. Make your way to pad seventeen."

"Affirmative, Control," Alexis replied. She cut the mike. "How much did that cost us?"

"Us? A few electrons may have been exploited, otherwise nothing."

"If this backfires…"

"As Sabrya would say 'chillax.' The funding was rerouted through official Surreal Tourney accounts from Malazi Phakani's assets. He is, after all, her sponsor."

The view of the domed city swung to their left as the *Malleus* drifted toward the indicated pad on the city perimeter. Below was an array of landing pads. Those further afield had much larger ships on them.

A slight beeping drew their attention to the console as they approached pad seventeen. Once landed, they felt a faint vibration as the pad descended. Soon, the surface was above them and the opening began to close.

"Seems elaborate for a small base," Alexis ventured after noting each pad became its own airlock.

"The information I got on their infocast indicates it's more practical than many tubes interlacing and linking the separate pads on the surface. As you saw, larger ships remain on the surface or remain in orbit and send shuttles down."

"Now, there's something we haven't got," Bradyn pointed out. "A shuttle could come in handy."

"And where would you put the hangar?" Alexis asked. "While we have got a lot of cargo space, we need to keep it for, you know, our future trading enterprise."

"True. I reckon we could dock it on top. Phillix, want to run a few design concepts?"

"Sure. What model shuttle were you thinking?"

There was a moment before the engineer replied. "Leave it with me."

"Okay, you two. We'll be clear to disembark shortly. Bradyn, see you at the loading bay in ten. You too, Torg." Alexis moved from the bridge and headed to her cabin for a change of clothes.

As they waited in the ship's airlock for the green light indicating air pressure equalization, Alexis noted the repairs on Torg had been completed and his chrome plating shone brightly. Bradyn had changed out of his work gear into some casual clothes he had picked up on Sylvanus. There was still some paint on his left ear.

"It never ceases to surprise me how paint or grease can find its way to the most unusual places," he commented when she pointed it out. Looking at his reflection in the glassteel viewport, he scraped the dry paint with his fingernail.

The green light illuminated. Alexis hit the button that raised the door and lowered the ramp, and the trio moved out.

"Phillix, what's the gravity here?" she asked, speaking into a small comms device pinned to her collar.

"Tataranga is 1.2 gravities to cater to those from high-G worlds. There are a couple of sections where the gravity is higher or lower, but this is the standard throughout the bulk of the dome."

"Treat it like a holiday," Bradyn said, doing little jumps.

At the blast door separating the pad from the station corridor, two beefy security guards awaited them.

"Halt here for weapons check," the taller guard said.

Hand scanners were used to detect any weapons on the *Malleus* crew.

"Your droid will need to remain on your vessel," the guard stated.

"Sorry, Torg. Want to put together a list of the recent stores? You can keep Phillix in line."

"Of course, Captain." The shining droid pivoted and strode back to the ship.

The guard continued, reading from his tablet. "With the Surreal Tournament Smash-fest being featured here soon, we are currently running an all-inclusive neutrality protocol. This means you'll not be apprehended for any offenses allegedly committed off-world. It also means you are prohibited from any retribution or violence in any way to any Surreal Tourney member or Tataranga spaceport patron. Failure to comply will result in either imprisonment or lethal force for contravening these rules and the impounding of your ship. If you agree to these terms, say so clearly."

"I agree," both said in turn, stating their names.

"As Captain, we'll also need to hear your verbal command to your ship droid or AI to power down any weapons systems and to not take any aggressive action within the spaceport area. To do so could also lead to imprisonment or lethal force against those contravening these rules and the impounding of your ship. If you agree to these terms, say so clearly."

Again, Alexis clearly and concisely spoke the instructions given.

"And your ship's AI?"

"I acknowledge and will comply," Phillix responded over the comm-link.

"Very good," the shorter guard said as the taller one stepped back. "Welcome to Tataranga Spaceport, where we hope you'll have a relaxing and enjoyable stay. On this level, you'll find our medical facility, with state-of-the-art equipment, security, and spaceport administration. The lower levels are for spaceport-authorized personnel only. Levels 1-4 are for registered business offices. If you'd like to negotiate office space, please make an appointment with spaceport administration during working hours. Levels 5-15 are for guest entertainment and relaxation, where you'll find top-class accommodations, restaurants and bars, cinemas, and virtu-rooms—where our facilities can provide any form of scenario to cater to all tastes and budgets. Elevators can be found at the end of the main concourse which is to your left at the end of this corridor. There's a floor plan at every major intersection if you need it." The officious guard stepped aside and waved them through. "Welcome again."

"Thanks." Alexis moved off, followed by Bradyn.

"That man takes his job far too seriously."

Alexis chuckled. "And you don't?"

They easily found the elevators, and there was a map at the next intersection.

"Phillix, you got any access to the base?" Alexis asked as she studied the map for any clue as to where to find Sabrya.

"Does space suck?"

"Actually—" Bradyn started.

"Since this is a big event for the tourney," Alexis cut in, "is there anything specific on the agenda or any indication of where the tourney contestants are?"

"I'm accessing the database now," Phillix commented after a short pause. "Here's something interesting. Sanctioned by the tourney hierarchy, all contestant weaponry augmentation has been nullified while on the station. There's a whole lot of paragraphs of legalese stating punishment for any infraction."

"So... these super-auged, cyborg-humans are now just mouth-breathing mannequins?"

"Seems so."

"What about Sabrya?" Bradyn asked.

"Calling her a mannequin will make you a head shorter," Phillix joked. "Technically, she's not a contestant, but even so, no doubt, as a patron, she is beholden to the same rules as any other civilian."

"Rules? This is Sabrya we're talking about," Bradyn stated.

"What can I say? If I had shoulders and arms, I'd shrug. I've uploaded schematics to your armpads and noted areas where there are weapon suppressants. I don't know if they'll affect her nanites."

Alexis tapped the button to call an elevator and waited, looking around. "And now, you're waiting for me to ask to hack into the security feed and locate her?"

Phillix replied, "Only if my Captain orders it, of course. I wouldn't dream—"

"Do it," Alexis said quietly as several other recent arrivals turned up to use the lifts.

"Level ten. Room 10156," their AI responded immediately.

Alexis rolled her eyes as Bradyn chuckled.

"Any sign of Necto or Bruiser?" she commed discretely.

"Nothing so far."

The elevator arrived. They took turns boarding with the other passengers. Bradyn tapped level ten. It was cramped inside the elevator with seven occupants. Other than mutual nods of greeting, no one said anything. The other occupants looked like spacefaring types, much like them, and there was a certain tang that was unmistakable.

Some occupants disembarked on other levels. Two remained when the lift arrived at the tenth level. Alexis and

Bradyn stepped off and glanced up and down the curved corridor, looking for room identification. The corridor curved away in both directions.

"Suite 10156 is closest to your left," Phillix informed them.

"Suite?" Alexis repeated as she turned and followed the number sequence.

"She has several million stellars at her disposal," Bradyn reminded her. "I think she's living it up a bit. I probably would, too."

Alexis nodded. "Phill, if what you say about these two brutes is true, they can't be trusted to keep the peace... maybe keep tabs on any tourney-registered ships, as well. Oh, and run a list of all the guests, highlighting contestants and tourney officials."

"Why?" Bradyn asked.

"Chances are Sabrya might be looking for some of them—Malazi Phakani in particular. She'll be pissed we're here... so it's sort of like a peace offering."

"And this ammo cache that's going to destroy the planet?"

"The message had an access code. Maybe she's after a ship to get to it?"

"She *had* a drocking ship."

"Yeah, but she didn't want us involved."

"We've been through some tough crap together. I reckon we could handle it."

"Perhaps she hasn't got that much faith in our abilities?" She stopped and turned to him. "Brad, I'm grasping at spacewhisps here. I've no idea what's going through her head, but if we've something to assist her, we might keep our heads, and she can keep her cool."

"We can hope. Sabrya isn't one to abide by the rules."

They soon found the door and tapped the doorbell. A couple of moments later the door swung open.

"What the frag are you two doin' here?" Sabrya asked with a

look of surprise—the first time either had witnessed it. The look instantly changed to a snarl. "That lyin' fraggin' piece of shit!"

"Nice to see you, too. If you mean Phill, he kept his word. Torg, however, is hardwired to obey his captain, so you can't get pissed at him."

"I can fraggin' try."

"Then, sadly, we'd lose two *Malleus* crew."

"Two? How so?"

"If you take your tantrum out on a droid who's incapable of striking back, you'd be no better than Franton Hobbs, that drunk lowlife back on Sylvanus. And, if that were the case, I wouldn't want you on my crew."

"That's fraggin' low."

"As low as ditching us and doing this alone?"

"I was tryin' to keep you fraggin' safe from those two maniacs!"

"Then you haven't heard?" Bradyn asked.

"May as well come in." Sabrya turned and strode back to the lounge area. "Heard what?"

As they walked through the short entrance to the living area, their earbuds blared loud static, and they had to quickly remove them.

'Jammer,' Bradyn mouthed to Alexis, who nodded.

They pocketed their earpieces, rubbed their ears, and moved into the room where a woman stood by the large window overlooking the moonscape.

"Noma, meet Alexis and Bradyn from the *Malleus*," Sabrya said as she slouched into the opulent lounge and grabbed her beverage. She drank it, but it didn't change the brooding look on her face.

The three guests nodded in greeting.

"Bradyn, heard what?" Sabrya asked.

"Not good news. Back on Plor—"

"I was about to tell you," Noma spoke up. She moved closer and sat beside Sabrya. "Word just in is Necto and Bruiser, along with a few others, recently attacked Brutus' homestead."

"They fraggin' did what?" Sabrya leapt to her feet.

"Seems Necto and Bruiser were as hell-bent on getting *you* as you are on getting them," Alexis said. "If you had stayed, perhaps none of this would have happened."

"Were you there? Did you see them?"

Alexis recounted their actions.

"The *Malleus* took out most of the skimmers and recorded it. One skimmer—no doubt with your maniacs—escaped. Nyka is the only survivor at the homestead, and Brutus is now in Cromyn Medical Facility." Alexis moved closer to her and added softly, "It doesn't look good. Be prepared for the worst."

"I'm always prepared for the worst." Sabrya turned and paced the room, swearing to herself. She stopped at the full-length window, which misted with the warrior's breathing.

"In case you're wondering, Phillix can't locate Necto and Bruiser on Tataranga. Not on the base, at least," Alexis said, glancing at her armpad for any updates and noticing the blank screen. She showed Bradyn her blank armpad. His was the same.

"I take it you saw the whole message?" Sabrya continued at their nods. "I didn't come here for them. I came to stop Grindstone bein' destroyed. That's why I contacted my old friends, the Sunfists."

"Did they respond?"

"We did. I'm their leader." Noma raised her glass to them. "We've worked successfully with Sabrya and Brutus in the past. Oh, I'm using a scrambler, so your armpads aren't faulty. Anyone could be listening."

"Sabrya became a slave as a result of working with you," Bradyn rumbled.

"And I lost some good people—"

"And some assholes," Sabrya commented.

"But we all knew the risks," Noma continued.

"What will you get out of it this time?" Alexis asked, leaving her armpad alone.

Noma remained quiet and sipped from her glass.

"It's all right, Noma. I've been with the *Malleus* crew for over six months now. We've been through some fraggin' shit together. I trust them."

"Not enough, apparently," Bradyn grumped quietly.

"Okay... chillax. Take a seat, have a drink, and we can discuss the details," Sabrya offered.

"Sab, are you sure?" Noma asked.

"Look, I tried to keep them out of it, but now they're here, it's not like they're goin' to walk away or talk to anyone."

They sat in the luxurious lounges once they had glasses in hand.

Bradyn looked at the contents dubiously. "This isn't any of that lethal concoction you drink, is it?"

"These glasses would fraggin' melt if it was." Sabrya chuckled. "This is the local moonshine, Tataranga Tequila." She drained the glass. "Tastes okay."

Sabrya poured herself another glass then began discussing her plans. "Each time there's a tourney, they bring in an ammo cache—a high-tech weapons platform where contestants gear up for each scenario. There's a dozen of them strategically scattered around the various sectors. This particular one's a fraggin' revamped relic waystation, which means it's locked in hyperspace."

"Hard to get to then," Bradyn commented. "Waystations tend to direct vessels away from them through the ship's AI."

Sabrya nodded. "This waystation also redirects spacecraft away, unless they have the override code and exact coordinates."

"Which were embedded in that message?" Alexis questioned.

Again, the warrior woman nodded. "As you heard, they want to use the waystation to wipe out Grindstone. The fraggin' fraggers." Sabrya drained her glass again. "I'm goin' to deactivate the AM-reactor, so when it hits Grindstone, it'll just crash like a ship."

"Sounds dangerous—"

"What you call dangerous, I call fraggin' 'fun times.'"

"And the Sunfists' part is to get you there?" Alexis asked. "We have a ship, too, you know." She tried to keep the irritation out of her voice.

Noma spoke up, knowing what it would be like to be a captain of a ship that was deemed unsuitable. Every worthy captain was proud of their vessel. "No offense to your ship, but from what has Sabrya told me, the *Malleus* isn't as large or powerful as the *Mulan*."

"And that's important because?" Bradyn looked confused.

"The ammo cache has a very strong repulsion field, strong enough to stop anything but large craft. Without it, a smaller craft could slip through the waystation's defenses, but not so a larger ship. If it has no access code, it'll be destroyed."

"The access code doesn't negate the repulsion field?" Bradyn asked.

"It opens up a narrow section to allow access to the specified dock, but it remains active in all other directions," Noma informed them.

"You should have more faith in the *Malleus*," Bradyn said proudly. "She may be old, but she can surprise you. Phill—" Bradyn started to call the ship, forgetting the scrambler.

"Other than the joy of saving Grindstone and sticking it to the tourney hierarchy—and no doubt in some way, to the Imperialists—what do the Sunfist get out of this?" Alexis asked.

"All that and as much high-tech ammo as we can carry."

Noma smiled and raised her glass.

"Even if you get on, surely there're security bots throughout to prevent any unauthorized access," Bradyn pointed out.

"Assuming the codes are correct, would the bots still be activated?" Alexis asked.

"I've never seen them." Sabrya shrugged. "From what I understand, as long as there's a legitimate code, the bots remain dormant."

"You've been there?" Alexis looked surprised.

"You'll recall, I was the fraggin' poster girl for the Sector 22 tourney. I know a bit about it. Mind you, I didn't need to go anywhere near the reactor, just the weapons lockers."

"So, you know about this repulsion field, then?"

"I know of it. I wasn't pilotin' any ship. When I went there, there was no problem gaining access." She shrugged.

Bradyn nodded, taking this information in. "When do you plan on starting?"

"The Smash-fest starts in two days, and Grindstone will be destroyed on completion—before the crowds frag off."

"And the tourney lasts how long?" Alexis queried.

"A day or two. Depends on the itinerary and how bloody it gets," Noma replied.

"I reckon three. These fraggers will drag it out to make maximum stellars." Sabrya turned to them. "I know you want to help, but most of the Sunfist crew are auged. They can cope with whatever's thrown at us."

"You do remember what we went through a couple of months back? Cyborgs, killer-bots, a rogue AI, all out to end us?" Alexis pointed out. "And we survived."

"Most of us..." Bradyn commented softly.

"This is diff—" Sabrya started.

"I say let them join us," Noma chipped in. "If their ship can't get there, no problem, we'll continue as planned, but if it makes it, they can help you do your thing—since you've already worked together—which frees up more of my crew to grab the ammo."

Sabrya looked troubled. "You got the access code?" she asked Alexis.

"Phillix made a copy," Alexis said.

"Of course, he fraggin' did."

Alexis put down her glass and stood. "Best we do this before the tourney starts. Are you coming with us?"

"This suite cost me a fraggin' fortune. I'm gonna get every ounce of luxury I can beforehand. I'll go over details with Noma and join you at the rendezvous."

"Fair enough," Alexis said after the briefest of hesitations. "Let us know the rendezvous coordinates when you're ready, and we can get this over and done with. We do have other plans," she said pointedly.

"I'll send it through to the *Malleus* once we're back on the *Mulan*," Noma offered.

"See you then." Alexis nodded.

The pair turned and made their way to the door.

"You didn't tell her about Malazi," Bradyn noted as they returned to the elevators.

"No need and better we didn't. She'd probably be tempted to go after him. Then there'd be more trouble than I care to worry about." Alexis pushed in her earbud. "How goes it, Phill? We're on our way back."

"I've been trying to reach you, but I'm guessing we were jammed? Quiet here, but there's sad news from Plorian. Brutus didn't recover from surgery."

"That's..." Alexis sighed and slumped against the wall. Bradyn was close by and reached out to support her. "Poor Nyka. Unless there's other family we don't know about, she's an orphan, now."

"Things are going to go to shit when Sabrya finds out," Bradyn said.

CHAPTER ELEVEN

"PHILL, I'm assuming you know where this weapons cache is?" Alexis asked when she and Bradyn returned to the ship. They made their way to the bridge in a sullen mood after hearing the news about Brutus.

"I've logged the location into the nav-comp. Any luck with Sabrya?"

Alexis took her seat and briefed him on their conversation and meeting Noma. "She'll be joining us later, after they send us rendezvous coordinates."

"She's living it up big time before her stellars run dry." Bradyn dropped into the seat beside her. It creaked in protest.

"It was a nice suite," Alexis commented. "Any other happenings while we were away? Any sign of Necto or Bruiser?"

"None," Phillix said. "A couple of very large vessels with Imperial drive signatures arrived. The *Romulus* and the *Remus*. They're part of the emperor's advanced retinue—"

"We're underground. How do you know that?" Bradyn asked.

"Think about what I do..."

"Ah." The engineer nodded.

"The arrival portends a few interesting days ahead. Two heavy warships appearing can only mean one of two things, and invasion is unlikely."

"It's a sure sign the emperor is going to visit," Alexis summed up.

"A high probability."

"Lucky for us, we won't be here. Small fish though we are, no doubt there'll be some notification with our and this 'stolen' craft's details on it." She patted her armrest.

"There's always the Bukshoga Qlan," Bradyn added. "They might not do anything to us while here, but they will be tailing us and striking whenever the opportunity arrives after our departure."

"It'll be interesting to see what happens to them if they follow us to the waystation," Phillix said.

"I'm more interested to see how our reworked drives perform," the engineer said. "When we jump, I'll be in engineering. I might need to calibrate them. This repulsor field sounds like it'll put the ship under some strain."

"The *Mulan* just sent a tight-beamed comm. Looks like coordinates. I gather they're still coming along. Are they needed now that we're going?" Phillix asked.

"Not sure of their arrangements." Alexis shrugged. "Maybe Sabrya feels she owes them. She said she wanted to keep us out of it."

"With these augmented maniacs on the loose, I'm happy for the extra muscle." Bradyn nodded.

"No arguments from me. I just feel shitty she didn't feel we were good enough. Phillix, take us out when you're ready... or is there a departure tax we need to consider?"

"Don't be silly." Phillix chuckled, which sounded weird over the speakers. "I already took care of that via the accounts of our generous beneficiary."

Alexis was on the bridge seat, still brooding. The jump into hyperspace—the kaleidoscopic swirl of light—was worth seeing, even if she'd seen it before. It picked up her mood a little. She was still watching it in wonder when her engineer arrived.

"How did the drive perform?" Alexis asked as Bradyn took his seat.

"Excellently. Not a hiccup to worry about."

"We certainly don't need another 'hyperspace hiccup.'" She recalled their ad hoc escape from the Qlan when they'd first used the hyperdrive.

"That was certainly an occasion to forget. Let's hope we don't run into the Qlan and have a repeat performance."

"I can assure you, Torg wiped that maneuver from the data banks," Phillix reminded them.

"The stealth shield should remove them from being a threat anymore," Alexis commented.

"We've arrived at the designated coordinates from the Sunfists," Phillix said a moment later. "Scanners are clear. The *Mulan* isn't here yet, though I'm picking up an unusual energy reading. It's quite massive, considering there are still several hundred kilometers to go."

"Sounds like the waystation Sabrya described." Bradyn glanced at the readings on the side of the display once the transition was complete. "An anti-matter reactor would put out significant power like that. Guessing AM also puts out an unusual signature?"

Alexis stood and stretched. "I'll leave you two tech heads to it and head down to go over the gear for propagating our food. Have to start sometime. Phillix, let me know when they appear on the scope. Torg, meet me at Charlie2 hold. Thanks."

"Very good, Captain," the droid responded over the comms.

"Should we remain uncloaked?" Phillix asked before she left.

"Yes. Our ability to cloak is something I'd like to keep secret. While the Sunfists do what they can to thwart the Imperium, stealth tech would tempt even the most devout rebel into making enough stellars to retire for several lifetimes." Alexis considered. "If we have the access codes, we shouldn't have anything to worry about. It'd be far too coincidental for any ship other than the *Mulan* to approach these coordinates. If that happens, go dark, but not before."

In Charlie2 hold, the bots had already unpacked the various containers, though their arrangement of the nutrient beds would need to be redone. Shelving had been constructed to store the items, which were stacked neatly, alphabetically.

Alexis studied the area, the bulkhead, and the deckhead, deciding the best place to install lighting and watering. She had been busy for an hour when Phillix commed her.

"I'm detecting a localized disturbance," Phillix informed the crew over the ship-wide comms. "The *Mulan* has arrived. We are being hailed."

"I'm heading up." Alexis removed her gardening gloves and headed to the bridge after leaving Torg with instructions. "Patch them through," she said upon arrival, as she dropped into her seat and swiveled to face the screen and viewport.

"*Mulan* to *Malleus* ..."

"*Malleus* here. Welcome. Sorry for the delay," Alexis answered.

"No problem. You've a shuttle inbound with your warrior girl, so don't shoot her out of the black. That'll just piss her off."

"Sabrya's always pissed off," Bradyn muttered, as he joined his captain.

The shuttle was a blue blip on the scope. "We see it," Alexis responded.

"Good. *Mulan* out."

Alexis muted the comms momentarily. "Stupid question, but is our shuttle dock serviceable? We've never needed to use it until now. Or does Sabrya enter via the airlock?"

"Union rules stipulate all spacefaring vessels must have a universal docking port. Rest assured, your underpaid engineer is earning his keep and maintaining all equipment and every inch of this vessel."

"Pfft. Remind me to double your rations."

"Lovely. More protein bars. My stomach's churning in anticipation."

"If you're especially nice, I'll even share some of the vegetables, once the garden starts producing." Alexis turned the comms back on.

As the shuttle approached, it slowed and turned. It was close enough that they could easily see it through the viewport. A hatch opened on the side, and a figure emerged and jetted across in a powered spacesuit.

"Still reckon we could use one of those shuttles," Bradyn said.

"You never know—"

"Hey you lot, get your hands out of your pants and open the fraggin' airlock," Sabrya commed.

"I guess that answers that question." Alexis reached over and activated the airlock. "Welcome back," she said when the warrior woman entered. "We'll be in the crew lounge. Bradyn's about to make a fresh pot of coffee."

"Of course, I am," the engineer muttered. "Underpaid engineer and barista."

In a few minutes, Sabrya joined them, still garbed in her spacesuit—one remarkably more updated than their own. She twisted off her helmet. "All forgiven?"

"We're a team. Nothing to forgive. Probably better, in the long run, to have the extra firepower. Have the Sunfists sorted themselves out?" Alexis poured three coffees and handed them around.

"They'll be fine." Sabrya nodded, accepted her drink, and took a sip of the hot beverage. Any animosity about tracking her to Tataranga was forgotten, but those that knew her could discern a darkness in her eyes following the news of the death of Brutus and his family. "Hey, Metalman, want to join us?" She asked Torg to come as she began to explain the plan.

"We're to follow the *Mulan* in. Both ships will be broadcastin' the code which'll deactivate a section of the repulsors, and then the AI will direct us in. There are landin' areas around the middle of the station. After we land at our designated spots, we'll be in the shadow of the repulsion field once it's reactivated. Even so, there are automatic magnetic clamps embedded in the pad."

"And if the code doesn't work?" Bradyn queried.

"Then we cloak. Noma and the Sunfists will be very pissed at me—if they survive—but I trust my colleague. Paceman was good—for a fraggin' coder."

"The code and coordinates embedded in the vid signal were elegant," Phillix complemented.

"If you say so." The warrior woman shrugged. "All I know is Paceman fraggin' died to give us this info." She continued, "From there, we'll suit up and head to the center of the area. Noma and her team will be grabbin' whatever they can take from the lockers as their payment."

"And these things aren't heavily fortified and secured?" Bradyn queried.

"You bet they are. It's a big, high-tech, heavily armed warehouse, but it's all on auto until the commencement of the tourney. That's when staff arrive. Anyone with clearance is safe. Just before the tourney starts, security's reduced, but there'll be so many auged fraggers around, it isn't needed."

"And they don't fight, blow each other up, and cause utter mayhem?"

"We've very few rules, but much like the temporary situation back on Tataranga, these are designated 'neutral territories.' Violence anywhere near these caches will lead to automatic forfeiture of all fraggin' awards, rewards, and any augmentation."

"I would've thought, considering who we're dealing with, it would be an immediate death sentence."

"We'd be so fraggin' lucky. Imagine our life… hero-worshipped around the galaxy, any and everythin' available on a whim, and so supra-auged that no norm person could fraggin' touch us… then they take it all away and throw you into the drift."

"You'd leave an empty shell," Bradyn surmised, answering Sabrya.

"Exactly. From Godhood to less than grunfer shit. A clean death would be fraggin' welcomed."

The lift doors opened, and Torg joined them in the crew lounge. "I am here," he announced, a smudge of dirt on his torso marring his otherwise gleaming surface.

"Okay, we get in," Alexis continued. "Then what?"

"That's where it gets a bit tricky, and it's another reason why I contacted the Sunfists—they have decent coders."

Alexis thought about this before commenting. "If you need to hack into their system, surely Phillix can do that."

"I'm sure Gadgetman's as good as he thinks he is—and I do not doubt that after seein' the way the ship has been functionin', no offense to Torg."

"A droid cannot be offended. It merely carries out its duties. Anything otherwise would be a flaw in the programming."

"Love how our Metalman never changes," Sabrya continued.

Torg pivoted to her. "With the new legs Bradyn has fitted me with, I am now 7.3 centimeters taller," the droid stated.

Sabrya slapped the droid on the back in jest. "Yes, I actually complimented the fraggin' coder."

"Who are you, and where's the real Sabrya?" Alexis asked the warrior in mock surprise.

"Ah yes, here comes the flattery," Phillix said. "By the way, for your reading pleasure, I have uploaded the recent highlights of the galactic and local infocast currently on the Mesh."

"And we care because...?" Sabrya asked, annoyed at the interruption.

"Because the emperor has just confirmed his attendance at the tourney. Security will be tightened. Just to let you know... It will still take us a while to arrive, thought you might like something to read."

"Good idea," Alexis approved, then questioned Sabrya. "Did you say those with the access code can enter? Why the need for hackers?"

"Getting into the waystation isn't the issue. We can't just waltz into unauthorized areas. We need a coder for that. The fun starts if they fail."

"And, no doubt, the reactor area is unauthorized?"

"You fraggin' bet."

"Any idea what'll be thrown at us?" Bradyn asked.

"Nothin' good. Definitely lethal. But, as you said, we handled the killer-bots on the *Iconic* —they were top Imp military droids—and nothin' here will be any fraggin' worse. We've better weapons, more of them, and you now know how to use them. At least there's no fraggin' maniac empress."

"And Torg?"

"We'll need the droid to do the hackin'."

"Why's that?" Phillix asked.

"To access and override the security control for the reactor."

"I can hack into it from the service interface on the pad," Phillix said, "assuming there is one."

"There is, but the reactor controls are air gapped. You have to be inside the fraggin' facility to access them. Want another ride in that node?" Sabrya referred to the node used to escape the wrath of Janus on the *Iconic*.

"I'll pass; I can assist Torg from here."

"I thought you'd say that."

"So, is that it?" Alexis asked.

"For the moment." Sabrya nodded. "Now, we sit back and wait."

"You staying in that suit?"

"Other than the last few months, I have lived in these things most of my time... fraggin' weird, but it's sort of homely. Wait till you see the suits I used to wear. Fit me like a glove."

"Poor girl has hit her head," Bradyn muttered to Alexis.

"I'll fraggin' hit your head."

"We're being hailed," Phillix informed them.

"*Mulan* to *Malleus*." They recognized the Sunfist leader's voice over the comm.

"Go ahead, *Mulan*," Alexis responded as she stepped up to the bridge.

"Just letting you know we're starting our approach. Codes working fine, and we're following the designated path."

"Concur," Alexis responded, looking at the readouts on her console. "We also have an approach path and assigned berth. See you there, in... forty minutes." She returned to the lounge with the others and continued reading the infocast Phillix had downloaded.

The infocast included data vids from the various sectors in the region. You could easily discern the allegiance of the particular providers: those that were pro-Imperium glowed eloquently about the happenings due to the beneficial guidance of the divine ruler; the reports from non-aligned sectors were more rudimentary and not as glowing.

Among the non-aligned reports, this 'beneficial guidance' was described as 'the only remaining choice the upstart emperor had due to the budgetary constraints of the ongoing conflict.' It was plain to see the inner planets loved him, while the outer regions utterly despised him, hence the massive security requirements.

When the waystation became visible, Phillix called them up to the bridge.

"It's not like any waystation I've ever seen," Bradyn pointed out. "Though, admittedly, I've only seen them on plans and schematics."

Phillix provided a summarized version of the news gleaned from the Mesh. "We know they're designed to ward off space-going vessels from navigational hazards and spatial anomalies during hyperjumps. They've been around for almost three thousand years and have changed dramatically in that time. As they developed, they became far more advanced, and AIs are needed to run them to prevent ships from crashing. When a vessel's transponder registers its route, the waystation will modify the ship's course to avoid a collision, but only if required. Otherwise, it monitors local hyperspace. This particular waystation is a relic, though now much larger. Considering they were designed to monitor and detour spacecraft, landing pads are not standard."

Sabrya nodded when she saw it. "As I remember, lookin' like one of those sea urchin things I saw on a vid-cast. All those spikes are weapons arrays."

"Looks a bit like your hair, but not blue and black?" Bradyn pointed out.

"That again? I'll turn you fraggin' black and blue?" Sabrya retorted.

"What are you picking up, Phill?" Alexis asked, smiling at the repartee of the other two.

"We're at fifty percent thrust to maintain our position, and we're still fifty kilometers away. When does this code activate?"

"No fraggin' idea. I've not piloted a craft in before, but it'll work soon enough."

"How's the *Mulan* fairing?" Alexis asked.

"Better than us, but considering she's a larger craft, that's understandable."

"Do you know much about the vessel?"

"I may have perused the files of all the ships docked at the Tataranga spaceport."

"And?"

"It's running twin Cerbrinka-Zaners drives, Wheinmarht scanners, Mark 4 Barrunta AI, enduro-armor, four tri-barrel plasma canons, and new supra-drive launchers for the AM-missiles."

Bradyn whistled, clearly impressed.

"AM," Alexis queried. "Anti-matter? They put that in missiles now?"

"We have 'em in grenades too," Sabrya added.

"Hand-held grenades... of anti-matter?" Alexis' jaw dropped.

"Yep. One well-placed AM-grenade can take out a spaceship, but you don't want to fraggin' be around when that happens."

"Um... how does that work, exactly?" the engineer asked.

"Open the airlock, toss, close the airlock, and get the frag out of there. There's no boom... just a nice shiny light that'll burn your retina if you look and a shock wave that'll make you paste into the fraggin' bulkhead if you get caught. It helps to have a fast ship."

"No doubt." Bradyn agreed.

The time to approach dragged on.

"There's our airlock." Sabrya pointed to a dark niche below one of the spikes.

The three crew were suited and waiting in the loading bay while the station slowly rotated. As described, the landing area was a platform encircling the station. Reducing the forward momentum, turning the *Malleus* around so the 'the head' was hanging over the pad's edge, all while adjusting to match the platform's spin so as not to plow into the structure required a delicate balance from Phillix. Eventually, the station and the *Malleus* were synchronized.

To the far right, they could see the *Mulan* having similar difficulties. In their case, the vessel was too large to fit lengthways, so it had to turn parallel to the station.

"Ten seconds to landing," Phillix warned them. "There could be a bump."

Bradyn squirmed, trying to adjust his girth in the powered spacesuits Sabrya had stripped from the Qlan mercs on the *Iconic*, the same mercs that had provided half the weapons in her ad hoc armory. She had also confiscated all the rebel weapons, but they were mostly small handheld laser pistols, with only one decent multi-rifle among them. The *Malleus* also had *Octavia* spacesuits, and they'd recycled the old suits from Jenna's team.

"Are these really necessary?" he grumbled.

"How good are you at holdin' your breath? We need them to search the station. No point havin' ongoin' fraggin' life support for an unmanned and fully automated facility." She had already taken them through a brief course on how to control the micro-thrusters in the suits. "Not that we'll need them afterward. Wait until you see the Kimichi Mk8. That's a suit to fraggin' dream about."

"You mean I have to adjust to another spacesuit?" Bradyn grumped.

"It'll adjust to *you*, big boy."

Everyone braced themselves as the two craft prepared to hit, albeit softly.

"Five... four... three... two... one..."

They felt the faintest of jolts. A Klaxon alarm blared for half a second before Phillix shut it down.

"We are attached and secured. I'll now begin hacking into the system."

"Good work. Let us know when you do. A schematic of the station would be handy." Alexis hit the door release.

"I'm in," Phillix said smugly as the four of them stepped onto the pad.

"How the frag can he sound so up himself... it's just fraggin' audio."

"It takes skill; it's all about the timing, tone, and pace," Phillix replied. "It requires almost as much skill to hack this AI, but it's got nothing on Janus."

Pings were heard simultaneously in each suit. Another highlight of these suits was the better graphics and interface the suits provided.

The trio scanned their armpads.

"These aren't schematics," Alexis noted.

"Harder to get to. Working on it. I thought some of you would like a list of the cache contents to peruse in the meantime."

"I thought we were here to save a planet... Sabrya?"

"Of course, we fraggin' are." The warrior still cast an eager eye over the list.

"Looks comprehensive, but I've no idea what I'm looking at." Alexis scowled. "Nothing for cultivation, I take it."

"There's a flame-thrower," Bradyn suggested jokingly.

"You won't be saying that when Sabrya and I have fresh

vegetable dishes, and you're stuck with those extra protein bars."

"Extra protein bars?" Sabrya looked at him curiously.

"I got a pay rise." His grin showed his white teeth which contrasted with his black beard and complexion.

"How unfortunate for you," Sabrya said as she scrolled up and down the list, creating her wish list. "Of course, there may be nothin' left by the time the Sunfists go through it."

"Lucky we're not here for ammunition then... at least, not as a priority." Alexis was aware they now had the capabilities to become a weapons platform, and some of the items looked quite devastating.

"Lucky you both have a fraggin' subject matter expert then, isn't it? I can pick the best of what there is to save space."

"Missiles are on deck three," Bradyn pointed out. "Phillix, how many can we handle?"

"The launch tubes we salvaged only had a rack of four each. But our maintenance bots can construct new racks to cater to our needs. The limit will depend on the size of the missiles and how many holds you want—"

"But there's so many to fraggin' choose from. There's—"

"Seriously, the whole point of the cloak is to avoid conflict. We'll certainly take what we can, *if* we can, but everything in moderation. See what else we can get before we make any final decisions. Make a list of what you feel we could best use out of what's available. Try to vary it. You never know what circumstances we'll come across later."

"We could trade weapons."

"We're going to trade supplies with colonists, not become arms dealers."

Sabrya held her tongue and returned to eyeing the lists.

"Surely, it's not only stuff to kill and blow-up things." Bradyn scrolled through the list to see what engineering parts he could use. His eyes widened when he spied a couple of choice items and added them to the wish list.

"Phillix, if there's anything you or the ship can benefit from, feel free to let us know," Alexis offered reluctantly. "Though it isn't a priority, I do accept missiles would be handy—especially where we're going—and this is an opportunity I doubt we'll get again."

CHAPTER TWELVE

BRADYN AND ALEXIS double-checked each other's suits, making sure the seals were correct.

"Don't fraggin' worry. I checked everythin', and then my Metalman buddy double-checked."

"Looks a bit loose here and very tight there," Alexis pointed out. "Should be okay, as long as you don't get too excited over the engineering specs. Phillix, don't let Bradyn see any pics of the station's inner workings."

"You're not funny. One size doesn't drocking fit all," Bradyn griped. "And they smell."

"Deodorized and sanitized, big boy." Sabrya glanced at him. "Any odors in there are all yours. So, quit your bitchin'."

The three of them waited as the lights in the loading bay dimmed.

"Time to go people. Everyone ready?" Alexis looked around. Bradyn's squat, stocky figure, in his ill-fitting suit, contrasted with the gleaming droid and their tall warrior woman in her body-hugging powersuit.

There were thumbs-ups all around.

At her signal, Phillix activated the door release once the

pressure equalized. Brandishing the charged gutpuncher, Sabrya, out of habit, stepped out straight away to check the area. While the breacher was her weapon of choice—it was a brute—the gutpuncher gave her more flexibility.

Strategically attached to her suit were a selection of pouches with grenades and other violent surprises. She noticed Bradyn looking at the bulging pouches. "When I know you can handle other ordnance, you can have a pouch, too."

He shrugged in his suit, which caused him to groan with discomfort. His scowl was barely visible through the faceplate.

They paused to take in their settings. The dull, kaleidoscopic display of hyperspace, the one that could make you crazy if you stared at it long enough, continued. The gridded metal sections of the landing pad stretched out in a dark flat ribbon around the circumference of the station.

"I'm thinking the Sunfists have started their shopping spree," Alexis noted.

About fifty meters further along, the tail end of the *Mulan* could be seen, its rear hangar door open. There was no other movement.

"The sooner we get this done, the more time we might have time to grab a few items." Sabrya moved off as she continued talking. "I can get us through most of it from memory, but once we get deeper, it's unknown territory to me."

The station loomed above, partly obscured by the 'spikes'—the large weapons arrays.

"Are those plasma cannons? They're huge," Alexis noted absently.

"The guns need to be big enough to deal with the most enthusiastic shopper. You've seen the list. What's available is mostly advanced R&D—prototypes for the military. Any psycho gettin' their hands on this lot could do some very serious damage."

They moved off warily, the experienced warrior leading and Torg in the rear.

"With all this armament, you reckon the Sunfists have got something up their sleeve?"

"If not, somethin' will no doubt come to mind once they see what they've got. Even with all the ramped-up security, the emperor being on tour offers many desirable opportunities."

"And you trust them getting their hands on this?" Alexis queried.

"I'm fraggin' sure. Wouldn't have called on them otherwise."

Alexis dropped the subject as it was bordering on the recent dispute.

The group moved to the nearest airlock, which cycled open at their approach. As Sabrya had stated earlier, the facility was fully automated, so there was no need to cater to biologicals, and the interior wasn't heated or pressurized.

"That took longer than expected." Their armpads pinged as Phillix finally uploaded the schematics. "Sorry."

"Thanks. Keep us updated," Alexis responded.

"Unless there's comms interference, I'll be assisting Torg with the hacking."

"This will be a system which I am unfamiliar with. Your assistance will increase our probability of success," the droid answered blandly.

The group warily ventured into a junction in the curving corridor, with another passage leading toward the center. The area suddenly illuminated as they entered. They looked left and right but saw no sign of the Sunfists.

"I don't give a drock if this thing is powered. I should've worn my old spacesuit." From Bradyn's grumbling tone, it was clear the suit wasn't to his liking, and his attitude was deteriorating by the minute. He had to reach down and readjust his suit every few steps. "Where the drock are they?" He looked down the darker passages for the *Mulan* crew.

"As we move, the lights behind us will go out, and those in front will flash on," Sabrya said, which is what happened when she moved further along the passage. The group followed, and the lights behind dimmed to nothingness.

Now and then, Alexis looked at her armpad to reference their location.

"Something's been bugging me—" Bradyn started as they slowly progressed inward.

"Yeah, it shows. That suit cuts in all those awkward places. I'm surprised your voice hasn't raised a fraggin' octave or two." Sabrya chuckled. "You haven't the body for space."

"Not that," the engineer continued, wriggling. "If we shut down the reactor, the anti-matter will no longer be contained. Once released, it will spontaneously annihilate everything within a vast radius. It would take a physicist to determine how that's going to go down in hyperspace, and whether it even affects real space. I doubt we'll have time to get out."

"Too deep for me, but I've gotta do somethin'." The warrior moved on to the next corridor after checking the surroundings.

Bradyn remained silent as they made their way cautiously to the next section.

"Perhaps we take the jump drives offline?" He said later. "That way, this thing will no longer remain in hyperspace. It will be visible to all and possibly stop their plans."

"If it's an option, you're just the person to do it," Alexis agreed.

Sabrya looked over her shoulder at the droid. "Why didn't *you* think of that, Metalman?"

"Nobody requested that particular information. The data is available, along with several terabytes of other data."

"Can it still be used as a planet-killer?" Sabrya asked the engineer.

"Yes, eventually. But it's a work in progress. Let's see how it's set up."

"Looks like I'll have to devise a Plan B," she muttered, clearly not happy with the current plan.

They continued, following the warrior woman toward the center of the station.

"We go up another couple of levels. That's when you'll need to start bein' cautious."

"Not you?" Bradyn checked the next intersection as he passed.

"I'm always fraggin' cautious. Here are the lifts," she said before the engineer could retort.

***

"This is it," Sabrya announced.

They had stepped out of the lift and walked another fifty paces before the corridor stopped, and a large area in front of them lit up. The floor, as throughout the rest of the facility, was a gleaming black surface. While the corridors leading inward were straight, as expected, those going around the station were curved, with the curvature becoming more accentuated as they progressed. In the center was a massive domed construct.

"I'll wager what we can see is only a portion of it." Bradyn examined his armpad schematics in detail.

"Do your thing, Chromehead," Sabrya said as she checked the area.

The droid stepped away and approached a pedestal terminal near where the domed construct met the floor. Several meters to the right were large blast doors.

"I will begin." Torg immediately interfaced with the console. His metal fingers rapidly tapped at the keys. They heard a weird undulating and intermittent tone in their helmets.

"What's that noise?" Alexis asked.

"Vocals are inadequate for this task. Instructions converted to electronic signals are far more efficient." Torg's fingers didn't flinch as he answered.

"Can't you geeks do it fraggin' quietly?"

With the exception of a minimal pause, the droid continued, though the volume in their ears was substantially reduced. Leaving the droid to do its work, the warrior strode off to cover the corridor and elevators. The remaining pair moved apart a few meters to cover the area and the other corridor.

Bradyn was beside the central bulkhead that separated them from the core. Behind the thick glassteel window was a railed gantry leading to a large, almost black sphere that disappeared above and below into darkness. The engineer nodded at his estimation of the massive structure. "That there's probably the largest electro-magnet in the Imperium. I wonder how much anti-matter is inside?" He squirmed again in a futile attempt to get comfortable.

"From the little I know of anti-matter, I'm sure it's enough to take us and the cruiser out," Alexis replied.

"Undoubtedly."

After a couple of minutes, Sabrya shook her head at the idle banter. She examined the schematics on her armpad. A glance showed Alexis and Bradyn watching their areas. She switched her comms to personal mode. "Phillix," she commed.

"Ah, first-name basis, are we? No longer Gadgetman? I deduce our illustrious warrior requires a favor."

"Frag off! This's for everyone's benefit. I'm thinkin' of a Plan B. Where's the weakest link in this AM core?"

"Easiest and most effective access would be via the power conduits for the station's plasma cannons. Another level up."

When she looked over at her companions, the droid was still busy at the terminal. Only his fingers were moving; the rest of his gleaming body was a statue. Alexis and Bradyn had barely moved and remained vigilant for security droids.

"I'm nippin' upstairs. I've got an idea." Sabrya started moving off.

"What are you up to?" Alexis asked.

"Just remembered somethin'." She strode to the nearest stairway down the corridor. "Cover my area. I'll be back before you know it."

"Wait."

Sabrya was gone.

"Why did we invite her?" Bradyn repositioned himself so he could see along both corridors.

"I'm back. Happy now?" Sabrya asked when she returned several minutes later. "Any progress? I thought we'd be ready to go by now."

"The AI controlling the core is substantially more robust than others we have encountered. It—"

The lights turned red, making the area gloomy and eerie.

"What the frag did you do, Metalman?" Sabrya turned to look accusingly at the back of the gleaming droid.

"I have not—"

Phillix interjected to defend the droid. "One of the Sunfist coders tried to hack into an unauthorized area. They're now engaged with combat-bots as they make a hasty retreat."

As he spoke, they could feel sporadic vibrations through the deck.

"Fraggin' coders!" Sabrya punched the bulkhead in frustration. "Access to a full armory of top-end weapons isn't good enough for them?" She paced quickly to cover the nearest entrance.

"Let's worry about that later. Torg, where are you up to?" Alexis asked. She noticed Sabrya's stance was far more alert, her movements quicker, a sure sign her nanites had kicked in.

"We have managed to get into the hyperdrive systems," Torg announced.

"Disconnect the drive and wipe the navigation comp data," Bradyn ordered. "It'll take them a long time to get that back online and up to speed."

"But they can still use it to fraggin' destroy Grindstone." Sabrya didn't break her concentration as she patrolled the corridor.

"Probably, but weeks down the track—"

"Which means we have time to come up with another plan to destroy the AM core. Currently, the only choice is suicide. Do it, Torg," Alexis ordered.

"Uh huh," Sabrya muttered.

"Captain, an Imperial cruiser has just appeared on the scanner," their AI informed them.

"That was drocking quick," Bradyn said, surprised.

"Perhaps they were on alert with the emper—" Phillix started.

"I don't want to hear another word about the fraggin' emperor," Sabrya vented.

"It is done," Torg informed them.

Both Alexis and Bradyn stumbled a step as the station jolted. Sabrya stood steadfast, as did Torg.

"The waystation has dropped into real space," Phillix informed them. "We're currently 0.2 light years from Grindstone and Tataranga."

"And the cruiser?" Alexis asked.

"Still in hyper. It's not registering on the scope yet."

"Good. Keep at it, Torg. Get that nav computer wiped; destroy it if you can."

"If I override the saf—"

"Just do it, so we can get out of here." Alexis was getting testy under the tension.

"The *Mulan* has just departed. It had to blow the mag

clamps holding it down. From its angle, the repulsor field is now in full effect and no longer accepting the code. I suspect our welcome has been revoked."

"I have completed my tasking," Torg stated calmly, stepping back from the console. "The navigational computer has been wiped and is now unserviceable. It will requi—"

"Let's get the frag out of here. Everyone, on me. We'll have to take the stairs." Sabrya clicked her powersuit on and, with the grace of a raptor, glided swiftly past the lift doors to the next corner and braked efficiently so as not to overrun the cover.

Alexis was less elegant but managed to follow closely.

Bradyn's ill-fitting suit caused him to spin, and he hit and slid along the bulkhead until he managed to turn it off.

Sabrya hissed, but knew there was no point in blaming anyone but herself. Amusing as it was, she berated herself for her lack of professionalism. She should have realized the loose suit would be inadequate for this sort of activity, especially with a novice, but she shared a grin with Alexis at Bradyn's antics.

"We'll work on that—" With her nanites augmenting her senses and actions, she instinctively ducked as the bulkhead where her head had been fused and melted when a laser coursed across its surface. Already pivoting, she returned fire and scored a headshot.

"This way!" She surged toward the sparking bot, spun at the last minute and thrust her legs toward the large bot's torso to stop. The bot was large enough that her impact made no impression. To avoid any further errors, the others decided to use their legs and not the powersuits to move. They had to take the stairs as the elevators were now offline.

Sabrya checked above then vaulted the railing and dropped to the lower level. Alexis moved in to cover from above as Bradyn made his way down. When he arrived, he covered her as she descended.

Sabrya stuck her head through the doorway and spied two

combat-bots—different models from those she had just destroyed—stationed side by side at the end of the corridor, blocking their egress. She swore and reported to the others what was waiting for them.

"Is there another way around?" Bradyn asked, quickly thumbing through his armpad's contents.

"This is the level we need to get out on. Our airlock is a bit farther, but it's still the closest exit. Let's not fraggin' risk unknown territory unless it's the last resort." Sabrya rapidly changed the ammo on the gutpuncher and selected a couple of HE grenades. She fired, and even before they detonated, she was peppering the bots with the high-powered laser. She ignored the minimal shrapnel that came her way when the grenades exploded.

The bots retaliated, though the targeting system on one was faulty, and its shots went wide. The other bot was in better condition and began lumbering toward her. Even concentrated fire with her laser wasn't sufficient to get through its thick armor.

"Frag it." She unclipped her EMP grenade and tossed it. "It's my only one."

The grenade detonated, causing both bots to go dormant.

"I doubt that'll last long before they reboot. Let's move." She quickly stepped out and glided to the closest bot, braced against it to stop. She began pulling at whatever she could and piercing it with her blades.

"You take care of the front one, I'll finish off this one," Bradyn offered. He moved his large frame and began rending the parts barehanded.

Alexis covered the other end of the corridor while waiting for the droid to catch up. When Sabrya gave the all-clear, she moved out and motioned for Torg to follow when he arrived. He had new legs, but he was not fast on his feet, especially descending stairs. Getting past the destroyed bots wasn't too much of a squeeze, and she was passing the furthest one before she looked back to check on the droid's progress.

Torg was a couple of meters behind her and about to push past the last bot.

After a quick look to her left, Alexis started making her way along the curved corridor that led to their airlock. As she neared, she noticed the airlock had closed and sealed, and her two crew mates were struggling to lift it.

"Phillix, override the airlock. We're hemmed in!"

"On it. The alarm changed the AI security protocols, and I was booted," he explained.

"All I'm hearin' is fraggin' excuses."

Alexis raced up to add her strength. Further along, evidence of the Sunfists' departure was obvious, with every surface scorched and pock-marked with laser burns and blasts. There were destroyed or sparking bots, both in the corridor and out on the landing pad near where the *Mulan* had been.

"Hey, Torg. Any time you—Shit!" She stopped mid-sentence, mouth wide, as she turned to look at the droid's progress. Coming up behind him was the largest bot she'd ever seen. It was double the size of the death-bot she'd faced on the *Iconic*.

Noting its approach, Torg had already turned and crouched in a defensive posture. One of the bot's thick arms batted him aside like a Plorian swamp bug.

As they left the airlock door, both Sabrya and Alexis had their weapons up and firing. They scored hits on the bot but with little sign of damage, and anything more powerful than a laser could potentially damage Torg as the droid leapt in to attack.

A panel opened in the bot's chest, and an intense laser immediately fired at the trio by the door.

Sabrya reflexively pushed her captain out of the way while she jumped in another direction.

There was a scream and groan as both Alexis and Bradyn dropped to the deck.

Sabrya landed elegantly on her feet and glanced back; Alexis was unconscious with a wound in her abdomen, and Bradyn's thigh had been seared by the same shot.

"Fuck you!" Sabrya swore as she brought her weapon to bear at the large bot. She changed the setting to something more powerful, but the bot and droid were moving erratically. "Get out of the fraggin' way, Metalman!"

Torg was clambering over the bot and avoiding its swinging arms.

The bot swiveled and careened into the outer bulkhead, attempting to dislodge him, but it only managed to crack the station's viewport.

Torg hung on then pulled his arm back and, drawing his fingers to a point, he drove them into the bot's laser cavity up to its elbow, bypassing the heavy armor-plating.

The bot began to spark. It turned and smashed into the bulkhead again, damaging the large window even more. Torg pulled his legs up to cushion the impact of the next ramming then kicked out. His mass and strength were insignificant compared to that of the bot, but moving the bot was not his intent. Instead, he used the effort to drive his arm up to his shoulder inside the bot and then proceeded to inflict as much damage as possible to the bot's internal circuits.

While the bot was preoccupied with the irritating droid, Sabrya chose her moment to click her heels to race in and assist. The blast doors along the main corridor crashed down as the bot exploded. She had little time to do more than duck as she slammed into it and dropped, stunned, to the deck, which shook with the massive explosion. When she managed to stand and peer through the blast door window, the corridor beyond was empty and open to space via a huge hole where the viewport had been.

"Frag it, no!" She looked stunned at the sudden outcome. "Hey, Phillix?" All she got was static. A heartbeat later, she pivoted and raced back to her fallen comrades.

Adjacent blast doors had dropped, separating her from the others. Repeated calls with no response proved the comms were still down. She dreaded seeing her friend and commander lying unmoving. Bradyn had already applied gel packs to slow the air leak from her suit, and he was working on his own. He looked up, clearly in pain. When he saw Sabrya through the window, he pointed to his helmet and shook his head.

"Don't I fraggin' know it." She showed him a grenade and motioned for him to move back.

He gripped the conduit running along the bottom of the bulkhead with one hand and pulled himself along while dragging Alexis with him. The engineer then moved so his bulk would protect her from any shrapnel or blast. Bradyn saw the flash of light off the bulkhead and felt a violent vibration through the deck. When he turned to look, there was a large hole where the corner of the blast door met the outer hull.

Sabrya glided over and took Alexis from his hands. She flew quickly and gracefully outside, then sped toward the open bay of the *Malleus*, sparing a glance at the discarded weapons and laden trolley abandoned in the hiatus. She landed quickly and carried her injured comrade to the medi-doc.

"Can you hear me?"

"I can now," Sabrya answered Phillix. She began telling him what had happened as she programmed the auto-doc. "You monitor her, and I'll check on Bradyn."

She met the engineer halfway to the ship and picked him up unceremoniously, returned, and sat him next to her captain before applying stimulants and painkillers. "Back in a minute."

"I'm in the system and have removed the docking clamp restrictions," Phillix commed.

"Flash up the drives, Phill, we're leaving," Bradyn ordered

from the captain's chair. At the first opportunity, he ripped off the ill-fitting suit and tossed it into a corner.

"Certainly, but, as reluctant as I am to say it, we should wait for Sabrya."

"Where the drock is she now?" Bradyn checked the monitor and external cams and saw Sabrya jogging up the loading ramp, pushing the abandoned trolley loaded with weapons.

"We fraggin' goin' yet or what?" she called out.

CHAPTER THIRTEEN

"NO FRAGGIN' way was I goin' to leave these babies behind!" Sabrya looked over the trolley with enthusiasm.

"I can assure you, they weren't required. But I guess it'll be good to have spares."

"Spares? What the frag are you on about, Gadgetman?"

"While you were away, during my continued search of the system, I came across some interesting items in a separate database. I suspect they're new additions that haven't been processed. Since I'm sure the Sunfists would've commandeered them from the maintenance bots if they had seen them, I directed them to take a different route."

"You're fraggin' laughin', aren't you? I can fraggin' tell."

"Leave that for later, Sab," Bradyn suggested. "We've got to work out how to get Torg back."

"On way." She clamped the trolley while waiting for the pressure to equalize then glided into the passageway and up the stairs. "How's Alexis?"

"She's doing well, and she's stable," Phillix responded. "The laser took out her appendix—at least, it's not where it's supposed to be, and I can't find it anywhere. As you know from your experiences, the laser cauterized the wound, so there's not much blood loss. We have some nano-bots that will help repair the minimal damage to her internal organs."

"Good. And you, big boy?"

"I'm sore, but—"

"Cool. So, what's the plan?"

"There's been no change in Torg's condition," Phillix said. "His database is still intact and undamaged as far as I can ascertain."

"That's good news." She slumped into a chair. "Let's fraggin' get him before anyone else shows up."

"The scanners are at max. You can see the *Mulan* is not hanging around and is now several hundred klicks away."

"Looks like your buddies didn't wait for you." Bradyn wiped his brow, the sweat indicating the meds were already wearing off.

"I'm accelerating to catch up with Torg, but I'll have to pivot the ship, open the cargo bay doors, and slow down, so when he enters, he doesn't smash into the bulkhead."

"When we get closer, I could go out and drag him in," Sabrya offered.

"Then you could take your time and match his speed," Bradyn said to Phillix.

"Uhm... we can't take our time." Sabrya glanced at the time index on the console. "We've got eight minutes and forty-four seconds to get the frag out of here."

"Why? What's going to happen then?"

"Plan B. I wasn't goin' to leave that waystation knowin' it was still capable of destroyin' Grindstone at a later date."

Bradyn then noticed that while she was still in her bodysuit, her utility belt of pouches was gone. "I imagine this is going to be bad?"

She stood and stretched. "Couldn't get much worse."

"The Imperial cruiser has just dropped into real space."

"You were saying?" Bradyn winked.

She gave the engineer the finger with one of her blades. "Can the fraggin' Imps detect us?"

"We cloaked the moment we left the station. We haven't been hailed or fired upon, so my confidence remains high they're unaware of our presence."

"So, let's grab Torg and frag off."

"We have a problem. The cruiser is turning toward Torg. I reckon they've pinged him and are curious. You'll be relieved to learn their codes are also voided. If I'm reading their drive signature correctly," Phillix continued, "Comparing it to the data I found on the dark Mesh, they are at approximately thirty-eight percent thrust, but that's not unusual considering its size and its relatively modern design compared to the *Malleus*. The good news is they did take some damage from the *Mulan*."

"Is that Torg?" Bradyn referred to the steady blue icon on the screen.

"Correct."

"How far away is he, and how long before we can get to him?"

"He's already thirty-three thousand meters distant. With the aid of the repulsion field, we'll be able to pick him up in seven minutes."

"That doesn't give us much leeway."

"Pfft. It's at least a fraggin' minute."

"I estimate the cruiser will reach him in six minutes and forty seconds."

Sabrya stood and paced the floor. "He fraggin' has every detail about us and the *Malleus*. We can't let them have him."

"She's right. If we can't save him, we can't let them have him. Besides our details, they'll learn about the *Iconic*, Sylvanus Colony, and the drocking stealth cloak."

"Are you suggesting we destroy him?" Phillix asked.

"Either that or the cruiser."

"I pick the fraggin' cruiser."

"We've not taken on the Imperials directly before. Mercs and the Qlan are one thing, but this would raise the stakes a few notches." Bradyn sounded dubious.

"Been there; done that. Do you want to see if the fraggin' weapons we installed work or not?"

Bradyn scratched his thick beard. "It has piqued my curiosity."

"Our target is already damaged and preoccupied. Can you think of a better time to test them?" Phillix stated.

"What've we got lined up that'll do anything to that cruiser?" Bradyn asked.

"The plasma cannons are functioning; however, we'd need to be much closer before they'd have any effect on their armor. And—"

"Tell me we got some fraggin' missiles in all that lot!"

"I do believe the bots brought some in. I'm not sure whether they've been unpacked and racked yet—"

"Why didn't you fraggin' say so." She was striding across the bridge when she added, "Bradyn, let's do this."

The engineer was at the door in three strides. "Sounds like a plan!"

"Use the rear launcher. I have a cunning plan," Phillix said to their departing backs.

Sabrya led the way to the Delta6 cargo hold in the rear where the new missile racks and launchers were. "Why don't they just fraggin' blast him?"

"Torg? Curiosity? Alerted by the alarm, they arrived and found a droid floating in space. It wasn't a waystation killer bot. They'll want to glean as much info from its database as they can."

"And they'll get a fraggin' lot. Wonder why they didn't chase the *Mulan*?"

"Maybe they're too damaged, or they're hoping to get enough info from the droid."

Sabrya looked at the new gear and then fist-pumped the air. "We now have missiles!"

"Dare I ask what sort?" Bradyn grinned. He rarely saw the warrior woman so animated.

"Armor piercing, high-explosive, nukes... and AM."

"Won't nukes and AM take out Torg? Or us? Do you know the yield of the warhead?" The engineer shook his head.

"Okay fraggin' fine. All we need to do is slow and distract them."

They loaded two of each of the HE and armor-piercing missiles.

"We'll target their already damaged sections. No point trying to make it harder for ourselves."

"The armor-piercing and HE-missiles are armed and loaded," Bradyn told Phillix as he limped after Sabrya toward the bridge. He stopped by the medi-bay to check on Alexis. She was still unconscious, but the readouts were all in the green. He noted the time; they had several minutes left. He continued limping to the bridge. On the way he heard a shriek, but it was one of joy, not pain.

"What was that?" Bradyn asked on arrival. "Where's Sab?"

"She's getting into her new spacesuit."

"Another one?"

"It was among some of the off-book items the bots collected. I think she's happy,"

"Sounded more like a grunfer in heat." Bradyn sighed and took the lift to the loading dock. Sabrya was donning a new suit, the previous one discarded in a corner. He thought the previous suit had been a body hugger, but this one was several notches clingier. Even he dropped his jaw. "You gaining weight?" he said to cover his staring.

"Frag off. You know you like it." She pirouetted as gracefully as any experienced ballerina, then she did a cartwheel. "Kimichi Mk8 combat spacesuit. Even better than my previous suit."

"You sure that's a spacesuit? Not the liner?"

"Nanotech at its finest. Tactical woven inner layer for impact protection, reflective external layer for energy weapon protection, and nanites that are capable of repairin' anythin' but major damage."

"Powered?"

"Yes, but not for long hauls. These lines and dots you see allow you to attach various modules like weapons and extra boosters for longer jumps. I haven't gone through all the specs yet. If Gadgetman got me this but not the modules, I'll be doing some reprogrammin' with my blades. I haven't taken a head for days, so I'm just itchin' to release some tension."

"He hasn't got a head, but I get your meaning. What are you planning to do, exactly?"

"I'm headin' out to grab Torg. Seein' another suit appearin' out of nowhere will no doubt get the fraggers' attention."

"And then we take them out with the missiles?"

"Either that or give them somethin' else to worry about."

"I'll get us as close as I can to Torg, and Sabrya will do her thing," Phillix said. "I'm about to fire the missiles. They'll hit the cruiser on their port side, where the *Mulan* damaged her in her escape."

"And they won't know where they came from?"

"The launch is internal, and the launcher tubes face out the sides. You know there are drives sticking out the rear?"

"You don't say." The engineer rolled his eyes.

"From what I'm reading on the specs, these smart missiles can be programmed to activate at given intervals. By the time they do that, even a minute, their drive signature will come from somewhere else. It'll make it hard to get a weapon-lock. At the least, it'll delay their response."

"And that's all we fraggin' need."

"Torg's now a hundred and ten meters to our port."

"I'm out of here." She strode confidently to the airlock, while hooking her breacher to the allocated slot on her back.

"Will you need that?"

"I can tell you from experience, you never know." Once inside the airlock, she clipped a tether to her belt. At the moment of depressurization, she opened the hatch and shot out.

"I have to say, sometimes she amazes me." He turned and started limping back to the lift. "Other times, she scares the crap out of me."

"Likewise," Phillix admitted. "But we won't let her know it."

"Can't have that."

"Missiles away. If they're not intercepted, the impact will be in two minutes."

On the bridge, after another dose of painkillers, Bradyn watched the viewport intently.

Directly in front of them, the medium-sized cruiser loomed three times as large as the *Malleus*, and it was closing in on Torg's location. Despite his gleaming plating, he was barely visible, there being insufficient light. Sabrya was even harder to see, but on the scope, she was the second blue blip.

Bright light flashed as the missiles struck the cruiser.

"Bet that surprised them," he said as the Imperial cruiser rolled to starboard.

"The cruisers launched fighters," Phillix stated. "You'll have company shortly."

"Lucky I brought the breacher." Sabrya hefted the weapon.

"How's our timing?" he asked Phillix.

"Two minutes to detonation... if the plan B chargers go off."

"I fraggin' heard that. They'll go off, all right. We don't want to be here for that. I've hooked Torg and am returnin'."

"Better be quick. Sorry to be the bearer of bad news, but two very large energy surges have appeared. I have a suspicion... yes, the *Romulus* and *Remus* just arrived from hyper."

"That's all we fraggin' need. Who the hell paints their spaceships black?" Even at the relatively close distance, they were hard to see.

"They're two big fraggers!"

"I'd be more impressed if I hadn't already seen the *Iconic*," Bradyn commented. "With all this activity too close to the emperor, it's bound to have happened."

"I've got a bead on the nearest fighter. He's not movin' that fast."

"No doubt struggling against the repulsors. You'll be within the cloak in ten seconds. Your disappearance will confuse them. Maybe, with all that's going on, they'll consider you a sensor glitch," Phillix replied. "I'm reeling you in as fast as I can. Don't do anything unless absolutely necessary."

"Are you my fraggin' mother?"

"How about your long-lost highly intelligent uncle?"

"The fighter's veerin'... is he goin' to hit the *Malleus*?"

"You know, I do believe he is," Phillix agreed.

Sabrya had the fighter in her breacher sights. The risk of him running into the ship was too great. She fired a long blast. Three seconds later, the fighter erupted in a fireball just before it entered the cloak.

"Any fraggin' damage to the *Malleus*?"

"Minimal... and... you're in. The cruiser and both dreadnoughts are now scanning this area. More fighters have been deployed from the cruiser and the dreadnoughts. In other news, the waystation is now firing plasma cannons at our big friends."

"At least that'll keep them distracted," Bradyn commented.

"This area will still be swarmin' with fraggin' Imps any minute. Why aren't we jumpin'? One of them's bound to run into us."

"A hyperjump in this repulsor field could become rather messy."

"It's goin' to get fraggin' messy here if those death-ships get a target lock on us."

"Good point. I have the coordinates loaded and ready. Our jump will be immediate."

"Phillix," Alexis called from the medi-bay, her voice raspy. "Do it, now."

Once the jump had been initiated, Bradyn asked Sabrya to take Torg to the workshop, then he made his way to see Alexis.

"How are you doing?" he asked when he entered the medi-bay.

Her smile was more like a grimace as she tried to adjust her position. "Still breathing, so I guess that's a good thing."

Bradyn went to the bed controls to adjust it for her comfort. "You missed out on all the fun."

"Apparently. You got shot too?"

"The same shot as you."

Sabrya joined them, still in her Kimichi. "It's Torg you should be thankin'. He took out that fraggin' death-bot himself."

"He did? How? That thing was huge." Alexis wriggled for comfort.

"While it was puttin' holes in the two of you, Torg drove his arm into the cavity where the laser was housed. It was the only way around that mech-monster's armor. Torg did sufficient damage for it to self-destruct. It blew out the window. You know the rest."

"And how is he now?"

"I'm about to check." Bradyn was looking everywhere but at the warrior. Her formfitting suit was still doing things to his mind. "Phill says he's offline but mostly intact, except for his arm and shoulder. I'll have a better idea once I've gone over him thoroughly."

"Good work, all of you." Alexis closed her eyes.

They left her to rest. "I'll be in my workshop." Bradyn limped aft and Sabrya went to the bridge.

"Where are we jumpin' to, Gadgetman?" Sabrya asked.

"I've a series of mini jumps in the works, so even the best AI will have a hard time tracking us. We'll be near the border of Sectors 43 and 44 in thirteen hours."

"That's not far."

"Not quite the other side of the galaxy, but a step in that direction. With Alexis and Bradyn injured, I thought we'd reassess our position before the big jump."

"We still fraggin' need to leave all this behind."

"I'm aware, but I'll wait until Alexis can take command. Besides, we've not defined our final destination clearly."

Two large plasma pulses from each dreadnoughts's array of weapons platforms lanced through the now-empty space where the *Malleus* had been seconds before.

In the distance, the waystation bloomed into a massive ball of released energy. The energy wave spread out quickly, too quickly for the Imperial vessels to avoid. The cruiser took the brunt of the blast broadside and vaporized. The dreadnoughts, although vastly larger, still took substantial damage. Minutes later, minuscule fragments of anti-matter impacted them. Large chunks of the ships disintegrated in a flash. A rain of shrapnel, large and small, peppered the remains of the hulls. The series of explosions that followed increased in severity as the power cores and weapons arrays were hit.

CHAPTER FOURTEEN

"PHILLIX, did you happen to find those items I selected for my wish list?" After removing the worst of the damaged components, Bradyn hooked Torg up to the computer interface for a complete diagnostic.

"The ones from the waystation? Aren't they there?"

"Not that I can see." The engineer limped around the hold he'd converted into a workshop then equipped with the help of Brutus before they left the homestead.

"All good. I've got the bots bringing it through now."

"Excellent. A 3D replicator should come in handy, especially now that we've got no spares."

"You still need to provide raw material."

"True. It depends on the item and the amount of power at our disposal at the time." He turned at the whirring sound near the entrance. The two maintenance bots carried a crate in their clawed appendages. He pointed, directing them to place the crate by the bench.

After setting the crate down, the pair of bots turned and whirred away, and Bradyn proceeded to unpack it.

"Hi everyone, this is your captain speaking. Meet me in the crew lounge when you can."

Surprised at hearing her voice and at her rapid recovery, Bradyn ventured out of the workshop and made his way along the length of the ship to the lounge. After a brief rest, the pain in his thigh was almost gone, as was the worst of the injury, which had left an angry-looking scar that would fade over time as the nanites did their work.

Alexis was pale. She was reclining on the lounge, with the mobile auto-doc—she was still linked to the Abbsolim S8 so the medi-nanites could carry out their programming—wrapped around her arm.

"What can I say?" she responded to his look when he arrived. "I needed coffee, and I'm not that much of an invalid that I couldn't do it myself." She took a sip and sighed. "So, where are we, and what are we up to?"

All three started talking until she raised a hand.

"How about we start with Phillix?" she suggested, "since he instigated this meet."

"We're sitting idle on the border of Sectors 43 and 44 and awaiting our illustrious leader to determine our final destination," Phillix said.

Alexis rolled her eyes. "You? Idle? Somehow, I find that hard to believe."

"I've hooked us up to a waystation and hacked into its feed to gather intel. I've interfaced with it. We made some minor repairs to the hull where shrapnel from the destroyed fighter hit us, then I had the bots go through and make a complete list of the goodies we collected from the weapons cache."

"Did we do good? I'm missing a few details," Alexis said.

"We did fraggin' awesomely," Sabrya exclaimed, as she lithely stepped in to join them.

"You're happy?" Alexis turned and looked the warrior woman up and down. "Who are you, and what have you done to the real Sabrya? Is that a new suit liner you're wearing, or have you finally succumbed to your true calling as a dominatrix?"

Bradyn laughed.

"You're still fraggin' injured, so you're forgiven. I'll have you fashion luddites know this is my new Kimichi Mk8 combat suit."

"Now that she's got her new toys, she's like a kid again," Phillix said.

"I was never a fraggin' kid." She scowled briefly. "And the 'new toys' Gadgetman refers to are the various attachments for the suits, includin' a shoulder-mounted railgun rifle, mini missile launcher with mini HE, thermal-incendiary, and disruptor missiles, and long-range propulsion packs."

"Somebody better quickly throw a bucket of cold water over her," Bradyn suggested.

"And," she continued, ignoring him, "there's a new thermal imagin' HUD, and the upgraded AI allows multiple simultaneous targets."

"Want to tell them the really good news?" Phillix coaxed her.

She huffed. "They don't fraggin' deserve it."

"True, but... you know... comrades in arms, buddies, crewmates and all..."

"Frag it. There's one suit for each of you," she said through a scowl.

"You're kidding?" both Alexis and Bradyn said.

"Won't Bradyn need two?" Alexis joked.

"Be nice, or I'll reprogram the auto-doc while you're asleep so you'll have large ears and a bulbous nose," the engineer replied.

"Neither of you's goin' to get in one until you satisfy me you're capable of usin' it without blowin' each other up. There's a module with extra nanites for over-large bodies."

"Yes, ma'am. We'll be very studious and careful." Bradyn bowed slightly.

"We're going to be traders, remember?" Alexis reminded them. "But... if there was ever a need, I guess these would be useful."

"'Useful' she says! If she wasn't my captain and friend..."

"Solidarity sister." Alexis grinned weakly and punched the air. "Anyway, other than to see your shining faces, the main reason I wanted you here is to determine where we're going next. I've had Phillix scour the Mesh while we've been waiting."

"If it wasn't hot enough for us before, this part of the rim just got worse," Bradyn considered.

"Actually..." Phillix started. "We aren't mentioned at all. Info-casts are laying everything on the Sunfists."

"What everythin' are you on about? I only took out a fighter. Big deal."

"You'll be pleased to hear; your Plan B took out the waystation."

"Yes! I fraggin' knew it! Oh, ye of little fraggin' faith."

"You had a Plan B?" Alexis asked. "What happened to Plan A?"

"How bad was it? That much anti-matter..." Bradyn looked intrigued.

"The reports are the cruiser and both dreadnoughts were taken out."

"Surely this isn't being broadcast officially?" Alexis queried over Sabrya's whooping.

"Correct. These are reports gleaned from the dark Mesh. The official version is the Imperial forces thwarted a pending attack on the emperor and the *Romulus* and *Remus* are now in pursuit of the scattered band of 'terrorists.'"

"We're not mentioned at all?" Sabrya asked when she calmed down.

"That is a good thing," Alexis insisted. "We want a low profile—preferably a non-existent one."

"With the waystation gone, there's no weapons cache. The Tourney's been cancelled. The emperor has 'modified' his plans and will now continue with his original tour."

Sabrya laughed. "I bet that pissed off the fraggin' tourney hierarchy."

"Indeed. You'll be delighted to hear Malazi Phakani has been disgraced, as his weapons platform was believed to be part of the 'assassination attempt.' The emperor has revoked any official support to the tourney."

"Since you mentioned fraggin' tourney scum... we still have Bruiser and Necto to deal with."

"Another reason why I called you here. Please look at the monitor."

Three heads looked up at the large monitor angling out of the lounge bulkhead.

"Interfacing with the waystation had its perks... the weapons cache was an absolute bonanza, which I'll go into shortly. So, back to the monitor. While this will no doubt be of interest to you all, I believe Sabrya will be even happier than she was with the arrival of her suit. The blips you see are real-time simulations representing two ships currently in hyper. One is Sabrya's backer—Malazi—and the other is Bruiser and Necto. I stumbled upon their transponder codes when we were on Tataranga. I'm sure you'll agree we need to deal with them before you leave this part of the galaxy. The simulation is only possible when interfacing with the waystation. When they jumped, a sub-program I initiated pinged, and here we are. Real video feed would take too long to get here, but Sabrya, we have comms access if you'd like to send them a final farewell."

"Final?"

"Remember the hyperspace monitoring I mentioned? Way

stations determine where and when ships jump and can manipulate any ship currently in hyperspace."

"You're saying you can send these ships anywhere?" Alexis asked.

"As long as they're in hyperspace," Phill replied. "Sabrya, channel A is to Malazi."

Sabrya stared, mute for a time, before deciding what to say. She activated the comm. "Malazi. Sad to say I can't see the look on your fraggin' pock-marked face. You once told me that without you I was less than nothin'. How things have fraggin' changed now we've come full orbit. Disgraced by the emperor, the Surreal Tourney in disarray? For the last few minutes of your miserable life, know that it was I who destroyed you and your valuable reputation. You are less than nothin' now." She disconnected and took a breath. "And this channel is for the other fraggers?"

"Correct."

"Recognize this fraggin' voice?" she said to them clearly. "You two are so cowardly, you murder norms and children to get your thrills and sate your fraggin' pathetic egos. You were Malazi's favorites until I came along, and you constantly failed to get back into his good books. Your deaths should be slow and painful, but that's not to be. Know this, though, my AI's goin' to go through every vid on the Mesh and wipe your names. No one will know you. You'll both be forgotten." She cut the channel. "You can do that?" she asked Phillix.

"I can, yes."

"End them," she said flatly.

The vid simulation continued for a few minutes, then the two blips blinked out of existence.

"Is that it?"

"Yes. They would be unaware I manipulated their routes while in hyperspace, and they were side by side. I thought it appropriate to crash both their vessels into Grindstone. No one is there to report it, and I ensured they had comms lockout the moment I found them. No one knows where they are, and they will soon be forgotten."

"Thank you," Sabrya said with the sincerest voice the crew had ever heard from her.

They needed something stronger than coffee. Bradyn got up and fetched the Arcturian whiskey bottle. He poured one for her, then one for Alexis and for himself before resuming his seat.

"When you decide where you want to be on the other side of the galaxy, I won't be coming with you," Phillix continued. "When on the *Iconic*, my eyes and mind were opened to a world I could only imagine. With hindsight, I now realize Janus, profound as she was, was a mere steppingstone. My body died, but you saved me by bringing my consciousness here to the *Malleus*. I was still naïve and inexperienced at being an AI, but I think I've adapted quickly. After the *Iconic*, I've determined the *Malleus*—such a combination of odd and mismatched components—is not big enough for me. Way stations, however, are interconnected across the galaxy—all fifteen hundred of them. I now have the room I need to expand and explore. And that's where I'm heading—"

"Who'll take care of the *Malleus*?" Alexis asked.

"Torg's quite capable and will continue to be once he's repaired. I've given him as many updates and as much reprogramming as I can."

"I witnessed Metalman save us by takin' out that death-bot. Was that you? Is that fraggin' normal for a droid?"

"He's not a security-bot, and I've not programmed him to be so. Somehow Torg's evolving... or reacting to the situation. It's an indication he's more than what he was. Some of the changes I've implemented have increased his AI capacity. I'm sure you've considered, given the things I've been doing on a whim, I'm not fit or suited to be running this ship... I'm more

Autonomous than Artificial Intelligence. I'm sure it's what Alexis suspects and fears—at some point there will be a conflict of opinions. If I move on, that'll never be a scenario you have to face. However, know that I'll always be contactable via waystations."

Their armpads pinged.

"These are the details of the newest areas opening up. The new sectors have not even been officially listed—several Imperial regional offices are squabbling over the borders. Until the regions have been drawn up and mapped, the area is known as the Cygnus Quadrant. But three sectors—49, 50, and 51—are on the cards.

"Also, since there's little info coming out of there, I've compiled a supply list of the newly terraformed colonies over the last two decades to get an idea what's needed. You can then scour the region to find out where we can get the goods, then the route can be loaded in the nav computer.

"One last thing. I've added a data file with numerous transponder codes. As long as where you're going doesn't have a visual on you, the identification should be acceptable, depending on the situation. For instance, there's a transponder code to allow you to approach any waystation as a maintenance rig. You'll then have access to refuel as long as you're in hyper.

"Bradyn, the refueling process is in a file on your armpad and on your tablet at the workshop, along with as many maintenance manuals as I could find for the components we have on this ship."

"This is you being idle?" Alexis asked.

"Consider it a farewell gift."

Sabrya was on her bunk, the turmoil of the last events going through her head, when a ping distracted her—a message on her armpad.

'Hey Sab. I've no idea where you are, but if you're getting this, you and the Malleus *have turned us into heroes out here. Great work and thanks. The* Mulan *crew have agreed to add a bonus to the fee. Good luck in your next endeavors. We've got your back if you ever need it.'*

Embedded in the message were account details to access the funds. She didn't look at the amount. It was irrelevant to her. She still had a vast portion of her two million stellars in a satchel at the bottom of her locker, and she had a ship, brand new 'toys,' and a crew she didn't want to kill every minute.

"Hey Phill, you still with us?" she commed.

"I am."

"The message I just received. It's got account details attached to it. Are you able to transfer whatever funds are in it to Brutus' daughter, Nyka?"

"I can do that. You do realize the account has five million stellars in it?"

"Then it should be enough to see her through with a bit of style. Thank you."

"No message?"

"No... Wait. Say 'From a good friend of your Da's. Choose your own path and make him proud.'"

"Consider it done."

Sabrya felt good; it was the best she'd felt for far too long.

PART II

CHAPTER FIFTEEN

IT TOOK them two months and several jumps to reach the Cygnus Quadrant. The route took them along the outskirts of Imperial space while avoiding the emperor's tour and those sectors with minor conflicts. No one wanted to get involved, and the crew was glad for the extended period of peace and quiet.

Initially, Alexis and Bradyn took it easy as they recovered with the aid of the auto-docs. Until Torg was repaired using Phillix's prosthetic arm, everyone took turns on the bridge, though after Phillix's alterations to the *Malleus*, most of the ship was fully automated.

Sabrya knew when she got bored or too inactive, her nanites went dormant, putting her in a foul mood. The only way she could maintain a semblance of civility was with a heavy training regime. Whether on-watch or not, she kept as active as she could, and other than meal times, kept out of everyone's way.

Alexis began setting up her garden area, and Bradyn, with substantial assistance from the maintenance bots, built the VR holo-deck with the gear from Brutus and some of the weapons cache surprises, courtesy of Phillix.

"It's amazing what he managed to get from the weapons cache in such a short time," he said to Alexis when he stood back at the finished holo-deck while waiting to surprise their warrior woman. "There was even some data on tourney training which I've tried to incorporate into this."

"We'll know soon enough. Here she comes."

"What have you fraggers been up to?" she grouched.

When she looked inside, she instantly recognized its purpose. Sabrya was so overjoyed, she gave them both a long hug. "I might be busy for a while."

Upon arrival in the Cygnus Quadrant, they remained in stealth mode and took their time checking the system surrounding them and assessing the sporadic infocasts they could get before they landed. As new arrivals, they thought it best to avoid the regions with higher populations until they had a better idea of what was what.

Blaranad Spaceport was little more than a hardened clay bed surrounded by prefabricated warehouses and a large expanse of ground, with some form of crop that was wilting in the dim glow of the reddish sunlight.

The air was breathable but had an unpleasant odor, which was only manageable for those not born to it through the wearing of nasal filters. They had been there for several days, scouring the local community for viable cargo. According to the data gleaned from the Mesh, this was supposed to be the 'go-to' region.

"And what is this, exactly?" Alexis joined her engineer at the market stalls.

Bradyn smiled and tossed her one of the crops, a fist-sized

lump of a strange-looking rootstock. "You're the botanist. They call it pumkoes, my guess is it's a hybrid... sort of... between a... I'm not sure, a couple of ancient Terran tubers? They say the original seeds were affected by the terraforming."

"Going by the name, I'd say pumpkin and potatoes?" Alexis looked at the produce dubiously and cut one open. "But the coloring and skin are wrong. I don't think they've ever seen a real pumpkin or a real spud. Texture-wise... and smell..." She licked it. "Starchy... it could be part potato... but the reddish hue. I don't know of any red pumpkins, maybe a beet." She waited a moment to analyze the taste. "Yes, a beet. Beetroot or something completely alien that looks and tastes like it. A chemical analysis would determine one way or the other." She looked at the stacks of sacks of the produce in the warehouse. "Is this all they've got?"

Bradyn shrugged. "It is in this town. I asked, and they said this was all surplus."

"What do they need?"

Bradyn shrugged again and wandered over to the vendor.

Alexis wondered at the language they spoke—a sort of pidgin version of Imperial Common—and guessed it stood to reason that halfway around the galaxy, the day-to-day trade language would change constantly. She made a note to see what language courses she could download to remedy her ignorance.

Bradyn strode back a few minutes later. "Either you're going to laugh, or you're not going to like it."

"Why is that?"

"Let me put it this way. I know Sabrya would get a chuckle. I have to say, it's sort of amusing."

"I'm a grown woman... and your captain. I suspect I can handle it."

"You talkin' about your sex life?" Sabrya asked as she joined them. "What's funny?"

"Alexis isn't keen on a cargo of... whatever these are—" He tossed the sample to her.

"You're kiddin'?" She bit into the raw vegetable and chewed with enthusiasm. "You don't know what these are?"

"No idea. You seem to like it. What is it?"

"I've no fraggin' idea either, and it tastes awful raw." She spat it out. "But I know what we can do with it."

"Well, don't leave us in suspense," Alexis said after a moment.

"We can distill it. I'm missin' my favorite booze and need to come up with somethin' before I go crazy."

"Hmm. That doesn't help. I think arms trader is a notch above bootlegger."

"Anyway," Bradyn continued, "our lovely captain suggested I find out what they need here."

"Well, trading works two ways," Alexis pointed out. "If they've got nothing to sell, maybe there's something they need, and we can try to get that."

"So, what do they fraggin' need?"

"Bodyguards and protection." Bradyn grinned.

"Tough guys, fighters, weapons..." Sabrya controlled her mirth. "And I'm sure you told them we were traders, not arms dealers or fighters."

"Oh, absolutely." Bradyn nodded with a wink.

Alexis huffed good-naturedly at being the butt of their joke. "You do know I'm stronger than either of you, with an armed vessel at my command?"

"Woohoo!" One of the locals nearby exclaimed and ran off shouting. "We've found our 'protectors.'"

"I think you just volunteered us to be their muscle." Bradyn paused, then started laughing again, along with Sabrya.

"Frack it," Alexis swore. "Bradyn. Get over there and find out what their problem is and how much they're willing to pay."

Sabrya slapped him on the back for good luck.

"And, Sabrya, they don't take stellars here. You'll need to do some currency exchange and they'll think twice about ripping you off."

"Yes, ma'am." Sabrya walked away, still chuckling.

Alexis stormed back toward the ship as the younger kids surrounded her, trying to sell her hats and scarves. She had no money on her and didn't want to encourage them, but some were very insistent and doggedly followed her. In the end, she felt sorry for the young girl who persisted all the way to the ramp where the shining figure of Torg appeared, scaring her. More as a reward for her determination than anything else, Alexis dug in her pocket and found a protein bar. The girl handed her the scarf and raced off with a huge smile.

"I see your trading skills are emerging, Captain," the droid offered.

"You can frak off, too." She stomped past him and threw the scarf around his neck.

"Yes, Captain. Thank you, Captain."

Her vexation lasted about a third of the way to the bridge before she started laughing at herself. She sat in her chair with a sigh and reviewed their itinerary on her tablet. Much of the data was either out of date or simply wrong; the Mesh out here was woefully inadequate.

For three weeks, they had shuffled from colony world to colony world, moving produce back and forth, even a dozen head of hybrid grunfers... though it was decided halfway through the short voyage that even if the maintenance bots did the cleanup, the lingering smell was not worth it. Her foray into the realm of interplanetary trading wasn't going as she had envisaged. She wondered what Brutus would think as she perused the selection of worlds to choose from.

She heard more laughter as her crew returned.

"Did Torg appreciate the souvenir?" Bradyn asked once he was seated in the lounge.

"Of course. He was delighted that it matched the color of his eyes."

"Well, we have good news, of sorts."

"I'm sure I won't like it, but—" she tossed her tablet onto the console "—there's not a huge number of options, so spill."

"Funny enough, it's not only these people that need the musc... protectors."

"Who does? And why?"

"A group of thugs pass themselves off as Imperial soldiers. They visit every month and take money from everyone, calling them Imperial fees."

"But this isn't part of the empire... not yet, at least."

"They know this but lack the ability to say no with force. They're farmers and merchants, not fighters. There's already a widow because someone tried to argue."

"And they want us to stop it?"

"This group is due tomorrow, so all they're asking is for us to hang around and watch. We can make up our minds then. They'd appreciate any assistance."

"It's not as if we've got anything pending."

"How'd the currency exchange go? I see you're not covered in blood."

"And they're damned lucky I'm being friendly! It went fraggin' lousy. One stellar gets roughly thirty-five novas."

"Thirty-five doesn't sound too bad."

"Tell her, Metalman."

"Official currency exchange rates range from 41.2 to 45 novas for one Imperial stellar."

"He started with twenty! I convinced him otherwise, but per my captain's orders, I decided not to spill any fraggin' blood and not push him too far."

"Amazing self-control."

"Pfft." Sabrya handed her and Bradyn each a wad of notes and a pouch of coins. "Try not to spend it all at fraggin' once."

The roar of the thrusters drew their eyes up to a descending craft. Deigning not to set down at the spaceport, it landed close to the market square, causing the stalls to flap madly. The dust billowed through the nooks and crannies of the adobe buildings. After uncovering their eyes and wiping their faces, much of the market crowd dispersed quickly, leaving the stall holders to tidy up their displays.

Sitting and observing at the cantina, the *Malleus* crew uncovered the drinks they were holding and continued imbibing. They had discussed whether they should openly wear their Kimichi Mk8 battle suits but decided that might change the dynamics of the visit. After more discussion, they wore the suits but covered them with clothes. The simple traveler's clothes wouldn't raise suspicion, and they'd have no need to change their routine of wearing suits.

A door slid open, and a ramp emerged from the craft. Soon, five men strolled down it. Their boots crunched in the dirt and gravel before they reached the paved area of the market. As they got closer, it was easy to see from their disheveled appearances that their uniforms were mismatched, as were their weapons. They were not up to Imperial standards.

They split into two groups and began harassing the stallholders. They rummaged through the wares and made a mess of the displays until the vendor dropped some local currency into the container they held out. If the vendor gave them insufficient funds, the stall was upended, and they moved on to the next one.

The young, female street urchin Alexis had purchased the scarf from the previous evening was working at one of the stalls. When the men messed up the produce, the girl ran to the front and kicked one in the shins. His comrade pushed her to the ground with his foot then laughed as he moved on.

Alexis put her arm out, knowing Sabrya was about to retaliate. The young girl was uninjured.

"Let's give them all the rope they want," she advised.

The harassment continued until the two groups converged at the end of the stalls, which brought them close to the cantina. They dragged two tables close together then sat and ordered food and drinks, whistling and leering at the young serving girl who took their orders.

The food and drinks arrived quickly, but it was an older male who brought them out.

"Where's the pretty?" The closest thug stood to confront him. Two other thugs stood nearby.

"I sent her home."

"You should've let her stay. She was good to look at while we ate and drank this swill."

"My daughter's not for your entertainment. None of us—"

The thug butted the proprietor in the stomach with his weapon. The man folded and dropped to his knees.

"You're gettin' beyond yourself there, old man. *We* determine what happens around... Hey!" he yelled at Bradyn.

The burly engineer calmly stepped in, shouldered his way through the group of thugs, and helped the man to his feet.

The couple of blows the thugs dealt were ineffectual as he escorted the man to safety then returned to his seat and his drink.

The surprised thug saw the look Bradyn gave him as he sat down. "What're you lookin' at?"

The other men moved closer to back their comrade.

"I'm not entirely sure. I don't believe there's a polite name for it." Bradyn shrugged. "Not even a collective noun."

"You bein' smart?"

"To be honest, I'm not even trying." Bradyn resumed sipping his drink. "It would be wasted on you lot."

Sabrya chuckled and fist-bumped him.

"Hey, I'm still talkin' to you!" The thug went red in the face.

"We're not fraggin' voice activated." Sabrya sat back, smirking.

Several pairs of eyes strayed to Alexis and Sabrya who were generally ignoring them.

"Looks like we've got more entertainment here." One leered.

"Not that you'll ever fraggin' know."

"Looks can be deceiving," Alexis added.

The leader of the group had remained seated during the exchange. He now stood and wandered over. He was clean-shaven, but his uniform was in need of repair. "Welcome to Blaranad. I'm Lieutenant Sladen of the Sector 46 Regiment. You're new here. There's a visitor tax of a hundred novas each."

"Sector 46 is a long way away. Are you lost?" Bradyn asked.

"A fee? Seems steep," Alexis observed.

The leader ignored the burly man and continued to address Alexis. "Hard times out here. Did you come by ship?"

"We fraggin' swam," Sabrya growled.

He looked at her, annoyed. "There's also a five hundred novas port fee."

Sabrya made a show of checking her pockets then looked at Alexis. "I don't seem to have that much cash on me. You?"

"Hardly anything. Enough for a meal and a drink, maybe a trinket." She dropped a few Imperial coins on the table. "Will this be enough?"

Before the man answered, Bradyn asked, "Is this a new Imperial policy? In all our travels, we've not encountered it before." He ran his eyes critically over their uniforms. "I can see you need it, though."

Seeing the disdainful look these three were giving them, the thugs grouped near their leader. One muttered in his ear, but the leader shrugged. "My man here doesn't like you. Reckons we should make an example of you for everyone else."

"Yeah, I get that a lot." Bradyn nodded. "But it won't turn out well for any of you."

The crew's armpads pinged at the same time Torg arrived and placed himself in the exact center of the group.

"Your droid needs to return to the ship," the leader said.

"Why's that? Don't tell me there's a droid tax as well?" Alexis looked down at her armpad message. *I am carrying a medium-range energy weapons suppressor to prevent any civilian casualties.'*

The thug leader continued, saying, "Ship's droids are forbidden to leave their vessels. It's a new bylaw."

"To what statute does this bylaw pertain?" Torg inquired.

The leader turned to the droid. "Statue?"

"Any droid must obey a lawful order issued by a bona fide Imperial Officer," Torg quoted.

"So, get back to your frakin' ship."

"Certainly. Please furnish me with your identity card to ascertain your credentials, and I will carry out your orders to the letter. It is also law that an Imperial Officer conducting official business is to prove his credentials to a captain or ship's droid. Has this occurred?" Torg turned to Alexis.

"I've not seen his credentials," Alexis replied.

Torg raised his slender arm. "Your identification card, sir."

After a pause, the man flashed an identi-card at the droid before sliding it back into his pocket. It was too quick for the human eye to detect the details, but not for a droid.

"Lieutenant Sladen, born on Glaarin in the year 5049. That makes you 73."

"Lookin' good for a fraggin' septuagenarian." Sabrya sipped her drink.

"Now, I order you back to your ship," the leader continued.

"The face in the card's image has blue eyes, but the jawline and earlobes are differently shaped from yours. I am not sufficiently convinced you are who you say you are. Are you aware that impersonating an Imperial officer carries a mandatory sentence under Imperial law of 10 years? This world, Blaranad, is not ratified Imperial property, nor has the region been officially declared a specific sector. Until taken/brought under Imperial rule, free worlds in these regions fall under the jurisdiction of the Free Alliance Act of 4505. Therefore, the Imperium has no jurisdiction on its surface or in its local space, and as stated, since this region comes under the umbrella of the Free Alliance Act of 4505, you and the Imperium have no jurisdiction at all within 12.7 light years—the official border of Sector 46 and the closest Imperial space."

"If this's your droid, you best get it back to the ship before I blast it. You're already in enough trouble. I should impound your ship until the fees are paid."

"I reckon this is the most entertainment we've had for a long time. Torg, please continue." Alexis put her boots on the table and crossed her slender legs.

As Torg continued, the stallholders and most of the small, rural community returned to see the outcome of the confrontation. The thugs were getting nervous at the unwanted attention.

"Stand down, droid, and shut the frak up!" Sladen shoved the droid but had little effect.

"Good luck with that." Sabrya chuckled.

"As stated, you have no authority to order droids or any citizen."

The thug brandished his pulse rifle. "This is the only authority I need."

The others brought up their weapons and covered the *Malleus* crew and droid.

The gathered crowd gasped and moved back, ready to run or take cover.

"Threatening unarmed civilians is an offense with a minimum of 5 years imprisonment," Torg stated calmly. "Also, your Ingman pulse rifles are not official Imperial forces issue. They should be Glaxon Mk3s."

"Frak you, droid." The thug tapped the trigger several times and was bewildered when nothing happened.

The other thugs did the same, with similar results.

Sabrya stood, and her blades were at Sladen's throat in the blink of an eye.

"Refrain from bloodshed," Torg stated, stepping back. "No violence has occurred. These men are guilty and should be held accountable for their crimes."

Alexis and Bradyn were also up and facing off with the others. They reached out, pulled the weapons roughly from the hands of the closest thugs, and bent the barrels.

"There's more of us out there!" Sladen threatened.

"More reward for us, then. Tell me there's a reward for this fraggin' trash?"

When one of the men turned to run, he tripped on the uneven ground and sprawled in front of the townsfolk. The nearest citizens kicked him until he stopped squirming, while others citizens came forward. Rope was quickly provided, and the men were bound securely together and left kneeling in the dirt with their injured comrade.

A portly older woman approached Sabrya and conversed with her in pidgin Imperial Common for several minutes. They knocked fists and parted, laughing.

"What was that about?" Alexis asked when the warrior joined her.

"She's the mayor—or what passes for a mayor in these parts. They haven't got a prison or secure place to hold them."

"So, what's to be done with them?"

"She says there's a bounty for them. We take them to the

Cygnus Quadrant Liaison Office, aka the 'Fortress,' and we can collect the rewards."

"We're now bounty hunters?"

Sabrya shrugged. "It's what they need. Demand and supply."

"I guess we'll need to devise a brig." Alexis turned to Torg. "That was well done."

"In your discussions last night to come up with a non-violent outcome, you set parameters, hence the weapons suppressor. The citizens here lacked the data to know these men were imposters. I provided that data."

"What led you to conclude they were imposters before you joined us?"

"I was monitoring your comms and heard the conversation. As stated, the vessel is not Imperial standard, and their landing was not in accordance with Imperial guidelines. Their actions thereafter proved beyond doubt they were not who they claimed to be."

"You're not going autonomous on me, are you?"

"I am conforming to a sub-program."

"And this is a new sub-program, I take it?"

"Correct. Considering where we were going—where we are now—I was furnished with complete files of Imperial and Free Alliance laws."

"I see Phillix's influence is still affecting us." She saw Bradyn and waved him over.

"It would appear so, though it has been to the benefit of the *Malleus* and its crew," Torg replied.

"True... so far."

"Did you have doubts about Phillix's motives?"

"Putting him in the *Malleus* was the only way he could survive. I had no other motive. But when he started doing his own thing without my say-so or input, I knew things would eventually come to a head. I'm just glad—and relieved—he found something that caught his fancy. Could have been very awkward otherwise."

"I will now arrange the modification of Charlie1 hold for a brig." He turned and strode back through the adobe buildings toward the spaceport and the *Malleus*.

"What's up?" Bradyn walked over, carrying a sack of local produce.

"Torg's making a temporary brig in Charlie hold. We'll need to arrange for plumbing and then find out where this Fortress is." Alexis eyed the sack curiously.

"A gift, for our efforts. Thought I'd give Sab's distilling idea a go."

CHAPTER SIXTEEN

LESS THAN THIRTEEN HOURS LATER, they were approaching the Cygnus Quadrant Liaison Office orbital, known locally as the Fortress, which was aptly named due to the armor-plating and formidable weapons arrays. The fortified orbital was a neutral area where Imperial officials and Free Alliance Council members could meet. The station also covered quasi-legal issues for the region, and while there was no law enforcement office at this point, it was the place to go to for registering disputes. Those disputes would be addressed once the borders and lines of jurisdiction were made clear.

Since they didn't have a shuttle, they had to wait until a docking tube was available. Alexis was nervous about the weapons platforms pointing at them.

The prisoners' ship was slightly astern of them. The mayor had informed Sabrya the captured ship might be included in the reward, so with Torg's assistance, Bradyn had slaved the ship's controls to the *Malleus*. Like the thugs' uniforms, it needed repairs and a thorough cleaning.

During the flight, Torg had hacked into and downloaded its

comp files. Some were encrypted and took time to hack. He rejoined the *Malleus* once they were stationary at the outpost. While going over the files, they found a couple that were corrupted or empty.

"CQLO to *Malleus*. Come on in. Berth 4. Leave your weapons on your vessel."

With relief, Alexis acknowledged the directions and slowly moved in and docked.

"We're in, people. Let's get these pieces of shit off my ship." She met Bradyn and Sabrya outside the make-do brig. They agreed that to show a level of professionalism, they'd all don the Kimichi Mk8s. Bradyn had his extra nanite module hooked up, so his suit was as form-fitting as that of Sabrya or Alexis.

So the prisoners didn't have to be carried, the gravity setting in the main corridor and loading dock was reduced to 3-Gs. For the prisoners, putting up any resistance other than a feeble grab for an arm required too much effort, but Sladen was slapped down nonchalantly and bound before leaving the loading dock. The prisoners were escorted off the ship and onto the station. A map on the bulkhead indicated the area for prisoner transfer. Within ten minutes of docking, they entered a large compartment at the end of a passage. It had all the indications of once being a machinery space, but whatever equipment was previously housed there had been moved. Even though it had been several years, the all-pervading smell of oil and grease lingered.

Now, an open area spanning eight meters separated rows of bare plastic seats from a long, high desk. Just to the side of the entrance lay a glassteel security area. With the aid of a shock-prod she found on their vessel, Sabrya shepherded the prisoners into it and closed the door. One bulkhead featured several small viewports showing space; the opposite wall had several bulletin boards. The main area was dimly lit and only over the desk was there more substantial lighting. Behind the desk were two heavy, metal doors. As they moved closer, they could see more details of the desk occupants. Two were dressed in clean, but well-used, Imperial fatigues. Unlike the recent prisoners, these were clearly up to date. The lone female's uniform was in far better condition and tailored to fit, and her dark hair was tightly plaited.

A male official at the desk waved them over, barely looking up. "You are the crew of the *Malleus*?" He shuffled through some papers, at a loss. "Bounty hunters? Here? You should've gone to level 4."

Alexis stepped forward and spoke calmly. "We aren't bounty hunters. Not yet. We were directed here from the docks."

"Not licensed?" The man huffed and lifted his head, clearly irritated. He pushed back his spectacles to glare down at them. "We can't have just anyone nabbing citizens when they feel the urge."

Torg stepped forward. "Free Alliance law—"

"Stand down, Torg. Thanks." Alexis turned back to address the clerk. "I am Alexis Nales, registered captain of the Free Alliance vessel, *Malleus*. You'll know, as a captain, I've the jurisdiction to arrest those breaking Free Alliance law in Free Alliance territories. These prisoners were impersonating Imperial officers and defrauding the citizens of Blaranad, as well as those of Vilos and Handrix." She passed him a thumb drive. "Here's our drone footage of the arrival of these men on Blaranad, their harassment of and use of stand-over tactics on civilians, including assaulting a minor and threatening unarmed citizens with energy weapons. There are statements from a dozen citizens, including the Blaranad mayor, detailing this occurrence and others over the last half year."

Upon hearing the details, the tall woman came closer. "I'll deal with them, Klauff, if you'd prefer."

"Ma'am." The clerk huffed, moved aside, and carried on with other work.

"I'm Lieutenant Strasser, the Imperial liaison officer here... until we know where 'here' is." She let a brief smile crease her lips before looking sternly at the prisoners. "And I can assure you, officers of the empire take impersonation extremely seriously."

She inserted the thumb drive into the computer and skimmed the contents. Her stern visage didn't improve at what she saw. "Do we know their real IDs?"

Alexis shook her head. "We asked, they declined, and I wasn't going to stretch the boundaries with... enhanced questioning techniques. However, these are the IDs they were carrying." She handed over several plastic cards. "We've impounded their vessel, too. Slaved it to ours."

Strasser checked the IDs by running them through the comp. "The cards are legit, but not for these scums. A quick biometric scan will identify your prisoners." She tapped a buzzer.

Shortly, four security bots came out of one of the doors behind the large desk.

"Escort these prisoners to the cells," she ordered them, then she turned back to Alexis. "Thanks for all this." She indicated the files and then proceeded to fill out a couple of forms and stamp them. "I mean it. Hard enough to eke out a living here without scum ripping people off. In my eyes, the impersonations were their biggest mistake; that'll put them away for a long time. Let's see what else they've been up to."

Sladen and his men struggled futilely against the droids.

"I'll remember you, bitches!" he called out.

"We've forgotten you already," Alexis replied as the door slid closed with a resounding thud.

"Now, as for my colleague you first spoke with. He has a

point—" Strasser put her hand up as Alexis was about to say something. "And you are both correct. To make things run smoother out here, we have a bounty hunter registry. A ship's captain has defined rights, as does a registered bounty hunter, but combining them makes you the nearest thing to law enforcement we have." She handed Alexis the forms. "If you go back the way you came, turn left, and go down one level, you'll find the Bounty Hunter Registration office. You can't miss it. Once you register with Mithum, you'll be able to receive and access the bounties on these men."

"I see. Thanks. And if we don't register?"

"Then you have the empire's sincere thanks, and mine, and the satisfaction of making the Cygnus Quadrant slightly safer." She smiled again and looked over their combat suits. Her eyes paused on Sabrya for a moment before moving on to Bradyn. "It's clear you're not farmers. And you look like you can handle yourselves. Simply having those combat suits puts you several notches higher than some of the more experienced bunters out there. And with your high-G colleague there, you have the muscle. So, unless you want to sign up to join the Imperium, I'm not sure what else you'll be able to do out here. Trading is difficult; profitable cargo can be hard to find, and then there's the long distances to haul it to people who probably can't pay except by their body weight in turnips. Mind you, almost anything can be distilled into alcohol of one form or another. Bootlegging doesn't pay that well either."

Alexis shook the proffered hand. "Thanks again, Lieutenant. We'll look into it."

"Here, if you need me." Strasser nodded and departed through the door the droids had used.

"Anyone want to sign up to join the empire?" Alexis asked. "I reckon Strasser will vouch for all of us."

"How can I put this politely?" Sabrya asked.

Alexis chuckled. "You never have before."

"True. Frag off, Captain."

"So, shall we go to this registration office?" Alexis walked out the back and retraced their path until the left turn to the stairs.

Bradyn shrugged. "Why not? Seems the only way we'll get the stellars—or novas—for the job. I wonder how much?"

"Only one way to find out." Alexis chuckled as they walked to the stairwell. "Torg, can you head back to the ship? Keep an eye on it?"

"Of course, Captain." The droid pivoted and made his way back along the passageway to the docks.

The trio continued down to the next level. At the end of one of the wider passages was a broken neon sign 'B_unty Hu_ters.' There was a substantial amount of noise coming from the far end.

"Bunty Huters. Not something that'll look good on a resume. You think this is it?"

"Going to take a wild guess judging by the ruckus inside," Alexis said.

"Bounty hunters aren't known for being fraggin' quiet and subtle."

The door swung open at their approach. While the machinery smell dissipated, the smell did not improve when they strode through the doorway, and the noise level increased substantially. They found themselves in a caged area. The barred door in front was locked, as was the door behind when it clicked closed.

"That fraggin' Imp bitch!" Sabrya was about to pull the door off its hinges.

"Sab. Wait." To Alexis, Strasser hadn't come across as the type to send them into a trap. Why would she when she had those large security bots at her disposal? "They could impound the ship if they wanted to."

"They can fraggin' try," the warrior fumed.

The trio took in their surroundings.

Several rowdy groups of disheveled men and women were scattered around the long, wide room. Many wore relatively clean clothes, some torn or bloody; others were more sloven in their appearance.

Heavy metal cages, like the one they were in, lined one side of the large compartment. Some of the occupants—the source of the noisome odors—were sleeping or unconscious, some were bleeding and yelling abuse at the others in the room.

High along the bulkheads, a long electronic board showed images of wanted criminals. The profiles flashed repetitiously across the screen, one after another. A circular monitor hanging from the center of the room highlighted several profiles resembling those recently captured.

A light was flashing above a desk inside a secure area at the far end. An aged man entered through the rear door. He put on his spectacles and seemed to look at something on his desk, then a speaker crackled over their heads.

"Weapons in the locker to the left."

The ruckus slowly stopped as the groups realized there were new arrivals.

"We have no weapons," Alexis called out.

The figure sat, then the cage door swung open a second later. "Move in and approach the desk."

Jeering from the cages started, this time directed at the newly arrived trio.

The *Malleus* crew warily left the caged entrance and strode down the center aisle. Alexis led, with Bradyn behind her and Sabrya covering the rear, watching warily for any threat. She pointed to the ceiling where several laser turrets followed their progress.

The various groups of bounty hunters parted, muttering among themselves. Though many of the comments were unintelligible, from the looks and pointing fingers, it was evident the combat suits were drawing their attention.

As they approached his barred desk, the old man's eyes ran over them before he quickly cleared his throat and shuffled the documents in front of him.

"I don't seem to have your details..." The man had graying hair and glasses, and his clothes looked too large for his slight build.

"Here." Alexis handed him the papers Strasser had filled out. "I guess you're Mithum?"

"From Strasser?" Mithum nodded, waiting until the papers were within the secured area before he reached for them and looked over them. "Ah. I see. You were supposed to bring your prisoners here." He frowned. "Well. Still, a good day. We've been after this group for a while."

"Someone hasn't looked too fraggin' hard then," Sabrya growled, looking at the groups behind her. "It was too damn easy."

"All good now." He offered them a seat. "Let's see." He tapped his console. "That Strasser woman's such a good lass. She's already IDed and processed your clients." He printed off several sheets and passed them to Alexis. "These are your bounties, yes?"

She looked over the documents and nodded. Sabrya looked over her shoulder and agreed.

"You already have their IDs?" Alexis asked.

"We do. They won't be causing mischief for a while."

A loud buzzer sounded, and the circular monitor displayed the profiles of their captives. Above the profiles was the reward amount. The gathered groups of hunters looked up. The mutterings grew louder, and the newcomers were further scrutinized.

"Ten thousand novas? Doesn't seem right for such fraggin' low lives."

"Oh, no. That's in Imperial stellars per head." Mithum beamed, making notes and nodding to himself. Then his eyes caught something else on the computer. "You impounded their ship?"

Alexis nodded. "We did."

"Any damage?" His eyes lit up at her shaking head. "Well, that's even better."

"Why's that?" Bradyn asked.

"After the auction, a quarter of the proceeds will go into your account." He rummaged through the files. "I can't seem to find your account though."

"I believe we're about to start one." Alexis leaned on the counter.

"Ah. Well. Good. We can arrange that now." He handed them a tablet and stylus. "If you'd prefer, there's a lounge through there. It's quieter and less odorous. Please fill out the details and bring the tablet back here when completed, along with the stylus."

Easily convinced the lounge was a better option, they nodded and left. The lounge was quieter, but the pungent smell of spilled ale filled the air. Above the bar stretched a leaderboard with the top ten bounty hunter groups. They ordered drinks and found a booth. The highest-ranking group, 'Juggernauts,' was nudging a million points, while the group at the bottom was on forty-five thousand. A board beside it listed the more recent felons, both individual and gangs, that had been captured or put out of commission, alongside the group of bunters responsible.

They weren't alone in the lounge, but the other groups kept to themselves. A couple of the bunters from the front office came in, went to the bar, and gave them a quick glance.

By the time they filled out the forms and finished their drinks, the registry office was empty, and the captives had been moved to their cells, awaiting transfer. Maintenance bots were hosing down the cages. They resumed their seats in front of the registration office, and Mithum explained another aspect of their new profession: the bounty hunter point system.

"For some bunters, stellars—novas—are all they want. Some just want a legitimate excuse to attack people, but they don't last long. The Watchkeeper doesn't take kindly to those that manipulate the system. Still other groups want more recognition and 'prestige.' The point system gives them that ego boost, but as they say, 'a happy bunter is a successful bunter.'"

When Sabrya laughed, he frowned at her.

"We learned this after several years of dedicated research and psychoanalysis," he added.

"Fraggin' psycho is the correct word."

Mithum only addressed Alexis and Bradyn after that. "Your team gets a point for each stellar. Also, depending on various factors—notoriety of the villains, duration of capture, injuries to clients and civilians, property damage and the like—our algorithm calculates the points based on all the details we have."

"What did we get for this lot?"

Mithum typed in the known details. "Ninety-four thousand stellars, not including the result of the ship auction. That could double if we get a good price for it."

"Sounds impressive. Is it?" Bradyn asked.

"For your first job, it is. Along with the points, there's a star ranking. Each year, the points revert to zero, but the group with the maximum points gets a star. There's still well over half a year to go for you to improve your status."

"How many groups are there?"

"With you, there's now twenty-six. Several groups aren't too serious; they're more opportunistic. Here's a list of your competitors. Consider though, some bunters have been doing this for years."

"Competition? Aren't we here to do the same thing?"

"Tsk, tsk." Mithum shook his head. "It might be different where you came from..." He looked over their papers. "And may I ask where that was? You all left that section blank."

"We got the impression from the fine print that our previous history wasn't necessary, as long as we abide by the rules here," Alexis answered.

Mithum nodded. "Your IDs would have been flagged if anything serious had come up, but it helps us help you if your history catches up." He shuffled the papers back into order. "Sometimes, people's past lives follow them. We do our best to look after our own. Anyway, to continue, take it from someone who has dealt with every one of these groups several times; they're not right in the head—present company excluded, of course." He licked his lips nervously. "You'll soon find some bunters take their position far too seriously and won't take kindly to a new group cutting in on their territory."

"Their territory? Who gave them exclusive rights?"

"I said, 'not right in the head,'" Mithum reminded her. "Now, have you a bunter name?"

"What name can you give a group that hunts down the dregs of society, scraping the bottom of the barrel?" Bradyn asked.

"Fraggin' Scrappers." Sabrya shrugged.

"I'm certainly not going to put that name down!"

"I think my friend means 'Scrappers.' I've got no idea. When do we need it by?" Alexis asked.

"It will do for now." Mithum tapped his keys. "Congratulations, Scrappers, you are now in ninth place. We have your contact details; you'll receive regular updates on rankings and other bunter news. Also, if a particularly notorious criminal or gang becomes active, their last known position will be promulgated."

"I reckon the 'Ion Maidens' won't be happy about being bumped." Bradyn looked at the updated leaderboard.

***

Within an hour of arriving, they were ready to leave the Fortress. They were officially in the system, and all had fresh bounty hunter licenses. The crew wandered back to the *Malleus*. True to his word, by the time they boarded, Mithum had sent them the updated bulletin of the most-wanted criminals. Attached to the message was 'Bunter Happenings.'

"Can you believe there's even a newsletter by Brianna DeCroix?" Alexis flicked through the document. "She calls herself the 'Buntress.'"

"It fits, I guess." Bradyn sat back, holding a steaming mug. "Where to now?"

"What do you think is the most active world here?"

Bradyn put down his mug and looked over the files on his tablet. "My guess is Quint-wil. It's close to an entry point and, no doubt, why CQLO is nearby. After a month or so of hyper, travelers will be looking for a place to ground themselves. The ads show minimal terraforming required, thermal pools, mountains, islands, beaches—"

"Why didn't we go there first?" she asked, bringing up the planetary details and reading them. "Torg, why didn't we go there?"

"We arrived at the coordinates set before I resumed my duties. I have no data as to the reasons Phillix chose those coordinates other than it was the closest entry point to begin trading."

"Since Quint-wil is near a busy entry point, there'll be a waystation nearby. We can take the opportunity to refuel."

"Well, let's go there then," Alexis decided.

"Yes, Captain. We will be there in... two hours," the droid said after setting course.

Alexis stood and stretched. "I'm hitting the shower then taking a quick nap. See you guys later."

"Yep, I might do the same. What about you, Sab?"

"Sleep is overrated. I reckon I'll go over some trainin' programs based on the info in this newsletter."

CHAPTER SEVENTEEN

WITH ALEXIS and Bradyn in their bunks, Sabrya ran through a couple of scenarios in the holodeck, then everything went dark.

"What the frag?" She picked herself up from the deck as red lights flashed.

Alexis bolted out of her bunk. It was dark. Red lights flashed on the console on her desk. "Torg, report."

"We have had a power surge aft. The sub-light drives are offline. Backup lighting now on."

"Bradyn?" she commed. "We're drifting."

"On it," the engineer grunted.

"Sabrya?"

"Already fraggin' patrollin'."

"Patrolling? Why?"

"Because I fraggin' can."

"I'm heading to the bridge." As quickly as she could, Alexis slipped into her Mk8. One of the advantages of the nanite tech was that once she'd donned it, it sealed itself. She raced to the bridge stairs.

"I have run a full diagnostic," Torg said by way of greeting her. "The sub-light drive is offline, and the power coupling to the hyperdrives is, as well."

"How is that possible?"

"Apart from direct manipulation from inside, a small, localized strike or electromagnetic pulse or severely faulty components would have similar effects."

"Didn't Bradyn recently replace outdated or dodgy components?"

"Correct."

"No way are any of us saboteurs. That leaves us with the other option. Who the frag's out there?"

"I have been monitoring sporadic glitches. Nothing is registering on the scope."

"What sporadic glitches?"

"This is the scope we had problems with back in Sector 22. The problems returned when we were at the CQ. I have begun a thorough diagnosis. Sporadic faults are notorious to pinpoint."

"Bradyn. Anything?" she commed.

"Slight acrid odor. Burnt circuits, I'd say."

"A fraggin' EMP could do it," Sabrya asserted.

"Yeah. Sure if—"

"Torg, deploy a drone to survey outside," Alexis ordered. "Activate external monitors."

"Yes, Captain. Done."

On one of the monitors, the external cameras came online in a split screen showing the loading dock, airlock, and sides of the ship.

"We've a couple of suits outside the main airlock." Alexis looked surprised.

"Fraggin' assholes. I'm on it," Sabrya commed.

The drone flew from its housing to the rear of the ship. The image encompassed the top section of the *Malleus* as it zoomed past, showing a couple of figures leaning over the entrance.

"And there's two more suits at the shuttle dock!" Alexis added.

"I'm closer to the shuttle dock." Sabrya clicked her heels and glided swiftly up to the gantry along the central corridor where the shuttle airlock was located. "It's how I'd do it, except I wouldn't get caught."

"Need a hand?"

"Pfft. I got this. Watch those fraggers at the main airlock."

"Both groups are attempting to hack into the systems," Torg said.

"Any success?" Alexis turned to him.

"Highly improbable without AI assistance. Phillix reprogrammed it all."

"I'm ready," Sabrya commed. "Open the shuttle airlock."

"Do it." Alexis nodded at the droid's hesitation.

On cam, the shuttle dock door swung open. The two suited figures looked at each other and then stepped inside one after the other. The door remained open.

Waiting inside, against the bulkhead, Sabrya lurked in the gloom. As soon as the two figures entered, she stunned them point-blank. They dropped heavily to the deck.

"Two down. I'm goin' out to grab those other fraggers." Without delay, Sabrya exited the airlock and flew gracefully over the ship toward the bow. She gave the thumbs-up as she passed a cam.

"The two by the airlock are moving. Must have heard something on their headsets," Alexis informed her.

"Chillax. They've got nowhere to fraggin' go." Sabrya had her stunner out, ready and powered up. The moment the pair of unsuspecting figures came within sight, she took them out. "This is too fraggin' easy." She yawned. "Open the loadin' dock." She flew down to the floating bodies and one by one, pushed them into the loading dock area.

Ten minutes later, four more prisoners were in the makeshift brig.

"The fraggers' suits look like those from the other group."

"That creep did say there were others out there. I thought it was an idle threat."

"Should have seen it comin'. I'm gettin' fraggin' slack."

Alexis informed her. "The drone has located a ship shadowing us about two klicks to our stern and running silent. No energy spikes. Once Bradyn fixes the drives, we'll search it, slave it like before, and head back to the Fortress. Torg, go see if you can assist Bradyn."

"Yes, Captain."

The thugs were still unconscious when the *Malleus* returned to the CQLO. This time, there were no other bunter vessels in view, and they were directed into the same dock as before. They laid the four prisoners unceremoniously on a couple of gurneys, found an elevator, and wheeled them to the bunter office.

Their new IDs allowed them to bypass the cage lock. There was no one manning the desk, so they locked the thugs inside the cages and went to the lounge to order drinks until someone turned up.

"Sorry, I was on a break. Back so soon?" Mithum appeared surprised to see them when he joined them in the lounge. He wiped his glasses then sat with a tablet. "I'll never get used to the hours of this job. But that's okay. It keeps me busy. You are running on Cygnus central time?" He continued at their nods. "Good. Now... let's see what we have." He began tapping his pad.

"Looks like these clients are affiliated with the previous prisoners. They generally remain separate and randomly harass outlying communities. There are reports from that area of one or two unsolved hijackings of traders—"

"Could be them," Alexis said, adding, "They took our drives offline before we knew it."

"If so, maybe we'll get them for those crimes, as well, after forensics have assessed your damage and compared it to the others and checked their ship's weapons. Which leads me to ask, did you find their ship?"

"Like before." Alexis nodded. "We'll send over the control codes. Here are their encrypted files and our statements."

"Very good." Mithum nodded. "Our tech teams will go over them for any intel. Dare I ask what your secret is?" he asked them. "Two bounties in as many hours?"

"Trouble fraggin' finds us." Sabrya shrugged.

"I'm sure you've realized we're new to the area. We came out here to become traders... and that didn't work out. We're going in blind on this new venture. Where can we find out who's who and what's what around here?" Alexis asked him.

Bradyn added, "The Quadrant's infocast is fairly slim. You sent us a list of other bunters, but who's doing the crime here? Any stats on that?"

"I will send what I can," Mithum said after consideration. "Though I wouldn't want to be seen as doing any favors."

"Don't then." Alexis drained the remainder of her drink. "You've got enough to deal with. We'll work it out. As my friend said, trouble finds us."

The leaderboard above the bar flashed their new score.

"Congrats. Scrappers, you're now in 6th place. This will set some tongues wagging the moment they see the updates. No doubt, they'll want to know who you are, more so now than before."

Back on the *Malleus*, Sabrya took her time to go through the haul of weapons from the captured ship. Bradyn had helped himself to whatever compatible spares he could carry. Some turned out to be no good, so the bots broke them down into their basic components. Soon, he had drawers full of various electronic components, screws, and other small hardware and parts for intricate repairs.

He left the bots to finish and ventured forward to the lounge where Alexis was making a salad. "The garden's going well?"

"Well enough. Could be better. Made a bit of a tweak to the nutrient solution. I got Torg to reduce the gees in there. The seeds aren't high-G viable, resulting in stunted plants or they just didn't take." She began slicing red carrots. "Speaking of Torg. Can you run another diagnostic?"

"Sure…"

"I'm not convinced he's all right," she explained. "With these thugs sneaking up on us. It's not like him. We came here to get away from being hunted, and I wasn't expecting it to be the same."

"Want to go back? At least we know the sectors."

"Hardly." She sat as he poured her a coffee. "We need to work at this if it's to be a success. We are now bunters. How do the opportunistic groups survive out here? Pretty sure it doesn't pay well enough unless they're doing something else to get by."

"It's not like we're fraggin' desperate for the stellars ourselves."

"I do think we have a fairly unique background, though. Not all bunters have an auged highly paid gladiator hero to work with."

"Fraggin' true enough."

"It might help to know the competition to see what we're up against. Torg, correlate as much data on the bounty hunter groups as you can find for the last four or five years. Probably easier to see any patterns that way. At least, we'll see how well the other groups have fared over time."

"Yes, Captain."

"Looks like someone's taking this bounty hunter routine to heart."

"After our recent incident, I'm open to suggestions. I know it was my idea to become traders, and we made a tentative start, but..." She shrugged. "As Strasser pointed out, trading out here is difficult, even for those with experience. On Sylvanus, we tried our professions—botany, engineering, and security—and they didn't work out for any of us. Of late, we've spent more time in space than on the ground, discovering some fantastic things, facing threats and violence, and coming out on top. I know I like it, and I think you do, too."

She counted the points. "Because of that, we have an armed stealth ship, weapons, and top-of-the-line combat suits. We've been trained by one of the best Surreal Tourney warriors this century in a state-of-the-art holodeck training ground. Unless there are other high-G bunters out there, we're all stronger. How can we not make this a success? Do you want to at least try, or should we turn around and head back to our old stomping ground?"

"Nothing's changed back there; we've still got bounties on our heads and the Bukshoga Qlan syndicate to worry about."

"Fraggin' ironic, we're bounty hunters evading a bounty."

"Not a legal bounty, just some crime syndicate, but true enough. We're here. May as well make the best of it. See if we're good at it, at least give it a bit of time to see what connects."

"I have correlated the information you requested, Captain," Torg said a few minutes later.

At a nod from Alexis, Bradyn began to check Torg's functions, while she started researching the new data. Although it would have been quicker with the droid, she wanted to do it old-school, as she felt a lack of physical connection with her current predicament. One of the drawbacks of automation and AI—everything is done for you. An ancient quote came to mind.

'It's the journey that's most important, not the destination.'

Even Torg pointed out he was only as good as his programming. If something was missed, she wouldn't know it until it was too late, perhaps not at all. This way, she'd see it all.

Frustrating as it was, some avenues of thought inevitably led nowhere; others began a bit of a pattern. In the end, she modified the spreadsheet she was working on to show region, time, and dates, then she matched them up with bunter activity. She found some interesting trends and decided to discuss them with the others when they joined her.

Alexis brought up the data on the monitor and explained her recent work.

"You fraggin' did all this?"

Alexis nodded. "You can see the columns, point tally, dates, injuries, etc. Doesn't look terrible. But if we dig further, correlating the dates with other important happenings, locations, and victims, half the incidents occurred at a crucial point in the ratification and trade discussions. When that happens, everything's thrown into turmoil for months.

"From my spreadsheet, these are the prominent groups. Some are vying for Imperial interests and others for Free Alliance interests, but there are several independent conglomerates that like the status quo. Some planets have mining colonies, and since they are in undefined territories, there's little jurisdiction and no taxes. They can reap what they want with few consequences.

"What if these groups are backing the 'opportunistic' bunters and direct them to do the jobs they do? They're well-resourced in many ways and have informants in high places who can notify them of talks or deals that will enable ratification."

"Surely, talks are going on in Imperial space as well as out here?"

"If they are, we aren't in the know."

"We could jump and send a message to Phillix and ask."

Alexis considered. "True. Is that what we want to do?"

"Handy to get the full picture from both sides. It's something I doubt anyone else has access to. Is Phillix that much of a worry?"

"I guess not, now that he's not on the ship. But I think he's... evolving."

She remained silent for a moment before continuing. "Anyway, I did find one group that made an appearance on many of these occasions." She highlighted the 'Quadranteers.'"

"Currently twenty-fifth in the tally. Seems hardly worth the effort."

"Barely makin' any fraggin' stellars."

"Yet they've been at it for almost four years. How do they survive? That's my point."

"Something else for income or maybe stay in stasis."

"Surely, there's no way anyone would volunteer to lay in stasis simply to wake up for some mediocre payment. How many members are in this group?"

"Officially two by the bunter registry, but other than the initial licensing, no one's seen them."

"Then how—"

"There are no survivors and no prisoners with their claims. No reason to go to the Fortress for the reward."

"And these names, Fernil O'plortex, and Driew Whal?"

"They're barely mentioned. Several years ago, Driew appeard on an infocast from Quint-wil, drunk and disorderly."

"Most of these anomalies are close to Quint-wil... not that one can get far away in the Quadrant."

"We've spoken of Quint-wil before. Reckon it needs a visit."

"I'll set it up." Alexis stood and put her plate in the washer. She sat at the console, began setting a course to Quint-wil, and noticed a message that had arrived while they were eating.

She opened it and was surprised to see it was from Strasser.

Torg returned to the bridge as she finished reading it.

"Torg, there's a new message from Strasser. Does the file look correct to you?"

The droid analyzed her inbox. "It is a marginally larger file for a simple message. There is embedded coding."

"Decrypt and display." Seconds later, the full message was available.

'I see from your rapid rise you'll be a good addition to the Quadrant. Some 'in the know' refer to me as the Watchkeeper. Unofficially, I take an interest in the bounty hunter groups in my sky. I know some—shall we say—very experienced ones are a step away from the dregs they're removing, but as long as they don't cross the line, I let them be. It wouldn't look good for the Imperium to be taking too much of an active interest out here, but once they go too far... well, we'll see.

'Why am I telling you this? Let's say I'm a good judge of character. My first impression of your group struck me as one of the better things to happen here lately. There are rumors that at least one of the bounty hunter groups is out here to disrupt the ratification process. While it's in the interest of both parties for the process to conclude swiftly, some wish it to remain uncharted, uncontrolled, and untaxed. They don't even want the Free Alliance to have any jurisdiction. So, no one's safe.'

"That's just too damn coincidental." Alexis sat back. She forwarded the message for Sabrya and Bradyn to read.

"Or... Strasser's a cluey chick for a fraggin' Imp and has done this for a while. Who's to say she's not got an AI lookin' into people lookin' for what we just did, but reluctant to say anythin'."

"If we go down that path, she'll be keeping tabs on us—new bloods," Bradyn considered.

"Torg, are you able to monitor whether anyone checks us out?" Alexis spoke into the comm then turned back to the others. "Two can play that game. If there's any group out there taking this as seriously as we are, they'll no doubt be doing the same thing. Hopefully, they haven't started."

"I will establish a list of keywords and set up to monitor remotely. When someone searches for us, they will not trace it back to us directly," Torg replied.

CHAPTER EIGHTEEN

"ANY RESPONSE FROM PHILLIX?" Bradyn asked when he returned to the bridge from the gradual organizing of his workshop.

"Nada. He could be on the other side of the galaxy for all we know."

"No doubt forgotten us fraggin' little people."

"Captain, I anticipated the probability of Phillix being delayed. As his location is unknown, it could take several hours for the message to be detected. As time is of the essence, I analyzed the latest infocasts across the Mesh and Grid. I used the same keywords and phrases you sent to Phillix. Here are the results."

"Good work, Torg. Not going autonomous on us?"

"It is not within my programming. I was being efficient with our limited time and resources."

"Just joking. Bradyn, have we got a sense of humor chip?"

"Not that I've heard of, no."

While they were drinking their coffees, they sat back and scrolled through the highlighted portions of the data stream.

"Torg, there are a few entries for Stenna McFee. Why is he

or his visit to Quint-wil of importance? It's a resort. People do go on holidays."

"If you correlate the dates with other worlds with certain other personages also highlighted you will see a pattern. The other people were listed as being involved with various Imperial mining interests were also at the same places, at the same time. There is an 84.3 percent chance mining and Imperium matters were discussed. Stenna McFee will be on Quint-wil in two days. Several representatives of mining conglomerates not currently invested in the Cygnus Quadrant are en route. Varga-Newton has a conference at the same location in a similar time-frame. Varga-Newton is also affiliated with Ironskin Mining—"

"I fraggin' remember Ironskin!" Sabrya sat up. "They were on Grindstone. They're an Imperial minin' front."

"I gather they didn't want to be associated with Imperial ties," Alexis surmised.

"They've probably used other fraggin' names, too. I'd like to get back at them."

"No doubt, but revenge isn't what we're here for."

"These reps may not have anything to do with what happened on Grindstone a decade or so ago," Bradyn pointed out. "New lives, remember?"

Sabrya let out a deep breath. "Seems fraggin' coincidental or what?"

"Perhaps," Alexis shrugged. "But consider, we're currently in an area under great scrutiny; we've accessed a waystation which gets infocasts from all around the galaxy—over a thousand planets, a hundred billion people—and we've got an AI scouring all that data filled with several thousand data points, specific phrases, and keywords. I'd think it unlikely nothing would turn up. Who knows? If we use different keywords, we might find other equally coincidental outcomes. We already consider Quint-wil a popular destination due to its climate, proximity to the border, and jump point.

"Is it just a coincidence an engineer, a tech whiz, and a warrior woman turned up at the same time as me, so we could team up and escape the slavers? If so, I'm glad for it. Coincidence is what we want happening right under our noses, and we had everything in place without even knowing it. In this situation, we're actively looking for it. Seek and ye shall find."

"Fair enough." The warrior shrugged. "Want me to come up with a plan of attack?"

"We should get more details first," Alexis said. "Full layout of where the meeting is and detailed background on all the names involved, motives, and weaknesses. Then we can brainstorm a plan." She motioned to the spreadsheet. "If we can put this together, perhaps others can too, and with what's happened before, those guys will probably have contingency plans if attacked."

"And other bunters might be involved, especially the Quadranteers," Bradyn added.

"Exactly. May as well get a full rundown on all the bunter groups and individuals, too."

"To continue," Torg said when the chatter stopped. "With this data, there is a 98 percent chance the meeting will take place in a large, public area close to the spaceport. An establishment named the Colosseum is one place that fits these criteria."

"Nowhere else on the whole planet?"

"The highest population density is centered around the spaceport. All other population centers are regional and do not fit the data profile."

"I guess we head there then unless something else crops up."

"Aye, Captain. Also, a message has arrived via our official bounty hunter box. It is an invitation."

"Is it clean?" Alexis asked.

"All incoming messages are thoroughly scanned. There is no malicious coding."

"Let's have a look."

Everyone looked up at the monitor.

'This is an invitation to officially welcome our newest bunters to the Cygnus Quadrant. The Scrappers are invited to join us at The Lair, the real bunter home away from home. See you at 8 pm, Chunta. We await your RSVP.'

"What or when is Chunta?" Bradyn wondered.

"On Quint-wil, Chunta is the 13th day of the month, which is tomorrow."

"What do you reckon?" Alexis looked at the others.

"Now that is another fraggin' coincidence."

"Who sent it? Any addressee?" Bradyn asked the droid as he looked the message over again.

"It is from the Juggernauts, but the address is scrambled and encrypted, like ours are, to make it difficult to locate us."

"Mithum did say they'd be interested. Stands to reason, so they can see what they're up against."

"How should we proceed?"

"Not goin' wouldn't help anyone. Stats are one thing, but better to see them face-to-fraggin'-face."

"Assuming we go, do we wear the Kimichis?"

"It'll look professional," Alexis said. "I, for one, don't have any formal wear."

"And it'll fraggin' piss 'em off, too."

"Torg, send a response saying the Scrappers appreciate the invitation and will be there, then find whatever information you can on this Colosseum."

"You think it's a trap? Maybe they just want to meet the competition?"

"It's what I'd fraggin' do. Hit 'em when they're off guard."

"Says here the Colosseum's on the rooftop of a large mall. It's located four clicks south of the Quint-wil spaceport."

"No landing pad? I find it hard to believe these people would willingly leave their ships behind."

"Looks like a built-up area—businesses and residences, no landing pad," Bradyn confirmed.

"Okay, we go to the spaceport. Torg will then launch, cloak, stay close, and track our suits. We'll keep an open communications channel. If he can't contact us, or vice versa, he can shoot something with the plasma cannon as a diversion, and we can get the frack out of there."

"If I was organizin' this, I'd have a scrambler and weapons suppressor in place."

"What do we have that counteracts that?" Alexis asked.

Sabrya drew her blades. "These, for starters. Those suppressors won't hinder my nanites or augmentations, or our strength. You've got unarmed trainin' behind you."

"Good. Will it affect the suits?"

"Only if we have the weapons options, but not the nanites or the protection they provide. The only way any of it's affected is if they completely envelop the area with a full fraggin' tech suppressor. But that'll stop everythin' other than natural strength—no electricity, no batteries, and no computers. I can't see them doin' that in a populated shoppin' mall. It'd be stupid and could potentially cost lives."

"What if we scan the area first? Surely that'll detect something—even if it detects a tech void," Bradyn suggested.

"We can do that. If we play this right, we can catch them off guard, if it comes to that. Torg, scan the area meticulously."

"Aye, Captain."

"But," Bradyn added, "maybe it's not a trap? We're paranoid of a simple meet and greet. Not everyone is out for our guts."

"Give 'em fraggin' time to get to know us. And there's nothin' wrong with a healthy dose of paranoia."

———

After landing at the spaceport, they hailed a cab. A couple

bypassed them. When one finally stopped, Bradyn sat in front for the leg room while the girls clambered into the back seat. They must have shown their surprise when they saw it wasn't auto-drive.

"You folks new here?" the driver asked, seeing their look. "We're not that sophisticated yet. Plans are in the works, though, for auto-cabs in a couple of years. Progress can be slow. Where we goin'?"

"The Colosseum Mall," Bradyn said.

The cabbie nodded and drove off, casually navigating his way through town. "Hey, I know you, girl," the driver said looking at Sabrya through the rearview mirror.

Sabrya rolled her eyes and looked out the window.

"Even way out here?" Alexis asked.

"Where do you think you've fraggin' seen me?" Sabrya asked eventually.

"Surreal Tourney match. Coupla years ago. You look good in the real; better than on maxi-screen."

"I'm fraggin' touched."

"It's a rough area you're goin', but I'm sure you'll sort it out. I don't reckon you're out there for the flix or shoppin'. You guys' new bunters? You sure look like 'em."

"What are they like?" Alexis looked curiously out the window at the buildings and neighborhood.

"I tell ya, they're all frickin' craz—oh." He stopped, realizing what he was about to say.

"Relax. I don't take the heads off my fans." Sabrya's chuckle was deep.

The cab resumed the speed limit, and the driver kept quiet until they arrived at the Colosseum.

"Here we are."

"What do we owe you?" Bradyn fished out some novas.

"We'll call it square for not takin' my head." He winked.

"Thanks." Sabrya nodded.

"Name's Durn. And it's no problem. See that woman over there?" Durn pointed.

They casually looked around and noted a plainly dressed, short-haired woman sitting in a café. The woman looked at them for a moment, made some notes, then continued to survey the main entrance to the mall.

"That's the reporter for the Bunter Happenings. She doesn't know you're bunters, yet. When she does, she'll pester you endlessly."

"No one's dealt with her?"

Durn shrugged. "If so, not enough. But she's only annoyin', not a physical threat."

"Thanks again." Alexis moved off with Sabrya.

Durn handed Bradyn a card. "Here, if you need me." He waved as he drove off.

Alexis looked at her armpad. "Want a coffee? We've got half an hour."

"Sure." Bradyn nodded, catching up.

"Goin' to get the goss from the source?" Sabrya's eyes scanned the crowd looking for any threats.

Alexis nodded. "Let's see how annoying she is. May as well get introductions over and done with on our terms."

"Fine. We can fraggin' deal with her another time when there are fewer witnesses."

The trio took a circuitous path to the café and looked at the wares in the shops near the main entrance. Eventually, they sat outside and waited for the bot attendant, and they were surprised when a young man came out to take their orders. Alexis had an idea and began tapping at her armpad.

Now and then, the Buntress looked their way but otherwise ignored them until she heard a faint ping. She looked down at her tablet then glanced their way again.

Alexis nodded when she caught her eye.

The lady stood. She was slightly shorter than average

height, but reasonably attractive, her dark eyes framed with glasses and a tanned complexion.

The waiter brought their drinks and then departed with a slight bow.

"I've not seen you here before. You must be the Scrappers," the Buntress said as she approached. "I'm Brianna DeCroix, but I suspect you knew that."

"We thought it best to meet before there is any angst. Please join us."

Brianna went back to grab her wine glass and tablet then sat opposite Alexis, between Bradyn and Sabrya. "Thanks for the invite." She turned to the warrior. "A pleasure to finally meet you in the flesh, Reaper." She adjusted her glasses. They weren't normal prescription lenses, but came with an inbuilt vid-corder.

"Looks like you have a good following here." Bradyn sipped from his mug. "Been doing the Bunter Happenings for long in the Quadrant?"

"I cut my journalistic teeth following the tourney," Brianna explained. "It started getting too commercialized, and larger media groups got involved, making crap up when they weren't distorting the facts."

"If you pissed off the fraggin' mega-media, I probably would have liked you if I'd known you."

"Speaking of introductions, I'm Alexis, and that's Bradyn."

"Pleased to meet you all." She nodded, shaking their hands. "Nice suits. They look familiar. Kimichis?"

"You've been payin' attention," Sabrya said, approvingly. "These are Mk8s"

"Impressive. I didn't know they were out already."

"How long have you been out this way?" Alexis avoided the subject of the suits.

"A few years. I came about the same time Reaper left the tourney, I guess. That was a story I would've liked to cover, but…" She shrugged. "Maybe I'll get a scoop yet. Fill in the details and quash the rumors you were running with the Sunfists?"

"Maybe." Sabrya looked away.

"Is that known out here?" Alexis asked.

"Doubt it. Was barely a rumor back home. I only chanced upon it because of my investigations. Other than major news— or the tourney—not much reaches us. What brings you out here, now?" Brianna asked her.

"Fresh turf. The Imperials gettin' under fraggin' foot even more. The Cygnus Quadrant might be less irritatin'."

"You're not a fan of the emperor?"

"Neither for nor against," Alexis said before Sabrya could vent. "To answer your question, yes, we are the Scrappers. We've been here almost two months. We were looking around for opportunities then stumbled into the bunter business by accident when we nabbed those thugs."

She glanced at her tablet. "The Skimmer gang? I see you've got all of them, now."

Alexis nodded with a shrug. "I'd love to say it was meticulous planning, but they fell into our laps on Blaranad." Alexis gave her the gist of the story.

"You found your way to the Colosseum quickly enough."

"Invited by the Juggernauts, no doubt to assess the real us."

"Especially your rapid rise to the top ten of the leaderboard. Any idea about the Challenge, yet?"

"Challenge?"

"They always test the new bloods with some silly quest. Maybe I could tag along…"

"Might be a bit early in our relationship for that."

Brianna shrugged. "Can't blame a girl for trying." She looked from Alexis to Bradyn and back. "I have a fair idea about Sabrya's abilities—and they're awesome—and I see from his stature, your man here is heavy-G. There are a couple of high-G worlds in the Quadrant, but with his complexion and build—and coming from the empire's regions—there's no one here to compare him to. Are you from Helios?" she inquired.

"Well done." Bradyn raised his mug.

Brianna blushed. "But you, Alexis, are an enigma. No offense, you don't look heavy-G, you're not a tourney fighter... what do you bring to the party?"

Alexis thought about how much she wanted to tell her about her origins. "Brains and a ship."

The three of them laughed. Brianna joined in the mirth after the briefest pause and began describing the other bunter groups. They spent a few more minutes chatting before Alexis' armpad buzzed.

"And that's time to go." Alexis finished her drink.

"I'd love to chat again." Brianna hesitated then pulled a card from her wallet and handed it to Alexis. "It might sound like grunfer shit, but I rarely give this out. Perhaps I'm giving it to you because you're new at this and not jaded and full of self-importance like the other bunters."

Alexis tapped the card to her armpad to read the chip. "Private number?"

Brianna nodded. "For what it's worth, I appreciate you reaching out and not making it difficult." She reached around to shake their hands in farewell. "If we're lucky, this won't backfire."

"Backfire?" Bradyn asked.

"Would you believe I'm not that popular with most of the bunters? You'd think I was the enemy. Most wouldn't have the fan base without my publication."

Sabrya turned back before she moved away. "Just don't become like the media back home, always fraggin' interferin'."

Alexis and Bradyn nodded goodbye and followed.

"That wasn't too bad," Alexis said as they approached the

mall entrance. "And we got a little bit of info about the other groups."

"No doubt her fraggin' biased opinion. Don't forget, fan or not, she's still a fraggin' reporter, lookin' for the next headline."

"Aren't we all a bit biased?"

"I'm not. I fraggin' dislike everyone equally." Sabrya moved on. "Until I take their heads."

"Right." Bradyn winked at Alexis.

CHAPTER NINETEEN

INSIDE THE MALL, they followed the signs to a bank of elevators. One labeled 'The Lair' was an express to the top floor, and it bore a sign with a warning of severe consequences for unauthorized use. As per the instructions, once inside, Alexis tapped her bunter credentials against the security screen. After a rapid ascent, the doors opened to the rooftop bar and grill, where a cacophony of noise and smells hit them. As soon as they stepped out, they saw four armor-plated death-bots nearby, focused on the entry.

"Chillax," Sabrya said a second later. "If they were goin' to shoot, you'd be fried. Must have us in their ID banks." She casually stepped between them and walked toward the bar. The bots didn't move or react in any way as the three visitors passed.

The center of the club was open to the night sky, and the perimeter was covered by large awnings that could extend or retract depending on the weather.

There was a band on the far stage playing what passed as pseudo-rock. A scream of pain came from a man who was tied spread eagle to a large circular tabletop. Four women were taking turns throwing daggers at him, aiming via a mirror as the table rotated. It was too far to see details, but from the sounds the man was making, he'd been struck by at least one blade.

"I wonder what he did to piss them off?" Bradyn looked like he wanted to find out.

"Let it be." It was Sabrya's turn to put her arm out. "This's their turf, not our business to keep the fraggin' peace. We're guests here."

Bradyn tensed but relented with a faint nod.

Sabrya looked at Alexis who also nodded.

"I defer to your expertise in this area."

"Don't worry. If they go too far, I'll bring the fraggin' house down around their heads."

"With our help," Alexis added.

"Wouldn't have it any other way." Sabrya kept moving toward the bar. Her colleagues followed, studiously ignoring the cries of pain.

"You got any Aeirlon-X Starbursts?" she asked the tall, thin barman.

"Sure do." He looked at the trio. "You want three?"

"Absolutely. And I better get two whiskeys for my friends while you're at it." Sabrya nodded.

"Two..." He started laughing then stopped when Sabrya didn't smile. "Right then. Three Starbursts and two whiskeys coming up. I'll bring them over to your table."

"Do that. I'm sure you'll find us." Sabrya pivoted and led the others to a high table near a wall.

They sat and waited, their eyes roaming the club. If the clusters of patrons were anything to go by, there were seven bunter groups there.

The barman had donned gloves and a face shield before he limped over carrying a tray. He deposited the drinks on the table—three bubbling glasses in front of Sabrya and two smaller glasses with brown, clear liquid in front of Alexis and Bradyn.

"Thanks. Who's who here?"

The barman removed the misting face shield and put it on his tray. "Oh, ah. The four dagger throwers are the Ion Maidens, the group near the stage are the Incredibles, and those five in the center are the Ghosters." As he spoke, one of the Ghosters tossed a bottle high in the night sky; one of his colleagues drew a laser and fired, hitting the bottle on the second shot. His colleagues commiserated, and he had to down a large glass. "Those creating the noise on stage are the Juggernauts. Hey, it's open mic tonight if you're up for it. Do us all a favor."

"Is that our Challenge? Reckon we'd fail."

"Nah. Those on top of the leaderboard determine that."

"The Quadranteers aren't here then?" Bradyn asked.

"They left just before you arrived."

"A shame. We must have missed them in the foyer."

"Nah. They always use the service lifts." He hooked his thumb over his shoulder, indicating a door behind the bar.

Sabrya gave him some novas. "That's not for the fraggin' drinks."

"Thanks." He pocketed the notes. "I guess, since the bots didn't melt you, you must be the Scrappers?"

"Guilty as charged." Sabrya tasted her bubbling drink and smacked her lips.

"Great. I'll set up a tab." He limped back to the bar.

"Probably an ex-bunter." Bradyn sipped from his glass, eyes raised at the quality of the drink.

"Well, we know several things, now. No scrambler, weapons, or tech suppressors activated."

"I turned mine off," Sabrya said. "They could still be fraggin' monitorin' our conversation, though."

The others nodded in agreement, then a spotlight suddenly flared at them.

"Hey, fellow bunters," one of the band members announced from the stage. "Let's give a big welcome to the Scrappers, our new high-flying bunters."

A round of cheers came from the crowd before they continued with their activities. Some groups looked toward them occasionally and muttered among themselves.

Recorded music started playing from the speakers as the four band members stepped down from the stage and wended their way through the scattered tables. All looked about the same—medium height, white hair, pale complexion, and heavyset.

It fit the heavy-G description from Brianna.

"Welcome to The Lair, Scrappers, a real bunter's home away from home," the lead band member greeted them. His voice resonated around the club. He looked at their drinks as he disconnected the mic. "You got a tab going?"

Sabrya nodded. "Haven't had a Starburst for a while."

"We don't get much call for that beverage. You must be Reaper, Sector 22 Surreal Tourney hero."

"Not any fraggin' more. Those days are just spindrift now." The forced smile flashed into a storm cloud.

"Fair enough. New turf, new persona. I get it. I'm Vlad, this is Verne, Filo, and Traj." He introduced his colleagues.

"Alexis and Bradyn," Sabrya introduced her crewmembers.

"Only three of you?"

"Does a fraggin' ship's droid count?" Sabrya asked.

"It better if it's navigating you through the galaxy," Traj quipped.

"Nah, droids aren't included. Three it is then." Vlad nodded.

Filo whispered in his ear and pointed to an image on his arm screen.

"I fracking know," Vlad hissed back. He turned back to the

Scrappers. "My overly excited brother here was reminding me of the bunter Challenge for all our newbies. We all do it. Most times we've been successful."

"And if we don't succeed?"

"Maybe we try a couple more until you pass, or we think you're not good enough to run with us."

Bradyn put his glass down. "I thought the CQLO determined that?"

The Juggernauts chuckled among themselves.

"They provide a login and give you a flashy card, but it'll take more than that to be accepted as a bunter out here," Vlad replied. "There are a few groups that failed or were unimpressive. They're still bottom-feeders or gone."

"Fair enough. And if we don't accept?" Alexis asked.

"Only a couple of groups have refused in the past; it got messy, and they're not around anymore."

"You'll find it much harder to get by without our support," Filo butted in.

"We seem to have done fine so far," Bradyn said.

"But now that we know who you are, we won't be as easy on you," Vlad said.

"I must admit, it *was* fraggin' easy. Still, can't see how you lot would be able to make it hard."

"Perhaps we got off on the wrong foot," Alexis said before the discussion got too heated. "We're not declining, just sussing out our options."

"Your options are simple, do it or leave." Vlad looked from one to the other. "Who's in charge?"

"Thought you said you know who we fraggin' are?"

Alexis held up her hand. "I'm the captain, so I'll determine whether we take on this Challenge of yours, or whether we need anyone else's support. So, what's this Challenge?"

Vlad stared at her for a moment then turned to the other Juggernauts for a brief discussion. Again, Filo pointed to his armpad. His brother nodded and addressed the Scrappers. "We saw you talking with the Buntress earlier. We want her gone."

"Gone? Permanently, as in dead?" Alexis said after a pause.

Vlad shrugged. "The method's yours to determine."

"That's a bit harsh. She write an unflatterin' article about you and your fraggin' singin'?"

"I shouldn't have to explain anything to you. She's a trouble-maker. We want her gone before she ruins our gig."

"Fair enough, we'll consider it."

"You'll consider...?" Filo's face flushed, but he held his temper.

Vlad leaned forward and spoke heatedly to Alexis. "You've got two Quint-wil hours." Sabrya was there in a blink, a blade at his throat.

"N-nice move, Reaper." He swallowed nervously as he slowly leaned back. "Do it, with proof, or your next visit will be brief."

"And bring her right hand," Filo added.

"I'm no longer fraggin' Reaper," she hissed at their departing backs.

As the trio finished their drinks, the speakers crackled to life with Vlad's voice.

"The Scrappers have accepted the Challenge. Within two hours, we will no longer be pestered by Brianna DeCroix. The Buntress and her interfering rag ends this night."

There was a resounding cheer from most of the bunter groups.

"Fraggin' asshole." Sabrya drained her second Starburst.

"Don't stress; we're not going to murder someone in cold blood," Alexis assured them.

"I reckon it's a fraggin' trap. If we do it, they'll use it to black-mail us. Fraggin' cowards."

"And if we don't?" Bradyn asked.

"Reckon we'll need more fraggin' ammo."

"These amateurs think they're so cocky in their lair." Alexis shook her head.

"What do you mean?" Bradyn sipped his whiskey.

"Remember when we suspected it was a trap? I've had comms open with Torg all this time, just in case," Alexis explained. "We've got the Juggernauts recorded for conspiracy to murder. The other groups present could be complicit."

"We've got two hours to work out what we're going to do, as well as make this rendezvous."

"If anything backfires, we can kiss any bunter plans good-bye. Nowhere here would be safe."

They finished their drinks and walked casually to the elevators. During the short trip to the ground floor, Alexis messaged Brianna's private number.

The Buntress was still downstairs, sitting at the café, waiting. "What was it like up there?"

Sabrya shrugged. "Just an open-air restaurant, with a lot of fraggin' testosterone."

"It's a crazy circus." Bradyn nodded.

"What do you know about the Juggernauts?" Alexis asked.

"Been active for about five years. Did well. Topped the leaderboard four years running. Four brothers from Itora, a local heavy-G world, but only three-gees." Brianna then listed a lot of stats. "Did you get your Challenge?"

"We did, though you won't like it."

"I'm a big girl."

"They want you dead or permanently removed," Alexis stated.

"They... Me? Dead?" Her face went white. "I..."

"What's so special about your fraggin' right hand?"

All eyes looked at it.

She conscientiously clenched it with her left hand. "It's a data hub. Everything I record and write is in there."

Alexis nodded. "I can probably add a recording for you. Why are the Juggernauts so pissed at you?"

"I've hardly ever spoken with them face-to-face. Not for a couple of years. Sure, I investigate and question, generally after whatever incident they were involved in, but I do that with all of them. I'm not biased; even the lowest bunter group gets a write-up." She watched them carefully.

"Try to relax." Alexis sat down. "We're not about to kill anyone just because some peroxide fools want it."

Bradyn looked at his chrono and sat, while Sabrya remained standing, glancing up occasionally. She typed on her armpad then kept watch. A few moments later, there was a distant flash high up. They heard a crash nearby as something dropped from the night sky and smashed onto the pavement of the mall.

A woman cried in fright, and the nearby crowd surged to look.

"Reckon someone just lost a drone," Sabrya said. "Better be quick. We should probably leave. Good work, Metalman."

"I can't go anywhere, yet." Brianna looked around, then at her watch.

"Expecting someone?" Alexis inquired.

"Yes," she said. "It's for my paper." Her voice was less shaky, though she still looked pale.

"There are some who don't want the empire to take control here—"

"Who'd want Imps fraggin' up their lives? We should at least move before they get another fraggin' drone here."

"I've got an idea about the hand. We can use Phillix's, now Torg's, arm," Bradyn suggested. "But I'll need some DNA. We have less than two hours to convince them you're dead."

"How about we get under cover?" Sabrya suggested.

Brianna nodded. "Let's go inside."

As they stood, the reporter dropped a few novas on the table.

"What do you need?" Alexis asked her engineer as they made their way through the crowded area.

"Blood, hair, skin tissue for the replicator," he said. "We can convince them with her DNA and fingerprints."

"I faint at the sight of blood." Brianna gave them a worried look.

"Better than the alternative. I'll be careful," Sabrya said softly as they approached the large revolving doors. They had to wait for a group of enthusiastic kids to push through.

Brianna knew the area well, so she moved to the side of the foyer and glanced randomly at the crowd until they were near the wall. The spot was away from the throng of shoppers, but they could still see the entrance.

"We need a quiet place to get what Bradyn needs. We could do it here, but that might create a scene, especially if you faint," Alexis said.

The woman hesitated.

"Look. I understand you're scared. You said you know me." Sabrya spoke softly and refrained from cursing. "You pose no threat to us, but you also know if I wanted you dead, you would be already. The longer you take, the harder it's goin' to be for Bradyn to get ready. Then we'll have a bunch of bunters clamorin' after all of us. Personally, that's somethin' I'd relish, but..." She shrugged. "I'm tryin' to start fresh here."

"All right... but I should warn you, everything you say and do is automatically uploaded directly to my secure hub in a satellite. It's on a timer. If I don't access it every hour, all the data is sent to the CQLO."

"Up to you." Alexis smiled reassuringly. "Pretty sure you'll be safer with us. I have a medi-kit in my utility belt."

"And you just might get that fraggin' scoop you're after if you play along," Sabrya added as encouragement,

The short-haired woman glanced at her watch. "Okay. Restrooms are over there."

"You all going?" Bradyn asked as the three of them walked away.

Alexis chuckled. "It's a girl thing."

"I'll wait here." He nodded.

"Good idea, big boy."

Bradyn rummaged through the brochures of a nearby shop until the ladies returned. Brianna looked slightly pale and sweaty, and she bore the telltale sign of tears. She was nursing her bandaged left arm.

"Thank you for doing this," he said to her.

"Didn't really have a choice." She winced as she checked her watch again.

Sabrya handed him a lidded coffee cup and a zip-lock bag. "Go do your fraggin' magic."

The engineer nodded and tapped Durn's number to order a ride. "I'll be back as quick as I can." He headed to the doors.

CHAPTER TWENTY

ALEXIS WATCHED her engineer's receding back as he cut a large swathe through the crowd. He may have been short, but his stocky physique was not to be ignored. "Torg, can you function without your right arm?" she spoke quietly into her comms.

"I can, though I will be down 15 percent efficiency," the droid answered.

"I assume you heard our plan. Anything you can do to assist would speed things up."

"I will communicate with Bradyn and remove the arm while he is in transit."

"Thanks."

The foyer was marginally less crowded now, as some of the flix were about to start. Alexis spotted a table in another café.

"May as well get more comfortable, and you should sit and have a drink to replace some of that lost blood, while we wait for whatever it is you're waiting for." Considering who Brianna was and her occupation, Alexis had a suspicion about what she was expecting.

The table in question had been cleared by the time they got

there. They weren't thirsty, but sitting idle could look suspicious, so they placed their orders and waited.

"Tell you what," Alexis decided. "To show you're a valued member of this impromptu team, I've a spreadsheet I'd like you to look at if you're interested."

"Sure. What's on it?"

"A comprehensive list of dates and bunter activities, especially those involving locations and the ratification process. If you're good enough at your reporting to get a death Challenge from the lead bunters, you might see something we've missed."

"What am I looking for?" the reporter asked.

"You tell us." Alexis put down her coffee and transferred the file to Brianna's tablet. "See if I've got something or whether it's all sheer coincidence."

Alexis sat back, resumed sipping her drink, and waited.

Sabrya, as usual, scanned the crowd. She fiddled briefly with her pouch and then shifted to readjust her utility belt.

Alexis looked at her, a question on her lips.

"I just activated the weapons suppressor," Sabrya informed her.

"Not taking any chances, then."

"Not in public, no. Like you said, we're here to start fresh. A public bloodbath isn't the best way to do that. We've got a bunch of unwanted attention already. That Strasser Imp is no doubt takin' a look, and now all these fraggin' bunters... like those." She looked to the entrance.

Alexis followed her gaze. "From upstairs, those with the blades and the guy on the table."

"Ion Maidens." Sabrya nodded. "I can handle 'em if need be. No doubt checkin' up on our progress since someone lost a drone." As she said it, one of the women looked in their direction.

"No doubt." Alexis could see, from previous experience, the

change come over Sabrya as her nanites geared up. "Let's not create a scene."

"You seem to be comparing ratification meetings with bunter activity." Brianna referred to the spreadsheet. She then showed her a split screen that aligned some of her research with Alexis' spreadsheet.

"Great minds... What's your take then?"

Brianna sipped her coffee before she spoke. "Most of these meetings involved mining groups. I know some of them are affiliated with companies in the empire."

"We—*I*—think the low-level bunters, like the Quadranteers, are bent on disrupting the ratification process," Alexis said. "They trick or force small-time thugs to disrupt these talks. Then the bunters come in to apprehend them, but they get the big novas on the side for the disruption of the meeting or the death of those assembled."

"So, they make an appearance to conduct 'bunter business,' but the main reason is made to look like collateral damage? Sounds plausible. Who pays them the big novas?"

"You'd be in a better position to answer that. Mining corps... anyone not wanting Imperial control."

Brianna nodded, then her attention was brought back to the crowd. "And there he is." The reporter used her head to point without being obvious.

"Who is *he*?" Alexis followed Brianna's gaze and saw a short man in a suit enter from the underground car parking area.

"That's Stenna McFee."

"Ah. Good. It's a relief to confirm the talks are here, and soon, from the looks of it."

"Why is this so important to you? You're new here, so jumping on your high-horse about Cygnus Quadrant remaining free doesn't gel."

"You're right. It's not just this Quadrant, it's... everywhere we go, there are these low-lifes who make everyone else's lives hell.

We came here to get away from that shit, but it looks like it's here too."

"We're runnin' out of fraggin' space. If this keeps up, we'll need another galaxy."

"So, we decided to make a stand here," Alexis finished.

"Can I ask why here? Why didn't you make a stand back home... your own turf?"

"*Here* because it's almost new territory; new beginnings. A powerful crime syndicate put a hefty bounty on us, and you know Sabrya wasn't popular with the Imperial Authorities. At the time, our resources were minimal. Admittedly, by the time we arrived here, our resources and abilities had improved, but we had already committed to start afresh."

"Sort of ironic, you being bounty hunters now. Have you considered going back?"

"Anything's possible. Let's see how we go." Alexis turned to Sabrya. "What's the plan?"

"You follow McFee, I'll head off these ladies."

"No bloodshed, unless absolu—"

"Startin' fresh. I fraggin' got it." Sabrya walked away and angled across the area to intersect the Maidens' path.

A mass of people were making their way to the elevators, which slowed down the four women. This gave Sabrya time to get where she wanted to be without having to shoulder her way through.

Alexis watched her disappear before she turned back to the reporter. "How's your arm? Are you feeling up to this?"

"I'm not going to get physical. I'll leave that to the experts. I'll just be listening and recording, as always."

"Good. Let's go. Must be a conference center somewhere." It was Alexis' turn to drop a few novas on the table.

There were a variety of shops on the periphery of the large foyer. The pair slowly made their way across the floor, browsing some of the shop windows now and then to obscure their motives.

McPhee slowly progressed through the crowd toward the far corridor that led to the business center and conference rooms. Only after he walked through the swinging doors did the women move faster.

Alexis could only make out the blue spikey hair of the warrior woman before the doors swung closed. "We're in the business center corridor, thirty meters behind you, past the hattery," she commed her colleague.

Sabrya acknowledged. With little option for a secluded area where she was, she moved to the same doors Alexis had used a minute earlier and waited to make sure the Ion Maidens followed. The business center seemed unusually quiet, but when she checked the notice board, she realized most of the conferences were either in progress or finished until tomorrow. The wide passage continued for about fifty meters and ended with two elevators and emergency stairs.

She quickly tried the nearest doors. The first two were full of mingling people, the third was locked. Little sound came from within. She forced the handle until the internal locking mechanism snapped, then she pushed the door. The room she entered was large, with tables and chairs throughout.

"McPhee entered the last door on the right." In her earpiece, she heard Alexis' voice. "The two security men by the door went in after and locked the door behind them... I can hear yelling."

Back in the corridor, the Ion Maidens spotted Sabrya.

"I'll be with you shortly," Sabrya replied then stepped inside.

A minute later, the door opened. The four women filed in, saw her, and fanned out.

"Lookin' for target practice?" Sabrya asked.

"Not anymore." The taller woman smirked. "Reckon we found what we're after."

"Thought you needed your targets tied down before you had a chance of hittin' them?"

"You thought wrong." A pair of daggers flashed in her direction as two Maidens ran forward.

Faster than they could blink, Sabrya swiped her arms left and right, sending the daggers into the walls. Using her suit, she soared toward them and met them head-on as more daggers deflected off her combat armor. She lifted the women off their feet, forced them back to the door, and held them firmly in place.

They were shocked at the sudden change in circumstances. Gasping for breath, they futilely grasped her arms to free themselves.

More daggers bounced harmlessly off the back of her suit as she spoke to the two women in a firm, deep voice. "You goin' against your Juggernaut buddies and takin' our Challenge?"

Unable to speak, one shook her head. The other nodded.

Sabrya shrugged, unsure at their contradictory responses. "You're fraggin' winded and confused. Relax, breath, and listen very carefully. You do know who I am and what I'm capable of?"

The two girls nodded nervously, white-faced.

"You're both a blink away from me rippin' you to fraggin' shreds, and your friends could be next, but... I'm tryin' to be reasonable. It's obvious none of you are auged or special in any way, and I'm not in the mood for a bloodbath with norms, so I'm goin' to let you go, but I promise you this, cross me again, and I will end all four of you. Got it?"

Again, the nervous nods.

Sabrya released them. The two women stumbled to the floor as she stepped back and turned to confront the others.

"Sab, two more men with blasters just showed up," she

heard Alexis say. "Your weapons suppressor would be handy now."

Sabrya stared at the sisters. "I'm not in the mood to be slaughterin' nobodies. Go tell your Juggernaut buddies we'll do what we need do in our own time, in our own way."

"No fracking way are they our buddies."

"Then why the frag are you down here followin' us? We said we'd do the job; we're fraggin' doin' it." Sabrya cocked her head as Alexis commed her an update.

"We're in the room. Those security guards were bogus. There's now four of them with blasters."

"We're here to stop you," one of the Ion Maidens said defiantly.

"To stop us? What the frag for? You want to do it yourselves?" She let her blades slide out. "You fraggin' want some of this too?"

They blanched at the sight of the blades and shook their heads.

"Didn't think so." Sabrya slid the blades home. "I've no time for this. I don't want to see you again." She pivoted and left the room. "On my way," she commed as she shot down the corridor. She got surprised looks from the couple lurking by the water fountain.

CHAPTER TWENTY-ONE

"I'M HERE." Sabrya glided to a stop outside the conference room and noticed the busted door handle.

"Oh, none of the blasters are working, now. Your weapons suppressor is taking effect, I reckon," Alexis informed her.

The doors burst open as Sabrya surged through. She came to an abrupt stop and looked around quickly. The room was the same size as the previous one, with the same decor. Brianna was to her left, crouching on the floor but holding her glasses over the top of the row of chairs. Alexis was moving down the left side.

A group of men at the far end, two dressed as security guards, jumped at the sudden noise.

"Four shooters, two left, two right. All are armed, but I guess that counts for nothing now. McFee and his friends are under the table. Two delegates are wounded," Alexis informed her.

"Cool. You about to put some of that trainin' to use?"

"Thought I'd better before I get rusty," Alexis replied. "I'll take these two. How are the sisters?"

"Still breathin'." Sabrya strode down the center toward two thugs. "Two wet their pants."

Stupidly, not realizing why all their blasters had stopped working, the thugs dropped them and pulled out smaller laser pistols. Two thugs concentrated on the men cowering under a large table, while the other two tried to fire at Sabrya. They started backing away at her continued approach. Just as they turned to flee, she kicked in her suit and raced forward.

As with the sisters, she slammed them into the walls, but headfirst. They dropped like stones to the carpet. When she turned, she watched her captain throw one several meters. He shattered several chairs when he landed.

Alexis then pivoted with a back kick and lifted the other thug off his feet. He, too, hit the wall and crumpled to the carpet, moaning.

"Too easy," Sabrya said at the quick dispatching of their opponents.

"Had a good trainer."

"Hey, Brianna, recognize any of these creeps?" Sabrya indicated the thugs.

"No one I know," the journalist called back after a moment.

"Hmm. Not the Quadranteers, then?" Alexis asked. "We thought we'd find Fernil O'plortex and Driew Whal."

"Our names sound so sweet comin' from your lips, don't ya reckon, Driew?"

"They certainly do," another voice answered.

Alexis and Sabrya spun at the new voices. Three more figures moved in from a rear door— two were broad-shouldered men taller than Sabrya.

Knowing no energy weapons would be functioning and having superior strength and combat training, the two *Malleus* women started making their way to confront the newcomers with confidence.

"Look what we have here," one of the taller men said. "Fernil, you forgot to mention we were partying afterward."

"Corpses can't fraggin' party," Sabrya answered.

Alexis looked at the delegates still under the table. "Might be a good time to leave; it might get messy."

The men under the table started moving, but when they saw Fernil pull a breacher out from under his coat, they froze.

Alexis spied several grenades on Fernil's belt before the coat flap closed.

"I don't think no one's going nowhere," Fernil said. His fellow Quadranteers drew their weapons and covered the two approaching women.

"Who's goin' to stop them?" Sabrya surged forward.

Too late, the thugs discovered their weapons didn't work.

Sabrya leaped at them. With a slight adjustment to her suit's thrusters, she spun sideways and bowled them over.

With the crazy warrior woman now looming over them, Fernil panicked. He fumbled for a grenade, tossed it, and began to crawl away.

Sabrya caught the grenade and stepped on his back a second later. "Like you fraggin' said, no one's goin' anywhere." With a quick stab of her blades, she deftly severed the tendons of his hands then popped the grenade in his pocket.

He screamed and writhed in pain, oblivious to the armed explosive now in his pocket.

Alexis ran the last few meters to her target, kicked the shorter thug in the head, and laid him out flat before turning to the other tall man.

He got to his feet and smiled as he pulled a large blade from a sheath under his coat. His lunge was surprisingly swift and caught her off guard. The point of the weapon hit her in the right shoulder, and the strength of his attack sent her spinning.

The wound ached like hell, but a quick look showed no puncture in the suit. Alexis fell, feigning an injury.

With a leering grin, the man stepped closer and raised his knife for a fatal stab.

Alexis' kick to his groin lifted him off his feet.

His face contorted as he fell to the floor, curled up in agony, and whimpered.

The far doors burst open as five mall security guards swarmed in.

"Everybody freeze," a guard yelled.

Ignoring them, Sabrya helped Alexis to her feet. "Nice one. Probably removed him from the gene pool, but you're not usin' your suit to its full potential."

"Next time."

"I said everybody freeze!" the guard repeated.

"You can put your weapons away, sergeant. They won't work," Alexis told him.

He hesitated then fired at the ceiling, to no effect. "Who's got the weapons suppressor? You?"

"Maybe." Sabrya shrugged.

"Turn it off," he ordered.

"No fraggin' way. This dude has a live grenade."

"Actually, he's got a few grenades strapped to his belt," Alexis warned them.

"Yeah, sure. I said turn it off!" When the blue-haired woman ignored him, he turned and said something to his men. They slung their energy weapons and drew handguns.

"Frag!" Sabrya noticed they were now brandishing projectile weapons. When she realized what his next step was, she grabbed Alexis, activated her suit, and rushed toward the far side of the room.

The chief spoke into his radio. A second later the large room was plunged into darkness as the lights went out.

The two women were halfway across the room when all tech failed. Sabrya let Alexis go as both women rolled to the floor and crashed through several rows of chairs and tables in the darkness.

The room erupted into chaos when the area they had been standing in seconds before exploded in an intense fireball.

There were screams of pain and confusion. A ten-meter area was engulfed in flames, with the body of the Quadranteers' leader at its center. The flames gave off a flickering light in all directions.

"That fool was usin' fraggin' incendiary grenades!" Sabrya picked herself up off the floor.

Several thugs and a couple of the delegates from the meeting were alight and screaming. Some were frantically rolling to put out the flames. Before the fire spread too far, sprinklers burst to life and covered the entire room in a cold, wet blanket that swiftly doused the flames before shutting off.

"We get less for deaduns don't we?" Sabrya asked as Alexis untangled herself from the furniture before climbing to her feet. The Kimichi had protected them from any injury, and the spray from the ceiling dripped off their suits.

"We lose about twenty percent, I think."

Sabrya shrugged. "It's still worth it." She looked over her shoulder as the doors swung open, casting more light into the room.

The Ion Maidens walked in.

Sabrya swore and strode toward the four women, pushing chairs out of her way. "What the frag are you doin' here? I told you what would happ—"

"And we told you, we don't want her dead." They quickly formed a protective ring around Brianna when they spotted her.

"And I told everyone to stop bloody moving!" the mall security chief bellowed. The guards around him tried to look menacing but were clearly unsure what to do. Their saturated uniforms clung to them and made their movements awkward.

Alexis said, "Sab, I'll deal with the security team, you talk—and I mean talk—to the Maidens."

"When you say *talk*..."

"With your mouth, using words." Alexis continued over to

the mall security chief and produced her bounty hunter credentials. To mollify his surliness, she complimented him on his swift and decisive actions, then she began explaining what had happened.

Sabrya stopped several feet from the Maidens as the lights came back on, although against her instincts, she refrained from extending her blades this time.

"Look. We're not here for trouble," one of the Ion Maidens said. "But you can't murder this woman just because those jughead cretins say so."

"Not that I need to explain anythin' to you, but it's lucky we're not." She looked at the reporter who was now standing, her hands resting on the back of a chair. "Hey, Buntress, it might be better if they hear it from your lips."

Brianna nodded and spoke quietly. "The Scrappers are going to great lengths to fake my death, but thank you for your concern."

"The Juggernauts are getting out of hand," the lead Maiden continued. Her posture relaxed slightly, as did that of the others. "And they're getting reckless. This Challenge to murder in cold blood was the tipping point."

Strasser walked in briskly with several men and a couple of security bots. She looked around quickly at the sodden chaos, the upturned furniture, the fire damage, and the groaning bodies at the other end of the room. She spoke into her comm then ordered her men to see to the thugs.

Moments later, several medi-bots rolled in to attend to the injured.

"What happened here?" the Imperial officer demanded. "And what idiot turned on the damn tech suppressor?"

The Maidens remained silent, still watching Sabrya warily.

Stenna McFee and the other delegates were now standing. Some wore smoking suits, and a couple showed signs of injuries. Fernil was dead, and most of the thugs were injured to some degree, some with burns, several with broken bones, and one big guy who was still having trouble standing straight.

Alexis moved over to meet her. "Hi, Lieutenant."

"Captain." Strasser turned back to survey the room while Mall security worked alongside Strasser's men and droids to secure the thugs, and administering treatment for those needing it.

Seeing how she wasn't going to get any coherent response from the mall chief, she looked back to Alexis. "Let's take this to my office," Strasser suggested since the room was now under control. She strode out before they could reply. Alexis and Sabrya followed. When Brianna pushed past the Maidens, they fell into step after a brief hesitation.

Strasser entered a waiting elevator. There was only enough room for four, so the Maidens had to use the next lift.

One level up, Strasser led the way to her unmarked office. They entered just as the other lift's doors opened.

"Please sit," the officer invited. "I only have one towel." She tossed it to Alexis, who dabbed at her hair and face before passing it to Sabrya. She in turn handed it to Brianna.

"We were working on a theory that the low-level bunters would have difficulty surviving unless they were moonlighting," Alexis began to explain her research. "It looks like our hunch was right. The Quadranteers get thugs with a pending bounty to do their dirty work, then they come in to grab them, killing them in the process, along with creating some 'collateral damage.' But it's the collateral damage that's the main target—in this case, McFee and his colleagues. I reckon the Quadranteers are on the payroll for some organization that is against ratification."

"Excellent work, and surprisingly similar to our research. Hence why I'm here, purely as liaison officer, of course. We were waiting for them to act but were delayed when some clown turned on a tech suppressor. Anyway, we'll sort through the personnel involved and the forensics and see what bounty is owed, if any.”

“Why did the grenade go off with your weapons suppressor in operation?”

Sabrya shrugged. “I reckon the tech suppressor counteracted the weapons suppressor. The grenade pin had already been pulled, so it couldn’t stop the spring action.”

“I dare you to tell her about your Challenge,” one of the Maidens spoke up from the doorway.

Alexis sighed and gave Strasser the details of the Challenge. “We have it all recorded. And, as we’ve stated several times already, there was no way we were going to accept it.”

“They were bound to overstep the boundaries eventually.” Strasser nodded. “Remember earlier, I said we were aware of certain bunters bordering on crossing the line? The Juggernauts couldn’t have become so successful without doing that. We just needed that one bump to do it, and a conspiracy to murder charge will do it. Might even be able to get them on other charges, too. We have legal precedence to seize and search.”

“They won’t fraggin’ roll over that easily.”

“True. There could be a bit of a fight coming up. If we have them committing a crime they haven’t been arrested for, we can post a bounty.”

“Is there a bounty on the Quadranteers?”

“No, as this is their first confirmed crime, and they’re now in custody, except for Fernil.”

“So, you can post a bounty on fraggin’ bunters?”

“Not straight away. First, we revoke their bunter registration. You’ll be interested to know there’s a bylaw—in the Bunter Registration fine print—that a group with a revoked registration will forfeit all rewards and goods. Those proceeds will then go to whatever department or group took them down. Once we do that, every bunter will turn on them.”

"Does that mean we get their equipment?" a Maiden asked.

"Quite possibly…"

"You guys aren't goin' to fraggin' nab the Juggernauts?" Sabrya asked Strasser.

"No, for the same reason we don't nab any other criminal group. It's a diplomatic issue. This isn't the empire, so we can't be seen taking an active role. Remember, I said you bunters were the closest thing to law enforcement in the Quadrant. Maybe not what you expected, but this is what you signed up for."

"You mean we're beholden to do this?" Alexis queried.

"Absolutely not, but the moment a bounty is posted, someone will try. It's going to be tough. They aren't push-overs, especially if their allies stick with them."

CHAPTER TWENTY-TWO

"YOU'RE PROBABLY NOT aware of what the Juggernaut's capabilities are," the leader of the Maidens declared. "If you want to go against them, you'll need our help."

Alexis looked at Sabrya before replying. "Let's see their reaction to the bounty on them. Taking on high-level bunters is not something we planned on, that's for certain. I suggest we discuss it another time, then we can compile our info and come up with a plan." She turned back to Strasser. "Lieutenant, what's the procedure from here? Hypothetically."

"Please, call me Ingryd. For starters, CQLO will want statements from all of you and a copy of that recording. A demand will be sent to all the groups in attendance this evening to get their statements, as well."

"And if they say no?"

"We have protocols for such an occasion, though they are rarely used. Refusing an official edict will initially result in resetting the points."

"That's fraggin' it?" Sabrya asked.

The four women quietly laughed.

"Someone doesn't fully comprehend the importance of the leaderboard," the Maidens' leader said.

"If a second demand is refused, that group's assets will be frozen," Ingryd continued. "Believe me, when the novas run out, there's a definite change in attitude."

They spent the next hour giving their statements. The procedure was simple—one by one, they were questioned by an AI, specifically programmed with every known law—Imperial and Free Alliance. There was also cross-referencing of the evidence occasionally for further clarity on minor matters.

"Can we keep this from reaching other bunters? At the moment, it's just between us. If the Juggernauts get wind there's an official investigation, they'll close ranks and lay low."

"It might not be that easy. You've reported a crime—"

"Have we, though? As much as we want them gone, let's give it a hard look. A death threat was *implied*... is that sufficient grounds to proceed?"

For the first time, Strasser looked annoyed. "I'll see what I can do before we go further. Go back to your ships. You'll be notified of the outcome. In the meantime, we will put Brianna under protective custody—"

"Actually, if I could, I'd rather stay with *them*—Alexis and Sabrya—if they'll have me."

Strasser scratched her head. "Well, you are a free citizen, and we have no right to hold you. If they are amenable..."

Alexis considered her options. "I don't see a problem. Maybe we can benefit from some detailed insider knowledge."

The Imperial officer nodded. "It's agreed then. Here." She gave them a pass. "This will get you through the service corridors out back. It'll reduce the chance the Juggernauts or one of their spotters see you leaving."

"Much appreciated." Alexis took the card.

"If anything happens—" the lead Maiden started.

"Then I'm sure the good lieutenant here will throw us all in the fraggin' brig," Sabrya finished heatedly. Sabrya waited for the Buntress to leave, then she followed.

"Torg, you there?"

"Affirmative, Captain. Comms were down."

"Sorry. Someone activated a tech suppressor, and then we had to disconnect for a legal interview."

"At last. I'm almost there," Bradyn said in their earbuds. "Just in time, too."

"We're heading down. We'll need to meet you around the back. I'll explain later." Alexis stopped before she entered the lift and walked back to the four Maidens. "Seems like this is the evening for reaching out. Sorry if we stepped on your toes. We never intended to harm Brianna. If anyone asks, can you ladies push the narrative that the Buntress was killed in the fire? Burnt beyond recognition would be a nice touch."

"It did get a bit heated… no pun intended."

Alexis' smile was brief. "It might be unorthodox, but you girls want to tag along? To see Brianna safely to our ship? If these peroxide knuckle-draggers are as tough as you say, perhaps we need to trust one another. Let this be a first step."

The four bunters spoke quietly before the leader answered. "Sure. We have a ride. We'll follow you to the port."

A few minutes later they saw Bradyn by the taxi near the rear service door, but they exited only after Torg confirmed there were no drones in the area.

Bradyn climbed out carefully, carrying a sealed container. "This is a work of art!"

"Ah… Bradyn… How should I put this?" Alexis broke eye contact, embarrassed to break the news.

"We don't need it now, big boy. Thanks anyway." Sabrya chuckled, slapping him on the back.

"You don't…" Bradyn went quiet. He put the container in Sabrya's hands and climbed back into his seat.

During the ride, the three women squashed in the backseat opened the container to examine Bradyn's hard work.

The arm had been placed in a sealed container with cryo-synth. The skin over the prosthetic limb was lifelike, but no matter how many compliments they heaped on him, Bradyn remained as quiet as a rock all the way back to the spaceport.

Alexis paid Durn the fare then waited for the Maidens before following her crew as they strode to the waiting *Malleus*.

Brianna even compared the arm to her own. She was still examining it as she walked, though the pad lighting was dim at best.

"How did you manage to make it so lifelike?" she asked enthusiastically. "I can only imagine how disappointed you must be after all that work."

"Well... it was the replicator, really... and your DNA." Bradyn gradually opened up as they crossed the large concrete pad. "It's almost like cloning, but on a very limited scale, and as it's biological, it will decompose unless we keep it on ice. Hence the container. But since we don't need it anymore, we won't have to put it back. I'll take care of it, and Torg can have his arm back."

The spaceport was quiet with no more scheduled launches that evening. Alexis heard most of the conversation as she walked toward the *Malleus* with the Maidens. They introduced themselves as Fyona, Bree, Doryne, and Quela.

"Before you ask, yes, she flies quite well," Alexis preempted the queries from the Maidens. "I, too, thought it was a piece of junk when I first came on board. You'd be surprised where she's gone and what she's been through in the last seven months."

The four women looked surprised.

"Seven months?" Fyona repeated. "How long have you been her captain?"

"Same."

"What did you do before that?" Fyona asked.

"I was a botanist on Mars."

In complete shock, the Maidens stopped walking. They were now at the foot of the loading dock ramp.

"It's complicated." Alexis shrugged. "Let's have a drink."

The others had already entered. On her approach, she spied Torg greeting Brianna, and the pair joined Bradyn and disappeared moments later, leaving Sabrya waiting for her.

"Gone to the workshop, no doubt. I'll have to make it up to him," Alexis muttered to her, as she waited for their guests to join them. She then escorted them to the lounge where she offered them coffee, wine, or whiskey. They all chose whiskey, and a few tense minutes passed as they sat, looking around and sipping their amber drinks.

"We don't normally get to see other bunter ships," Fyona started. "It's very... generous of you."

"Not at all," Alexis reassured them. "I'm hoping it's one way to build trust, which is what we'll need if we are to become allies."

Sabrya leaned against the bulkhead, keeping quiet.

"There's just the three of you?" Fyona asked.

"We do have a ship's droid." Alexis nodded. "I'd like to think he is part of the crew, too."

"Not meaning to offend, but... how did a botanist become captain of an armed, though run-down, warship and team up with a disgr—an outed Tourney champion?" Fyona looked nervously at Sabrya, who didn't bat an eye.

"Oh, that was a fun time. We're all escaped slaves." Alexis sipped her drink and smiled at their incredulous looks.

"Fun times," Sabrya echoed.

The women consumed several more drinks as they got to know more about each other.

Alexis glossed over a lot of the previous activities' details, but even so, it was cathartic to talk about the events to complete strangers.

During their tour of the non-sensitive parts of the *Malleus*, the Maidens touched on their backgrounds. Fyona and Doryne were sisters, and Glyn and Quela had been friends in the military. All were Quadrant-born and bred, from Sidria, an agricultural world with a few other resources.

Farming life wasn't what they were cut out for, so when the opportunity presented itself to hire a ship and become bunters, the two sisters jumped at the chance and sought like-minded people to help crew the *Raquech*.

With the promise of a tour of their ship tomorrow, the Maidens bid their farewells.

"One thing, if I may ask before you go, why the name 'Ion Maidens'?"

"You'll see tomorrow." Fyona waved.

Several hours later, Bradyn and Brianna stepped wearily into the crew lounge.

"Okay," said Bradyn. "My peevishness is over. Why did I waste half the night for nothing?"

Brianna looked tired but happy to listen in. Torg continued to the bridge, his arm as good as new.

Alexis poured her engineer a large glass of whiskey with ice and waited for him to sit, relax, and drink before she started detailing their eventful evening.

"We can fraggin' argue there was so much goin' on with security bots and Strasser's people scourin' the place, we couldn't retrieve the arm."

"There is a vid call for Captain Nales. It is from Lieutenant Strasser," Torg announced.

"Now? Put her through." Alexis paused until the overhead monitor came to life. "Hello, Ingryd."

The Imperial Liaison Officer was still in her office with several datapads lined up on the desk. She was still fully dressed in her uniform, and even after all that had gone on, not a hair was out of place.

"Captain Nales, sorry for the lateness of the call. I have the results of the Judicial AI investigation. Not surprising news. I've embedded further details, but in short, it deemed there's only a 68 percent chance of a successful prosecution of the Juggernauts based on the available criteria. The news is not totally discouraging; it's yet another crack in their slowly fracturing lifepod. Day by day, they seem to be getting closer and closer to losing it. Then they'll fall. I just hope no innocents get injured beforehand."

"So, life goes on. Thanks for the update. We have Brianna with us, and I've already notified the Juggernauts she died in the fire."

"Fair enough. I'll deal with anything on this end. Strasser out."

The monitor went back to the cyclic views from the external cams.

The coffee was already on by the time Alexis made her way to the lounge the next morning.

"Morning, Bradyn. Sleep well?"

"Well enough." He poured the steamy hot liquid into her mug.

Brianna stuck her head in the doorway. "That smells good."

"Tastes better." Bradyn offered her a seat then fetched a mug.

During breakfast, Alexis broached something troubling her.

"I tossed a bit during the night... my mind couldn't grasp a couple of things, one in particular." She looked at the Buntress. "You've been working on your paper for several years, at least. Sure, some might get annoyed with your questions and reports. No one likes their bad side laid open to the public. What I'm not comprehending, though, is why they wanted you dead. A bad photo, even an embarrassing story, wouldn't warrant anyone's death. So, what is it you know, or they think you know, that would make them want your death?"

"What makes you think I know or saw anything?"

"They not only wanted proof of death, for which a photo or your head would have sufficed, they specifically wanted your right hand, your data hub. Whether you consciously know it or not, there must be something on there that will cause great harm to them or their interests. We need to find out what that is if we want a chance to remove these assclowns."

"Have you interviewed them or followed them recently?" Bradyn asked.

Brianna shook her head. "The last time I had anything to do with them was over a month ago."

"Hopefully, you trust us enough, that when I ask if we can access your recordings, you'll understand we're trying to determine what you may have seen or overheard," Alexis assured her.

"How do you work, exactly?" Bradyn continued his line of questioning. "How do you come up with the information for your paper?"

"Other than possessing a curious mind, good contacts, and fairly deep pockets, I'm adept at working with tech. Generally, I watch the comings and goings at the Colosseum. Sure, I might not get all the juicy details of the bounties captured—I do sometimes resort to buying info from those in situ—but these assclowns, as you call them, always return to the Lair with their boastful talk. While his attention has waned of late, Kyle, the younger one was always open to a drink and a flirtation. I've got no objections to sharing the data, but since you're new here, do you know what to look for?"

"Other than fresh eyes and perhaps a different perspective, we also have access to one of the greatest AIs in the Quadrant."

"Torg?" Brianna looked questioningly toward the bridge.

Alexis smiled when Sabrya rolled her eyes. "Not Torg, though he's adept when it comes to analyzing data."

"Can you promise me none of this will get out?" the reporter asked.

"Absolutely," Alexis stated without hesitation. "We've no interest in your scoops, other than to find out why the Juggernauts put a hit out on you."

Brianna looked unsure and toyed with her breakfast.

"I reckon you'd come up with a fraggin' good story how you helped in bringin' down… whatever it is we're bringin' down."

"We understand your reticence," Bradyn said to assuage her doubts. "Fascinating company that we are, I'm sure you will soon want to get back to your life. Imagine the sales when you returned from the dead!"

"My sales will no doubt improve." The Buntress smiled. "And yes, the company is certainly *different*."

"Do you have any family here in the Quadrant?" he asked.

"No, but I have a sister back in Sector 19." She pushed her empty plate away. "Okay, then. What needs to be done?"

"Can you transfer the data to our computer? Torg can cross-reference it with everything we have, and we can look at the recordings. Fresh eyes…"

"Let's start fast-tracking backward from last night. We'll slow down when we see any bunter activity, see what happens." Alexis commed the bridge. "Torg, can you analyze the data and cross-reference it with what we already have, as well as facial recognition?"

"Affirmative, Captain."

"There." Alexis pointed after only twenty minutes of watching the recordings. "Isn't that the clerk from CQLO?"

"Klauff Peinkoph," Brianna confirmed. "He visits once or twice a month. Most of the time, he goes to the office we were in last night with Strasser, but on occasions, he pops up at the Lair."

"Is that normal? Does Mithum do it?"

Brianna shook her head. "I've never seen the old man there. There might be a perceived conflict of interest, since he's the one who basically controls the leaderboard. I think he lives in the Fortress."

As she spoke, they continued backtracking the vid feed recorded from her glasses.

"Hold there." Bradyn sat up and leaned forward.

"What is it?" Alexis asked.

"I've seen that face before." The engineer pointed to an average-looking male who was speaking with the Juggernauts as they exited the lift. "From... before we met."

"Any idea who?" Alexis asked before comming the droid. "Torg, reference the vid at 1305, 24:08:5123."

Torg came back seconds later. He read off the names of the Juggernauts and Klauff, but not of the fellow in question.

"Why's a fraggin' Imp pen pusher, a bunch of loud-mouth bunters, and some fraggin' shady dude from the empire meetin' for?"

"Phillix would know."

Brianna looked at them. "Who's Phillix?"

"Want to go on a trip?"

"As in... off-world?" Brianna looked excited, though pale.

"Sure. You've done it before?" Alexis queried. It didn't occur to her until now that some people rarely left a planet's surface.

"A couple of times, back in the empire, but not since my arrival here."

"No fraggin' way!"

Brianna shrugged. "Lots of nothing to do out there. This is where I get the info that pays for my meals."

"Remember I mentioned one of the greatest AIs in the Quadrant? How would you like to meet him?" Alexis asked Brianna.

"I can't fraggin' believe we're goin' back to him," Sabrya grumbled.

The Buntress noted the friction. "Did you have a falling out... with an AI?"

"Let's say he outgrew the *Malleus*." Alexis laughed. "Torg, can you arrange our departure with FlightCon?"

"Aye, Captain."

Brianna spoke quietly to Alexis. "Your ship's droid... he's... different."

"You think he's different? Wait until you meet his mentor."

CHAPTER TWENTY-THREE

TWO HOURS LATER, the *Malleus* launched. The crew had continued going over the recordings, but the footage they had found with the unknown visitor was the most likely cause of any possible angst.

Alexis sent out a message to the Maidens before liftoff. "Something has come up. We'll be back in a few days for the tour of your ship. Shite news from Strasser, but we will persevere. Alexis, out."

As soon as practicable, Torg set course for the waystation then jumped.

Brianna, on the bridge with Torg and Alexis, was amazed by what she saw with the jump. "I was on a passenger ship before. I barely managed to see anything as I was in a low berth, unable to afford much more, especially the luxury of a viewport." She stared with wonder. "And you get to sit here and do this every day."

Alexis nodded. "I do love it, and it is amazing, but the luster can wear off. Just like watching sunrises and sunsets over and over—yes, they look beautiful, but after the first dozen or so, you don't lose sleep if you miss one. Now, if you'll excuse me, I'm going to get my hands dirty in the garden. I believe it's time to harvest some vegetables for another real dinner."

As she stood to leave, she turned back to the Buntress. "Roam around, do what you want, and thanks for sharing that data."

They sent a message to Phillix in the hope he'd receive it and respond in time. It turned out to be fortuitous timing, and he was there to greet them when they docked at the waystation using the provided transponder code.

"I was only a few sectors away, so relatively close."

As it had been several months since they had last heard from him, they made themselves comfortable in the crew lounge and filled him in on their activities up to the latest incident.

"You may or may not believe it, but I do have access to millions of infocasts across the galaxy. I'm even conversant with your guest, Brianna DeCroix. I trust you're enjoying your trip?"

"I am, very much." She blushed. "You know of me?"

"Very much so. You did some wonderful pieces on the tourney back in the day. A shame you didn't get the full recognition you deserved."

Brianna's face turned even redder with the praise. "I can't believe you are so widely read."

His chuckle sounded weird over the speakers. "You would be astounded by what I've read and what I know."

Sabrya coughed. "Here we fraggin' go."

"Miss me, Sabrya?" he greeted the warrior.

"Well, Mr. Well-read, we have a question for you." Alexis told him about the recordings and death threats toward Brianna. "We need you to identify this fellow. Bradyn recognizes him, but he says you'd know him better." She played the recording.

The speakers were silent for longer than expected.

"You there, Phill?" Bradyn asked.

"Comms are working at 99 percent efficiency," Torg offered.

"I'm here." There was another pause. "His name is Giono Halmar Shobianu."

"And?" Alexis asked when more information wasn't forthcoming.

"He's the one who double-crossed me and put me into slavery. He is also, I later discovered, a middle-level member of the Bukshoga Qlan."

It was the crew's turn to pause their comments.

"The Bukshoga Qlan? Aren't they a small-time crime syndicate?" Brianna queried.

"Maybe back in your day. They're no longer small-time," Phillix informed her. "They're now quite powerful and spread out. They even have a bounty on all of us, which is not a concern for me anymore."

"And that, in a nutshell, is why we're here—to avoid a face-to-face with such a large syndicate," Alexis reluctantly admitted.

"What the frag are they doin' here in the Quadrant?"

"New turf? New pickings?" Phillix offered. "If I understand it correctly, the bounty hunter fraternity is the nearest thing to any form of enforcement here. No doubt it would be a boon for them to get their leg in the door before the Imperium takes charge." Again, Phillix paused for several minutes. "I've just gone over the infocasts for the last four years. Giono has been here several times, the first being—coincidentally—just before the Juggernauts made their first breakthrough. Here's a condensed version."

A file appeared on the side of the monitor. Upon activation, a column of text ran up the right of the screen.

"The Juggernaut's first big bust was—"

"The Blood Reign," Brianna interjected. "They'd been attacking settler ships for several months. Back then, with only one waystation online, they lurked near the entry point, and the moment a ship arrived, they hit them. At least 30 percent of all passengers were killed, and they hauled off several million stellars worth of equipment, stores, and machinery. The Juggernauts turned up during one of the attacks and cleaned them up. After that, they rocketed to the top of the leaderboard and have had a steady supply of successful bounties ever since."

"I wonder what the current status of the Bukshoga Qlan is here, in the Quadrant?" Bradyn wondered.

"And how Strasser would feel about bunters making deals with a crime syndicate." Alexis considered for a moment. "Phill—"

"At a guess, you want the dirt on these Juggernauts, a detailed dossier on any and all of their dealings?" Phill asked.

"Also, what can you find on this Giono clown, as well as a Klauff Peinkoph? He might be nothing, but it doesn't hurt to find out, especially since he's Strasser's right-hand man here. As you saw in the recording, Klauff already has an acquaintance with your Giono, and also seems to be in the pocket of the bunters. Is he stupidly innocent or a conniving genius under Strasser's nose?"

Sabrya scoffed at genius.

"I'll send a message to Strasser, asking her if she crossed the Qlan within the empire, and what she'd do if they came here."

"Are you going to tell her they're here already?" Brianna asked.

"Are they, though? One lowly minion doesn't make a syndicate. He's just only another asshole causing mischief."

"Or a mischief-causing asshole," Brianna quipped.

Alexis nodded and looked at them. "If we can't get the

Juggernauts convicted of conspiracy to murder, you think a chat with a nothing bit of riffraff will turn the tables?"

"I'll put the coffee on. This could take awhi—"

"All done," Phillix stated as their armpads pinged with the details of Giono and Klauff.

Sabrya laughed. "Don't you fraggin' hate it when he does that?"

"Klauff's records are a tad harder to get, since they're stored deep within the empire. The records I can locate are minimal. His parents were administrators, moving from planet to planet when the need arose; their forte being great troubleshooters. It seems they were highly regarded in many circles and slowly moved into the inner sanctum of the emperor—probably another reason his records are hard to find. Since he's not greatly featured, I'm of the opinion Klauff was not the favorite child, hence the low priority of this position. Perhaps his posting here was a matter of convenience for the rest of his family.

"He was one of the first Imperial staff members to arrive at the CQLO to set things up for Strasser. After that, his performance has been mediocre day after day. High-ranking administrator siblings were generally given prestigious positions within the Empire. If I were to hazard a guess, I'd say he was doing this to spite his parents and the empire.

"Now, as for Giono. He was born in Sector 10 on Frallon in 5088 as Rubern Shorak. At the age of 24, he was an up-and-coming clerk with a large importer-exporter in Poross, Frallon's capital city. An investigation of his suspiciously rapid promotion led him to flee and change his name to Giono. He found himself on Ieoni, where he managed to secure an assistant manager role. When the Qlan moved in—a much smaller yet zealous enterprise back then—they killed off several of the Orbital's senior management before he capitulated to do their bidding. From that time on, the reputation and influence of Ieoni Orbital and the Qlan grew."

Brianna sat quietly while they discussed this latest info.

"What are your thoughts, Brianna?" Alexis asked, still wondering how Phillix became involved with the likes of Giono. But it was something for him to decide to share or not, and she respected that.

"The wealth of the data is certainly impressive, but I'm confused on several issues." Brianna's bewildered look passed from person to person. "An AI that hazards guesses? Why would there be a bounty on an AI, and how is it possible an AI was sold into slavery?"

"As I said, I'll get the coffee started." Bradyn quickly retreated to the counter.

"Coward," Sabrya sniggered.

"Tell you what," Alexis said. "Since you've only known me and Bradyn for a couple of days, I'm sure you'll believe Sabrya more than us."

"Cow..." Sabrya grinned as Alexis went to assist Bradyn. "Funny how makin' fraggin' coffee suddenly requires a starship captain and a hyperdrive specialist." She sat down in the chair Alexis vacated. "Okay Bri, got your recorder goin'? You'll need it because I'll relate this once only. There'll still be some parts I'm not goin' to fraggin' tell you about." She put her hand up as Brianna opened her mouth. "No fraggin' questions until I've finished, and no, the parts I don't tell you about are for your own protection as well as ours. What I'll tell you though, is if that info gets out, the whole fraggin' Imperial Navy, every fraggin' bunter, crime syndicate, and Surreal Tourney player would be houndin' us to the edge of the galaxy and beyond."

Brianna was silent for a long time afterward. Her third coffee had gone cold.

"That's what you could tell me?" she finally asked, looking at each of them with, perhaps, a clearer understanding. "I thought I'd seen quite a bit. I apologize for underestimating or doubting you all."

"Nonsense," Alexis chided softly. "You couldn't possibly have known who to trust or what our capabilities are."

"Except Sab, of course. I knew of her capabilities; I just never thought I'd be this close to her. Perhaps, when you're ready, we can discuss the Sunfists?"

Sabrya slowly shook her head. "The fraggin' ramifications of any of those stories gettin' out could endanger their reputation, if not lives."

The reporter nodded. "I understand."

"Now that you mention it, I also have an update on the Sunfist," Phillix said.

"You're tellin' us now?" Sabrya sat up.

"I have to say, Giono threw me off a bit," Phillix apologized. "Since the destruction of the waystation, they have gained themselves a reputation. You'll recall they took the blame—or admiration—for an attempted assassination of Nero—"

"Someone tried to assassinate the emperor?" Brianna asked, awestruck.

"No, but the fraggin' Imps are playin' it that way. Continue," she directed the AI.

"So much so, the Qlan is now taking an interest. For Brianna's sake, the Sunfists were a low-level rebellious group, who took on the Imperials where they could in matters of social injustice and the like. With the weapons haul, they've slapped the Qlan in the face by disrupting some of their activities. And as you know, the Qlan react swiftly and decisively—"

"Or try to," Bradyn added.

"So, the Sunfists have their hands full, fending off increased Imperial attention, as well as a large crime syndicate."

"We know how they feel, but they better not come here," Alexis said. "For all her decency, Strasser can't possibly sit back when suspected terrorists appear. There will be a bounty for sure and a hefty one."

"Every fraggin' bunter will be after them."

"Everyone but one group," Phillix said. "Congratulations on becoming licensed bounty hunters."

"Speaking of which—and knowing it's not legally binding—any word on *our* bounty?"

"You have a bounty on you?" Brianna asked.

"More of an order to kill than a bona fide bounty."

"Because of the escape from slavery?"

"That, the deaths of several Ieoni and Qlan crew, and commandeering this ship."

"Your bounty is still active, though the Sunfists have taken precedence," Phillix stated. "I might stick around here for a while," Phillix suggested.

"Not much happening back there?" Bradyn inquired.

"On the contrary, there's half a galaxy of activity. There's the continuing fallout of the Surreal Tourney debacle. No one seems to be able to locate Malazi Phakani. The remnants of the board are trying to get back into the emperor's good graces, and there's a proclamation that they will no longer have armament stored in waystations.

"People are wondering what happened to the *Romulus* and the *Remus*, since they've been absent for so long. Our friends on the *Iconic* are slowly dealing with the vastness of the ship. Danders and Co. are still having a bit of trouble with the freedom faction, but nothing too problematic for now."

"Captain, there is a message from the Juggernauts," Torg commed.

Alexis acknowledged and rolled out of her bunk to activate the comp at her desk. They had returned to Quint-wil spaceport. She was in a surprisingly good mood, knowing Phillix was nearby.

"Congratulations, Scrappers. The Buntress is no more. Too bad you didn't get the hand, but the fire damage will have to do. So, while not exactly what the Challenge stipulated, the result is the same. Feel free to pop into the Lair anytime, your home away from home. We've an opportunity we'd like to discuss. Vlad out."

She let a smirk cross her face. Letting the 'conspiracy to murder' slide had turned out better than expected.

"At least we're not at war with half the bunters," she commented later when she let the others read the message over their breakfasts.

"What the frag are they up to now?" Sabrya queried. "Whatever it is, I'm up for it and hope to catch them in their own fraggin' trap."

"They probably want to check out the *Malleus*, see what she's capable of in a fight."

"There's also an update from the CQLO regarding new bounties. We could get back to earning our keep," Bradyn commented.

"So, we go over the list while heading back to the Lair, see what the boys want—probably say no—then knuckle down, get a few more bounties under our belts... and live a little."

"Hmm... we can but try."

CHAPTER TWENTY-FOUR

WITH BRIANNA REMAINING SAFELY aboard the *Malleus* with Torg, they ventured to the Colosseum to meet with the Juggernauts. Phillix notified them that Strasser was currently in her planetside office, so they made an impromptu visit first.

"What do you know of the Bukshoga Qlan?" Alexis asked the Imperial officer. All three were invited to sit as the officer cleared her desk.

Strasser sat back and steepled her fingers. "They're a crime syndicate lurking on the fringes of the empire with a tad too much influence, and it's getting bigger. Why do you ask?"

"How much of a background check did you do on us?" Bradyn wriggled to get comfortable in his chair.

"Minimal. None of your names red-flagged anything Imperial. I'm not naïve enough to think those opting to come here are saints, but I keep an eye on those with a violent history and those the empire is interested in. With minimal ability to do anything, I let sleeping dogs lie until they snap."

She stood and stretched, then went to a cabinet and returned with a bottle and several small glasses.

"And yes, I'm aware of Sabrya's history, but I also have other sources of data to go by, not only the official word." The officer poured a drink for each of them. "I know I keep saying it, but with the limited resources at my disposal, I can't lock up everyone the empire has a grudge against. I do what I can until I have to act. Treading water and collating data. What happens if and when the empire takes over is anyone's guess."

Sabrya looked at her when she mentioned her history. "Just so you know, the fraggin' empire was usin' mercs to enslave Grindstone workers."

"And as I said, I have other data to go by. I don't condone what some factions of the military do or who they work with. As far as I'm concerned, nothing you've done, there or here, has caused me to think any less of you."

They quietly sipped their drinks while Strasser resumed her seat. "What brought up the Qlan?"

"We believe we know why there was a hit on Brianna." Alexis was careful about the information she revealed. "It concerns her witnessing a Qlan member here, in Quint-wil."

The Imperial officer nodded. "Bound to happen, I guess. Care to pass on any details?"

"Giono Halmar Shobianu, but he was born in Sector 10 on Frallon in 5088 as Rubern Shorak."

Strasser made notes on her tablet. "If this pans out, I'd be interested to know where your info comes from."

"Like you, we have various sources. However—" Alexis paused, knowing the next part might not be so pleasant "—it might be best to keep the name to your most trusted people."

"As in not telling fraggin' Klauff." Sabrya put her empty glass down and reached for the bottle.

Strasser's stylus stopped. "Why? I take any accusations of impropriety by my staff seriously, but he is a pen-pushing pest with high-ranking parents."

"Anything we have is circumstantial at best..."

"Go on."

"He's been seen chumming up with the Juggernauts, and he also seems acquainted with Giono," Alexis stated.

"Not trying to disparage his reputation, you understand," Bradyn tried to quell any argument. "We thought it unusual, that's all."

Strasser sighed. "The way we're chatting and drinking now?"

"That's one way of looking at it." Alexis shrugged. "And one appearance with Giono could be purely coincidental, but not three."

"Okay then." Strasser put the stylus down and sat back. "I'll keep him out of the loop in this instance."

Alexis' armpad buzzed. "We have ourselves another appointment with the Juggernauts."

"New friends? You're back in their good books?"

"For now." Alexis stood.

Bradyn pushed his chair in. "Reckon they're just chumming up to us to glean our secrets."

"Keep your enemies close..." The officer nodded. "Fair strategy. It's what I do." She winked.

With the weapons suppressor activated, the three *Malleus* crewmembers emerged from the lift into the Lair.

This time, since it was still daylight, the area was almost empty, except for a pair of Juggernauts and the barman. When he saw them, he anticipated their order and brought the drinks over as they approached the other bunters.

"Welcome, Scrappers," Vlad greeted them. "Have a seat. Been out and about?"

Sabrya took a long draft of her Starburst and smacked her lips. She gave him the briefest of looks then burped loudly.

Verne moved to the opposite chair, so he was looking directly at her.

"We prefer it in space." Alexis sat back and sipped her drink. "Out of everyone's way and staying out of trouble."

"Just looking for it, I bet." Vlad chuckled.

"You never know until you do," Bradyn offered.

"So then... what of this proposition?" Alexis swirled her whiskey.

"Straight to it." Vlad nodded. "I like it."

"Yeah, that way we can get back into the fraggin' black quicker."

The lead Juggernaut scowled at her, then focused on Alexis. "You've seen the list of the new bounties?"

Alexis nodded.

"What we have isn't on it, and it's a beauty," Vlad continued. "Enough for both to equally share."

"Interesting. I have to ask... why us? We're new here. Relatively untried and tested."

"New is good. You haven't any fixed allegiance to the others."

"Is that a concern?" Bradyn asked. "Your group's miles ahead of anyone on the leaderboard."

"Points are one thing; ability is another beast."

"You're sayin' being top of the leaderboard doesn't make you that good?" Sabrya smirked.

"No!" Verne spat. "We're better than all of you! That's a ridiculous thing to say."

"Your bro basically fraggin' said it." Sabrya finished her drink and put the glass down. "I'll fraggin' explain it to you in simpler terms if you like." She blew the wafting vapors from her glass towards Verne, making him lean back quickly.

Verne was about to stand. "Chill, Verne." Vlad stopped him from rising. "I mean the bounty we're after will be hard for us but doable. Add the Scrappers to the mix, and it should be easy enough."

Sabrya's second drink arrived. "Want a sip? No hard feelin's."

Verne frowned and shook his head.

"Want to give us the rundown on this bounty?" Alexis got them back on track.

"If you're in, we'll send you the details."

Alexis thought about it. "Can't promise we're in then. We're not going into anything blindly."

"No problem," Verne said. "We'll be there to help."

"Help isn't the issue. Like Vlad said, ability is another beast. You know what you're up against, and you've already stated it'd be difficult for you, yet you want us to join you without that info? Maybe you need to speak to others. I'm not in that much of a rush to risk my ship and crew on your whim or to climb the leaderboard."

"There's very little risk," Vlad insisted.

"Good. Send the data, and I'll give you my answer once I've gone over it."

"I'm curious. If it's not on the bounty report, where did the bounty come from?" Bradyn asked. "CQLO promulgates the official bounties... so, is this official? If not, from what source? Who pays?"

"He's got a point," Alexis agreed. "Do they pay on unofficial bounties? Does the top of the leaderboard get preferential treatment?"

"This could make you guys," Vlad said encouragingly. "Then you'll know all about preferential treatment."

"Seems like they're almost beggin' us to play," Sabrya muttered.

"Beg?" Verne stood up. "We don't need to beg."

Sabrya remained sitting, unphased. "But here we are..."

"We're offering it to you out of courtesy," Vlad said placatingly.

Verne spoke to him in a quiet but gruff tone and stared daggers at Sabrya.

"Have I hurt his feelings?" she asked.

Vlad scowled.

"Tell you what—" Sabrya put her elbow on the table, arm up "—I challenge big boy to an arm wrestle. I'll apologize if he beats me."

"Bet she's not heard of Itora." Verne grinned. Vlad grabbed his shoulder to get his attention, but Verne had already nodded. "I'll try not to hurt you."

"You can try as hard as you want."

Alexis and Bradyn shook their heads at each other and ordered more drinks.

"Or, you could just send us the details," Alexis repeated.

"Nah. Your girl made the challenge. She can't back out now."

"Actually, I was giving *you* the option."

"Left arm though." Verne's grin was sly. If he thought he'd upset her in any way, he was disappointed.

Sabrya moved her bottle and swapped arms without hesitation. "Fine by me."

The large Juggernaut sat and put his arm out. The two clasped hands.

"You can hang onto the table if you want," Sabrya offered.

Her opponent shook his head.

"On my mark," Vlad said. "Ready?"

Both nodded.

"Mark."

Instantly, Verne tensed, his arms bulging with muscle.

Sabrya's strength, on the other hand, didn't only come from muscle, but from her auged nanites.

Slowly, Verne pulled her arm down, but it was a struggle.

Then Sabrya reversed the situation. She watched the surprised look on his face as he realized his competitor had much greater strength than he had imagined.

Verne started sweating. Try as he might, he could barely budge an inch.

"Come on, Verne," Vlad coaxed. "She's a grown girl. You don't need to be soft on her."

The big man's arms started shaking with fatigue and strain. Verne's eyes briefly glanced at her calm face. He took a deep breath and tried harder. When he grabbed the table, his arm moved incrementally, but Sabrya stopped him. She reached across to her bottle and took a long swig, followed by another burp.

"How about we call it a draw?" Alexis offered.

"You can't back out now," Vlad replied, perplexed as to why his big brother was toying with the blue-haired woman.

Alexis shrugged. "Sab, can we end this? Just don't break his arm."

She nodded. "Last chance, blondie? Draw?"

He shook his head, unwilling to back down.

"Like he said, ability is another beast." Sabrya's arm slowly and steadily pushed his down to the table and held it there for a few seconds before she released him. "I guess you've not heard of Grindstone?"

Verne rubbed his arm and shook his head, looking ruefully at the warrior.

Vlad glared at his brother for a moment, stunned at the loss, before pushing his chair back noisily. "I'll send the details. Give me an answer by morning." He stood and left. Verne followed, favoring his arm.

"Care to explain what that was about?" Alexis asked her, unimpressed.

"They were annoyin'. Just wanted to slap them down a notch."

"You did, without a doubt. Not sure you did us any favors, though."

The trip back to the ship was subdued. Sabrya went to the holodeck to burn off her annoyance.

"What happened?" Brianna asked when she saw the blue-haired stormcloud stomp down the central passage.

"Just our warrior woman venting." Alexis gave a brief description of the meeting.

"She probably needs to get laid," Brianna surmised.

"Don't we all?" Bradyn muttered as he walked away. "I'll be in my workshop," he said louder.

"So, how did the other meeting go?"

"I understand this can't be easy for you. We'll try to get through it as quickly as we can." Alexis and Brianna made their way to the lounge as she brought the reporter up to date.

"Oh, it's not so bad. Getting to know a bunter group in detail has its merits."

In the lounge, they sat opposite each other across the table.

"The Juggs say they've a bounty, but it's not on any of the lists," Alexis said.

"Can't say I've heard of that before. If it's not an official bounty…"

"I agree. Sounds more like a hit, and anyone taking it would be criminals. So, two things come to mind—they're trying to frame us, or they have another surprise up their sleeves."

"Do we know who it is?"

"Still waiting for them to send it through. In the meantime, I've been remiss with the Maidens and their offer to tour their ship. Want to tag along if they're still around?"

Brianna nodded.

Alexis sent them a message and got a quick response.

"Hi, team," she commed across the ship. "Anyone wanting to tour the Maiden's ship, you've got ten minutes."

"Welcome to the *Raquech*," Fyona said proudly. "You'll understand, like the *Malleus*, a girl's got to keep her secrets." She looked pointedly at the Buntress. "We might not want you dead, but we also don't want our ship all over the paper."

"Not a word will be written or recorded." Brianna pulled a glove from her pocket and slipped it on, then pocketed her glasses.

"How old is she?" Bradyn asked, looking keenly at the clean and streamlined interior. There was a bit of a shuffle so the stocky engineer could carry out his examination.

"As far as we can tell, about ninety years old. We got it at auction, though, and we're still paying it off. Another year of good bounties, and she'll be ours outright."

"There's an auction house out here?" Alexis looked surprised.

"We can't all fraggin' steal 'em."

"It's from the commercial arm of the CQLO."

"Of course." Alexis rolled her eyes. "They have the two ships we captured to sell."

"And, no doubt, after a bit of a diagnosis and refurb, they'll sell them off." As Fyona spoke, they walked around the interior in the company of two of the crew.

"Just the two of you here?" Brianna noted the absence of the other crewmembers.

Fyona led them upstairs. "Doryne and Quela are off getting supplies. We don't all have the luxury of our own hydroponics garden."

"Or a botanist," Glyn added.

"Heading out?" Alexis asked.

"Lucky you called when you did." Fyona nodded. "You saw the list of the new bounties?"

"We did," Alexis replied. "But the Jugheads have something different for us, apparently."

"A partnership? With them?"

Alexis shook her head. "They seem to think so, but I made no promises. They're being coy with the details."

Fyona looked at Glyn before replying. "Do you think they know about Brianna?"

"Hard to say. They seem pretty oblivious about some things."

"Put it this way. You ladies know my fraggin' history?" She continued at their nods. "I challenged Verne to an arm wrestle. I reckon his arm's still hurtin'."

"He accepted?" Fyona and Quela laughed. "I would've loved to have seen that."

Sabrya grinned. "He's not too fraggin' bright."

"Even so, I don't want to underestimate them," Alexis said. "They didn't get to where they are today by being totally inept."

"Reckon they had a fraggin' helpin' hand, though."

The bridge was smaller than that of the *Malleus*, and Alexis took a few moments to admire it.

"Bradyn, we need a refurb," she said.

The engineer shook his head slowly. "I'll put it on my schedule."

"If your ship is what, four centuries old, why not sell it and get another, newer one?" Fyona asked.

"Everyone underestimates her. She's built to last, though she's not pretty."

"Maybe one day we'll see her in action."

"Maybe. By the way, I'm curious about your name?"

"Ion Maidens? That's simple enough. It's because we have an ion cannon. We fire it at low power—a hit will cut a ship's electronics, like an EMP. We then hit them with our tech and military expertise... albeit not to the level of Sabrya. She's a platoon all on her own."

Alexis' armpad buzzed. She gave it a cursory glance. "They have to be bloody kidding!"

"What is it?" Bradyn asked.

She showed them the message.

CHAPTER TWENTY-FIVE

"THE FRAGGIN' Sunfists? They're the new target?"

Back on the *Malleus*, they went over the details of the Juggernaut's message. The plan was to hit the Sunfists when they arrived in the Quadrant.

"How the frag do they know where and when they are going to jump?"

"We should send them a message. Find out what the frag's goin' on and why they're comin' here."

"I agree." Alexis called the bridge. "Torg, do you have comms with Phillix?"

"We have an open channel," the droid responded. "I have signaled him."

"Phill, when you get this, can you give us the status of the Sunfists?"

They didn't have to wait long for his reply.

"I can track them, of course, but then, I do have a unique perspective. The only other ways of following a ship in hyper are an extremely good AI or a tracking device."

"So, they've been compromised?"

"All the more fraggin' reason to message them."

"It will take me a moment to hail them."

"Must be great, having those resources to call on," Brianna said.

Alexis considered. "Definitely, but when you remember Phill used to be a living man and a friend, I'd rather have him as a person than as an AI." She went to the bridge to receive the call on the encrypted channel.

Sabrya joined her.

"*Mulan* to *Malleus*. What a coincidence. Is that you, Sabby? How are you all?"

It was only an audio signal. The static was minimal, but getting a visual signal through the vast distance and through hyper could be difficult.

"Hey, Noma. Not a coincidence. Where are you?"

"Deep in the gray."

"No, I meant on your fraggin' ship. Are you secure?"

"My quarters. It's late. What's this about?"

"We reckon you're bein' tracked by the fraggin' Qlan."

"What? How the frak are they doing that?"

"Have you any new gear or personnel?"

"Well, yes to both. We've had some interesting tim—"

"Noma, Alexis here. Let's keep this brief. I'd go over your ship, stores, and personnel thoroughly. There's a welcoming party waiting for you."

"You know where we are?"

"We don't, but others here know where you'll be. We think they're being fed info by the Qlan, which is why you need to check everything, everywhere, and everyone."

Sabrya moved closer to the mic. "Why the frag are you comin' here in the first place?"

"Thought a slight reprieve was in order, and we'd encourage you to come back. As I said, it's been interesting since you left."

"Once you've checked everything, change course. Call us when it's done. Out."

Alexis sat back, thinking. "Phill, remember when you took care of Malazi?"

"Of course."

"When Noma gives us the all clear, are you able to reroute them?"

"I can control any ship in hyper."

Scary. "Okay then. How about bringing them to the waystation? We can catch up with them there."

"Consider it done. I'll get to work on it—"

"But not before they contact us."

"Roger."

Alexis turned to Sabrya. "They want you back."

"Us, I reckon. Too hot for them alone, but together..."

The captain looked dubious. "I don't know. While not much, we do have a fresh start here."

"Which will mean nothin' once the Qlan gets here... and they'll come. The Quad's ripe for the pickin'. I'm surprised they're not here already."

"It wouldn't be easy to start a new business enterprise, especially covertly, but they must have been here before us if Briana's recordings of Giono are accurate. Who knows what went on before that?"

"*Malleus* to *Dominator*."

"Vlad here. What's up?"

The Juggernauts had finally shared a rendezvous time and location.

"It's half an hour after the scheduled arrival." Alexis lounged back in the chair on the bridge. "How good's your intel?" She already had confirmation the *Mulan* was safely docked at the waystation.

The *Dominator* was several kilometers off their port bow. It was slightly larger than the *Malleus* but more streamlined and newer. While they waited, she ran the data Phillix had found on the *Dominator's* specs. Fore and aft had Ylonda armor plating. There were two weapons arrays—twin Orpenus plasma cannons in front and Slithosa Ion Cannon Mk3s in the rear. Their jump drives were something Bradyn could only dream about—twin Cerbrinka-Zaners Mk2s. She recalled him saying the *Mulan* had a Mk1.

"Intel has always been ace," Vlad said. "Give 'em a bit more time. They probably had some trouble."

"Trouble? In fraggin' hyperspace? May as well pack up now," Sabrya muttered.

"Keep your bra on, Blue." Vlad chuckled. "This's worth the wait. You'll see."

"That's what they all say." Sabrya laughed. "And they always disappoint."

Alexis cut the link and stood to stretch.

"Hey, what the frag?" Sabrya pointed to the scope.

"You have an incoming vessel," Phillix stated, sounding surprised.

"That's fraggin' obvious!" Sabrya vented as sat up in her chair.

The ship now materializing was unknown to them, but it was four times their size. The many weapons arrays were visible. It was a warship in every sense of the word.

"Who are they Phillix?"

"I cannot say at the moment..."

"You what? Never mind. Later." She turned to the droid by the weapons console. "Torg, load the launchers and get ready with those cannons."

"Cannons are warming up. It will take seventy seconds to load the launchers."

"Bradyn, are we good to jump if need be?"

"We are, but I'll head back there anyway."

"Sab. Your reflexes are faster than mine, even Torg's. If that thing opens up, we're jumping."

"Not stealthin'?" she whispered.

"Too late for that now. A missile will still hit—"

"Hey, *Malleus*. Meet our new partners." Vlad's image came on the screen. His grin stretched from ear to ear.

"You've got some very big friends," Alexis said. It was the first thing that came to mind.

Sabrya couldn't resist a jibe. "You know, where I come from, that's an indication of your own inadequacies."

"And where exactly do you come from... Reaper?"

"Finally! I was startin' to think I'd lost my infamy." She shrugged at Alexis' look. "You know my old name, so you know where I come from and what I'm capable of."

"And so do my buddies. They are very keen to catch up, but they also think you've got some interesting gear that would be good for us." He nodded at something said off-screen.

"It takes a certain type of man to admit he likes girl toys," Sabrya teased.

"Well, Vlad, if you'd said you needed help, we could have worked something out. What do you need help with?"

Sabrya laughed. "Ya know, with bein' top of the leaderboard, you'd think they wouldn't need our help."

"Ah." Alexis slapped her forehead. "What was that I heard about points and ability?"

Sabrya nodded and made a display of rolling her eyes. "Somethin' like 'you could have lots of points, but no ability.' Now we know for certain."

Alexis turned back to Vlad. "I can see why you need big friends, now." She smiled to cover her nervousness.

"Okay, okay. Enough chitchat. My buddies here—"

"Haven't been introduced." Alexis turned to view the Qlan commander. "Quite rude, since they think they know who we are."

"They know quite a lot about you," Vlad persisted.

"Blah-fraggin'-blah. Captain, all I'm hearin' are words." Sabrya winked at Alexis.

A new, deeper voice came over the comm, but there was no image. "Heed these words, then. I am Gravid Xionus, Commander of the Qlan battlecruiser *Invictus*. You would do well to surrender before we annihilate you and your vessel."

"You see, I know you won't annihilate us for fear of destroying this wonderful toy you boys in the Bukshoga Qlan dreamt up," Alexis retorted, mind churning at how the hell they got themselves a battlecruiser without anyone knowing. Crime does pay!

"So, you do know who we are. Good. That should make things easier."

"Tell you what—" Alexis stood and leaned on the counter "—run back to the black hole you came from, and we promise not to get too offended. Sorry to say, Vlad, that alliance you were after... it isn't going to work. But I'll offer you the same deal before I unleash your worst nightmares."

"She's bluffing, Vlad. Like Blue did." They heard Verne in the background.

"And how'd that work out for ya, Vernie? How's the fraggin' arm?"

"You have thirty seconds to comply," Alexis warned as she cut the comms. "Helmets up. Torg, the moment they twitch, open fire. Let's hope our armed ship's good enough. That cruiser looks damn tough. No doubt a thick hull." Her voice changed tone slightly as the nanotech helmet and faceplate formed around her head.

"AM doesn't care about thick hulls," Bradyn called. "I got the bots here to put a couple on the rear launchers."

"Good. What's on the front?"

"Amor-piercing and HE. Two of each."

"They have weapons lock on us," Torg stated mildly. "They have fired. Launching countermeasures."

"Probably warning shots, but I'm not taking any chances. You have two targets. Fire. Unload the lot, and jump."

"Firing both plasma canons and launching missiles."

Instantly they felt the slight rumble as the missiles launched and the pulsing as the canons began a barrage on each vessel.

The two enemy vessels drifted to the starboard of their view as Sabrya hit the jump sequence. "I've thrown in a couple of evasive maneuvers!"

The *Malleus* shook, and the lights dimmed when they were struck by several plasma cannon bolts. The board lit up as alarms buzzed.

"Torg, keep firing the canons," Alexis commanded. "Reload missiles."

"I've programmed for only a short jump," Phillix's voice came on.

"The bots are on the way to assess and repair," the droid reported. "Fifteen percent loss of hull integrity starboard aft. Delta cargo hold is depressurizing. Blast doors activated."

"Keep the external cams on them. I want to see what we can do. Cloak us, as well."

"What if they survive?" Bradyn asked. "The stealth tech will be confirmed."

"They're not going to survive. None of them are. We came here to get away from this. They brought this on themselves."

"I'm proud of you, girl!" Sabrya was watching her board. "Missiles inbound!"

"Jumping in three... two...one..." Phillix counted.

Their view blinked into the kaleidoscopic miasma of hyperspace.

"Captain, with your permission, I will go an assist in repairs."

"Granted."

"Let's play back the last of the cam feed," Sabrya said as the droid left the bridge.

They saw several of their missiles hit as the image turned gray.

"Frag it. We don't know their damage," she voiced her disappointment.

"Can't be helped, but at least we gave them something to think about, and only a couple of their bolts hit. How are we doing, Bradyn?"

"Glad we're wearing these suits." His image came on the monitor. The engineering space was a bit of a mess. "One of those stray bolts hit some of the piping. We've a lovely mix of toxic gases here."

"How long before we can return?" Alexis was looking at the scope, which showed their current location compared to the previous.

"You want to head back?" Bradyn questioned.

"I do," she said firmly. "I told you they're not going to survive, and I'm guessing their egos will think we ran, so they won't be expecting us."

"Yeah, their brains are the same size as their balls." Sabrya nodded.

"Give me ten minutes." Bradyn turned off the vid.

"Good. Long enough for them to think we've bolted." With nothing else to do, Alexis lowered her helmet and went to the lounge to see Brianna. "How are you holding up?" she asked when she stepped inside.

The reporter was belted into one of the chairs, looking pale and nervous. "What the hell was that all about?"

"Follow me, and I'll tell you." Sabrya helped her undo the restraints, and, together, they headed down the stairs.

"Where are we going?"

"We had an unexpected visitor—which I'm still waiting for

Phill to explain—so you'd better get into one of our suits. Should've done this before this started. My bad."

"Didn't we just jump?"

"We did." Alexis nodded. "But we're going back."

"Seriously?" The reporter looked incredulous.

"We have to. They know who we are, and what we've got. We can't afford to let them get away."

"Who are *they*?"

"The Qlan. Here's that scoop you wanted." From her personal wardrobe, she handed the reporter the spare suit. "Can't let you keep this, you understand, but you'll get to feel what the Kimichi Mk8 is like."

Brianna held it like it was gold as she took it to the cabin they had assigned her.

"It'll basically dress you itself." Alexis walked with her. "Just strip beforehand so the coolant works properly. It needs skin contact."

Alexis left her and continued aft to check the area. The blast doors were still down, and there wasn't much to see through the thick window. By the time she returned, Brianna was opening her door.

"This is amazing!" she gushed. "Is there a helmet?"

"When it's programmed, it can be voice-activated, but in your case, just touch that tab." She indicated an orange button.

Brianna's squeal of delight faded as the helmet and face shield enclosed her head. She tapped the button to remove it.

"Captain, the bots have finalized the worst of the repairs."

"On my way." She headed to the bridge, and Brianna started to follow her. "Later, depending on how this goes, I'll invite you to the bridge to see what's going on. I'm sure you understand."

"You'll be busy kicking ass. Good."

Leaving Brianna in the lounge, Alexis strode the last few meters to the bridge. "How's engineering?"

Bradyn commed, "All clear here."

Alexis took her seat. "We'll keep the blast doors down. Are all launchers loaded?"

"Affirmative, Captain. Same configuration as before," Torg replied.

"Phill, you've been quiet," Alexis noted.

"I've been investigating the anomaly of the Qlan's surprise arrival."

"And?"

"I'm at a loss. A form of signal or drive suppressor I guess."

"Could be useful. Want to jump us back?"

"Sure. We'll be there in fifty seconds. It doesn't look like they've moved, so we'll appear behind them and move between both ships."

"Even better. Helmets up everyone," she commed. "Brianna, you on?"

"I-I am."

"Good. Listen only, and don't talk or question, otherwise, I'll mute your comms." Alexis turned to Sabrya. "Hyped?"

"I wouldn't have it any other way."

"If anyone survives, we'll need to go across and deal with them personally."

"I was hopin' you'd say that."

Torg returned and took his place by the weapon controls.

"Twenty seconds," Phill said.

"Warm up the cannons. Remember Torg, if they twitch…"

"I will launch everything. Aye, Captain."

They watched the timer and the screen.

"Maintain radio silence. Passive sensors only." Alexis went cold as she double-checked they were still cloaked. She sighed with relief as normal space appeared.

Coming into view, still several kilometers distant, the two ships drifted, one dwarfing the other. There was little movement, other than the sections of hull scattered between them.

Incrementally, Alexis fired maneuvering thrusters to get

closer. It was a delicate operation to match the slow roll of the *Dominator*.

The *Invictus* had a large hole in the rear starboard quarter.

"Looks like anti-matter damage," Sabrya whispered. "Cool."

"We did some amazing targeting. Any communications?" Alexis asked Torg.

"Negative, Captain. I am detecting energy spikes, indicating power." A schematic of the *Invictus* appeared on a monitor. "Similar to when we first came upon the *Iconic*, the large ones are without doubt power sources—weapons, shields—whereas the smaller ones are likely combat suits. I can determine their hyperdrives are offline, but not their sub-light engines."

"So, they're not going anywhere fast. Good." Alexis counted twenty-three smaller spikes. "And the *Dominator*?"

The battlecruiser image faded, as the smaller ship came on screen. There were four small spikes; only two showed indications of movement.

"We could jump across and get in via that lovely big hole."

"Won't they see our movement, like we can see the shrapnel?"

"Not if we get really close, like, next to them."

"Risky, especially with the drift."

"You say risky; I hear fraggin' fun times."

"Of course, you do, coz you're not right in the head. Just the way we want you to be. Torg, get us in as close as you can," Alexis stated.

"Aye, Captain."

"Bradyn. I need you on the bridge."

"On my way."

With bated breath, she watched as they closed in on the damaged bunter vessel.

As Torg compensated for spin, several metallic pings could be heard along the hull, some louder than others.

"Shrapnel?" Alexis asked.

"I concur," the droid said.

Several minutes later, the *Malleus* slowed.

"Brianna, how are you holding up?" Alexis asked.

"F-fine. Can I get a drink?"

"Sure, but strap yourself back in straight away."

Alexis continued to watch the screen and monitors, noting who was moving and where. It looked like two of the Juggernauts were on an upper level dealing with a problem, while two others were separate and not moving.

"Any chance those two are still alive?" She tapped the monitor, indicating the two Juggernauts in the lower section.

"No life signs, Captain," Torg reported

She kept watching the others until Sabrya returned, Bradyn behind her.

"What's happening?" Bradyn asked, eyes shifting from monitor to viewport. "We did that?" He pointed to the gaping hole in the battlecruiser's hull. "Told you AM doesn't care about armor-plating."

"Sabrya and I are going to board the *Dominator*. We want you here as backup. Get Brianna away if things look bad. This isn't her fight."

"No, but it is mine as much as yours." Bradyn turned to her.

"If we can't take out the Juggernauts quickly, the *Invictus* will probably be aware of us. We can't let them succeed. They know—or strongly suspect—we can cloak, and they no doubt have a plan to capture—not destroy—the *Malleus,* so we'll use that to our advantage."

"Well then, to optimize our success, I'm coming, too. Torg can unleash the missiles and get Brianna out of here."

"No—"

"We've come this far. Don't I deserve to finish it?"

Alexis looked from one crew member to another.

"Sucks to be fraggin' captain, Captain."

"Fine! Torg, if we don't return, unleash everything we've got at that battlecruiser, and then you are ordered to destroy the stealth shield generators. No one can get their hands on it. Understood?"

"Affirmative, Captain."

"Phillix. If things don't work out, jump us to the Fortress and report to Strasser. Tell her what happened here. Got it?"

"Yes, Alexis. You can count on me."

Alexis kept her thoughts to herself as she looked back at the monitor. There was little change in the movements on the *Dominator*. "Let's go and get some weapons."

"Frag yeah!" Sabrya whooped as she raced downstairs, followed by the others at a more sedate pace.

When Alexis walked through the lounge, she paused and spoke to Brianna. "No doubt you heard? You may as well head up to the bridge. Most of the controls are locked but best not touch anything. You might kill us or yourself."

Brianna nodded. Her face looked pale even through the faceplate. "I'll see you all again, I'm sure."

Alexis smiled, nodding. "Of course. But just in case, I've made plans to keep you safe. Torg and Phillix will look after you. Relax and enjoy the ride. I'm sure you'll get some good stories out of this." She turned to head downstairs.

"And this cloak thing?" Brianna asked.

Stopping, Alexis looked back at her. "Best to be forgotten. Believe me, it's too risky for anyone if word gets out about it."

"Is that why the Qlan is here?"

"Mostly. Let's continue this discussion when—if—we get back."

CHAPTER TWENTY-SIX

"YOU'RE all adept with the breacher, the gutpuncher, and various pistols, but we've not used this lovely beast before, except in simulation, so I'll go over it again." Sabrya methodically pointed to the various parts of the add-on weapon. "Your shoulder-mounted mini-launcher. A mag of six mini HE-missiles sits across the back of the shoulder. As long as you're five meters away from any impacts/boom-booms, your suit should be enough protection. Activated by voice or tab, beware when in use, this unit will rise a hand-width above your shoulder. Since we're all high-G, we shouldn't need to brace, but in zero-g, or flight mode, a launch will spin you like crazy."

"That's drocking amazing," Bradyn noted.

"Reckon so?" Sabrya shrugged. "Thought you'd know more about physics than me."

"I do, but I meant you didn't swear once in all that. Surely that's a record?"

"Frag off." She punched his chest. "Everyone *fraggin'* got it?"

Both nodded with a grin.

"Let's fraggin' dance." Sabrya turned to the door.

"The ol' *Malleus* two-step," Bradyn muttered.

The trio stood on the edge of the airlock. The *Dominator* loomed ten meters away. Behind them, the backdrop of stars moved as both ships slowly twirled around each other.

"It looks more like a waltz," Alexis offered quietly.

"Let's up the fraggin' beat. Ready? On me," she said at their nods. Deftly, she jumped from the *Malleus* dock toward the dark opening that was coming into view. She used her suit's thrusters to match the spin. The rupture in the hull opened into what looked to be a storage compartment, now empty, which would explain the many crate fragments drifting nearby.

"Your suits should be okay, but watch those edges for snags," Sabrya warned as they moved closer. She grabbed hold of a section of the hull and waited for the others to do the same.

"We'll deal with the live crew first, then check on the others," Alexis ordered. She climbed in carefully after the warrior woman. "Any change, Torg?"

"Negative. Two unmoving spikes, two moving, same location."

"Let me know if their status changes."

Sabrya landed with the aid of her mag boots. "Zero-g. Remember what I said about the launcher." She swept her helmet light across the bulkhead. There was a hatch a couple of meters ahead, but no handle on their side.

"Hey, big boy. Reckon that fraggin' goes against union regs?"

Bradyn moved closer. "Only if it's a compartment used for habitation or manual entry, but judging from the size—"

"Though fascinating, can we please discuss ship design another time?" Alexis suggested.

In short order, Sabrya used the breacher to cut around the hatch, then her blades to lever the still-hot metal aside, catching it before it struck the deck or bulkhead.

"Captain, two figures are moving toward your location. My estimate is they will be there in forty-three seconds."

"Come to the party, boys," Sabrya muttered. She stuck her head out to check the corridor.

"Could they be heading toward the unmoving figures?" Alexis asked.

"In all probability. They will need to pass you to get there."

"Boss, how about you and big boy move back into the corner, and I'll wait over there." Sabrya pointed to an intersection.

"Okay then. Be quick." Alexis dowsed her light and readied her gutpuncher, as did Bradyn.

"Better not fraggin' shoot me," she warned as she glided through the gap. She was in position eight seconds later.

They waited in the darkness. A short time later, torchlight played sporadically along the corridor. As the Juggernauts passed the hatch, one stopped then reached out to the other. They turned to view the new hole, and the circles of light moved along the deck, closing in on the corner where Alexis and Bradyn were hiding.

Suddenly, the pair of bunters were hurled against the bulkhead and their faceplates smashed. There was rapid decompression and a spray of blood before both suits went limp.

"Done. Thanks for the distraction."

Alexis and Bradyn came forward.

"Better I do this. It's what I trained for," the warrior said gruffly, then her voice softened. "You don't want it to be you. Stay here."

Three minutes later, Sabrya returned.

"Just confirmed, no survivors. Shall we do a quick search? Split up and see what we can find?"

"Torg, status?"

"No change here. Minimal movement from the *Invictus*. From the lack of activity, I conclude our presence is still unknown to them, and they are concentrating on internal repairs."

Slowly, they combed the ship for anything useful. Alexis went to the bridge and found a few portable hard drives, and Bradyn made his way to the engineering space to look over the engines.

When they regrouped, they saw that Sabrya had a load of weapons.

"I see that look. You can fraggin' never have enough. Bradyn, we might need a bigger armory."

The trio floated back to the *Malleus* airlock and returned to the bridge a couple of minutes later.

"That went well?" Brianna greeted them. She had found the whiskey and had a glass ready for each of them.

"Well enough." Alexis picked up her glass after putting the hard drives down. "This is a bad idea, though." She raised her glass and took a quick drink.

"The Juggernauts aren't a fraggin' problem anymore. You can go home, Bri." Sabrya clinked the reporter's glass in celebration.

"They're…"

"Dead. They were goin' to kill us, have no fraggin' doubt." Sabrya drained her glass and looked at Alexis. "What's next?"

Alexis sipped her drink, deep in her thoughts. "Next? We tackle the *Invictus*."

"It's a big ship with at least twenty-plus experienced crew," Bradyn pointed out.

"I didn't say we'd do it easily. Not without help." Alexis finished her drink and headed for the bridge. "Torg, can you hack into the *Dominator*?"

"Once I establish a hard connection, affirmative."

"Happy to assist," Phillix offered.

"Good. Get the bots to arrange the connection. In the meantime, design a program so it begins unloading whatever ordnance it has left into the Qlan vessel, especially its drives, weapons, and comms. If we're lucky, and they're unprepared, it might even the odds."

"We could use that ordnance." Sabrya joined her on the bridge.

"And then we'd use it exactly the same way. This way, we're not the ones being shot at."

"Where will we be?" Bradyn asked as he joined them.

"On the sidelines, watching and waiting for a result. When it's over, we will move in and take care of the rest."

"There probably won't be much left of the *Dominator*. No novas..."

"That was never the issue." Alexis turned to Brianna in the doorway. "There might be a nice reward for that, though. What would it mean to you if you had exclusive footage of the Juggernauts taking down a Qlan battlecruiser?"

Brianna balked. "I could write my own ticket."

"You want to make the fraggin' Jugheads heroes?" Sabrya asked, perplexed.

"Not particularly, but are we after fame? We have the Buntress with us. No offense, Brianna. Knowing what it would cost her, how long do you expect her to keep quiet about this?"

Sabrya had no answer, knowing the only way to keep this silent was a permanent solution.

"I'm still for keeping a low profile, especially where the Qlan is involved. If that means the Juggernauts posthumously get recognition for it, that's a win in my book. Look what happened when we took out that weapons cache, the Sunfists got the credit, and look where it got them."

"There goes our hyperdrive upgrades." Bradyn grimaced.

"I'm going to assume the battlecruiser's drives..."

"I would say far too big."

"Let's hope the *Dominator*'s drives remain viable then. I gather they looked okay?"

"Repairable, yes, if we had a spacedock."

Alexis considered the options. "Okay, I put forward my suggestion, but given the circumstances, what are your ideas?"

Sabrya took a deep breath then exhaled. Thinking. "It's a fraggin' big ship."

"Torg, what's our ordnance like?"

"We have eight missiles remaining—three each HE and armor-piercing, two anti-matter."

"Can you target the already damaged sections to bypass the armor?"

"The vessel is motionless. I calculate an 87 percent success to hit."

"Let's look at that then. Program the *Dominator* as I suggested. We'll keep our own ordnance, just in case."

"Aye, Captain."

"Won't that make us a target?" Brianna questioned nervously.

"Our smart missiles can be programmed. When we were up against an imp... enemy ship, we launched the missiles with a programmed delay. By the time they activated, we had moved, and the ship didn't know where we were."

"Because you were cloaked?"

"Yes, but that has to remain a permanent secret. Word getting out—"

"I know. You said."

"And I meant it!" Alexis looked at her and then at Sabrya. "Okay then. Like before, if we're cloaked, hitting us will be extremely difficult. And, of course, we can always jump; they can't."

"Bradyn?"

"It worked last time, and the Cerbrinkas are very nice. I prefer your second option."

"You reckon the fraggin' Cerbrinkas are worth it?"

Bradyn replied with a forced smile. "I feel as much for the C-Z drives as you do for the Kimichis."

"Ah, well, frag that! Why didn't you say so? I'm with him. Let's save the *Dominator*!"

"Phillix, what do you think?" Alexis rolled her eyes at her two crew.

"Both plans are feasible, and both plans are good for different reasons. The Juggernauts don't become heroes, just victims of a very large invader. They gave their all, but it wasn't enough. However, we then arrive and take care of the rest. Bradyn gets his drives; the Qlan battlecruiser is destroyed. No doubt a thorough search will reveal much about the Qlan. That by itself would be worth it. If we're fortunate, and the *Invictus* has something to think about, they may not even detect our sub-light thrusters."

"What about the Sunfists?" Sabrya suggested. "They can help."

"We'll keep them out of it if we can. We're doing this because we're cloaked. They aren't, and I don't need them to know about it. Given the choice, I'm sure the *Invictus* will prioritize on what it can see."

"You do know the Sunfists are on our side?"

"Perhaps... but they are compromised. Look. The cloak is a tremendously advantageous bit of kit. The more people that know about it, the more risk others—the Imperials—get wind of it. We can't let that happen."

"You think the Sunfists want that?" Sabrya asked at the thought of her allies being untrustworthy.

"No, of course not, but I trust me more than I trust them."

"They did leave us behind when the Imperial dreadnaughts arrived," Bradyn reminded her.

"You faced the *Romulus* and *Remus*? That was you?" Brianna's jaw dropped.

"Another story for another time." Alexis sighed. Having a reporter on the ship was becoming a nuisance. However, she considered, the longer Brianna remained on the *Malleus*, the longer all this could be kept under wraps. "I need to eat. Torg, keep me informed of any Qlan progress."

"Aye, Captain."

"Phill, anything you can do to help would be appreciated."

"Of course."

Alexis stood and stretched before making her way to the lounge.

Brianna turned from the doorway and led the procession back to the lounge.

After consuming several protein bars, the crew sat and waited for the next phase. Sabrya drank whiskey, but Alexis and Bradyn declined and consumed water instead. Only Brianna shared a glass with the warrior.

"The programming is complete, and the cabling removed," Torg announced. "On your say so, the *Dominator* will open fire with everything it has left before it is destroyed."

"Good. And our missiles?"

"Target locked and programmed to activate in increments of two minutes after launch," Phillix stated. "I also gleaned quite a bit of intel from their comp."

"Great work. Both of you."

"Torg, take us out slowly." Alexis headed to the bridge, with the others following. She was about to stop Brianna but thought otherwise. She took her seat, as did Bradyn and Sabrya, with the reporter standing behind the warrior.

Alexis waited until the *Invictus* was five kilometers away. "Torg, activate the *Dominator*'s ordnance."

The *Malleus* continued as all the *Dominators*' missiles were deployed.

"That's it, Captain. All missile ordnance has been depleted."

"Very good." She tapped the controls to bring her ship

about in a wide arc. "Let's see how this plays out." Still cloaked, Alexis then cut the *Malleus'* drives and coasted closer.

They counted eight impacts on the *Invictus.*

She enlarged the images of the two ships on-screen for a detailed view, but it was only moments before they all witnessed the response. When it happened, it was spectacularly devastating.

The *Invictus* blossomed with each explosion. As expected, the battlecruiser returned fire at the only viable threat; two of the forward batteries targeted the *Dominator.*

With no ability to evade, the *Dominator* was struck many times. The vessel was already rolling, so much of the damage was to the underside of the hull.

Bradyn's hopes of salvaging the Cerbrinka-Zaners hyperdrive remained alive.

"Torg, when you can, scan and update on *Invictus* life signs." Alexis kept watching intently.

"I can only detect their energy spikes." As before, a schematic of the *Invictus* appeared on a monitor. "Weapons are still online; life support is offline, as are the hyperdrives. Hard to determine the number of personnel until we are closer, but there are indications of movement."

"Comms?"

"Offline also."

Alexis took a deep breath. "So, no call for help."

When the ships were a thousand meters apart, Torg added, "There are still twenty-six small energy spikes. Only eight of those appear to be moving, now."

Alexis turned the ship slowly to match their vector and speed. She decided to bring the *Malleus* in closer herself. *Better than sitting and waiting.*

"There are several access points," Sabrya said, observing the damaged hulk.

"Captain, I am picking up a very large energy surg—"

"Torg! Jump. Get us the frak out of here!" Alexis turned the *Malleus* away, full thrust, but she was only using sub-light drives. They wouldn't make it.

"What—" Brianna started in shock at the outburst.

"Fraggin' self-destruct. Nice."

"Nice? Are you ins—"

The viewport screens dimmed as the *Invictus* blossomed.

The *Malleus* rolled when the blast hit them side-on.

Brianna screamed when she was tossed down the stairs. The crew was strapped in. Alarms blared and lights blinked an angry red across the board. The moment the Kimichis detected toxic fumes or depressurization, the faceplates and helmets rapidly formed, and the inbuilt auto-docs kicked in.

"*Mulan* to *Malleus*. Come in. Where the frag are you?"

"You're sure they're here?" Noma asked Zintan again.

"Look at the damn readings yourself. That's definitely the *Malleus*' drive signature."

"Chillax, girl." Noma breathed away her frustration. "Just can't damn see them."

They kept scanning the area, following the rough trail the signature left, but it was fading.

"*Malleus* to *Mulan*. We read you."

The *Mulan* bridge crew sat upright, not recognizing the voice.

"Who is this?"

"I am Torg. Ship's dro—"

"Where the frak is Sabrya? And the crew?" Noma asked.

"Where the frak are you?" Zintan asked over her.

"I can inform you the crew are unconscious but stable."

"And your location?"

"I am not at liberty to say—"

"What the frak! As a ship's captain under the legislation of the Free Alliance to another Free Alliance vessel, I order you to comply."

"Nope. I repeat, the crew is stable. Once they regain consciousness, I am certain they will be in touch. *Malleus* out."

Noma sat stunned. "Did that droid just cut us off?"

"It did."

Noma fumed for a few more seconds. "Find the damn signature and follow it."

CHAPTER TWENTY-SEVEN

WHEN ALEXIS WOKE, she was in her bunk, her Kimichi on its hanger, recharging. She couldn't recall... she looked under the sheet. *Naked.*

When she sat up, her head spun. She lay down again. "Torg? Anyone?" she croaked.

"Yes, Captain. Good to have you back."

"Where are we? Where are the others?"

"The location of the *Malleus* is 4.5 kilometers from the Quadrant border waystation, following a circular trajectory. Bradyn is in his cabin. Sabrya is outside. Brianna DeCroix is in the medi-bay."

"She is? How is she?"

"Stable, but she sustained a fracture to the humerus in her left arm when she fell down the stair—"

"Wait. Sabrya's outside? What the frag's she doing there?" She winced as her raised voice brought on a headache.

"Conducting repairs."

"How's my ship?" Alexis rubbed her temples.

"The ship sustained damage to the aft port side. It would have been worse if not for the jump."

"And the *Invictus*?"

"I am unaware of that vessel's condition, due to the afore-mentioned jump."

"Of course." She took a slow, deep breath and pulled herself upright. Her head throbbed but was bearable. With careful, deliberate movements, she pulled the Kimichi on, grateful it almost donned itself. She couldn't wait until the inbuilt auto-doc kicked in.

"I do not think it wise for you to be up and moving, Captain."

"Me neither, but here we are. Captains do that sort of thing." *And if Sabrya can do it, I can too.* She knocked then went into Bradyn's cabin. She was glad he was still unconscious; he had rolled in his bunk and his sheet was now on the floor. Feeling silly for tiptoeing, she quickly picked it up and covered his body. Sabrya's cabin was empty. *Fraggin outside! Crazy woman.*

"Why is she radio silent?" Alexis asked after attempting to call her.

"I am unaware but will go inform her of your recovery."

Slowly, Alexis made her way to the bridge where she could view the external cams. She passed the droid on its way to the airlock.

"I should also inform you the *Mulan* has been hailing us," he said.

"They have? Where are they?" She stopped and turned, swaying slightly, as a bout of dizziness hit.

"They were attempting to follow our drive signature, but as we are circling the waystation, they have drifted off course."

"Huh? Why are they following our signature?"

"We are still cloaked, Captain. I was of the understanding they were not to be aware of it."

"Oh, of course. Okay. Thanks."

"Not required, Captain. I will now attend to contacting Sabrya."

Alexis nodded. When she finally reached the bridge, she slumped into her chair. Her world stopped spinning, and she looked at the cams and out the viewport. Sabrya was easy enough to locate, as was Torg when he waved to get the woman's attention.

From this angle, the ship damage didn't look too severe, but perhaps repairs had been conducted sufficiently. Reaching across, she deactivated the cloak.

"*Malleus* to *Mulan*. Hi, girls."

"Alexis? This is Noma. How... How the frak did you do that?"

"Do what? Want to pop over?" Alexis was able to slow the ship to a virtual standstill. By that time, Sabrya had bounced up the stairs.

"Hey, you," she announced upon her arrival. "Glad to see you up and about."

"I gather you were hardly injured?"

"Me? Fraggin' out cold, like the rest of you, I just recover quicker. When everyone was taken care of, I helped do a few repairs."

"Oh. Good. Um, the *Mulan* is on its way. Your comm is out."

"Thanks for remindin' me." She turned it back on.

"You knew they were calling?"

Sabrya nodded. "But you were adamant they not know about the cloak, so I thought it best to shut the frag up and keep them guessin'." She grinned.

"Well, I decloaked, and they're on their way."

"Knew you'd come around."

"I won't tell them how evil you are."

"Appreciated. Noma can be such a spoilsport."

<hr>

Noma and Zintan entered via the shuttle dock and dropped down to the central corridor. They looked around with surprise and interest at the ship's interior.

"Welcome aboard the *Malleus*. Not what you expected?" Alexis asked. "You should've seen her when I first joined."

The visitors were escorted to the lounge where the reunion was boisterous, until Noma turned her wrath on Torg.

"That frakking droid disobeyed a direct order. My direct order! I want it diagnosed and reprogrammed."

"Noma, he was acting on *my* direct orders. It isn't your call to determine what should be done to a droid not in your charge."

"Want to sell it to me?"

"You fraggin' hate droids," Sabrya commented.

"Exactly. It wouldn't be around long."

"The answer's no. Torg's part of my crew. I'll defend him as much as I would defend any of them."

"You are one weird captain."

"I'll take that as a compliment. Being weird has its privileges... or is that drawbacks? I'm never sure, but it means I can change my mind on a whim. You never know what'll set me off —a hangover, someone wanting to reprogram my obedient droid, or even being left for dead when three Imperial vessels appear."

"Yeah. What pissed me right off was you had superior ordnance at your fingertips, and yet your fraggin' coder fragged the mission up. What the frag were you thinkin'?"

"Okay, okay. We got greedy. I saw those maintenance bots grabbing stuff from other areas and thought there was more than what was offered. Not blaming you, just that frakking AI."

"That fraggin' AI has saved our asses more than I care to remember. He fraggin' saved your asses, as well."

"He did? How? When?"

"Why did you end up at this waystation?" Sabrya asked them.

"I... we made an error in our jump?" Zintan offered, not sounding convinced.

"Pfft. Phill detoured you in hyper, knowing about a fraggin' Qlan trap."

"A frakking AI *detoured* my ship?"

"Don't start gettin' all *droids-are-takin'-over*. Waystation AI do it all the time so ships don't collide. It's their fraggin' job. Believe it or not, some of them have our interests at heart. This one, in particular." Sabrya stopped for a minute. "I can't believe what I'm fraggin' sayin'."

"It sounded good," Phillix commed. "I thought you were genuine. Thank you."

Bradyn and Alexis smiled at the inside joke.

"What did I miss?" Noma asked. "Was that the AI? This *Phillix*?"

"I'm still waitin' for an explanation for why you left us for dead!" Sabrya vented.

"Knew you could handle it." Noma shrugged. "And here you all are."

Sabrya was about to retort, but Alexis cut her off.

"No point arguing."

"Care to enlighten us on how you seemed to be invisible?" Noma asked.

"Were we?"

Zintan nudged her. "Rumor has it you came across some form of advanced tech."

"Fraggin' rumors." Sabrya laughed. "And where did you hear that crap?"

"We can't say," Zintan retorted.

Sabrya turned to Alexis. "No doubt the fraggin' Qlan assholes spreadin' their shite again."

"Are you denying it?" Zintan fumed. "We were tracking your drive but couldn't see you for over an hour!"

Alexis shrugged. "It's not for me to speculate on what's wrong with your ship—"

"There's nothing wrong with our ship," Noma declared, echoed by Zintan.

"Maybe optics? Had them checked lately?"

"Everything is working fine!" Noma insisted.

"Yet you couldn't see us?"

"Reckon it must be more than optics," Sabrya offered. "If what they say is true, they couldn't see us with their eyes, either."

Alexis shrugged. "It's definitely an anomaly. Still, I'd get the *Mulan* overhauled."

"There's nothing wrong, dammit!"

"Noma, I can't say why you didn't see us—wait. Phillix might be playing games."

"That AI?" Noma questioned, eyes showing concern.

"He's a clown, loves a joke," Alexis confirmed, using the woman's fear and prejudice against her.

"That must be it." Sabrya turned to Noma. "I reckon you've got a virus. Nothin' sinister, he's not that mad, but still worth gettin' fraggin' checked out."

"Glad we got that sorted out." Alexis sighed her relief.

"Now, let's have another fraggin' drink. We have some catchin' up to do."

"Sabrya, you have more catching up than I do. I'll leave you to it for a few minutes while I check on Brianna."

Sabrya nodded as she opened another bottle.

"You've someone else on your crew?" Noma asked.

"Hardly. The boss took a reporter under her wing for protection."

"From?" Zintan accepted the refill of whiskey.

"Some local dudes wanted her dead."

"Some reporters need deading as much as droids and AIs."

"Fraggin' oath, but not this one. She's cool."

Noma looked at the warrior. "You've changed."

"Have I? Good. I was a fraggin' monster."

"Don't you miss it?" Zintan asked, swirling her booze.

"I'm not in the tourney anymore, so no. Being a monster in this life isn't the way to go. These are good people." She raised her glass to Bradyn who was sitting quietly in the corner, still recovering, nursing his amber liquid.

He smiled back, acknowledging the compliment.

"So," Sabrya queried. "What have you been up to these last fraggin' months? Oh, thanks for the stellars, too."

<hr>

Alexis quietly stepped into the medi-bay. The Buntress was still unconscious, but her vitals were stable. An image of her arm showed the break. The prognosis for a complete recovery was good.

Ensuring the passage was clear, she opened her private comm channel. "Phillix?"

"Yes, Alexis."

"Sorry for making you the scapegoat. I had to make an excuse for the shield generator."

"Think nothing of it. The Sunfists aren't the allies you expected. I understand."

She chuckled wryly. "I'm not convinced they're as sincere as they're making themselves out to be."

"Then may I ask what you're going to do about them?"

"It's unclear. They can't stay here. Not with their history— true or not." Alexis sat and shrugged. "They did abandon us the moment the Imps turned up."

"When it comes to a question of survival, very few people are selfless. My experiences may have jaded me somewhat, but as I recall, you stayed behind to look after me, even though I was already dead."

"And you sacrificed yourself to save the *Malleus* from Janus' self-destruct."

"We must be good people, then." He laughed.

"Perhaps. What I'm about to ask you to do, though, isn't what a good person would do."

"I think I know where this is going, but I'll wait for your suggestion, lest I reveal how much 'not a good person' I can be."

"Can you listen in on the Sunfists? I stand by my argument from a while back—the stealth tech is too good for someone to ignore."

"You think Noma wants it?"

"Oh, I'm certain she would take it if she knew. She didn't come all the way out here for a reunion. But I still think she's a decent person."

"One who left you for dead…"

"True enough. Not sure about her crew though, especially Zintan. She's up to something, and then there's the new crew."

"Consider it done. It was what I was thinking, too."

"Thank you. I know we've had our differences—"

"Pfft. And still will. It has never been, nor ever will be, an issue with us."

"Good." She cut the link. *Time for a drink.*

Her head still throbbed, but her dizziness was easing. She sat there for a few moments, listening to Brianna's steady breathing and the various soft beeps of the Abbsolin S8 auto-doc. To think, over seven months ago, she had been in that chair on her way to the Ieoni Orbital slave markets.

She shuddered to think what their lives would have been like if not for the actions she and the others had taken to escape. After a deep breath, she composed herself and headed back upstairs. Approaching the lounge, she heard the chuckles.

"Good reminiscing?" she asked upon entering.

"Yah. Old times." Noma clinked glasses with Sabrya.

"How's the Buntress?" Sabrya asked, with the slightest slurring.

"Still out, but her recovery is looking good." Alexis looked at her briefly. *Why is she feigning being drunk?*

"I guess we should go." The Sunfist leader drained her glass. "Let you all recover properly."

Alexis smiled. "That's a good idea. And thanks for looking out for us."

"No problem," Noma replied as she stood and motioned to her second.

"Once we're fully functional, we'll arrange to head back and see what we can do regarding the Qlan ship," Alexis suggested.

"Good. See you then."

Sabrya escorted her friends to the shuttle dock, which was situated in the deckhead of the main passage. With a quick wave, they closed the door. Shortly after, she felt the vibration of the shuttle departing.

"They're fraggin' up to somethin'," Sabrya swore on her return.

"We've ordnance left, if need be, and the plasma cannons." Alexis considered their options. "We could handle them if it came to that. Look what we did to that mother-fragging ship."

"Pretty good plasma cannons, too," Bradyn offered.

The two women nodded.

"But we don't know what they have left after their weapons haul. There were nukes in the cache," he reminded them.

"Any attack will be non-destructive for fear of damaging the stealth shield," Alexis observed.

"What about the Ion Maidens?" Brianna offered from the lounge doorway.

They turned in surprise at her arrival.

"Should you be up yet? How's the arm?"

"Throbbing but mending. Amazing thing, this." She looked at the cylinder enclosing her upper arm.

"Come, have a seat before you fall again," Alexis offered, moving to another chair.

Brianna nodded her thanks and sat, gratefully. "The Ion Maidens would help if you asked."

"This isn't their fight..." Alexis said.

"You know, there's a way we can do this without our needing to be in the crosshairs." Bradyn suggested. "We even touched on it before."

"My mind isn't up to this at the moment, Bradyn. Spill."

"Let CQLO know the Sunfists are in the area," he suggested. "With the supposed assassination attempt, they're a big enough concern for the empire to take notice. Pretty sure Strasser would put a bounty on them immediately."

"The trouble is, Strasser isn't an idiot. You don't think she'll start putting together some link between us, the Qlan, and the Sunfists? We might have another bounty on us if we're not careful. No. We can't afford to be associated with the Sunfists. New beginnings, remember?"

"Not forgetting, though we have that message from the Juggernauts. They're the ones who initiated this. It's not of our doing. As the 'nearest thing to law enforcement,' we're simply doing the right thing by the Quad."

"It's risky." Alexis hesitated.

"Risky? No more than half the fraggin' things we've already done," Sabrya said.

"Do you want to do that though?" Brianna chimed in. "They were allies? You said you worked with them? I know it's not my place, but do you want them to be destroyed?"

Alexis shook her head and regretted it, then she turned to Sabrya.

"Not destroyed. But it'll give 'em somethin' to fraggin' think about. In the end, they are mercs... more beholden to stellars than anythin' else."

"We're bunters, so we're 'in the know,'" Bradyn said. "As allies, we could warn them. They'd get away, no harm done, with an indication of what they'd cross next time. I doubt it would get back to us."

"Not forgettin', since the fraggin' Jugheads knew about them. Their presence could be anonymously leaked to some beady-eyed clerk."

"Which reminds me, we should go back to see what's left of them," Alexis suggested.

"You ready for that?" Brianna asked.

"We can look, if nothing else. Want to tell them?" she asked Sabrya.

"On it."

"I'm going to sit and relax and let the Kimichi and its in-built auto-doc do its magic."

"Good idea." Bradyn sat back and closed his eyes.

"I knew you'd come around to wantin' to wear 'em all the time. They're like a fraggin' second skin, only better."

CHAPTER TWENTY-EIGHT

THIRTY MINUTES later they were all back on the bridge.

"*Malleus* to *Mulan*. I've sent you the coordinates. Ready to jump?" Alexis commed.

"Roger, *Malleus*. All set."

"See you on the other side." Alexis nodded for Torg to initiate the jump.

Bradyn sat back, getting comfortable. "Years from now, some psych's going to come up with Kimichi Syndrome—an addiction to wearing these suits."

For a few minutes, the opalescent, gray light of hyperspace dazzled their eyes as it stretched across the viewport but was quickly replaced by a scene of devastation.

Seconds later, the *Mulan* appeared near them.

"Frakking hell," Noma exclaimed. "You survived this?"

"Just caught the prelim of the blast before jumping," Alexis commed back. "That hulk to our port is—was—the *Dominator*. Everything else was the *Invictus*."

"That's what was chasin' us." They recognized Zintan's voice.

"Yep. We reckon the *Invictus* was about four times our size, over twice yours."

Alexis moved the ship in, slowly aiming toward the *Dominator*. She tapped a message on her armpad. *'Anyone got any idea what a hyper negator would look like?'*

Bradyn typed back. *'No, but it's probably something connected to their hyperdrives that shouldn't be.'*

'You're our expert.' "Who feels like going outside?" she said aloud.

"Finders fraggin' keepers," Sabrya whooped. "I'm in."

"*Mulan*, better grab what you can. If the Qlan knew about your visit, no telling who else will be calling or when."

"Will do. Thanks for the heads-up. *Mulan* out."

Alexis cut the comms again. "When we leave the ship, make sure you're fully armed."

"Before we head out, I'm gonna show you the long-range add-on."

"We're not goin far..."

"No, but if we need to get back quickly, we can fraggin' max burn the whole way."

"Can I come?" the Buntress asked.

Alexis turned to Brianna. "Another time. You need to be trained in these suits, and this definitely isn't the time or place. All they know is you're injured, probably still unconscious. Let's leave it that way." She turned to the droid. "Torg, monitor all cams and scanners. Anyone comes within a hundred meters of the *Malleus*, warn us."

"Will do, Captain."

As she got up to leave, she paused and checked to see where the *Mulan* was situated. It had moved incrementally closer to the sections of the Qlan battlecruiser.

"Tell you what—" she turned to Brianna "—I know there's no point in telling you to not record any of this, but... want to be the one with the scoop on the Qlan arrival in the Quad? You can say you gleaned the info from some intel leaked by the Juggernauts, and your moral compass just *had* to let the CQLO in on it."

"I could do that, yes." Brianna nodded eagerly.

"Do us a big favor, though. Maybe arrange a message relayed via somewhere other than our ship?" Alexis winked. "I'm sure Torg or even Phillix will assist."

With that, Alexis joined the other two by the airlock. Sabrya had already donned her gear and was finishing affixing the long-range fuel canister to Bradyn's suit.

Bradyn and Sabrya both completed setting up Alexis' suit.

"Good to go," Sabrya said after a quick once over.

"Torg, if the bots find anything, let us know."

"Aye, Captain."

"What's the plan, Sabby?" Alexis entered the airlock and ducked slightly to prevent the mini launcher from hitting anything. As soon as the others entered, she started depressurizing. Their helmets snapped up instantly.

"Well, they need to fraggin' see all of us out there for starters. I'm hopin' our friends don't try anythin', but while we're here, I think the priority is ordnance and the hyper negator thin'. I'll head to the *Dominator* and check missiles, etc. If the bots are around, I'll get them haulin' them back. Big boy, here, goes and checks the Qlan hyperdrive. And you... fly around lookin' pretty, keep an eye out, or—"

"Frag that. I'll see if those C-Z drives are intact."

"If we can't use them, the Sunfists can use the spares," Bradyn suggested.

"Always thinkin' of others." Sabrya punched his chest. "Remember, no fraggin' good deed goes unpunished."

"Not sure that's how it works." He shrugged.

"Time to go people." Alexis opened the airlock the second the red light came on.

The door swung open, and they zoomed out silently. Alexis went left and was quickly overtaken by the far more experienced warrior, and Bradyn, at a more sedate pace, headed toward the *Invictus*, which reminded him of a vid he saw as a kid of a massive, fossilized skeleton.

The huge ship was in three large sections. The blast did catastrophic damage to the bulkheads and decks. Minute to car-sized debris was scattered among the larger chunks of twisted metal rolling and colliding with other chunks of wreckage.

From memory, he tried to put the pieces together to determine what went where. The engineering space was easy enough to recognize. No way could the huge thruster tubes be confused with anything else. He made his way toward them.

'*Torg,*' Bradyn typed. '*I think we've a couple of drones from the cache. Can you send them my way and slave them to this suit? Might be a good time to put them to use.*'

'*Affirmative.*'

The engineer was combing through the Qlan battlecruiser hull fragments when he got the message the drones were on their way. He sat on one of the many exposed decks of the vessel to take a few moments to check their capabilities and to link their visuals to his HUD, then he sent one into the engineering spaces behind and below him to begin surveying.

He'd never seen this model before, but he had an idea where some mandatory manufacturer details had to be placed. It was union regs. He directed the drone to locate the identification plate.

One of the other aspects of the HUD was the depiction of friend and foe. He had already identified and marked his two crewmembers as pink dots, though he thought Sabby would cut his balls off if she knew she was designated hot pink. While not foe, any other suited figure his HUD detected would be orange.

He didn't want to think ill of the Sunfists, considering their association with Sab, but they were mercenaries, and they had left the *Malleus* behind. Maybe not enemies, but definitely not friends—unless there was something in it for them. *No good deed goes unpunished.*

Two orange dots seemed to be roaming aimlessly nearby, but they remained close. Now that he was sitting, it appeared they had also found something worth their consideration. He moved one of the almost invisible drones to hover thirty meters above him and survey. Once done, he concentrated on observing the images sent from the other drone.

His recent ordeal still had his head aching, and concentrating on the various HUD images didn't help. Though annoying, it kept him alert. Bradyn sighed and decided not to inject any painkillers.

***

Alexis glided to the hulk of the *Dominator*. The side facing the *Invictus* was peppered with shrapnel, and some metal fragments the size of a door were embedded several feet into the hull. Entry was simple enough through the gaping holes. She made her way aft.

"Do you know what you're fraggin' lookin' for?" Sabrya commed.

"Hey, I'll have you know, I'm a starship captain. I think I know what a hyperdrive looks like. Even this damned Cerbrinka-Zaners that has Bradyn drooling."

"Uh-huh."

"Maybe you should concentrate on what *you're* looking for."

"Yeah. Long bits of metal cylinders with little fins, funnel-things at one end, and pointy at the other. They go fraggin' boom if you hit them."

"Sounds about right. Good description, too. I'm sure Bradyn will be proud."

"I'm overwhelmed with the tech lingo I'm hearing," their engineer commented.

Alexis typed to them, *'You know they're watching us?'*

'I have a drone surveying the two on me.'

'Duh,' was Sabrya's comeback.

"As your captain, I recommend you take a language course with sublim training."

'Pfft.'

'Excellent. Use those bigger words, sister.' She looked at the next reply. *'Ooh, regressing to cute pix now.'*

"You know they can't fraggin' hear us?"

"They can't?"

"Our suit's comms are encrypted."

"Now, you tell me."

"I thought, you bein' a fraggin' starship captain and all..."

"Pfft."

"Now you're speakin' my language. And I found them."

"The long pointy things?"

"Yep. There are a few here. I'm callin' in the bots. You havin' luck?"

"Well, I found the engine room, and I found these big thingies that are welded to the back of the hull. Lots of tubes and conduit. It isn't a toilet." She flicked the tab to share her visual.

"Bradyn would be proud of your techno-lingo, too. They look to be in pretty good shape."

Bradyn stopped his task for a moment to check the feed on his armpad. "That's my assessment. There's no visual damage."

"Well, look at that." Alexis zoomed in on a manufacturer's plate. "Make, model, and date. Bradyn's going to wet his pants."

"As long as he's in these Kimichis, we won't know either way."

"Not a bad thing." Alexis laughed. "Heading over to you now."

"I'll have you ladies know I have amazing bladder control."

"Uggh."

"You brought it up," he replied.

"Hey," Sabrya said. "There're still quite a few missiles. I guess the launch sequence was aborted when the ship took damage. If you can find somethin' to tie them together, even better."

Alexis checked the compartments on either side of the corridors as she passed. She jumped when her helmet light panned across a suited body floating in the dark. With no idea which Juggernaut brother it was, she moved on quickly. The next compartment had rolls of strapping for containers and such. She grabbed several rolls and continued along the corridor to the entrance point. She avoided the debris field and took a wide path toward the *Invictus*.

"How many pointy things are there?" Alexis asked when she located the missile room, which was not too difficult considering half of it was exposed to vacuum.

"There are a dozen in this room, alone. No doubt there are, or were, a couple of other missile rooms around the hull. We'll strap six together, and the bots can't take them back. I'll let Torg know to open the loadin' dock. Maybe, when we're refittin' those new drives, we can install loadin' hatches for missiles. Saves us heavin' these things through the ship. You know, boom?"

"That's going to cost."

"I—we—have the stellars."

"Which reminds me. I wonder what the salvaging rights are in the Quadrant."

"Captain, we have two *Mulan* crew attempting to enter via the airlock."

"We're heading back now."

"Lucky their coders are fraggin' useless." Sabrya abandoned the missile she was moving and followed Alexis.

As they were watching, they saw a brief flash as the airlock exploded.

"Fraggin' amateurs, blowin' their way in."

"Captain—"

"We know. Tell me Brianna is in her Kimichi!"

"Affirmative."

"Good. Keep her safe. Bradyn?"

"I heard. Also returning."

Nearby, they could see several more suited figures moving toward the *Malleus*.

"Noma. What the frag are you doin'?"

"This is Zintan!" the *Mulan* responded immediately. "We didn't come all this way for scraps of metal!"

"Where's Noma?"

"I'd be more worried about your ship. Better tell us where the device is."

"You've been listenin' too much to Qlan lies, you stupid fragger!"

"There are several thousand stellars in our accounts that say differently."

"Corpses can't fraggin' spend stellars."

"Zintan, Alexis here. Some of your crew are heading toward my ship. If they know what's good for them, they'll back off. There are three mini missile launchers aimed at them right now."

"Mini missiles?" Zintan sounded doubtful.

"Wanna test us?" Sabrya launched a HE-mini missile at a large chunk of the *Invictus*. Her skill in the battle suit kept her from deviating from her course. "You'll soon see how fraggin' advanced these Kimichi Mk8s are."

"Torg, what's our missile status?"

"Still loaded and armed, Captain. Awaiting your orders to fire."

"Target the *Mulan*. Send weapons control to me." She checked when her armpad vibrated. "Listen up, all *Mulan* crew, unless you want to be left behind, head back to your ship."

Two crew heading toward the *Malleus* hesitated, made wide arcs, and moved back to their ship.

"Captain, th—"

"Torg?" The abrupt silence concerned Alexis. She checked to see if her comms were online.

"Here's your pet droid," a voice declared.

While still distant, they saw the silhouette of a figure push the shiny droid out of the blown airlock.

"Fraggin' assholes."

The three *Malleus* crew raced for their ship, closing the distance rapidly. Being the more experienced with the suit, Sabrya was in the lead by far. Alexis trailed by thirty seconds, and Bradyn, having to navigate around large pieces of floating hull, wasn't halfway yet.

"I'll get Torg." He changed his path slightly to intercept the droid.

"And now, say goodbye to your ship," the same voice said.

"Good fraggin' luck with that."

"Sab, you aim for the closest figure, I'll target the next."

Simultaneously, the mini launchers rose and fired. Two mini missiles shot away into the dark. Seconds later, they detonated.

As soon as her fist missile was away, Alexis tapped her armpad. The plasma cannons swiveled and started pounding the side of the *Mulan*, two kilometers distant.

"Missiles are coming next!" Alexis warned.

Sabrya took out three more crew with her launcher.

"You're currently down at least five crew, Zintan."

"You'll regret every death!" Zintan shouted back.

"No I fraggin' won't."

The *Mulan* began moving, aiming to put the *Invictus* between them. The two returning crew floundered in the turbulence of the maneuvering thrusters.

"Come on out here, then. I'll happily destroy your ship, knowing you're too desperate to destroy the device you think we've got. But I'm just as likely to let you go if you call your hounds off."

"You don't think I won't take out the *Malleus* and comb through the wreckage later?"

"Sad to say, you won't be around." Alexis released the missiles.

'Phillix, can you jump, or cloak?' she typed then looked up to gauge Sabrya's progress.

The warrior woman stopped herself by pivoting and slamming into the hull boots first. After a glance to check the airlock was safe with no traps, she slipped inside.

CHAPTER TWENTY-NINE

ALEXIS SLOWED and landed in a similar, but not so elegant, manner. She checked her private comms channel setting before she spoke. "Brianna, can you hear me?"

"I'm here."

"Where's here, exactly?"

"Torg took me to the holo-deck. He activated some sequence to make it harder for anyone to find me if they look."

"Okay. Stay there. How many are on board?"

"I only know of two," the Buntress replied.

Alexis looked 'up' at the area around her. The two wrecks rolled and yawed silently. The plasma cannons ceased firing the moment *Mulan* was out of sight. Seconds later, she saw a series of bright flashes, indicating her missiles had hit something.

"I'll be with you in a minute." Before she turned to go in, the scene changed, as the *Malleus* started moving.

"We are cloaked and jumping in twenty seconds," Phillix announced.

"I was wondering where you had gone." Alexis sighed and entered.

Sabrya activated her HUD in combat mode. It would now detect a threat and do an instant assessment if required. Movement and heat sensors were set to max. Slowly and methodically, she glided inside. "Loadin' dock clear." She tapped for the lift as a decoy then moved on to check the main corridor and stairs.

With the airlock blown, the interior up to the first blast door was in vacuum. She looked to her left and saw the blast doors down, as she'd expected. To her right were the stairs leading up to the lounge and the bridge and down to the cabins.

Knowing the intruders had virtually zero chance of hacking into the console, she was in no rush. She fully expected they'd become desperate and do something stupid and probably fatal, so she turned left to collect some gear as a precaution. At the first blast door, she punched in the override code then used her suit's thrusters to counteract the sudden depressurization.

Her small armory was in this section. She was happy with her array of accumulated weapons and gadgets, but she would always be happier to have more.

Can't have too many toys.

She opened a locked drawer and quickly extracted the weapon and tech suppressors, then she clipped them to her utility belt, one on each hip. Back in the corridor, she resumed her approach to the bridge. Alexis appeared in the doorway to the loading dock and indicated she was heading aft. "We're about to jump."

Sabrya nodded. "Better wait there. This won't take long."

Alexis nodded, understanding the reason she needed to remain, but hating it all the same. Seeing someone getting sliced open wasn't something she'd ever want to see again, if possible. It was silly, she knew. These people were trying to steal her ship. Blowing the airlock was a sure indicator they had no qualms about hurting or killing anyone inside. It was just good fortune Brianna was already in her Kimichi. While they deserved to pay, them versus Sabrya was no contest.

Once Alexis passed through, Sabrya slowly glided forward to the top of the stairs then across the lounge to the door leading directly to the bridge.

One figure was hunched over the console working hard at the keyboard, the other was brandishing a gut-puncher. The figure turned just as Sabrya's helmet appeared.

"Get back." He fired where her head had been, but he only scored the bulkhead.

"We've got a bomb. Try anything, and we'll blow it."

And there it is, desperation makes people stupid. "And kill yourselves for nothin'?" she responded.

"If we leave without the device, our families are dead. This is the only way to save 'em."

"Too bad, so sad. Should've thought about that before." Sabrya activated both the weapons and tech suppressors. All electronics stopped. The lights went out, with only the dimmest glow from outside to shed any illumination. "Do what you reckon you need to do. But you're not takin' this ship." She rose to the top of the stairs in full view.

The first guy tried to fire his weapon again, but it failed. "Damn!" He shook it in frustration.

"You dudes are new to the *Mulan*? That's a shame. I've got no loyalty to you. Have you heard about me? Sabrya Reaper Smith." There was enough ambient light from the viewport for them to see her blades slowly extend.

"Th-that's *you*? I thought..."

"Think again. Here's the rub. I'm turnin' a page here, in the Quad. I could end you, and you know it. Might even be doin' you both a favor, but I don't want my bridge covered in your blood and guts. My boss is squeamish about that. So, your choice is to scoot back to the *Mulan* or die painfully."

"Or I could blow us all!" The female coder turned and stood, holding a device in her hand. "If I release this, the front half of this ship disappears. You with it." She indicated a large pack on the captain's seat.

"You're not too fraggin' bright." Sabrya slowly shook her head and stepped forward. "Sorry, Captain. I'll do my best to keep it tidy," she muttered.

The coder hesitated before releasing the detonator.

Nothing happened.

The warrior leaped, leading with a two-handed punch, and hit both helmets simultaneously. The mag boots held them to the floor as her razor-sharp blades pierced their glassteel face-plates without shattering them. When she slowly withdrew them, only a few drops escaped before the congealing blood sealed the punctures.

One by one, she dragged the bodies to the loading dock and out the open airlock. The coder, with the bomb pack now attached to her belt, was first. Sabrya activated the powersuit and pushed the coder away. After twenty meters, the suit powered up as the bomb went off.

The warrior went back inside to collect the gunman. She spotted Alexis and Brianna behind the blast door, looking through its thick window.

Alexis shrugged at the silence, indicating the door wouldn't open.

Sabrya grinned and showed her the tech suppressor as she passed.

Back outside, she repeated the process and pushed the gunman's body away. When his suit came to life, the gunman spiraled off in a random direction.

Only then did she deactivate the suppressors and climb back inside.

"Hear me now, boss?"

Alexis nodded. "And that explains why we didn't jump."

"Knew it wasn't me," Phillix said.

"Zintan, you there?"

There was a pause. "You're not dead yet," the rebel replied.

"A damn traitor. Looks like Noma was the only decent one, after all."

"She had it coming. Always pussyfooting around, not facing the big issues."

"Your fraggin' coder just faced a big issue, and the other one's headin' toward Sagittarius."

"He almost hit me as he passed," Bradyn commed. "I'm back, and I've got Torg. Looks like he was tagged with a localized EMP stud. Shouldn't be hard to remove."

"Good to hear," Alexis said.

"What did you do with Noma?" Sabrya asked Zintan.

"She always wanted a space burial. She probably thought she'd be dead beforehand, though."

"You're a piece of work." Alexis shook her head sadly and headed to the bridge, followed by Sabrya.

"Looks like the workshop—again—for me and Torg." Bradyn punched in the blast door code.

Once the maintenance bots were recalled to repair the airlock, Alexis cloaked the *Malleus* and began moving it in a wide arc to the far side of the *Invictus*. The *Mulan* was nowhere to be seen.

"Phillix? You on?" She deactivated the missiles and plasma cannons.

"Loitering in the background and ready to assist, like any good AI. Want the *Mulan* to go somewhere else, perhaps?"

"So, they did manage to jump?"

"I can confirm they did."

Alexis sat, looking at the empty space.

"You want them to 'not be'?" he asked when there was no response.

"Fraggin' oath, Gadgetman," Sabrya answered.

"Alexis?" Phill prompted.

"Since they were so keen on stellars, let them find a star."

"As you wish."

<hr>

Several minutes later, Alexis took a deep breath and began looking over her ship via the internal and external cams. There was no doubt about it, the ship needed work. More than they could hope to do out there with just the bots. A glance around showed Sabrya had left her alone.

After a last look, she ventured to the lounge where the others were filling in Brianna on the details outside. She slumped into a chair opposite Bradyn.

"What do we know of salvage rights in the Quad?" she asked when the conversation died down.

"Should be the same as in any other non-empire region. The *Invictus* is clearly not an issue, as it has no legal right to be in the region, especially if it's established it is from the Qlan, and, therefore, a bona fide gang-related vessel," the engineer said.

"As for the *Dominator*—" Brianna looked up from her tablet and twirled her stylus across her fingers as she spoke "—they were bunters who had a bad day. There's no bounty, so like the Skimmer gang or the Quadranteers, a percentage of the proceeds will go to whoever calls it in."

"I thought as much."

Torg was standing nearby.

"Torg, no after-effects from the EMP?" she asked.

"My CPU shut down a nano-second before the EMP. I am at 99 percent capability."

"Good to hear it. What's the real story of my ship?" she asked her engineer.

"She'll hold. The bots already repaired the worst of it," Bradyn replied. "I'm running a full diagnostic on the engines, and so far, so good."

"I am also running diagnostics on all areas, and we are at 93 percent efficiency. The port rear missile launcher tube is currently out of commission, as is the airlock. Navigation, comms, weapons, life support, secondary—"

"Great, Torg. Good job. Both of you."

"Now, we've got all that taken care of, let's go and get our bang sticks." Sabrya stood.

"How'd you do with the hyper device thingy," she asked Bradyn.

"Just before the attack, I found something suspicious, an add-on, that needs investigating."

"Can you do it in situ?"

"There's no power source. I could hook something up, but what if it does something different from expectations and fires up a damaged drive? I'd rather carefully remove it and bring it here for a thorough diagnosis in the workshop."

"Good. Take what you need and do it." She inclined her head toward the Buntress. "True to her word, Brianna sent her message. I've no idea how long before we'll get a response or whether anyone will turn up. I would prefer it if that device were on board before that."

"Roger." The engineer stood. "Torg can finalize our engine diagnostics, and I'll grab my tools and take a bot."

"Done." She turned to Sabrya. "That leaves you and me."

"Let's get the bang sticks unless you've got somethin' better to do."

Alexis shook her head. "I'm sure I *could* find something, but more hands and all."

Once the missiles had been retrieved, Alexis left Sabrya to arrange her new toys, while she flew about the wreckage, taking vids and pics of most of what she could. It would be a fairly simple editing process to collate them into separate Qlan vessel *Invictus* and Juggernaut vessel *Dominator* files.

"Oh... crap." She was moving among the debris on the far side of the battlecruiser hulk.

"What is it? You okay?" Sabrya asked.

"I just came across what's left of the two crewmembers who headed back to the *Mulan*."

"Bad?"

"Never get behind a spaceship's thrusters." She moved on from her gruesome find and continued until she covered the length of the ship then headed back.

"Which reminds me," she noted on her way in. "What should we do with the Jughead bodies? Brianna?"

"Umm. Space burial, as far as I'm aware. I've not covered any bunter funerals before."

"Good. I wasn't relishing hauling four corpses back to Quint-wil or the CQLO." Alexis nodded. "May as well get it over and done with, then I'm calling it a day."

"And corpses could lead to fraggin' questions. I'm on my way."

It took both twenty minutes to transfer the bodies to the *Malleus* forward launch tubes to jettison them.

"Why not just push them away?" Brianna asked, watching from the doorway as the first two departed.

"At some point, someone will come here to assess these ships for salvage or market. Shunting the bodies off via the launcher sends them far and fast. By the time anyone arrives, they'll be long gone," Bradyn explained.

"Did they die from the damage to the ship?"

"Yep." Sabrya loaded the last bunter and stood back. "Asphyxiation does that."

"Ready, Torg."

The tube closed, there was a woosh, and the tube was empty.

———

"We could spend days here; the wreckage is so large," Alexis commented later as she examined the footage. The others were with her, looking up at the lounge monitor.

From the schematics they had, they determined the *Invictus'* self-detonation was near the bridge. It appeared the hyper-nullifier wasn't the main target, but the computer with Qlan records. Still, they could use the bots and drones to go over every piece to get what they could.

Brianna spent time compiling her story, adding some details and removing others at the crew's suggestion.

"Remember, you won't be doing us any favors if our association with the Sunfists is known," Alexis reminded her.

"You've done so much for me. Shown me an aspect of bunter life I could never have imagined. I promise to edit out anything relating to them and you completely. However, I need to get back. With the Juggernauts gone, I can finally get my life and my paper back in order."

"She's right. I guess we could all do with a break. We've laid claim to this wreckage for salvage, and only Strasser knows the location. We can take a break and be back in a couple of days to finish up."

"I'll get Torg and Phill to program the maintenance bots and drones to check as much of the wreckage as they can in the minute hope of finding one or two CPU components. We might get a bit of data regarding the Qlan."

"Umm, have you looked outside? There's a fraggin' lot of debris to comb through."

"I don't hold any great hopes."

"And our damages?"

"A day or two, at least, in the shop to get the worst of it." He shrugged. "The bots have done what they could with what we had, so they won't be needed. Once they're recharged and programmed, we can send them off again."

"How long for that?"

"I'm thinking an hour. Phillix?"

"Already working on the programming."

"Fine. I'll arrange a jump to Quint-wil in sixty-five minutes."

CHAPTER THIRTY

THEY LANDED at one of the ship repairers close to the spaceport after arranging for an assessment and repair.

"You guys see some action out there?" A workman came out with his tablet and began assessing.

"You could say that. You should see the other guy, though," Bradyn finished the ancient line. "If your quote's within reason, we could have some more work for you in the future, or I could take her to McDurmotts." Bradyn looked across the road.

"I dunno." The man looked skeptically at the old hull. "Not seen this model for years. Didn't know they were still flying. The hull's pretty beat up. Tsk... Look, I could give a generous quote for salvag—" The man nearly fumbled his tablet when he looked over the stocky man's shoulder.

Sabrya was standing there, nonchalantly using her blades to etch a sad face in the tarmac.

Sparks were flying.

"Um. Sure," he stammered. "I'll give you a good quote. I remember now, you're the new bunters. Bunters get a special rate. Shoulda said. I'm Hank."

"Good man, Hank. Now, we don't expect everything done at

once. We're off again in two days. Do what you can by then. As long as she's space worthy. Don't mind the droid."

Sabrya waved as her blades retracted.

"Y-you bet." Hank waved nervously.

"Time for you to go home, Brianna," Alexis said. "We're heading to The Lair if you want to join us. Could be a great way to announce your return."

"Thanks, but I need a bath. And a long sleep. And food, though your vegetables were great."

"You have our details. Call if you need anything. As you heard, we'll be here for two days. And we'll be letting Strasser know officially about the Juggernauts."

With a final wave, they went their separate ways.

They booked rooms in a local hotel, and after freshening up, paid a visit to the Lair.

The Ion Maidens were there and came over. It seemed that, without the Juggernauts lingering in the background, the other bunters became more sociable. After quite a few meet-and-greets, the bunters went off to their respective tables, but the Maidens remained.

"Did you get any of the new bounties?" Alexis asked.

"We got into a couple of scraps," Fyona replied. "Two small bounties in the bag, but one managed to get away. I'm sure we'll meet them again."

"I think we bumped you down a notch." Glyn showed them the new leaderboard tally.

"So, you did. Good for you," Bradyn congratulated them.

"How did your rendezvous go?" Doryne asked. "We looked up the Sunfists. Were they tough? More Juggernaut shite?"

"They were a no-show," Alexis lied. "But those Jugheads had other ideas. Heard of the Qlan?"

"You mean the Bukshoga Qlan? Bad-ass crime group? Not much, just a bit of chatter and rumors. Why?"

"What have they got to do with the Quad?" Fyona asked.

"Or the Jugheads?" Glyn looked from one to the other.

"Speaking of which, we've not heard their bragging for a while. Any ideas?" Doryne queried.

"Umm. Some. Before we get into that, you'll be pleased to know Brianna is back and safe."

"Will she be safe? The 'Nauts think she's dead."

"About that..." Alexis decided they might as well be told. "We suspected the Jugheads were up to something, so we were sort of prepared. Well, they were, and it sort of backfired—"

"In a big fraggin' way," Sabrya added with enthusiasm.

"The Juggernauts are dead; the *Dominator* destroyed."

"No frakking way!" Glyn hissed loudly.

Fyona gasped with shock. "Who could do that? You? This Qlan group?"

In turn, the crew shared the bulk of what had happened with the Maidens.

"Does the CQLO know?"

"Of course. I'm sure it'll be made official shortly. How will the other bunters feel?" Alexis looked over at the four other groups milling about and having a few quiet drinks.

"Well, most of us didn't like them much, those overbearing and cocky loudmouths. One minute they were your buddies; the next they would spit on you."

"Is there any bunter ritual for the passing of a group—liked or not?"

"Yeah, nothing much, just a round of drinks, maybe a toast."

Alexis conferred quietly with Bradyn. He shrugged and nodded then went to the bar.

"I know they were one of us, but... glad they're gone. Was it gruesome?" Quela asked.

"Come with me." Alexis motioned the Maidens closer to the

large screen above the silent and empty stage. "Hey, bunters. Gather round. I guess we've had some recent adventures lately with the new bounty lists coming out. Some successful, some not. You'll have many questions about what I'm about to reveal. Some of you will disbelieve. So, we have ship recordings of our activities over the last few days. We've all had a run-in or two with the Juggernauts. I'm sure you know the Challenge they set for us to murder the Buntress. I'm here to tell you, for better or worse, this will never happen again."

Some bunters looked dark and shook their heads.

Sabrya stood ready to act if need be.

"I can also assure you Brianna DeCroix is alive and well, and she will have much to write about in the next few weeks, if not months."

This news cheered the dark faces. Her armpad buzzed with a message from Bradyn. *'Good to go.'*

The barman came around, accompanied by a bot with a tray loaded with drinks. The bunters were eager and chatty as they grabbed a glass of their favorite booze.

"We were suspicious of our 'friends,' especially when they invited us, the new Scrappers, to rendezvous with the promise of a big job. It was a trap, one which we sort of expected, but even we were surprised with the outcome. We have compiled our ship's recordings of what happened." She nodded to Bradyn. On their return, they had gone over and over it, removing any footage of the Sunfists and the *Mulan*.

The large screen lit up, revealing the sequence of events.

The *Dominator* was idle in space. They'd even added some external cam views of the *Malleus* for perspective, so everyone could see the two ships near each other.

The Lair echoed with the loud gasps of shock of the bunters when the battlecruiser appeared. Many could barely believe its sheer size, and some of the more gun-frenzied bunters were awed by the weapons array.

"This is a Qlan battlecruiser. They had arranged with our friends to capture us and the *Malleus*. Yes, it's hard to believe." Alexis nodded at the doubters. "As to why? Our history isn't for you, but what you need to understand is bunters were betrayed by bunters.

The vid continued, showing the initial attack. "We were outmatched in every way, but one. The moment they locked their weapons on us, I did what any sane captain would do. I fired a salvo of what we had then jumped like hell to save my ship and crew."

Some of the bunters shrugged and shook their heads lightly. Some nodded and cheered.

The vid showed some of the impact on the *Malleus* before she blinked out with the jump.

"We did a quick reload and repairs and headed back."

The bunters gasped again, disbelieving that anyone would willingly return to face that behemoth, especially when damaged. The next part of the vid unfolded. Coming into view, still several kilometers distant, the two ships drifted. There was little sign of activity other than sections of hull drifting between them. The huge amount of damage was easy to see, as were the large chunks of debris.

Since the *Malleus* was now cloaked, Alexis came up with an explanation as to why the ship was no longer in view. "We sustained quite a bit of damage. Our comms took a hit, so most of our external cams went down."

"Why aren't they shooting back?" one bunter asked.

"You're in plain sight!" another pointed out.

"I can't say. A big ship with inexperienced crew? They definitely aren't military." Alexis shrugged. "Maybe lucky shots took out their weapons or sensors? Or perhaps we were confused with shrapnel?

The vid continued, and they witnessed the many explosions, then the self-destruct.

"We were in closer at this point, and we didn't realize they'd blow themselves up. We jumped but copped substantial damage. And here we are. The Qlan aren't a myth. It might take a while, but they will be back, and they can be beaten."

Bradyn cut the vid feed, and the gathered crowd began muttering about what they saw.

"Quiet please." Alexis waited for everyone to pay attention. "When the fireworks were over, we moved in. We checked the *Dominator*, but the Juggernauts were all dead by the time we got there. Like them or not, they were fellow bunters, so, a toast to their passing. May they find their far horizons." She raised her glass.

"Far horizons," they all intoned and drank. Some looked slightly relieved, others remained neutral. More drinks were ordered, but this time, the other bunters were doing the buying to congratulate the Scrappers for getting through their ordeal relatively unscathed.

The following morning, only Sabrya was in high spirits.

"If you're so damn cheery because of your nanites, I want some." Alexis groaned as she rolled out of her bed. She ordered breakfast, and by the time it arrived, she'd showered and felt almost human. She was picking at her food when Bradyn emerged. He was already showered and dressed, ready to face the world, his white teeth contrasting against his dark Helios complexion.

"I hate you both," she grimaced at them.

"Pfft. I've got nanites, big boy's got a heavy-G constitution. You'll cope."

"If it makes you feel better, I approved some of the work for the ship," Bradyn informed her. "As long as his workmanship is up to it, the price was quite reasonable."

"Any plans for the day?" she asked. Both shook their heads. "A good day by the pool, then." By the time she was showered and ready to face the world, a message had arrived from Strasser.

'Heard you were in town. I'll be in the Colosseum office all day.'

"There goes my pool relaxation."

"Pfft. You know you'd get fraggin' bored in an hour."

"Probably," she agreed. She replied they'd be there soon.

After a light lunch, they walked the short distance to the Colosseum Mall.

"Brianna DeCroix is alive and well," Alexis informed Strasser once they got through the brief pleasantries.

"She's probably in her office, as we speak, with her new scoop." Bradyn nodded.

"I know. She called but was coy with the details," Strasser said. "Please, have a seat."

Alexis took a deep breath to give her time to sort out what she'd say and how to say it. "You know about our dubious relationship with the Juggernauts. We were playing along with them when they invited us to join them for a 'big score.'" Alexis showed her the note from the Juggernauts about trapping the Sunfists. "Not sure what was supposed to happen exactly, but these Sunfists were a no-show, and then a Qlan vessel appeared. No doubt, that can be linked to Giono. As to how the Qlan knew we were there... I suspect an interfering clerk with bunter friends. Essentially, it was a trap, specifically for us."

"Looks like you escaped relatively unscathed..."

"The *Malleus* took a beating from both ships, even though we were alert and suspicious. We've some experience with the Qlan and their tactics, albeit not with such a massive ship. Our weapons systems were primed and ready, and we had some pretty cool and formidable smart missiles at our disposal."

"Our hyperdrive was also hot and ready to go," Bradyn

added. "Torg was interfaced with all aspects of the ship. The moment it got crazy, we unloaded a barrage of smart missiles and jumped."

"And you say, after all that, you went back for more?" Strasser shook her head in disbelief, as she went over and over Brianna's recordings.

"As you can see, we did. We had to finish this. Because of our various pasts—everyone on the *Malleus* has a history with the Qlan—we came here to escape and, possibly, lead normal, if not exactly peaceful, lives. We know, now, from this trap they'd never have stopped. If we had let them escape, this would have been repeated over and over. So, yes, we surprised them by retaliating.

"We jumped back with our smart missiles ready. As expected, we caught them unaware. Who in their right mind would have knowingly come back, outnumbered, outgunned, and outmassed ten to one? We even boarded the *Dominator* to check for survivors. After that, we came up with the idea to use their missiles for a quick hack-job. We moved away and used their ship to unload everything they had.

"Our AM-missiles inflicted some initial serious damage on the Qlan ship, and what the *Dominator* did compounded their problems. Knowing they weren't going to escape, I assume the captain, Commander Gravid Xionus, gave the self-destruct order. The *Dominator* took quite a bit of damage. When we noticed the energy surge, we jumped immediately, so we only copped the forefront of the blast."

"You must have Lady Luck on your side to have survived."

"I don't know about that, Ingryd, but I do know I have a damn good crew and a damn tough ship."

"My turn, I guess." Strasser leaned forward and looked at each of them. "As you'll be aware from other dealings, the Juggernauts were not convicted felons and had no bounty against them. Like the Quadranteers, they were caught in a criminal act—in this case, working in cahoots with known Imperial enemies, the Bukshoga Qlan crime syndicate—so, their membership is revoked. In that regard, you'll get a percentage of their proceeds since you took them down.

"As for your salvage claim on the *Invictus*, while I'm sure my Imperial counterparts would have an apoplectic fit, we have no jurisdiction in the Quad, and given the limited power and resources at my disposal... I assume there was no illegal contraband or anything of the like found?" she queried.

"You can see the images. It's scrap metal value only."

Strasser looked again at the images and shook her head. "I'm not going to quibble over it." She sat back, reviewed her tablet, and used her stylus to add a few notes before putting it in a locked drawer. "You heading back to your ship after this?"

"Assuming all the paperwork is up to speed, yes."

"If you don't mind, I'll walk you out." She checked her chrono. "I need to stretch my legs anyway."

"Um... sure." Alexis and Strasser led the others into the corridor, and then they slowly made their way to the foyer via the lifts.

"My office sometimes has ears, and I didn't want this on any official record," Strasser explained. "I'm putting a few things together."

"About... us?" Bradyn asked. He and Sabrya were following his captain and the Imperial liaison officer as they spoke.

Strasser nodded. "I said at the start, I thought you were the best thing that has happened to the Quad in a long time, and I will stick by that. Others, though, will eventually put two and two together." She put her hand up before Alexis or Sabrya could say anything.

"If you say anything, I'll have to act, but speculations aren't something I can act on.

You arrived here just over six months ago. My office did its checks, as you know. And yes, of course, Sabrya's alleged history of working with the Sunfists came up, but as I said, with nothing concrete to go by, I chose to overlook that. I have no regrets.

"Flash forward to the Qlan battlecruiser's arrival as part of this trap set up by the Juggernauts. The obvious question is why are the Qlan interested in you enough to send a battlecruiser? Why the ruse with the Sunfists? Why would a known terrorist group, believed to have made an assassination attempt on Emperor Nero, come all the way out here?

"One of my subordinates—one we are all acquainted with and a mutual friend of some bunters—was heard mentioning he knew the Juggernauts were up to something. Not officially, of course, and he didn't mention the coordinates. It's an amazing coincidence to hear about two traps in the same area, involving you and the Sunfists, instigated by the Juggernauts and Qlan.

"We also know—rumors of course—that a group of individuals uncannily similar to you in appearance caused a lot of mayhem at a disreputable orbital in Sector 38 and stole a *Bolide*-class vessel."

"It was a slave market!" Bradyn whispered forcibly, wary of making a scene.

"And believed to have been run by the Qlan. I know. But that was there, and, therefore, not the Quadrant's problem. How uncanny it is that Giono, the manager of said orbital, was seen exiting the Lair in the company of our leading bunters? Another amazing coincidence. And, if I'm thinking about it, others will too, eventually."

"You're saying, there'll come a time when the Quadrant becomes part of the empire, someone will put this together and come after us?"

"Everyone leaves a trail. A bloodhound will follow it relentlessly. The empire employs people with a certain skill set. They are good, and they are ruthless, and nothing will be left to chance. Especially when suspected assassins or their associates are mentioned. When they have their prey, the whole force of the empire will be behind them."

"I see. Any chance the Quad *won't* go all Imperium on us?"

"Very unlikely. Some of the ratification talks are duds, some are successful. In my estimation, it will be finished in a year, two at max. As it grinds to its culmination, the empire will start sending in more... personnel. A slow beginning to arranging infrastructure and all that."

The lift deposited them in the foyer, among the ever-present, mingling crowd. They wandered outside in silence.

"This battlecruiser salvage claim might get some interest, but it should still go through okay. I'll keep in touch." Strasser said her farewells and wandered off to enjoy the sun and fresh air.

"What do you think?" Alexis asked her crew as the bunters made their way back to the hotel.

"She knows a lot about us." Bradyn shook his head slowly. "Too much."

"And I was fraggin' startin' to think she was okay. But she has to go. I'll try to make—"

"What? No. Yes. She has put it together, but that was a friendly warning to grab what we can and go."

"Leave? We just got here, sort of."

"We have too much baggage, it seems. Too much of a trail. The Quad was going to be a clean break for us. Looks like that's not going to happen, now. It looks like the Quadrant is going to become Imperium, so we might be safer back where we were."

"Fraggin' bloodhounds... far worse than fraggin' coders."

"Bloodhounds? You've heard of them?"

"Well... rumors. They're assassins. Fraggin' auged to the hilt, but you wouldn't know if you looked at them. Even Klauff could be one."

"You're kidding."

"If you didn't want to look like a fraggin' assassin... but yeah, I'm kiddin'. Klauff's an idiot." Sabrya laughed at their looks. "Seriously, if a bloodhound was on our trail, we'd be dead."

"But your augmentation—"

Sabrya smiled. "Poor Bradyn. I thank you for your support and admiration, but I tell you now in all sincerity, a bloodhound attacking me would be like me attacking a norm child, asleep, in a straitjacket."

"Why would you be in a straitjacket?"

"Fraggin' idiot." She punched him in the chest.

CHAPTER THIRTY-ONE

WHEN THEY RETURNED to the repair yard, they were greeted by Hank. The head mechanic showed them the completed repairs. Bradyn was impressed with what had been done in so little time.

"Sorry Sabrya, looks like he gets to keep his head."

"This time." Sabrya grinned evilly.

"Wh-what was that?" Hank asked, looking worried.

"We had a deal that if your workmanship was shoddy, or you duped us, she'd take your head. It's okay though." Bradyn put his hand on the man's trembling shoulder. "She takes pride in her work. She sharpened and oiled her blades last night. But she's used to disappointments, aren't you Sabrya?"

"Only because I'm disappointed all the fraggin' time." She retracted her gleaming blades and wandered up the loading dock ramp.

Hank was still pale.

"Seriously though, you did very good work," Bradyn praised. "And we'll be back again to finish off the other stuff. Have you any vacancy for another appointment? Could be a big one."

Hank nodded at the encouraging words, and a smile slowly crossed his visage.

"Let me check my schedule." He started swiping across his surprisingly clean tablet, though it had a cracked screen.

"While you're at it, can you direct me to a scrap metal merchant? We have quite a large salvage claim that needs processing."

"Oh, I can take care of that too, if you'd like," Hank offered.

"Sure..." Bradyn looked over the yard. "Is this your entire factory?"

"I have a much larger yard and warehouse on the edge of town. Cheaper rates out that way, but lots of work here next to the port."

"Good, you'll need it." Bradyn flicked through some of the prepared images and vids of what was to be salvaged. "We had an encounter with a very large battlecruiser. While I'd love to check it out bit by bit, I just haven't got the time."

"A battl—" The man's jaw dropped when he saw the size of the ship and the amount of salvage. "That's a lot of metal."

"Sure is. Too much for you?"

"N-no... but it'll take a while to bring it all in. I'll need to go and assess its total mass. Probably need to use the spacedock."

"Perhaps not. Here are the specs of the ship model. We found the manufacturer's plate." Bradyn showed him the details Phillix had located during the return trip.

"This was the *Invictus*. *Gorgon*-class battlecruiser. As you can see, it has a mass of 1.5 million tons. With the damage and cost of retrieval, let us drop that to 1 million tons of various metals, including exotic alloys."

Hank ran through the numbers. "Look. It wouldn't be right or professional if I just popped out a figure on the trot. I'll get back to my office, do the number crunching, and give you a reasonable price."

"Not forgetting, I'm allowing for a .5-million-ton loss. I'd hate to see Sabrya visit. She can be quite formidable when she's on the prowl."

Hank paled again but stood firm. "Mister—"

"Bradyn."

"Look, Bradyn. Yeah, she sure scares the crap out of me, but I said I'd give you a fair price, and that's what I'm gonna do."

Bradyn smiled. "I had no doubts, Hank. Looking forward to your wave. If the boss approves, we'll send you the coordinates." He shook his hand and returned to the *Malleus*. "We heading back out?" he asked on his return.

"We are indeed. What did the mechanic say?"

"Sabrya will need a new dance partner. Hank's sure to be reasonable. He'll send through his best price once he's crunched the numbers."

"Right. We've got clearance to launch in ten minutes," Alexis informed him.

"Fine. I'll do a quick walk through on the inside."

"You good to go?" Alexis checked with Sabrya.

"Fraggin' always."

<hr>

The return trip to the area was uneventful. Once they positioned the ship in a convenient and safe location, Torg recalled the droids and bots. The debris field had spread, but only the smaller pieces were at the perimeter.

"It should not take long to process the debris to determine if we managed to locate anything resembling computer tech," the droid stated. "I will let you know the moment I have gathered all pertinent data."

"I'll gladly assist, too," Phillix chimed in.

"Fine with me." Alexis nodded. "Keep an eye on the scanners, just in case we happen to get some sightseers."

"You expecting someone?" Bradyn called from the lounge.

"No, but the Juggernauts may've had other contacts or informants. We already know Klauff was their lackey."

———

It took a whole day to gather the few bits identified as possible computer parts from the debris field.

Bradyn looked at the amount of scrap being brought in. "We've got a fair bit of work ahead of us—analyzing anything we picked up just now and the add-on to the hyperdrive, and going over the Juggernaut data."

"I've already gone over the Juggernaut files we collected," Phillix informed the engineer. "I've sent the data to your inbox."

"Excellent. I'll look at it shortly."

"Captain, we have an incoming call. It is from the CQLO," Torg announced.

"Put it through."

"*Malleus*, this is Lieutenant Strasser. I have a request for a Free Alliance rep to personally inspect the location to verify the salvage."

"Hey, Ingryd. What a surprise. You have the coordinates from our claim?"

"Correct. I've forwarded you his drive signature, so don't blow him out of the sky."

"See you when you get here."

"I won't be accompanying him."

"Ah. I guess it wouldn't look good. Imperials and FA working side by side..."

"Worse things have happened. ETA's about two hours. Strasser out."

"Well, there we go," Alexis muttered, switching the comms to ship wide. "Listen up, we have a Free Alliance official coming to check the area. We've got a couple of hours."

"Is that fraggin' normal? I reckon she's up to somethin', or both of them are."

"Maybe, maybe not. To be honest, there was a lot of stuff happening here. I'd be surprised if no one took notice. Glad to see the FA are taking an interest. First time I've heard of an in-the-flesh representative doing personal visits. Let's make sure we've got everything they don't need to know about stowed and secured."

"Want me to divert them?" Phillix asked.

"Uh no, Phill, thanks all the same." Alexis shook her head. "Not everyone needs to disappear." She spun out of her chair to grab a mug of the fresh coffee Bradyn was brewing. She found both crewmembers lounging about.

"Am I the only one working here?"

"You did fraggin' volunteer to be captain."

She sat with her steaming mug. "Not sure it was exactly volunteering. Torg, can you search the infocasts for anything about this Joran Fershain?"

"Aye, Captain."

"Hey, Gadgetman, can you also take a peek at this FA rep's ship, since Strasser was nice enough to send his fraggin' drive signature?"

"You suspect something, too?" Alexis asked.

"I'm fraggin' curious at the sudden interest. With all the other stuff happening at these ratification meets and nada from them—and yeah, with the recent warnin' from Strasser—any new player is worth a checkup. These reps are secretive fraggers, which's why you hardly hear about them. He might not use his real name, but if he uses his ship, we might get a better picture."

"I'm on it," Phillix replied then went silent.

"In the meantime, assuming he's legit, he might want a tour, so let's make sure he only sees what we want him to see."

Several hours later, Phillix had some information. "Torg and I have checked. Joran Fershain is a bona fide Free Alliance representative, born here, in the Quad, on Handrix, a small terran-type world that's predominantly water."

"Ah well, had to fraggin' check—"

"However, in the last few months, he's made several trips to the Imperial fringes."

Alexis shrugged. "That's not unusual, I guess, for his line of work."

"Except for the uncanny coincidence of the places and times..."

"For an AI, he is so melodramatic. Just spill it, Gadgetman."

"His hyper-trail has been to nearly every place you've been. He went to Sector 22—Plorian, to be specific—just after the death of Brutus and Tataranga. He somehow visited the hyper-space location of the weapons cache. He's been to Frallon, where the Surreal Tourney HQ is. And he has even gone on a trip to Sector 34."

"Where the *Iconic* is... was? How the hell did he do that?"

"I can only guess he has links with the Qlan or some other source of knowledge. Several of his trips have been to orbitals within known Qlan territory."

"In brief, his trail started with Ieoni Orbital in Sector 36, so he must have some knowledge of the *Malleus*, and, therefore, all of us. Anywhere the Qlan has followed us, he has been. However, there are some areas he's been to that the Qlan don't know about, or at least, not about our involvement, but the Imperials may have as they were also in Sector 34."

"Our guest is on approach," Torg informed them. "I am powering down the plasma canons."

Alexis was double-checking that her Kimichi was fully operational. "Oh, better drop the gravity to Terran standard," she advised. "Everything set?"

"Our stealth tech is well concealed, as is the new hyper-device. All data from the *Dominator* and the *Invictus* has been encrypted."

"You heard Phillix. This guy's not to be trusted," Bradyn stated.

"A bit of fraggin' paranoia always helps."

Bradyn and Sabrya waited on the main deck of the central corridor. Alexis was up on the gantry, a few paces back from the shuttle dock.

"Joran Fershain, welcome aboard the *Malleus*." Alexis met him as he stepped off the ladder. She reached to shake his hand, but he refrained from taking it. She frowned, disliking him already. "Pleased to meet a Free Alliance representative," she continued her banter. "We were beginning to think you guys were myths. This way." She led him to a ladder to the main deck.

"You'd be surprised how much distance we cover. We spend half our time in hyper from one place to another," he said as he followed.

Alexis nodded. *I bet!* "All the more reason to thank you for coming out here for this minor matter."

"Not at all. We in the FA HQ take incursions into our space by crime syndicates very seriously. I saw the wreck while flying over here. I must say, that ship is huge. You took it out all by yourselves?"

"We used some clever tactics, and we had the *Dominator* up our sleeve. This is my crew, Bradyn and Sabrya, and Torg at the back there, which you must have read in the report we sent."

Having seen his response on the gantry, no one offered to shake his hand.

"Ah yes. Quite sneaky. Strasser spoke highly of you all, the new rising stars in the Bounty Hunter world." He may have sounded friendly, but his smile looked forced.

"Right place, right time." Alexis shrugged. She was about to reluctantly invite this rude individual to tour the ship, but he cut her off.

"Exactly. So, to business." Any friendly demeanor was swiftly buried. "I'd like to refrain from any violence. However, considering who you are and your amazing capabilities, I'm leaving nothing to chance. I am under orders to bring Sabrya Reaper Smith back to face charges laid out by the Surreal Tournament Group." He turned to the warrior who was staring through him. "These charges are in the fine print of the Surreal Tournament Charter, countersigned by the previous emperor, Nero XXXIII. Failure to comply is not only a criminal act, it will be regarded as treason. This includes accomplices or anyone aiding in non-compliance. The punishment can range from a fine and exile, to commandeering any vessel involved with the accomplice or aid, or death."

"Frag all of that!" Sabrya spat.

"This is ridiculous! What has this got to do with our salvage claim, and how is the Surreal Tourney in any way related to the Free Alliance?" Alexis asked.

Joran ignored the salvage reference. "It's in the new charter to abide by Imperial laws that do not directly oppose or hinder the laws or contractual agreements of the Free Alliance."

"How does the FA new charter have powers over any alleged previous crimes within the empire region?" Bradyn queried.

"The how is simple enough—an agreement between the FA and Imperium hierarchy. The charter has no statute of limitations and has the formal backing to include the last ten years."

"Why are we even fraggin' talkin' to this meatbag?" Sabrya stepped forward.

Joran put his arm up. "Before you decide to be too impetuous, I should warn you of the ramifications. Your Ion Maiden friends..." Joran tapped his armpad. It showed an image of the *Raquech*'s interior. The four women were sitting on the floor, backs against the bulkheads. Each was wearing a neuro-collar.

"I know you're all very familiar with this device. If anything happens to me, they get the full treatment until it kills them. All I need is compliance from you, Sabrya, and everyone remains alive and unharmed." He continued when there were no comments. "Now, this is especially designed for *you*." He handed her a familiar black collar, slightly thicker than the last one she'd worn. "You'll note it's not just a simple neuro-collar; it will suppress any and all ST augmentations, including your nanites. All you'll be is an angry, ineffectual woman."

"And if I fraggin' don't?"

A tap on his armpad made the Ion Maidens writhe and scream.

"Enough! Frag you."

"So, you'll comply?"

She nodded reluctantly. The agony of the fellow bunters stopped, though their cries and moans could be heard.

"You do realize, though, coward that you are to hide behind defenseless captives, you're a fraggin' dead man walkin'."

"Ah, yes. The idle threats of those with little power. If anything should happen to me before we arrive at ST HQ, I can assure you we've other tricks up our sleeves. For starters, all your assets will be seized, although some of them will be directed to the accounts of Ingryd Strasser, old Mithum, and Brianna DeCroix. I'm fairly certain the FA investigation that follows will find evidence of corruption and inside dealing. This, I'm afraid will ruin their careers and prospects for future employment—a very unfortunate occurrence for an old man, left destitute and alone. Ms. DeCroix still has her youth and womanly charms, I'm sure she'll find suitable employment. As for Ingryd, being an Imperial Officer, she will be court-martialed and made an example of what happens to those who usurp their powers. It might not mean much to you, but her family will be in disgrace and, no doubt, lose their high positions. Finally, being close to ratification, Klauff will probably be promoted and take over command of the CQLO, as appointing another officer for such a short time would be in no one's best interest."

"Where are the Ion Maidens now?"

"Currently drifting somewhere in hyper. Once I'm safely away from here, I'll send you their coordinates. Be warned though, if anything should happen to me, if I don't send the code, the collars are programmed to activate for ten seconds every fifteen minutes until the batteries die. And you all know, ten seconds on even a minimum setting is excruciating."

"Drocking asshole," Bradyn fumed.

"What about Strasser, Mithum, and DeCroix?" Alexis asked.

"Going about their daily routines, which won't be interfered with unless our arrangements are compromised."

"You've thought of everything, haven't you?" Alexis watched with trepidation as Sabrya put the collar on. They heard a snap as the latch locked.

"I like to be thorough. And like I said, seeing how resourceful you've been, I can't take any chances. You must realize what a compliment this extra effort is to you all. The lock is coded, of course, and I'm the only one with the combination. Same with your friends."

"So, let me get this straight, you're a Free Alliance representative working for the Surreal Tourney Group?"

Alexis and Bradyn watched as Sabrya tested her abilities.

"Let's say I'm a Free*lance* Alliance rep. The old paradigm of Free Alliance space is fading. One needs to look to the future."

"Yours will be a lot fraggin' shorter than you reckon." Sabrya lifted her hand and studied her fist, but try as she might, no blades appeared.

"I know you want to hit me, so get it over with, and we can drive home how truly ineffectual you are."

Sabrya reacted quickly with a punch toward his face. With her augmentation and nanites, he wouldn't have stood a chance. However, Joran moved his head to the side and slapped her arm away with barely any effort, causing her to stumble toward the bulkhead.

She used the momentum to pivot, bring her leg up, and kick him in the chest as she spun.

Joran fell back and landed awkwardly on the deck.

"Not so fraggin' ineffectual." Her victorious grin turned to a grimace when Fershain activated the collar. She dropped to her knees, hands instinctively trying to claw it off.

"So, now we know what happens." Joran climbed to his feet, red-faced, but smiling at seeing her pain. "You will, of course, be locked and secured in a cabin. Weak as you are, I'm sure the idea of stabbing me and taking over my ship will cross your mind during the trip." He rubbed his chest.

"Why not just fraggin' drug me or stick me in stasis?"

"I could do that. I still might. It all depends on you. Just imagine what could happen to you, alone and unable to raise a hand for over a month..."

"You're one sad, fraggin' creep."

"Yes, yes, it's true," he replied testily. "Now, shall we go? The sooner we're on our way, the sooner your Maidens can be free of those collars."

Sabrya gave Bradyn and Alexis a curt nod in farewell as she was about to walk away, but her friends would have none of it. First Alexis, then Bradyn reached out to hug her.

"Frag off you two. I expect you to be helpin' me kill this limp dick soon."

"Of course. This is to give him a false sense of security," Bradyn muttered.

"Tick tock," Joran muttered.

If looks could kill, the FA representative would have been a dismembered corpse a hundred times over. Sabrya shoved past him. "See you guys soon," she said before climbing the ladder to the shuttle dock.

Fershain chuckled. "I love this sense of camaraderie and bravado."

Alexis scoffed. "Tell the truth, you're a sad loner with absolutely no idea what camaraderie is like."

Joran's face clouded slightly, then he turned and climbed out.

Bradyn was about to move forward, but Alexis restrained him.

"He won't get far," she said.

"I know, I just wanted to knock that smarmy grin off his face."

"Don't worry. We will."

They heard the clamps disengage and felt the vibration of the shuttle as it powered away. Both quickly headed for the bridge and watched the shuttle make its way to the other vessel.

"Phillix?"

"I heard every word. Once he's in hyper, we've got him."

"But then we'll still need to get on board and free Sabrya."

"One thing at a time."

"True. Can you patch me into the Maidens? Do you know their location?"

"I can and do, as they are conveniently in hyper."

"Joran was right to be worried about us, and he has no drocking idea about Phillix's capabilities," Bradyn seethed.

CHAPTER THIRTY-TWO

"THE *RAQUECH* WILL BE HERE any second now," Phillix advised.

As planned, the Maidens' vessel appeared a few kilometers away from the debris field.

"*Malleus* to *Raquech*. Anyone acknowledge?" Alexis commed immediately.

"I will match speed and come alongside," Torg informed them. "I estimate we will be there in four minutes."

While waiting, hoping for a response, Alexis checked her suit. "We'll shoot over in the Kimichis. Can one of you override their airlock?"

"Difficult without a hard connection," Torg replied.

"And I can't access their nav-comp now that they're back in real space," Phillix added.

"Ale-xis, this is Fyon-a... We're—"

Alexis could hear the pain in her voice as she spoke. "We're alongside. Can you open the airlock?"

"Huh? Um... yeah." Her voice sounded like it was fading.

"Good girl. Hang in there. We're coming over."

"Airl-ock rele-as-ed. How...?"

"I'll explain later. See you soon." Alexis shot out of her chair. "Keep us close, Torg. Ready, Bradyn?"

"All set." The engineer had packed several auto-docs in a medical bag.

With their airlock still out of commission, the pair quickly made their way to the shuttle dock. It took a moment to activate the airlock and get out, then a quick kick and minor adjustments of the suit's thrusters to align themselves with the *Raquech*'s airlock.

Shortly after, with the airlock sealed behind them, they made their way onto the bridge. Just as they entered, the collars activated.

The four women writhed. Their screams and cries filled the bridge, but the moment Alexis activated the tech suppressor everything stopped. The bridge was plunged into darkness, and they had to grope around, guided by the groans of pain, until they could manually release the collars.

Once they were free, Alexis deactivated the suppressor. The interior lights flashed on. "That's one handy gadget." She marveled at it as she put it aside.

"Brought to you by the drocking auspices of Surreal Tourney R&D. They make monsters, then a device to control them. Sabrya excluded, of course." Bradyn grinned as he quickly unpacked the auto-docs and, together, they applied them to the Maidens. Once the women were being treated, Alexis and Bradyn lifted them easily and carried them to their cabins, leaving them to rest in their bunks. They knew all too well the effects of the collars, but they hadn't had to endure the pain and agony anywhere near as much as these women.

"Their vitals are looking good," Alexis read off the small screens. "Now, it's just a matter of giving them time to recover."

"And every minute is a minute that creep has Sabrya."

Alexis nodded, looking forlorn. "It can't be helped, but I

promise we'll get her back as soon as we can work out how. Joran will pay, have no doubt."

It was over an hour before the four women were up and about, though their necks still showed red welts.

"How did you know where we were and that he had put collars on us?" Fyona croaked.

Alexis explained their situation.

Glyn winced as she spoke. "So, he's... got Sabrya with him... now?"

"He's taking her back to the empire? I thought he was Free Alliance?" Fyona's voice was a whisper. She sipped some water regularly.

"He's a bona fide rep, but he's sold out to the highest bidder," Bradyn explained.

"We can... report—"

"We could, but I can guarantee he won't be around to face charges."

"What? You said he's in hyper..."

Alexis looked at them then Bradyn. "You have a lot of questions, and we've got a lot of explaining to do, but it would be best if you all come across to the *Malleus* before we do so."

"The *Raquech* is quite capable of jumping, too."

"Ladies, look out the window. Torg, stealth mode, please."

With looks of bewilderment on their faces, the Maidens watched the *Malleus* drift alongside them.

"I don—" Fyona stopped mid-sentence as the *Malleus* was no longer visible.

"Where the frak is it?" Glyn coughed.

"Still there. Thanks, Torg."

The ship reappeared instantly.

"I can't explain how it works," Alexis said at their incredulous looks, "or where we got it from, but you're now a part of this, and I'm sure you want to see it through to the end. This is easier than keeping it a secret from you. We can track Joran, and if you want to be there, you need to come with us. We can't take the *Raquech*."

The women looked at each other and exchanged a few quiet words before deciding.

"We're with you," Fyona stated. The others nodded.

"Great. Thought you would be. This has become your fight as much as ours. We're sorry you were dragged into it. This lowlife has used every tactic to get to us, even to the level of threatening Brianna, Strasser, and Mithum."

"Do we need weapons?" Doryne rasped.

"We have plenty." Alexis shook her head. "Unless you have an absolute favorite."

"Your spacesuits will be needed, just in case," Bradyn added.

"We'll head over now. You ladies take your time to get ready. Do what you need to do to keep the *Raquech* secure. We'll head off the moment you join us."

The ship became a hive of activity as the women organized themselves.

Alexis and Bradyn packed their gear and left them to it.

"We need to come up with a plan to get onto Joran's ship," Alexis stated.

"Could be tricky without him knowing. We know crap about his ship. Has he got a crew? Is he alone? Droids?"

"We won't know for sure until we're alongside. Only then can we come up with a definitive plan."

"*Raquech* to *Malleus*. We're coming over," Fyona called.

"Access is via the shuttle dock on top."

"Roger."

Ten minutes later, the four women were aboard. Glyn and Quela still looked a bit ragged.

"How about we sit you down with the auto-docs a bit longer?" Bradyn suggested. "Your trauma from enduring those collars will require ongoing attention. We'll need to be on our toes in case things don't go according to plan... when we have one."

While Bradyn set up the devices, Alexis brought out some of the fresh vegetables and made a quick salad.

"These are from your garden setup?" Quela asked.

"There's not enough for every meal." Alexis nodded. "It's a work in progress."

Soon everyone was having a nourishing bite to eat while waiting and recovering.

"We'll be closing in on the Free Alliance vessel within the next thirty minutes," Phillix informed them.

"That didn't sound like your droid," Fyona remarked.

The women looked around for the origin of the voice.

"That would be Phillix, our AI," Bradyn said.

"You have a ship's droid and an AI?"

"Remember a while back when I said, 'it's complicated?' I wasn't joking."

While they waited to come alongside Joran's vessel, Alexis and Bradyn touched on some of their past.

"He used to be a man and is now connected to all the waystations?"

"If you could call him that. He was a coder." Bradyn laughed.

"Hey, be nice. I might disappear and wander the waystations for a while."

"You know you'd be bored without us." Bradyn smiled at the looks the Maidens were sharing.

"Hmmm... life would be less complicated, for sure. Still, I guess I need a few biologicals in my life to stay sane."

"To answer your question, yes. That's how we're able to track ships in hyper," Alexis said.

"I am close enough to begin scanning. Two small energy spikes which can be determined as human. Several large ones for powerplant, weapons array, life support. However, there are several that are neither."

"Explain." Alexis pushed her plate away and chewed the last mouthful as she went up to the bridge to look at the screen in greater detail.

"As you can see, Captain, they are similar to previous scans of bots, like on the *Iconic*."

"Ah. Okay." Alexis hoped the Maidens hadn't overheard or asked too much about the *Iconic*.

"Looks like he has four bots," Bradyn said behind her. "He's not taking any chances."

They spent a few minutes going over the readouts before Alexis returned to the lounge.

"Have you done this before—boarded a vessel inconspicuously?" she asked them.

"Well, not inconspicuously. Do you have a breaching pod?"

Alexis looked unsure. "Phillix? Torg? Any idea about a breaching pod?"

"As it happens, we do have a small one from the cache. However, none of you would fit inside."

"What's the point?" Alexis showed her frustration.

"We don't need to be in it if we are accurate," Bradyn considered. "Can I see the specs? Maybe you ladies can assist with your experience?" The pod specs came up on his armpad.

Alexis studied the rough outline of the vessel they were shadowing on the overhead monitor. "Is that Sabrya?" She pointed.

The others glanced up.

"The probability is high. Based on these energy spikes, these are the four suspected bots, and this is presumably Joran Fershain on the bridge, so these must be cabins and, therefore Sabrya."

Alexis thought about it for a few moments. "Right. We'll go with that."

"We've decided the tech suppressor and a Kimichi should be sufficient for the pod."

"No weapons?" Alexis questioned.

"Sabrya *is* a weapon, but when the suppressor is activated, it will take out some of the bots. That will leave only her and Joran."

"I almost feel sorry for him," Alexis said. "Almost."

"If we're accurate, and if the breaching pod is successful with a decent seal, Sabrya can activate the tech suppressor and be free of the collar. She can then don the spare Kimichi, but she'll have to be quick. I think you know what'll happen after that."

"We get our girl back."

"And the Free Alliance loses a representative. Exactly."

"Going by his comments, he might wear the uniform, but the Free Alliance lost him a while back."

"Once the pods are connected, we'll fly across and get Torg to hack the airlock."

Everyone gathered in the loading dock as there were far too many to use the shuttle airlock. This way, the six of them could render aid if needed.

"We move as soon as the pod breaches. Once Torg gains access, we'll board. He'll then establish a hard connect with the ship's computer and download everything from it."

"Your droid is that good?" Glyn asked, looking at the innocuous metal man.

"Torg's very adept, but our prime hacker will be Phillix."

They nodded. Impressed.

"I can see how you did so well," Fyona praised them.

"Thank you." Alexis hoped her red face wasn't easily discernible through her faceplate. "We muddle through."

"Two minutes to breach," Phillix advised.

The pod was a small container on the front of a short-range, but powerful, missile. The head was toughened graphene, designed to shear through a foot of metal plating before opening to allow access to its contents. Their biggest concern was that in trying to target her cabin, Sabrya might be injured if she was too close to the breach point.

They heard a distant rumble and whoosh.

"Pod away," Phill informed them.

Bradyn hit the button to open the door and ramp and stepped out as soon as he could fit through the opening, Alexis behind him. They looked at the ship.

Bradyn pointed at the protruding end of the pod. "Looks like a good seal. Hardly any vapor emission."

"Let's hope Sabrya can get to it."

"The energy spikes are moving toward the breach location," Phillix updated them. "Two are now near her cabin. Our man is also quickly approaching. Must be a different level."

"Torg, do your thing."

The droid jumped, expertly aiming for the FA ship's airlock. On arrival he grabbed onto the edge, opened the control panel, and began his work. Moments later, the airlock door cracked open.

"Time for us to go." Alexis jumped, then Bradyn.

One by one, the Maidens followed.

"A large section of the ship has suddenly gone blank," Phillix commed.

"Great. That means Sabrya has the tech suppressor activated." Alexis sounded relieved.

"Ah, well, we might as well pack up and go home," Bradyn quipped.

"What?" one of the Maidens cried. "Are you kidding?"

"Sorry, love. Yes, I'm joking." Bradyn chuckled. "Can't let Sab have all the fun. Imagine what goodies this guy could have."

"Hey, Sabrya. You on yet?" Alexis called.

"Should I point out that her comms won't work until the suppressor is deactivated?" Phillix asked.

"Ah. A facepalm moment."

"We all have them. Well... not me, anymore."

"Okay, people, that means when we enter the affected area, nothing electronic will work. So, no light, no comms, and no gravity," Bradyn said.

"From memory, we go in and turn right. After that, we'll see what we see... so to speak." Alexis shrugged in her suit, then had an idea. "Hey Phill. Are you able to aim a spotlight on the entrance? Maybe we can see by the reflected light once inside."

"On it."

Torg returned to the ship to pull in the cable for the hard connect.

The airlock was only big enough for three suited people. Alexis, Bradyn, and Fyona went first. Cycling through the airlock was slow, and the door had to be opened manually. By the time they were ready to enter, a beam of light from the *Malleus* lit them up.

After a short passage, the main corridor went left and right, or aft and forward. As they were now within the tech suppressor zone, there was no gravity, but there was enough reflected light to pull themselves along the passage without difficulty.

At the next corner Alexis came upon a large inert bot. She found a way past, then Bradyn worked his way around, but with more difficulty. After several more meters, the lights flashed on, and everyone fell to the deck.

"What the frag!" They recognized Sabrya's voice.

"The suppressor is off." Fyona used the bulk of the bot to

pull herself to her feet. She backed away quickly and brought up her breacher anticipating an attack.

"I've pulled the powerpack out of the bot near the airlock. So don't stress if you come across it," Sabrya commed.

"Glad to see you're okay," Alexis called as she regained her feet. "Where are you?"

"A bit further forward."

"Can you hold up? We have the Ion Maidens with us." Alexis looked back to see the progress of the others.

"Oh... frag it. I guess they can watch. Looks like he's holed up in the bridge. By the way, I knew you'd come. Thanks."

"Wouldn't have had it any other way," Bradyn said. "Didn't want the holo-deck to go to waste."

"I have made the hard connection with this vessel." Torg commed. "With Phillix's assistance, we will hack into the computer and download the data."

"Good work," Alexis said.

Another ten meters, and they could see a familiar Kimichi battle suit slouched against a bulkhead.

"About fraggin' time." Sabrya waved briefly. "This is about to get interestin', I reckon." She pounded on the door. "Hey, Joran. Time to die."

"Sab. How many bots did you deactivate?"

"Two."

"Drock. I'll go back." Bradyn turned. "Lucky you brought that breacher, Fyona. Might come in handy. Want to join me?"

"Why not?" The Maiden turned and followed the large, swarthy engineer as he made his way back. The other Maidens let them pass, then they, too, followed.

There was another bot at the intersection, but like the first, it was dormant.

Further aft, they spied a larger bot in the corridor to the engine room.

"I'm no expert, but it looks like it's powering up after a

reboot. Time to hit it before it's fully operational. Everyone, set yourself up." Bradyn brought his laser up. The others followed suit.

"Fire."

The bot didn't stand a chance. Before it could get any of its defenses or weapons online, it was riddled with energy bolts that easily penetrated its metal skin. Everyone ducked when it blew up.

"Ah, good. Not a death-bot then. Pretty low-key."

"Wasn't there another one?"

"Yes, but we didn't pass it, so it's either further back and stuck because this thing is blocking the passage or it's up in the bridge. You hear that, Sab? Could be a bot in the bridge."

"Who wants it fraggin' easy?"

"Is she always like this?" Glyn asked as they turned to head back.

Bradyn nodded. "That would be a yes."

Soon everyone was gathered near the bridge door.

"What are you fraggin' up to in there, Joran?"

"Torg, you're still on the *Malleus*?"

"Affirmative, Captain."

"What's Joran doing? Is he alone?"

"There is another large energy spike present on the bridge."

"There's our last bot." Bradyn nodded. "If it's like the other one, it won't be too hard to put down."

Sabrya pounded on the door again, denting it. "I must say, I'm very disappointed," she called out. "All that tough talk and bravado, and, now, you cower behind a bot and a locked door."

"You know we can easily open it," Alexis suggested.

"Yeah, but you asked me to wait, and I'm just fraggin' toyin' with him." She extended her blades and punched them into the door deep enough to get a good purchase. "You know when it opens, all hell will fraggin' break loose?"

"If you just open it a bit, we can pepper the bridge with these," Fyona offered, waving her breacher.

"Ready then?" Sabrya put a boot against the bulkhead and began to tense so the door slid a little bit.

The slim opening lit up when energy bolts riddled the area. Some bolts hit the bulkhead above her boot.

"Fraggin' lucky!" She laughed as she dropped her boot.

A scream of pain came from behind her. Quela fell, clutching her thigh. Glyn and Alexis immediately went to her to check the wound and seal the suit.

"Flesh wound," Glyn said. "Hurts like hell, but not serious."

"I'll give you frakking 'not serious.'" Quela grimaced in pain.

Alexis helped Glyn drag Quela further back and sat her against the bulkhead. Glyn then groped inside Quela's belt pouch and took out a stim-pack—an adhesive pad loaded with antibiotics and painkillers. She applied it to the wound and used a bandage to help secure it in place.

Cursing, Fyona moved in closer, pointed her weapon through the gap, and opened fire. There came an instant return of fire which left scorch marks along the bulkhead and door frame, but none of it struck the breacher. She continued until she heard a scream.

"We can do this for ages," Sabrya taunted.

"Someone else want a turn?" Fyona offered. The other Maidens were all eager for a bit of payback.

They took turns opening fire through the gap.

The return fire gradually dissipated.

"Is your bot gone yet?" Fyona asked.

"The larger energy spike is—"

The door buckled out slightly with the explosion. A strip of light flashed through the gap.

"Bot go boom." Glyn smiled.

"Hmm. Not the way I fraggin' thought it would turn out."

Sabrya tried to pull the door a bit further, but the buckling prevented it. She chanced a snap look inside.

No energy bolt took her head off. The bridge was a mess. The bulk of the bot was intact, but the side casing was blown out and had jagged edges. Joran was on the floor in a small pool of blood.

"Is he dead?" Fyona asked. "I thought there'd be more blood."

"Lasers fraggin' cauterize wounds. Generally."

Fyona nodded.

"Both energy spikes have been extinguished," Torg answered.

Sabrya chuckled. "That's droid speak for they're fraggin' dead." She stepped back as Alexis and Bradyn moved closer.

Together, they heaved on the door until there was enough room to get through.

"I see you bring more to the group than brains and a ship." Fyona looked impressed at the strength Alexis showed.

"Not always fraggin' brains," Sabrya slapped her back.

CHAPTER THIRTY-THREE

AFTER TAKING the Maidens back to the *Raquech*, the *Malleus* flew to Quint-wil. On the trip, they devised a story to explain everything.

It was clear Strasser knew about Joran's visit to the *Malleus*, but the dilemma was how far the Imperial Liaison Officer would bend the rules, considering she was also a target. They were prepared to reveal the truth to her, but they would play it slow until they were sure it wasn't going to backfire and land them in the brig.

They needn't have worried. Once Strasser heard the recording of what Joran was going to do and his statement about being freelance, she was on their side.

"Before we do or say anything we'll regret, we need to do this properly," Strasser said. "First, we'll take this recording to the Free Alliance headquarters, which is conveniently located here, in Quint-wil. Yes, there are many FA offices scattered around, but for the Quadrant, it's located in the most populated city on the most populated planet.

"It would be good if we all go in person," Strasser continued. "I can vouch for Haruld Whirash, the head administrator there. We've known each other for years, and he is FA through and through. The statement from Joran will not be tolerated in the slightest." Strasser waved at the file recording. "I'd be surprised if Haruld doesn't denounce him immediately and revoke his license. I reckon he'll even backdate it to negate anything Joran has said or agreed to under the FA banner in the past year or so."

"Where does that leave us?" Alexis queried.

"You were protecting your own, so, basically, it comes down to self-defense. As licensed bounty hunters, given his threatening and coercive behavior, you were within your rights to go and get her. Those neuro-collars are banned for good reason. Sabrya and the Ion Maidens are well within their rights to apply for compensation."

"And Joran's vessel?" Bradyn asked.

"To be impounded and assessed. After that, probably sold off. And, yes, you'll get a percentage. Same as you'll get for the *Dominator*."

"About that. Could we purchase it ourselves?" the engineer asked. "It has a nice hyperdrive I'd be keen to put into the *Malleus*."

"Shouldn't be a problem. I guess your commission can come off the price. You'll have to liaise with Mithum on that. Now, let me organize on my end. How about we meet up here tomorrow afternoon, and we can all visit FA HQ?"

"Sounds like a plan." Alexis stood, satisfied with the outcome. She led her crew to the Lair for a celebratory drink with the Maidens.

On the return from the bar, Bradyn detoured via the repair yards to follow up on their arrangements. He booked the

Malleus in for a complete overhaul, which would now include replacing the old hyperdrives with the latest twin Cerbrinka-Zaners modules.

Hank sent the assessment of the *Invictus* salvage to his armpad.

"Gonna do it in the spacedock, mostly," he said. "That mother's too frakking big to bring down to the surface in one piece."

Bradyn nearly fell over when he saw the assessment, and he wandered back to the ship in a daze.

"People, we are officially rich," Bradyn announced when he sat at the lounge table. He had poured everyone a whiskey and transferred the assessment to the monitor so everyone could see it.

"How rich?" Alexis asked, looking up. "That has far too many digits. You sure it's not a contact number?" Alexis' eyes went wide at the amount.

"The price per ton of various metals, minus haulage and cost of operation. We'll still pocket nearly ten million stellars each."

"We could retire—"

"Pfft. Frag that. A slow death isn't what I signed up for."

"Besides, where could the likes of us retire?" Bradyn asked, slightly mellow now that he had a whiskey in hand.

"Yeah, the moment we set roots anywhere, we'll start makin' friends—well, not me obviously—and then questions about our past come up. People start talkin'. Yada yada. And the next thing you know, you've got those bloodhounds bayin' at your door."

"Well, in that case, we know what's potentially coming our way, so we'd better prepare."

It would take a month to fully repair and overhaul the *Malleus*. They booked suites in the hotel down the road from the Lair and tried their best to relax. In less than a week of idling around at the pool, sightseeing, and evenings at The Lair, they realized retirement wasn't going to work, even if they wanted it.

The meeting with Haruld Whirash at Free Alliance HQ was unnerving at first, and it felt like walking into a trap, but a few minutes after meeting the highest-ranking FA representative in the Quadrant, all suspicions were thrown out the airlock.

Haruld almost had an apoplectic fit when he heard the recording.

They even brought in the neuro-collars which had Joran's DNA all over them, as proof.

As Strasser had speculated, all interaction with Joran Fershain was to be nullified and reassessed.

"We have some other data for you, but I'm not sure of the legalities of its procurement. We had our AI trace his vessel's drive signature. It depicts a history of all the locations he visited, including those within the empire."

"I can assure you, there'll be no repercussions for any information you provide, even if it falls in a gray area. You have stopped this agent from doing further damage to our organization. And for that, I will personally take responsibility for the data."

Part of the proceeds from the takedown of the Juggernauts included ownership of the Lair. Bradyn helped out with retrofitting and repairs of their ship, while Alexis and Sabrya, with not much else to do, spent much of their time going over the business structure and leasing arrangements of the club. Anything that looked dodgy was stopped, and new arrangements were made.

"And we need to find someone we trust to manage this while we're away," Alexis said to Sabrya as they were having a drink with the Maidens and Brianna.

"Frag, yeah. It's not somethin' I care to do. I'd be drinkin' the bar dry of Starbursts!"

"Exactly. What we need is someone—or *someones*—who'll happily and comfortably spend their time looking after it. Perhaps another bunter group we know and trust."

"Ya know, if we find the right people, maybe we could consider makin' them equal partners."

"Now, there's a thought. That way, they'd have a vested interest, not just a regular salary." Alexis looked meaningfully at each of the Maidens. "Anyone here know any suitable candidates?"

"Umm..." Fyona tried to hide a grin. "I might know of some girls." She looked at the others. "Interested?"

"Are we what!" Glyn jumped up, nearly spilling her drink.

The four women all seemed excited about being partners in the establishment.

"On one condition, though." Fyona hesitated in taking Alexis' hand to clench the deal. "The Challenges are off the table."

"I never thought they were on it in the first place. We won't be revisiting any of the stupidity of the Jugheads."

Finalizing the paperwork for the various proceeds of the bounties and revoked bunters meant another visit to the Fortress was required.

"Congratulations. The Scrappers haven't been bunters a full year, yet, and you've already managed to upset the status quo— removed a traitorous FA rep, taken down the reigning bunter champions, and took their place—"

"They had to fraggin' die first."

"Ah, yes. Umm... if you maintain the lead, you'll get your first star in a couple of months."

Mithum had become aware of the threat that loomed over his head and the role they had played in its removal. For that, he bought them a round of drinks when he managed a break.

"I looked deeply into the Free Alliance charter that representative spoke about. While some of it was utter crap, an equal amount is true. One of the bonuses created with the emperor's input is that any Free Alliance registered Bounty Hunters are now legal to follow leads into Imperium space if required."

They discussed the ramifications of that outcome.

"Do known crime syndicates fall within our jurisdiction, then? Do they have bounties on them?"

"Bounties, no, but there are rewards, which amount to the same thing. I'll look into it and send you a wave once I have more info."

"It'd be great if you can, but we don't want to burden you with any extra work."

"Nonsense. It's because of your efforts, I still have work to do. So, you have *my* thanks."

"We haven't seen Klauff." Bradyn said.

"Ah yes. Klauff. Poor boy has been transferred to the New Territories."

"New Territories?"

"Yes. It's like the Quadrant, but much closer to the inner regions."

"Is it a promotion?"

"Yes and no. While on the surface it might look like it, with better conditions, those within the empire hierarchy will see the move as a reprimand. He was supposed to initiate the set-up of this liaison office, and once ratification passed, Strasser would have moved on, and he would have become the Quadrant Ambassador. The new position is the same as this, but several years behind."

The new *Malleus* was almost ready. The hull had been completely repaired, painted, and polished. The new hyperdrives had been successfully installed and calibrated; the ad hoc missile launchers had been replaced with state-of-the-art launch tubes, along with proper stowage for two dozen missiles; the plasma cannons had also been overhauled; and a new shuttle had been procured.

Once the official work had been completed, Bradyn, Torg, and the maintenance bots got to work on installing the stealth-tech and the hyperdrive signature diffuser.

They were at a restaurant in the Colosseum Mall, one they had been frequenting for the past couple of weeks.

"Want to stick around the Quad a bit longer and revel in our new popularity?" Bradyn asked them during dinner. "The ship will be ready in a couple of days."

"There are only so many 'scoops' one can handle." Alexis forced yet another smile, as a family group recognized them and came over to take a snap-vid. "I wish Brianna every success with the Bunter Happenings, but this 'hero' status she's bestowed on us is a bit much."

"Maybe we should look into that wave Mithum sent," Bradyn suggested.

"True. It would feel great to head back as legitimate bounty hunters and deal some justice, along with a few missiles."

"Sounds good to me. We came here to get away from the Qlan crime syndicate, a bogus bounty on our heads, and our past. But now, we have not only the skills, knowledge, and equipment to bring the game to them, we have legal backing."

"You want to go back?" Alexis played with the last portion of her meal.

"If you want to. Sab?"

"Frag yeah. Let's kick some more Qlan ass." Sabrya fist-pumped the air, scaring a group of children. "But let's get dessert first."

ABOUT A. J. GORDON

AJ Gordon (Andre Jones) has been dabbling in writing for many years, but only got "serious" after his early retirement from the Royal Australian Navy where he served for almost 20 years as an Electronics Technician.

Now sharing time between Australia and France, Andre is able to write full-time when not drawing or gardening.

To date, he has written eleven novels (co-authored three) including Seven Portals series epic fantasy; The Death Wave Chronicles urban fantasy; Gnome Henge, a children's book; Red Sails; and now The Outer Reaches sci-fi series.

Did you like this book?
Please write a review!

EXCERPT FROM "SECRETS OF THE DEEP"

RED SAILS BOOK ONE

Now and then, Alexis looked at her armpad to reference their location.

"Something's been bugging me—" Bradyn started as they slowly progressed inward.

"Yeah, it shows. That suit cuts in all those awkward places. I'm surprised your voice hasn't raised a fraggin' octave or two." Sabrya chuckled. "You haven't the body for space."

"Not that," the engineer continued, wriggling. "If we shut down the reactor, the anti-matter will no longer be contained. Once released, it will spontaneously annihilate everything within a vast radius. It would take a physicist to determine how that's going to go down in hyperspace, and whether it even affects real space. I doubt we'll have time to get out."

"Too deep for me, but I've gotta do somethin'." The warrior moved on to the next corridor after checking the surroundings.

Bradyn remained silent as they made their way cautiously to the next section.

"Perhaps we take the jump drives offline?" He said later. "That way, this thing will no longer remain in hyperspace. It will be visible to all and possibly stop their plans."

"If it's an option, you're just the person to do it," Alexis agreed.

Sabrya looked over her shoulder at the droid. "Why didn't *you* think of that, Metalman?"

"Nobody requested that particular information. The data is available, along with several terabytes of other data."

"Can it still be used as a planet-killer?" Sabrya asked the engineer.

"Yes, eventually. But it's a work in progress. Let's see how it's set up."

"Looks like I'll have to devise a Plan B," she muttered, clearly not happy with the current plan.

They continued following the warrior woman toward the center of the station.

"We go up another couple of levels, that's when you'll need to start bein' cautious."

"Not you?" Bradyn checked the next intersection as he passed.

"I'm always fraggin' cautious. Here are the lifts," she said before the engineer could retort.

\#

"This is it," Sabrya announced.

They had stepped out of the lift and walked another fifty paces before the corridor stopped, and a large area in front of them lit up. The floor, as throughout the rest of the facility, was a gleaming black surface. While the corridors leading inward were straight, as expected, those going around the station were curved, with the curvature becoming more accentuated as they progressed. In the center was a massive domed construct.

"I'll wager what we can see is only a portion of it." Bradyn examined his armpad schematics in detail.

"Do your thing, Chromehead," Sabrya said as she checked the area.

The droid stepped away and approached a pedestal

terminal near where the domed construct met the floor. Several meters to the right were large blast doors.

"I will begin." Torg immediately interfaced with the console. His metal fingers rapidly tapped at the keys. They heard a weird undulating and intermittent tone in their helmets.

"What's that noise?" Alexis asked.

"Vocals are inadequate for this task. Instructions converted to electronic signals are far more efficient." Torg's fingers didn't flinch as he answered.

"Can't you geeks do it fraggin' quietly?"

With the exception of a minimal pause, the droid continued, though the volume in their ears was substantially reduced. Leaving the droid to do its work, the warrior strode off to cover the corridor and elevators. The remaining pair moved apart a few meters to cover the area and the other corridor.

Bradyn was beside the central bulkhead that separated them from the core. Behind the thick glassteel window was a railed gantry leading to a large, almost black sphere that disappeared above and below into darkness. The engineer nodded at his estimation of the massive structure. "That there's probably the largest electro-magnet in the Imperium. I wonder how much anti-matter is inside?" He squirmed again in a futile attempt to get comfortable.

"From the little I know of anti-matter, I'm sure it's enough to take us and the cruiser out," Alexis replied.

"Undoubtedly."

After a couple of minutes, Sabrya shook her head at the idle banter. She examined the schematics on her armpad. A glance showed Alexis and Bradyn watching their areas. She switched her comms to personal mode. "Phillix," she commed.

"Ah, first-name basis, are we? No longer Gadgetman? I deduce our illustrious warrior requires a favor."

"Frag off! This's for everyone's benefit. I'm thinkin' of a Plan B. Where's the weakest link in this AM core?"

"Easiest and most effective access would be via the power conduits for the station's plasma cannons. Another level up."

When she looked over at her companions, the droid was still busy at the terminal. Only his fingers were moving; the rest of his gleaming body was a statue. Alexis and Bradyn had barely moved and remained vigilant for security droids.

"I'm nippin' upstairs. I've got an idea." Sabrya started moving off.

"What are you up to?" Alexis asked.

"Just remembered somethin'." She strode to the nearest stairway down the corridor. "Cover my area. I'll be back before you know it."

"Wait."

Sabrya was gone.

"Why did we invite her?" Bradyn repositioned himself so he could see along both corridors.

"I'm back. Happy now?" Sabrya asked when she returned several minutes later. "Any progress? I thought we'd be ready to go by now."

"The AI controlling the core is substantially more robust than others we have encountered. It—"

The lights turned red, making the area gloomy and eerie.

"What the frag did you do, Metalman?" Sabrya turned to look accusingly at the back of the gleaming droid.

"I have not—"

Phillix interjected to defend the droid. "One of the Sunfist coders tried to hack into an unauthorized area. They're now engaged with combat-bots as they make a hasty retreat."

As he spoke, they could feel sporadic vibrations through the deck.

"Fraggin' coders!" Sabrya punched the bulkhead in

frustration. "Access to a full armory of top-end weapons isn't good enough for them?" She paced quickly to cover the nearest entrance.

"Let's worry about that later. Torg, where are you up to?" Alexis asked. She noticed Sabrya's stance was far more alert, her movements quicker, a sure sign her nanites had kicked in.

"We have managed to get into the hyperdrive systems," Torg announced.

"Disconnect the drive and wipe the navigation comp data," Bradyn ordered. "It'll take them a long time to get that back online and up to speed."

"But they can still use it to fraggin' destroy Grindstone." Sabrya didn't break her concentration as she patrolled the corridor.

"Probably, but weeks down the track—"

"Which means we have time to come up with another plan to destroy the AM core. Currently, the only choice is suicide. Do it, Torg," Alexis ordered.

"Uh huh," Sabrya muttered.

"Captain, an Imperial cruiser has just appeared on the scanner," their AI informed them.

"That was drocking quick," Bradyn said, surprised.

"Perhaps they were on alert with the emper—" Phillix started.

"I don't want to hear another word about the fraggin' emperor," Sabrya vented.

"It is done," Torg informed them.

Both Alexis and Bradyn stumbled a step as the station jolted. Sabrya stood steadfast, as did Torg.

"The waystation has dropped into real space," Phillix informed them. "We're currently 0.2 light years from Grindstone and Tataranga and 0.5 light years from Plorian."

"And the cruiser?" Alexis asked.

"Still in hyper. It's not registering on the scope yet."

"Good. Keep at it, Torg. Get that nav computer wiped; destroy it if you can."

"If I override the saf—"

"Just do it, so we can get out of here." Alexis was getting testy under the tension.

"The *Mulan* has just departed. It had to blow the mag clamps holding it down. From its angle, the repulsor field is now in full effect and no longer accepting the code. I suspect our welcome has been revoked."

"I have completed my tasking," Torg stated calmly, stepping back from the console. "The navigational computer has been wiped and is now unserviceable. It will requi—"

"Let's get the frag out of here. Everyone, on me. We'll have to take the stairs." Sabrya clicked her powersuit on and, with the grace of a raptor, glided swiftly past the lift doors to the next corner and braked efficiently so as not to overrun the cover.

Alexis was less elegant but managed to follow closely.

Bradyn's ill-fitting suit caused him to spin, and he hit and slid along the bulkhead until he managed to turn it off.

Sabrya hissed, but knew there was no point in blaming anyone but herself. Amusing as it was, she berated herself for her lack of professionalism. She should have realized the loose suit would be inadequate for this sort of activity, especially with a novice, but she shared a grin with Alexis at Bradyn's antics.

"We'll work on that—" With her nanites augmenting her senses and actions, she instinctively ducked as the bulkhead where her head had been fused and melted when a laser coursed across its surface. Already pivoting, she returned fire and scored a headshot.

"This way!" She surged toward the sparking bot, spun at the last minute and thrust her legs toward the large bot's torso to stop. The bot was large enough that her impact made no impression. To avoid any further errors, the others decided to use their legs and not the powersuits to move. They had to take the stairs as the elevators were now offline.

Sabrya checked above then vaulted the railing and dropped to the lower level. Alexis moved in to cover from above as Bradyn made his way down. When he arrived, he covered her as she descended.

Sabrya stuck her head through the doorway and spied two combat-bots—different models from those she had just destroyed—stationed side by side at the end of the corridor, blocking their egress. She swore and reported to the others what was waiting for them.

"Is there another way around?" Bradyn asked, quickly thumbing through his armpad's contents.

"This is the level we need to get out on. Our airlock is a bit farther, but it's still the closest exit. Let's not fraggin' risk unknown territory unless it's the last resort." Sabrya rapidly changed the ammo on the gutpuncher and selected a couple of HE-grenades. She fired, and even before they detonated, she was peppering the bots with the high-powered laser. She ignored the minimal shrapnel that came her way when the grenades exploded.

The bots retaliated, though the targeting system on one was faulty, and its shots went wide. The other bot was in better condition and began lumbering toward her. Even concentrated fire with her laser wasn't sufficient to get through its thick armor.

"Frag it." She unclipped her EMP grenade and tossed it. "It's my only one."

The grenade detonated, causing both bots to go dormant.

"I doubt that'll last long before they reboot. Let's move." She quickly stepped out and glided to the closest bot, braced against it to stop. She began pulling at whatever she could and piercing it with her blades.

"You take care of the front one, I'll finish off this one,"

Bradyn offered. He moved his large frame and began rending the parts barehanded.

Alexis covered the other end of the corridor while waiting for the droid to catch up. When Sabrya gave the all-clear, she moved out and motioned for Torg to follow when he arrived. He had new legs, but he was not fast on his feet, especially descending stairs. Getting past the destroyed bots wasn't too much of a squeeze, and she was passing the furthest one before she looked back to check on the droid's progress.

Torg was a couple of meters behind her and about to push past the last bot.

After a quick look to her left, Alexis started making her way along the curved corridor that led to their airlock. As she neared, she noticed the airlock had closed and sealed, and her two crew mates were struggling to lift it.

"Phillix, override the airlock. We're hemmed in!"

"On it. The alarm changed the AI security protocols, and I was booted," he explained.

"All I'm hearin' is fraggin' excuses."

Alexis raced up to add her strength. Further along, evidence of the Sunfists' departure was obvious, with every surface scorched and pock-marked with laser burns and blasts. There were destroyed or sparking bots, both in the corridor and out on the landing pad near where the *Mulan* had been.

"Hey, Torg. Any time you—Shit!" She stopped mid-sentence, mouth wide, as she turned to look at the droid's progress. Coming up behind him was the largest bot she'd ever seen. It was double the size of the death-bot she'd faced on the *Iconic*.

Noting its approach, Torg had already turned and crouched in a defensive posture. One of the bot's thick arms batted him aside like a Plorian swamp bug.

As they left the airlock door, both Sabrya and Alexis had their weapons up and firing. They scored hits on the bot but with little sign of damage, and anything more powerful than a laser could potentially damage Torg as the droid leapt in to attack.

A panel opened in the bot's chest, and an intense laser immediately fired at the trio by the door.

Sabrya reflexively pushed her captain out of the way while she jumped in another direction.

There was a scream and groan as both Alexis and Bradyn dropped to the deck.

Sabrya landed elegantly on her feet and glanced back; Alexis was unconscious with a wound in her abdomen, and Bradyn's thigh had been seared by the same shot.

"Fuck you!" Sabrya swore as she brought her weapon to bear at the large bot. She changed the setting to something more powerful, but the bot and droid were moving erratically. "Get out of the fraggin' way, Metalman!"

Torg was clambering over the bot and avoiding its swinging arms.

The bot swiveled and careened into the outer bulkhead, attempting to dislodge him, but it only managed to crack the station's viewport.

Torg hung on then pulled his arm back and, drawing his fingers to a point, he drove them into the bot's laser cavity up to its elbow, bypassing the heavy armor-plating.

The bot began to spark. It turned and smashed into the bulkhead again, damaging the large window even more. Torg pulled his legs up to cushion the impact of the next ramming then kicked out. His mass and strength were insignificant compared to that of the bot, but moving the bot was not his intent. Instead, he used the effort to drive his arm up to his shoulder inside the bot and then proceeded to inflict as much damage as possible to the bot's internal circuits.

While the bot was preoccupied with the irritating droid, Sabrya chose her moment to click her heels to race in and assist. The blast doors along the main corridor crashed down as the bot exploded. She had little time to do more than duck as she slammed into it and dropped, stunned, to the deck, which shook with the massive explosion. When she managed to stand and peer through the blast door window, the corridor beyond was empty and open to space via a huge hole where the viewport had been.

"Frag it, no!" She looked stunned at the sudden outcome. "Hey, Phillix?" All she got was static. A heartbeat later, she pivoted and raced back to her fallen comrades.

Adjacent blast doors had dropped, separating her from the others. Repeated calls with no response proved the comms were still down. She dreaded seeing her friend and commander lying unmoving. Bradyn had already applied gel packs to slow the air leak from her suit, and he was working on his own. He looked up, clearly in pain. When he saw Sabrya through the window, he pointed to his helmet and shook his head.

"Don't I fraggin' know it." She showed him a grenade and motioned for him to move back.

He gripped the conduit running along the bottom of the bulkhead with one hand and pulled himself along while dragging Alexis with him. The engineer then moved so his bulk would protect her from any shrapnel or blast. Bradyn saw the flash of light off the bulkhead and felt a violent vibration through the deck. When he turned to look, there was a large hole where the corner of the blast door met the outer hull.

Sabrya glided over and took Alexis from his hands. She flew quickly and gracefully outside, then sped toward the open bay of the *Malleus*, sparing a glance at the discarded weapons and laden trolley abandoned in the hiatus. She landed quickly and carried her injured comrade to the medi-doc.

"Can you hear me?"

"I can now," Sabrya answered Phillix. She began telling him

what had happened as she programmed the auto-doc. "You monitor her, and I'll check on Bradyn."

She met the engineer halfway to the ship and picked him up unceremoniously, returned, and sat him next to her captain before applying stimulants and painkillers. "Back in a minute."

"I'm in the system and have removed the docking clamp restrictions," Phillix commed.

"Flash up the drives, Phill, we're leaving," Bradyn ordered from the captain's chair. At the first opportunity, he ripped off the ill-fitting suit and tossed it into a corner.

"Certainly, but, as reluctant as I am to say it, we should wait for Sabrya."

"Where the drock is she now?" Bradyn checked the monitor and external cams and saw Sabrya jogging up the loading ramp, pushing the abandoned trolley loaded with weapons.

"We fraggin' goin' yet or what?" she called out.

Get "Red Sails" at all great bookstores. And find out more about Andre Jones at: https://alienpress.org/.

"There," the dropskiff pilot announced in his emotionless baritone.

He gestured at his helm, and a reticle appeared on the forward window, singling out a distant building positioned just below the apex of the Hill. The villa. Its longer sides faced east and west, downslope and upslope respectively. Other homes were spaced along the hillside in line with it. Below them, a barrier of artificial pine forest—artificial because of the planet's water scarcity—kept them sequestered from less expensive properties.

The skiff's nose swung down and across, bringing the reticle and the villa to the middle of the window. "Keep the thrusters idling while we're down," she told him as she rose and eased her way to the back of the cockpit.

"Of course, Madam Quaestor."

Anticipating the debarking, Proselyti troopers had already risen from their benches and were standing in a double line along the troop cabin, each with a hand on the ceiling rail. Although many of them were tall, and some were broad and heavily muscled, her adjutant Caiu who stood at the very back was the most imposing. Her adjutant had clad himself in easy-fitting green and gray tactical clothing bearing pouches that bulged with supplies, making him look like some kind of pack animal, like the corpiformed gorillas she'd once watched working on Artemis XII. The Proselyti, by contrast, were lightly armed and armored. Their small arms consisted entirely of Glaxon Mk3 pulse rifles, adjustable for stunning or for lethal force. Aurelia didn't expect any stunning unless it was of Ectorius or his wife. None bore sidearms—an oversight, perhaps, by the *Maelstrom* commanders who'd armed this team or some form of passive-aggressive undermining of the way she'd commandeered nine of their soldiers. But Aurelia could see the handles of the knives and batons that were their backup weapons. The lightweight vests they wore over their light tan fatigues were made to 'resist' ballistic and energy fire. No matter about the lighter form of armor or the missing sidearms; Aurelia didn't seriously expect more than the most meager opposition. The Proselyti vests and belts bulged with pouches of extra rifle charge packs and the individually chosen contingency materials Saito had given them permission to carry. None had grenades; grenades were expressly forbidden by her orders.

Aurelia glanced down at her simple one-piece jumpsuit—black, and its only adornment was a narrow belt holding her sidearm. With her orgments, it was unlikely she'd need anything else, and if she did, her insertion team would provide it.

From the middle of the group, Sgt. Saito caught her eye and nodded politely. Her side of the uncarpeted patch of deck between her and the closest Proselyti would soon drop away, forming a ramp for the team to debark. Saito said nothing, and Aurelia said nothing, for there was nothing to be said. They'd made their plan, she trusted the team knew their jobs, and most of what would transpire rested on her shoulders.

Abruptly, the deck tilted several degrees to starboard, and the shuttle lurched, as power rerouted from gravity and dampeners into the braking and landing thrusters. Then the deck righted itself before, a moment later, a double clank-and-thump announced they were down. The egress ramp unsealed with a hiss then whined and shuddered its way down, hinging on the troopers' side. Bright daylight seeped in.

Again, no words were uttered as the first four in the team surged down the ramp. Aurelia half-smiled in approval at their professionalism and confidence. These four—two males, two females—would secure the stairwell exit housing at the far end of the roof and any staff who might appear through it. The hospitality staff had arranged with Aurelia's fake catering company to have two people waiting to assist them with a quick transfer of the provisions. Now that she thought about it, the glimpse she'd caught of the rooftop hadn't shown *any* personnel waiting. They were late or arrogant enough to make the off-worlders wait.

Well, she thought as she jumped halfway down the ramp and turned to face the roof, *their lateness just bought the poor things a few more moments of existence.*

Aurelia's graceful, long-legged gait brought her out under the skiff's nose and onto the eternicrete surface of the rooftop, and she focused on the stairwell exit ahead. The remaining team members followed at her heels. The sky and the air had a sand-colored quality to them. It was cool enough up above the desert. She tasted the tang of pollution on her tongue. To her side and past the roof's eastern edge, the view stretched out over the smog haze of the city toward the distant Panlands, which were a mere smudge of yellow-tan. She had no time to utilize the zoom and resolution-enhancement abilities of her left eye; she wasn't there to sightsee. It was late morning, which put the local sun high above the pollution haze and off to one side because of their latitude. Halfway to the stairwell exit stood one service droid. Still no hospitality staff. Two troopers stopped by the droid to deactivate it; the others continued toward the structure projecting up through the roof which protected the stairs from the elements. The door remained closed, and the first alarm went off in Aurelia's gut, causing her to slow to a halt as she came alongside the droid. *Was* this a simple power play by the local servants, or was something wrong? She felt and heard the rattle and skid of the insertion team behind her battling to halt without slamming into her or each other.

Ahead, the first two troopers reached the stairwell housing, and the door burst open in front of them, causing them to drop to one knee with weapons up. Two people lunged into the sunlight, a man with deep black skin and a paler woman with black hair tied back and some kind of maintenance droid on her shoulder. The pair wore dark brown maintenance coveralls, but both had the bearing of highly exercised, well-trained people. Their shoulders were back and their legs braced, and they'd stepped out to either side of the door as if preparing to clear the rooftop.

More rattling and grunting came from the troopers by the droid and the ones behind her, more weapons snapping into position. Aurelia signaled she was about to move to avoid friendly fire from those behind, then edged that direction, out of their way, in the direction opposite the view of the cityslope.

The man who'd exited the stairwell shouted a short message, and the translator clipped to her ear lagged only a second behind as it interpreted. Belatedly, she realized he'd spoken in the Proselyti private language, Terran True.

He called out, "Sgt. Saito Shimada! Do you remember me?"

From behind her, Saito made a startled noise, not something she expected of him. He called back, "*Lieutenant? Lieutenant Jabari?* What in the hells?"

Jabari? The Jabari who'd vanished with Scipio's rogue

mission? For a moment, Aurelia found her jaw hanging open. *Now this is curious.*

Jabari had one hand raised while the other clutched a long, rectangular shape—a device she didn't recognize—to his side, non-threateningly. One Proselyti near the droid shouted for him to drop it, but others appeared to recognize either Jabari or the woman with him and lowered their weapons.

Shifting to Imperial True, Jabari called, "We need to get into your ship and get off this rooftop, now!"

Aurelia continued slipping to the side, the alarm in her gut turning into a red-hot warning. Whatever was afoot here, she was in no way disposed toward following this stranger's orders.

Saito had recovered, and he hadn't lowered *his* weapon. Straightening, he responded to Jabari with a sharp, "Why?"

The woman with Jabari used both her empty hands to point out over the city. "*That's* why."

A deep thrumming shook Aurelia's bones even before the sound registered in her ears and a moment before the two *Charon* gunships rose into view from the cityslope side, fifty meters out with their noses and weapons nacelles angled menacingly toward the rooftop.

Troopers swore. Two broke rank and stumbled back toward the shuttle. When one of the gunships fired a missile, Aurelia was already sprinting, except she was making for the opposite edge of the roof. There came multiple shouts of "Down!" or "Drop!" and then the quaestor was vaulting over the safety wall at the roof's edge and into the empty space beyond it.

The missile impacted above her, the explosion limited enough to indicate the strike had been confined, surgical.

For a moment, Aurelia's feet speared toward the rocky ground three stories below, before she twisted in midair to face the building, and her machine arm latched onto a rough eternicrete sill. She'd caught the edge of a window on the top floor, and her feet swung in to find purchase on the lumpy facia below it. A cool wind from across the summit snatched at her, but she held firm with her mechanical hand. She had a choice: draw her razorslinger from its side holster and shatter the window for easier access or continue dropping to the ground one windowsill and one level at a time.

Sounds flowed down along the wall from above: a five-second patter of distant weapons-fire, the violent thudding of impacts into the roof's surface, then people shouting in distress when the weapons fire ceased. Somewhere off to the rear of the building, creaking and crunching sounds announced a structural collapse of some kind. No doubt, it was the damaged skiff sinking through the damaged roof, and vibrations in her window, her sill, and her patch of wall seemed to confirm this.

This precise and deadly response to Aurelia's team's presence had come far too quickly to be a routine reaction to a security breach. Three things were obvious: her skiff was out of commission; the local garrison had been fully prepared for her arrival and waited in ambush; and the lieutenant she'd executed hadn't been Ectorius' only spy aboard the *Maelstrom*.

She ground her teeth. The Proselyti were on their own now, along with her Corfids, if any were even alive up there. None of this changed her mission. Betrayed or not, stranded alone or not, Aurelia Cossea still had a verdict to serve.

QUAESTOR
By Peter J. Aldin
(The Outer Reaches, Book 2)

In the year 5122, maintaining law and order across the Imperium's vast reaches is extremely complex.

Enter the Quaestors. Judges. Law bringers. And, when needs-be, executioners.

When imperial Quaestor Aurelia Cossea enlists Proselyti troopers to depose a corrupt governor, Sergeant Saito Shimada willingly accepts. A convert to imperial ways, he has devoted himself to a safer, more united galaxy.

But when the assignment is interrupted by betrayal and the bizarre appearance of troopers from an earlier Prosyleti mission, Saito's commitment to his Imperium masters is sorely tested.

Under-equipped and cut off from support, the hunters will become the hunted, forced to navigate the twisted maze of an ancient city in a desperate bid for escape, hampered by bad intel, the governor's minions ... and unsure about these two deserters who've returned apparently from the dead.

Pick up a copy where you bought this book. And find out more about Peter J. Aldin at petealdin.com.

ALIEN
PRESS